HEAT

OTHER COLLECTIONS OF SHORT STORIES
BY JOYCE CAROL OATES

The Assignation
Raven's Wing
Last Days
A Sentimental Education
All the Good People I've Left Behind
Night-Side
Crossing the Border
The Seduction and Other Stories
The Poisoned Kiss (Fernandes/Oates)
The Goddess and Other Women
The Hungry Ghosts
Marriages & Infidelities
The Wheel of Love
Upon the Sweeping Flood
By the North Gate

HEAT

AND
OTHER STORIES

JOYCE
CAROL
OATES

A WILLIAM ABRAHAMS BOOK

DUTTON

DUTTON
Published by the Penguin Group
Penguin Books USA Inc., 375 Hudson Street, New York, New York 10014, U.S.A.
Penguin Books Ltd, 27 Wrights Lane, London W8 5TZ, England
Penguin Books Australia Ltd, Ringwood, Victoria, Australia
Penguin Books Canada Ltd, 10 Alcorn Avenue, Toronto, Ontario, Canada M4V 3B2
Penguin Books (N.Z.) Ltd, 182–190 Wairau Road, Auckland 10, New Zealand

Penguin Books Ltd, Registered Offices: Harmondsworth, Middlesex, England

First published by Dutton, an imprint of New American Library,
a division of Penguin Books USA Inc.
Distributed in Canada by McClelland & Stewart Inc.

First Printing, August, 1991

10 9 8 7 6 5 4 3 2 1

Copyright © The Ontario Review, Inc., 1991
All rights reserved

For acknowledgments, please see page 399.

 REGISTERED TRADEMARK—MARCA REGISTRADA

LIBRARY OF CONGRESS CATALOGING-IN-PUBLICATION DATA:
Oates, Joyce Carol. 1938–
    Heat & other stories / Joyce Carol Oates.
      p. cm.
    "A William Abrahams book."
    ISBN-0-525-93330-1
    I. Title. II. Title: Heat and other stories.
    PS3565.A8H43   1991
    813'.54—dc20   91-8007
                                            CIP

Printed in the United States of America
Set in Garamond
Designed by Eve L. Kirch

PUBLISHER'S NOTE

Once again, for William Abrahams

CONTENTS

I

House Hunting	3
The Knife	24
The Hair	39
Shopping	54
The Boyfriend	69
Passion	82
Morning	101
Naked	123

II

Heat	141
The Buck	154
Yarrow	169
Sundays in Summer	185
Leila Lee	195
The Swimmers	223
Getting to Know All About You	241
Capital Punishment	262
Hostage	284
Craps	295
Death Valley	311
White Trash	322

III

Twins   333
The Crying Baby   349
Why Don't You Come Live With Me
   It's Time   360
Ladies and Gentlemen: 373
Family   381

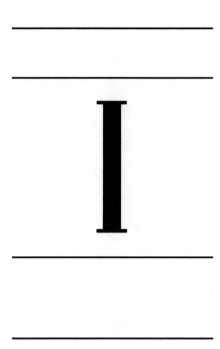

I

I

HOUSE HUNTING

How subtly the season of mourning shaded into a season of envy. To their knowledge they had never been envious people but suddenly they caught themselves staring at families, young parents with their children, a mother holding her baby—strangers whose happiness grated with the irritation of steel wool against the skin. One Sunday in a city park Joel saw Kim staring at a couple with very young twin girls, her eyes narrowed and her pale lips drawn back from her teeth. He looked away as if he'd seen something forbidden.

It was a season too of opaque skies, wet air, slick dead leaves underfoot. Rain drumming against windows in the night, mists that rarely burned off before noon. They had lived in this beautiful city on the West Coast for nearly eight years, and this was the first winter they found nearly unbearable. And the routines of their lives, which had once seemed so exciting. And the routines of their friends' lives. And the handsome little Victorian house they'd bought at such a bargain on a street not then fashionable, and renovated, and decorated, and furnished—nearly unbearable. The period of their young adulthood was finished and they decided to move back east.

It was not difficult for Joel to arrange to be transferred to the Philadelphia branch of his company; he was a salesman, but a salesman of a very high order. The products he sold cost millions of dollars and were contracted for years in advance of delivery. Kim

---

3

was a commercial artist who could find work anywhere. Or maybe, since they had money, she might not work at all . . . that period of her life too seemed to be winding down. She was thirty-four years old. She looked, as she said, precisely her age. She had intended to take only a month's maternity leave from the small public relations firm with which she worked but, as it turned out, she had been away twice that long, and at an unscheduled time—the baby had been born six weeks premature. Now, as she said, she was permanently out of the rhythm set by her co-workers and rivals. New seasons, and new promotion campaigns, and new strategies of selling: she couldn't keep up because she'd become repelled by it, and she wondered if she had been repelled by it all along, without knowing.

"You hypnotize yourself into loving your life because it's what you are doing and because it's life," she said. There was an edge to her voice these days, a perpetual bemusement and irony, that Joel had come to dislike. He particularly disliked, and feared, pronouncements of this kind: flat, abstract, impersonal. They allowed of no access, no quarrel.

But he said, "I love you."

He said, "We'll do whatever you want to do."

He was thirty-six years old. Young for his age. Athletic, aggressive, affable. With sandy graying hair trimmed short, small shrewd alert features, his skin rich, warm-looking. He loved to laugh and people loved to hear him laugh, his pleasure in happiness seemed so sincere. He had a quick temper which he kept in control, in public; as a small child he'd been susceptible to violent tantrums, short-lived but frightening. Even now, in his maturity, he was susceptible to a flaring up of what he thought to be his "other" self, his childish despicable ignorant self, erupting as it seemed out of nowhere and leaving him exhausted and guilty and ashamed afterward. Kim said, "I hate you in that state. I'm terrified of you." She said, "You should see your face when you're shouting—so *ugly*." She told him she felt at such times that she couldn't trust him, that she didn't even know him; she wouldn't want such a man, so little in control of himself, to be the father of any child of hers. And Joel was angered the more but knew to keep it hidden, swallowed down hard. He apologized; he was hurt, baffled, repentant, but resentful, accustomed since childhood to being forgiven. Wasn't there a natural rhythm, a ritual, of transgression and forgiveness, the loss of control of one's self and the restoration of control?

She wasn't serious, Joel said. Speaking quietly, with what he knew to be exquisite control.

She had better not say certain things, he said; it was impossible after all to unsay them.

"I say what I think," Kim told him.

She was by nature a quiet girl, very quiet, still and premeditated, but at such times, her cheeks flushed as if they'd been slapped and her eyes bright, she seemed to take pleasure in defying him, in prolonging their quarrel. If he began one of their scenes, she must end it.

He embraced her, and she pushed him away. He embraced her again, and she pushed him away. Then a third time, perhaps, burying his face in her neck, murmuring Sorry sorry sorry until he could feel her begin to relax, still tense and in defiance of him but beginning to relax, and often he dared run his fingers up and down her sides, tickling her, making her laugh, breathless and flushed as she was. Once he made her laugh, he had her won. They wrestled together like puppies. Kim would slap at him, pummel him; he'd allow her to get the better of him, taking pleasure in being slapped as he deserved, so long as the blows were harmless, playful, affectionate. Sometimes, heated and aroused, they felt a sort of anarchy between them, for what was there to prevent them from doing anything they wished, anything they knew to do, to each other? If they made love at such a time, wordless, clutching, triumphant, it was as if they didn't know each other; they were strangers, suddenly intimate, rather heartless. And what pleasure in being, for once, heartless—as if the body was after all the only way they could know each other.

After they lost the baby Joel's temper tantrums stopped. Or were temporarily in abeyance. Weeks, months, nearly a year had gone by and he hadn't flared up in the old way, nor did they make love in the old way but were apt to lie together in each other's arms in a state of mutual exhaustion or melancholy or, oddly, contentment, a sense that they'd come to rest after grief, played it out, drained themselves of sorrow as they'd drained themselves of tears. Of course this wasn't really the case and they both knew it, but what pleasure in their lying together in each other's arms, adrift in separate dreams, on the very edge of sleep or extinction.

One day in March they were packing to leave for a three-week visit in the East—to see relatives, to meet with Joel's new associates in Philadelphia, to begin house hunting—when Kim told Joel she wasn't going with him; she couldn't do it.

He was dazed, stunned, having thought in that brief instant that she meant their marriage was over. That she wouldn't be going east with him at all.

But she meant only that she wasn't going now, for the three weeks. She wanted to stay by herself in the house; she wanted to be alone.

Joel smiled instinctively as he always smiled when he was thrown off balance. Several times he said, "I don't understand."

Kim said there was nothing to understand.

"But what's wrong?"

"Nothing is wrong. I want to be alone for a while."

"Why didn't you say something before now?"

"I didn't know before now."

"Before this *instant?*"

"Don't talk to me in that tone of voice," she said, turning away.

Her copper-plated earrings, the size of silver dollars, swung and flashed against her cheeks. Her voice rose sharp and despairing.

She began to pace around their bedroom, not looking at him, resisting him. She lifted her heavy hair and beat at it from beneath with her fists as she sometimes did when she was anxious. She said she wanted him to go alone; she wanted to stay behind, alone; she was exhausted.

"Exhausted by what?" Joel said, dreading her answer.

"Just exhausted."

She shrank from him when he tried to touch her.

Still, his instinctive reaction was to smile. Like a skull's smile, Joel's wide staring grin.

She told him she needed space to breathe in. Always, they were alluding to the baby even when they spoke of other things. There was no escaping it—no escaping each other. She wanted to be alone for a while, for three weeks or maybe more; she was desperate to be alone and if he loved her he would respect her wishes.

When he tried to touch her she shrank from him. He felt her frantic heat, heard her quickened breath. He said, hurt, stung, angry, "You want a separation—you don't love *me*." She said, "I love you but I don't know if I want to love you." "What does that mean?" "I'm exhausted." "What does *that* mean?" She backed away. She was still slapping at her hair, breathing hard. When her stony gaze moved onto him it seemed she looked at him without recognition; he was simply something standing in her line of vision.

"You know what I mean," Kim whispered.

They were to leave for Philadelphia at seven-thirty in the morning but he ran out of the house, stayed away until nearly two. When he came back, mildly drunk, still angry, Kim was asleep in their bed, breathing now deeply and heavily. He envied her, resented her. He too was exhausted, after all.

In the bathroom he checked Kim's barbiturates but couldn't judge how many she had taken, or if she'd taken any.

He avoided looking too closely at his face in the mirror. When he drank too much his skin became mottled and flushed; the veins in his eyes pressed forward. He had been a beautiful child for what seemed a very long time and now, as an adult man, he worried he was still too attractive for other men to take seriously.

But he made them take him seriously: didn't he know how!

He went into the bedroom and woke Kim and she shrank from him, terrified, as if she'd forgotten their quarrel. As if she thought he might strike her. Her cringing, her high wild little screams, provoked him the more but he knew enough not to lose control. He shouted at her but did not hit her—drew his hand back—stood frozen, transfixed. "All right, I'll go alone. I'll leave you alone if that's what you want," he said. "If that's what you want." Kim was too frightened to speak. She lay with one arm raised to shield herself from him. He felt immediately repentant; he felt like a damned fool.

He said, "If I don't have you I don't have anything. You know that." He spoke bitterly, calmly. It was not a statement of love or even of reproach but a mere statement of fact.

Their baby, whose name they never afterward uttered, weighed only three pounds eight ounces at birth and had not lived a week. Despite the ingenious medical strategies, the costly machinery, the suffering. For there was suffering. You could tell yourself that an infant so absurdly small, born with malformations of the heart, lungs, and kidneys, very likely brain-damaged as well, did not possess the consciousness to register pain in the usual sense of the word. Without awareness of self, can there be awareness of suffering? And if the self *is* mere suffering . . . ? Joel was to wish he had not seen the tiny creature encased in its glass cage, since seeing it involved seeing also the strawlike translucent tubes hooking it up to life, tubes feeding both the body and the head. The infant was "premature" yet had the look of being prematurely aged, bearing the doom of the species.

Joel stared and stared, unable to break away. The creature was not so much his as it was himself.

He was in the east, he said, to see about buying property. In Bucks County, perhaps, or in a suburban village. He wasn't a wealthy man but he had a fair amount of money to invest and would have considerably more when his house in San Francisco was sold. What he wanted was—well, it was difficult to say. Something unusual, unconventional. Not necessarily in perfect condition; he and his wife liked to remodel, decorate. He would know it, he said, when he saw it.

Ordinarily he and his wife would have been house hunting together, Joel added. But his wife wasn't well at the present time.

The real estate agent, a Mrs. Brody, was all business and quick empathy, exhaling smoke as she jotted down information on her clipboard. A woman of indeterminate age, in her late forties perhaps, trim, attractive, stylishly dressed, with hair tinted the color of champagne, frosted nails, a husky throaty voice. She was sorry, she said, to hear that Joel's wife was unwell. Did they have any children? Plans for children? And could Joel be slightly more specific about the kind of house he wanted?

Joel said defensively, "As I told you, I'll know it when I see it."

Quickly Mrs. Brody said, "I understand." If she heard the emotion rising in her client's voice she gave no sign; she busied herself taking notes.

So began the brief intense period of Joel's house hunting.

For the next several days Mrs. Brody drove him about in her maroon Mercedes-Benz to look at properties, as she called them, of particular interest, in the country northeast of Philadelphia and in one or another suburban village. Joel had sorted through what seemed to have been hundreds of listings and selected a generous number, reluctant to discard any that seemed halfway promising. He was keenly excited yet also rather tense, edgy, acutely uncomfortable at first, sitting in the passenger's seat of Mrs. Brody's car, Mrs. Brody at the wheel. It seemed unnatural for him, particularly in his keyed-up state. If he and Kim were going somewhere it was invariably Joel who drove.

And when Mrs. Brody brought him to the first house—red-brick, Federal-style, "restored," and rather shabbily grand—Joel felt an instant's panic at the prospect of going inside. Why was he here? What right had he to trespass? His heart was beating heavily and his face felt unnaturally warm. Mrs. Brody unlocked the door and turned to him with a smile. "This is a beautiful house," she said. "It's a shame your wife isn't with you, to see it."

There had been a derelict house in his grandparents' neighborhood, years ago; he'd passed by it a thousand times as a boy: weeds in the front yard, diseased trees, boarded-up windows and barricaded front door, and that look of abandonment—patches of moss growing on the rotted shingles, tiny trees sprouting in the rain gutters. What was there about the house that so fascinated him as a child? He had sat on the curb staring. He prowled about. Threw stones that fell clattering down the steep slant of the roof. Once, ten years old, he'd dared poke about the rear of the house, stepping through mounds of broken rubble and glass, squatting to peer into a cellar window caked with grime—he'd frightened himself imagining a face staring up at him, waiting for him; he'd run away and never come back.

Even as he knew there was no one, nothing, there. For what would it be, all those years? No one, nothing. Eventually the old house was razed, the debris hauled away.

He telephoned Kim. He apologized for not having called sooner; he was excited, restless—couldn't sit still even with the phone in his hand—interrupting himself several times as he reported to her how his meetings with his associates-to-be had gone, how much they liked him, or seemed to, what sort of reputation he had. It was an excellent idea, their coming back east. This transfer was the wisest decision he'd made in years.

"Yes," Kim said in a neutral voice. "I think you're right."

"I *am* right," he said. "You'll see."

He waited for her to say something further—even to chide him for not having called until now. But she was silent.

He told her with suppressed excitement that he was house hunting. Again, she didn't respond. Then she said in a faint voice, "You are? Alone?" He said at once, "But I'm here alone." And again they fell silent. Joel stirred his drink with a forefinger: Scotch on the rocks. He'd bought his own bottle that afternoon, ordered ice cubes from room service. Remembered too late, when the busboy delivered them, that ice cubes by way of hotel room service were enough for a dozen people.

He wanted to tell Kim about Mrs. Brody, joke a bit about the houses he'd seen that day, blurred now in his memory, each so promising at the outset and finally—in some cases, immediately—so disappointing, but she was vague and evasive, sleepy-sounding. He wondered if she had taken a barbiturate, if in fact he had woken her from sleep. He said, "Are you all right?" and she said, "I'm fine," and he said, "I hope so," and she said, "Yes—I'm fine," and he said, "As long as you're all right," and she said, that slight ironic nettlesome edge to her voice, "I didn't say I was all right, I said I'm fine," and he laughed as if she had said something witty, which perhaps she had. "As long as you're fine, then," he said lamely, feeling clumsy and blunt as if tumescent (which he was not), "—with me gone." Kim made a sound that might have been assent or protest, mild protest, mild and fleeting as a sigh. "The house empty," he said. But this too was wrong, not what he meant to say. He corrected himself: "I mean—empty of me."

There was a pause. Kim said, "Who else would it be empty of?"

Joel said quickly, "Look—you *are* all right? Would you like me to come back home?"

"No," said Kim. "I'm fine. Didn't I tell you?"

After they hung up Joel sat on the edge of his bed and drank his drink. His thoughts followed one another slow and dense as clots in the blood but were not clear, could not have been translated into words. He felt both sick and elated. He tried to sift through a stack of property listings Mrs. Brody had left with him but he was too distracted, couldn't concentrate. He finished his drink and poured another and realized that he was waiting for the telephone to ring, but why was he waiting for the telephone to ring? He and Kim had just spoken. And there was no one else likely to call him, here.

Are you going to try again? he was asked. His parents asked him, and his older sister asked him, and even Kim's mother asked him, fearing, perhaps, to ask her daughter directly. The question was always tactfully raised; Joel grew to anticipate it. He told them frankly that he didn't know. He hoped so. But he didn't know. It was up to Kim after all, Kim was the one who had suffered most, or did he mean more: she'd suffered more than he had. (Obviously the baby had suffered most, but that was another story.) No, Joel said, speaking carefully so that he wouldn't be misunderstood; no, he didn't know. He wouldn't know for a long, long time.

"Vacant houses are harder to sell than furnished houses," Mrs. Brody said, unlocking the door, leading him inside. "They look smaller, for some reason. Why, do you think? Why, if there's more space, do they look smaller?"

Joel said he didn't know. Maybe it was an optical illusion.

"It *is* an illusion of some kind," Mrs. Brody said. "I suppose it must be psychological."

He was shown vacant houses, and he was shown furnished houses. A Dutch colonial, and a brick Cape Cod, and an English Tudor, and another English Tudor, and a California-style house built around an atrium, and a glass-and-redwood split-level, and a French Normandy, and a renovated stone farmhouse, and an aggressively modern house designed by a student of Frank Lloyd Wright. . . . Each was promising but none was, upon inspection, quite right.

"I hope I'm not exhausting you," Joel said gallantly. Though in fact it was he who felt the strain.

"Not at all," Mrs. Brody said, with a quick smile. "It's my job."

The woman was tireless, or seemed so. Brisk, pert, cheery, su-

premely in control. In her high-heeled shoes, handbag in the crook
of her arm. She had the key to every lock; only let her fit it into the
door and the door opened and she led her client inside: Mr. Collier,
who was made to feel uncharacteristically passive, helpless. He didn't
like the feeling. Then again, he did like it; there was something
intimate and brazen, heady, as if with the air of the forbidden, about
being led by a woman he didn't know into the houses of people he
didn't know, escorted through rooms in which strangers lived their
secret lives. The first several minutes were the most acute; he felt
shy, absurdly ill at ease, excited. As if he was being brought to a test
of some kind, a challenge or a riddle, and would not be equal to it.

Living rooms and dining rooms and kitchens (many gleaming with
smart new tile floors, copper utensils that looked unused) and stair-
ways and corridors and bedrooms and bathrooms and glassed-in
porches and wood-paneled basements and washer-drier rooms
(where the soiled laundry of strangers, in inglorious heaps, was frequently in view), and again living rooms and dining rooms and kitchens, and sometimes, in the older houses, butler's pantries, and
bedrooms and bathrooms and maids' rooms and staircases, and two-
and three- and even four-car garages. . . . Everything held promise
but nothing pleased. Everything held promise but nothing pleased!
He grew irritable, impatient, panicked that he wouldn't find what he
knew was there, somewhere, waiting for him—if only he could find
it. Several times he rejected houses with a flat "No, sorry," not
troubling to get out of Mrs. Brody's car. Then again, he asked to
see one of the houses a second time even as—as he asked—he suddenly knew it wasn't the right house and he was wasting his and Mrs.
Brody's time.

Though Mrs. Brody kept assuring him, "It's my job."

She assured him, "The customer knows what he wants and what
he doesn't want."

She asked him to call her Charlotte. (" 'Charlotte Brody'—the
name sounds like something out of a nineteenth-century novel,
doesn't it?") He asked her to call him Joel but didn't insist; she
seemed more comfortable calling him Mr. Collier. Joel liked her,
was inclined to trust her, yet at the same time had to remember that
she was trying to sell him something—hoping to sell him property

that would cost a half million dollars or more—and what, he wondered, was the agent's commission on such a sale?

He tried to keep this fact in mind. It was a fact no salesman would ever forget.

On the morning of the third day Charlotte Brody drove twenty miles into the country to show a house she thought Joel might like. And so it seemed as she parked her car and he stared—how his heart began to pound!—as much intrigued by the house's location as by the house itself. It was a modified Cape Cod, not, as Charlotte Brody warned, in the very best condition but an excellent bargain, on the market for only twelve days and sure to be sold soon. Its location was the odd, intriguing, charming thing: built on the downward slope of a steep hill beneath a graveled road, overlooking a small lake, no other houses visible in the area. To reach the house you had to descend a considerable flight of steps. There were railings on both sides painted a gay brash green; the house's shutters were the same color. As they approached the front door Joel's heartbeat accelerated—he could see right through the house, through a front window to windows at the rear overlooking the lake! The air was wintery, still, fresh, invigorating; the lake was glassy, dimpled near shore with thin discontinuous sheets of ice. Joel glanced back and up, at the stone steps. How vertical they were, how steep. He could see Kim making her way down, cautious, gripping the railing (which was not very steady), worried of losing her footing—was she pregnant again? Charlotte Brody said, "*Isn't* it delightful? A honeymoon cottage. And intelligently priced."

Joel followed Mrs. Brody inside in a haze of apprehension. For some minutes he seemed scarcely to see what he was looking at or to hear what he was being told. . . . Was this *the* house, but oddly altered? The rooms cramped and rather shabby, the ceiling too low, a smell of cooking in the air, dog hairs on all the furniture? The kitchen fixtures antiquated? The colors all the wrong colors—bold, primary, "arty," "modern"? Joel could scarcely follow Mrs. Brody's animated talk of a mortgage available at 12 percent, boating privileges on the lake ("But no motorboats allowed, I think that's wise"), the convenience of a shopping center only five miles away. Off the main

room was a weatherized but drafty porch, and in a corner was an old
spinet piano, badly out of tune as you'd imagine; Joel struck several
notes. He had not played piano since going away to college. A sensation of extreme weakness rose in him, as if he were about to cry,
or had in fact been crying.

The occupants of the house had tried to decorate it with a certain
flair: Turkish carpets, outsized pillows, walls crowded with art. Joel
had a vision of Kim rearranging the pillows, Kim drawing the drapes
back from the windows, Kim kneeling on the hearth in front of the
stone fireplace. . . . But was the woman Kim? Her husband entered
the room as if at a gallop, tall, husky, big-shouldered, sweater draped
over his shoulders—no one Joel knew. He was faintly revulsed by
them, disapproved of how they'd ruined this house of such promise,
wanted only to be gone. To be led out.

Beneath the cooking odors and the dog odors there was an undercurrent of decay as well. Joel's sensitive nostrils picked it up. Was
the lake polluted? Did it flood the house? He interrupted Charlotte
Brody to say, "I assume it floods here sometimes, doesn't it? That
isn't much of a retaining wall."

"I suppose—sometimes," she said. With a slight drop of her voice.

Later that day she asked whether Joel might want to call a temporary halt to house hunting? It was such an intense, exhausting
activity after all.

Joel said quickly and coolly, "Do you want to give me up? And,
if so, could you suggest another agent to take your place?"

Charlotte Brody was startled into silence, perhaps even stunned.
For a moment she couldn't even reply. Then she said, in her level,
throaty voice, "Certainly not. I was only thinking of you."

A split-level glass-brick-stone-stucco with cathedral ceiling, enormous fieldstone fireplaces, 180 degrees of plate glass overlooking a
"sylvan woodland scene," "fully equipped wet bar" on the ground
level—and Joel, suddenly impatient and thirsty, suggested to Charlotte Brody that he make them a drink.

Naturally Mrs. Brody demurred; that sort of thing wasn't done.
Joel said, "Oh, what's the difference?" He poked about behind the
bar, whistling, ignored Mrs. Brody's protests. What difference could

it possibly make? And who would know? The liquor cabinet was lavishly stocked; there was even a container of fresh ice cubes in the freezer. "Scotch on the rocks, Charlotte," he said. "Who deserves it if we don't?"

She was staring, smiling, fiddling with the strap of her handbag, uncertain of how to respond. Joel simply pushed the glass in her hand. "I insist," he said.

She accepted it reluctantly. Joel clicked his glass against hers and said, "Here's to—the future."

"Yes," Mrs. Brody said.

Joel took a large grateful swallow of his drink. "Assuming there is one, of course."

Mrs. Brody sipped at her drink, or pretended to do so. With an air of mild reproach she said, "There will be, Mr. Collier."

She was a handsome woman with a fair, just perceptibly faded skin. Fastidiously made up, the eyes especially—shrewd, intelligent, watchful. Her kidskin gloves were the color of vanilla and gave off that scent; her suit might have been by Chanel: a fine, fine wool, rosy-brown, expensive. Joel had been smelling her subtly astringent perfume for days; he didn't know if he liked it or disliked it. If he liked her very much or disliked her. She held her glass high between them as if judging the innocence, or the danger, of the moment. She was cordial, still—Charlotte Brody couldn't be anything but cordial: the stamp of the professional—but not altogether at ease in his presence. Preparing to sidestep him should he—

As if, Joel thought, annoyed, he was that kind.

He strolled whistling about the recreation room, drink in hand. Asking Mrs. Brody a barrage of questions though it was clear to him, and very likely to her, that he had no intention of buying this house: it was not *the* house. Glass walls overlooking a redwood deck overlooking an oddly shaped swimming pool, now covered with a tarpaulin; in the near distance a dense stand of pine. In one of the windows a woman's shadowy reflection defined itself but he knew it could not be Kim's. It was no woman he knew.

He, in this house, was no one he knew.

But he *did* feel good. The drink *did* hit the spot. In a few minutes he'd make himself another.

He said, abruptly, "I'm so lonely."

He said, "Oh, God, I'm so scared."

He was sitting in a leather chair with queer chrome tubular legs, his knees weak and head spinning. Only one drink and his head spinning.

In weak moments the image of the glassed-in baby rose to consciousness, transparent tubes attached to its head because veins elsewhere were too tiny to endure the pressure of the IV fluids. Incubation, but the incubation period was over and this was the result. No one to blame. He was a reasonable man, knowing this was so, but still. His wife had said quietly, What have we brought into the world together except Death? And he had had no reply.

He was leaning forward, his head on his crossed arms. Playing at being maudlin drunk though certainly he wasn't drunk, not so quickly. He felt a woman's hand nearing the back of his neck. Her lacquered fingernails about to dig, lightly, into his flesh. Or would she lean over him to kiss him, exposed, vulnerable, hopeful as he was? But when he looked up Mrs. Brody was at the far side of the room, as if unaware of him, checking something on her clipboard. She wore half-moon reading glasses perched low on her nose; he couldn't quite see her expression. The room was very quiet. The windows were too high, too insistent. Dull wintery-white light, eye-aching yet not illuminating, heavy with moisture. Joel wanted to shield his face.

It seemed to him that a good deal of time had passed, yet of course it was no more than two or three minutes.

His glass was empty, on the table before him. Mrs. Brody's glass, scarcely touched, was on the bar.

He heaved himself to his feet, sucking in his breath, in robust high spirits again. He would have walked out without thinking about the glasses but of course Mrs. Brody remembered, washed them carefully at the sink, dried them, tidied things up.

That was the last house but one. He'd forget it by the next morning.

The final house Mrs. Brody was to show him had been on the market, she said, for three years. And it was rather overpriced. She didn't think, in fact, that it was a property quite for him.

But Joel wanted to see it nonetheless. He was intrigued by the blurred photograph, the description of a "stately brick Georgian" with "historic" significance, a "Bucks County estate." Six bedrooms and a part-finished attic, "ideal for large family."

The drive took a half hour, beyond Jenkintown, beyond Abington, up north and east of Huntingdon Valley. Mrs. Brody was quiet as she drove, and Joel was quiet, drumming his fingers on his knees. He stared out the window and saw nothing. Traffic, roads, stubbled snowy fields, then again traffic and hilly farmland and a sky the color of tarnished silver. His nerves were taut and alert, his eyes burned, he felt himself on the brink of a revelation—though he had slept fitfully the night before, an alcoholic stupor for a few reliable hours, then broken-up patches of sleep until morning. At one point he woke dazed and groggy, not knowing where he was. He'd felt someone touch his shoulder, as Kim sometimes did when he snored loudly. Or when, as she said, he seemed to stop breathing—she would be wakened by the absence of sound, the sudden quiet. A sharp clicking sound in his throat and he'd stop breathing and after what seemed like a very long time he drew in a deep snorting breath as if he was desperate to suck up all the air in the room. . . . He had felt someone touch his shoulder, but of course there was no one there.

The evening before, Kim had told him on the telephone that she was going to spend some time with her married sister in Arizona, her sister was recuperating from some minor surgery and had invited her down, and Joel said that sounded like an excellent idea—she always enjoyed visiting there, it seemed to do her good. He didn't ask immediately if she wanted him to join her in Arizona but talked for a while of other things, that day's house hunting, for instance, keeping the talk general and vague and upbeat. Before they hung up he asked if she wanted him to fly to Tucson instead of going directly back home, and Kim said, "I didn't think you could spare the time," and Joel said, "I suppose I can't."

Three acres of land, mainly woods, came with the house in Huntingdon Valley. As Mrs. Brody pulled into the circular driveway Joel stared and stared, unable to believe his good fortune. He thought, This is it.

Told himself extravagantly, Coming home!

"The architecture *is* distinctive, isn't it?" Charlotte Brody said, to break the silence. She couldn't determine if her client was deeply offended by the weatherworn look of the house, the crumbling foundation and sagging shutters, or whether, seeing past such contingencies to the solid structure beneath, he was deeply stirred. "Of course it needs work—"

"Yes," Joel said quickly, as if to shut her up.

"In the hands of the right owners—"

"Yes," Joel said. "I was thinking that too."

Inside, Joel was sharply disappointed that the house was very nearly vacant and smelled of neglect. Only a few pieces of furniture in the downstairs rooms, draped in dusty sheets. No heat, of course; the air was damp and chill, colder, seemingly, than out-of-doors. A beautiful house, or it had been at one time, with large airy rooms, carved archways, hardwood floors. The ceilings were high, the floors bare: their footsteps sounded discomfortingly loud and their voices echoed, particularly Mrs. Brody's. The woman was talking nervously, incessantly, as if frightened of the silence. Joel wished violently he had come here alone.

He walked through the downstairs rooms, slowly, reverently, staring and blinking. Coming home! Coming home! His vision misted over; he felt weak, shaky, yet altogether certain of what he must do. He would buy this house: make a bid, a shrewd but reasonable bid. Already he could imagine how the living room would look, the floors sanded and polished, the walls freshly papered, perhaps in William Morris wallpaper. Near-transparent curtains at all the windows to let the light in, and the marble fireplace restored, if marble so discolored can be restored. They would buy new furniture in light neutral colors. . . .

He was intensely excited. He unbuttoned his coat, tugged at his collar. It seemed he could not look hard enough, yet he was having difficulty seeing clearly; his eyes had begun to water. And when Mrs. Brody fell silent he could hear something, or someone, in the background: singing? children singing? or was it a radio? upstairs? in another wing of the house?

"What is that? Do you hear that?" Joel asked Mrs. Brody. She cocked her head, stood very still, heard nothing. The old house was silent. Outside, the sporadic cries of birds, crows—Joel had noticed a field of crows, close by—and in the distance, nearly inaudible, what

sounded like the low dull roar of machinery. "It sounded like
singing," Joel said. But now he heard nothing.

They walked on. Into the dining room: French windows facing
a lawn that sloped to a border of junipers hundreds of yards away.
Joel's vision misted over; he swallowed hard, seeing the lawn in
summer, the grass freshly mowed, beds bright with flowers—

He heard the singing again, faint and teasing. He interrupted
Charlotte Brody's chatter to say, "There—there it is! You must hear
it."

Charlotte Brody said cautiously, "Where is it coming from?"

"It sounds like children singing."

They listened. And now, to his annoyance, Joel couldn't—quite—
hear it. "It might be coming from upstairs, or from the carriage house.
Does someone live in the carriage house?"

"Not that I know of."

"A radio left on—"

"Yes. That might be it."

Joel was staring at a chandelier—brass and crystal, Irish-made—
that hung down from the precise center of the dining room. It was
layered in cobwebs and dust but still beautiful. How sad, though,
that the dining room was vacant, the wallpapered walls discolored,
the hardwood floor in such poor condition one might think it had
been deliberately battered: hammered at, chopped at, with mysterious instruments.

Mrs. Brody led him through to the butler's pantry and into the
kitchen. Here, the sound was stronger: Joel decided it must be made
by wires vibrating in the wind. A high maddening humming.

"Of course, the kitchen needs to be completely remodeled," Mrs.
Brody said apologetically. "Modernized. Would your wife like a
country kitchen?"

"What?"

"Country kitchen."

Joel discussed kitchens with Charlotte Brody, hearing his voice
level and clear and unhurried, his logic impeccable, even as he felt
a tightening in his chest, a sickish apprehension. Each of these rooms
was unknown to him—yet oddly familiar: he seemed to know what
he would see, though in fact as he looked about he saw nothing

familiar; the house was totally foreign. He'd never felt so disoriented and yet—and yet!—so certain of himself. He was arguing with Kim, telling her they must make a bid on the house before someone else did; the house would be snatched away from them if they didn't hurry. A down payment of $200,000 could be easily arranged if their San Francisco house was sold quickly. . . .

They would have children to fill the empty rooms. Whose children, otherwise, would fill them?

They were climbing the uncarpeted stairs and Joel heard a faint scurrying overhead and saw, or seemed to see, a shadowy figure in the hall above. Mrs. Brody noticed nothing, but then perhaps Mrs. Brody was not as alert as her client. She was telling him of the house's history: old misfortunes and more recent ones; the difficulty the owner, an elderly widower who had disinherited his children, had given a number of local realtors over the years. He would not budge from his unreasonably high price and he would not, or could not, keep the house in a salable condition. . . . The shadow broke into shadows as Joel and Mrs. Brody approached, dispersed as if running for cover. Playful figures, very likely children: but of course nothing but light, refracted sunlight, a tricky play of light and shadow. The original house had been built in 1840, Mrs. Brody said, by one Icabod Dieter, Squire—he'd insisted upon calling himself a Squire—and subsequently added to, remodeled, renovated over the decades. Its heyday, so to speak, was in the twenties, when the owners had plenty of money, owned five hundred acres of land; there were no taxes, servants came cheap. She glanced sidelong at her frowning client. Could she sense the intensity of his interest? How improbably close she was to a sale? "Of course," she added, carefully, "a good deal of work needs to be done. In the hands of the right people—"

"Yes," Joel said. "You've already said that."

It should not have been surprising, yet it was, and keenly disappointing, that the upstairs—the "master bedroom" in particular—was in far worse condition than the downstairs. Bedrooms, bathrooms, a sewing room: the wallpaper was stained, the windowsills warped, the floors badly scratched. There were ghostly rectangles on the walls where mirrors and paintings had hung. Apart from fireplaces in several of the rooms there were no unusual features on this floor; Joel looked in vain for something to admire. Of course, everything would have to be redone, in any case: new plastering, new wallpaper, new plumbing, new windows. The floors were so bad they would have to be completely carpeted. And the lighting fixtures—

He was standing in the doorway of a large high-ceilinged room speaking intensely with Mrs. Brody even as he stood in the intensive care ward for premature infants, "preemies" as they were called, being told something by a doctor that ran through his head like a piece of short thread through a needle; try as he might he couldn't retain it. Too much! Too much to be borne! He had understood that the floor beneath him could fall away at any instant; that was what he had to concentrate on. Like this floor, in Squire Dieter's house.

The physical body is the "floor." The head imagines itself floating but is in fact merely balanced on its stalk: a desperate device, staring and blinking, taking in information, monitoring the avalanche of information that constitutes the "world."

Mrs. Brody's voice trailed off as she sensed her client's inattention. She was opening a door that connected two rooms. "The nursery through here," she said, "I would guess."

Joel heard the high fine humming again, heard a teasing scuffle down the corridor. He began to whistle. Went to stand at a window, hands on his hips. I own this, he thought. The sky was mottled, deep crevices of cloud, pockets of sunshine. Oh, help me, God. God help me. It was another man's prayer—another man who had stood here, at this window, long ago. In a house so "historic," in these upstairs rooms in particular, a good deal of living had transpired.

It was damply cold. Their breaths steamed. Yet Joel was perspiring inside his clothes. Mrs. Brody had slipped on her tight kidskin gloves that smelled of vanilla.

Mrs. Brody was about to suggest that they leave—Joel had stood so long without speaking, rubbing his forehead with the back of a hand—but he said, turning to her, "There's more to the house, isn't there, than we've seen? A third floor?"

"A partially finished attic, yes," Mrs. Brody said. She hesitated. "Would you like to see it?"

"Of course," Joel said.

Was it *there* he'd meant to go all along?

Mrs. Brody led him along the hallway to a back stairway, where they climbed wordless up into the dark; the light switch evidently didn't work. A powerful smell of mildew, mice, dirt assaulted their nostrils.

Mrs. Brody pushed a door open cautiously. She said, "I believe I saw this part of the house years ago, but I don't seem to—" The room was flooded with light, which was a relief. They stepped in. Joel blinked and stared, wiping his forehead with a tissue. He was really quite agitated and no longer cared if Charlotte Brody noticed. She was speaking quickly, walking about in her clattering high heels as if to distract them both. "Excellent for a study of sorts, a hideaway for the man of the house . . . guest room . . . room for a teenager who values privacy. . . ."

The room was large but undefined, a mere rectangle. Dormer windows on one side, a large circular window on the other. Flooded with light, but mere space. Very dirty, cartons and mismatched furniture in one of the corners, dust balls, the dessicated remains of insects. That strong rank smell of mice and age. Joel, breathless from the stairs, stood with his hands on his hips. He'd climbed up so impatiently, with such dread and anticipation, and—was this the room? *This*—the last room in the house—the place of revelation? Even the faint teasing singing had stopped. He heard only the crows somewhere close by, their raucous cries lifting and fading.

The circular window was unusually large, perhaps five feet across, like a porthole, but with elaborate leaded spokes suggesting a wheel or a stylized spider's web. The glass was layered in grime but sunshine streamed through nonetheless: warm, dazzling.

The floor was covered in worn linoleum tile in which there were deep scratch marks, from a bed perhaps. Joel could see the bed clearly—plain, merely functional, no headboard, exposed metal rollers. A figure lying on it, too weak to move. Too weak to turn his head.

Somewhere close by, improbably, an insect was buzzing. Joel discovered a wasp on the windowsill of the circular window—tiny convulsive death throes. He said, his voice lifting in faint bemused wonder, "How can a wasp still be living at this time of year?" but Mrs. Brody was speaking of other things and did not hear.

Joel stood very still. There was nothing in this room but the space itself: mere space delimited by four walls.

But what otherwise might there have been? What had he hoped to see?

Sunlight spilling through the window, churning with dust as with maggots, atoms. Joel closed his eyes and felt the warmth on his eyelids. His heart was pounding very hard; he knew why he was here.

He stood swaying on the balls of his feet, sunshine beating on his face. Light, feathery, insubstantial as a breath, or a kiss. He knew: his life was pointless, yet he wanted to live. There was no purpose to it, yet he wanted to live. He was desperate, greedy, shameless—he wanted to live.

Mrs. Brody cleared her throat nervously. She asked him if he had any more questions about the house, and after a while he turned to her and said no. He'd seen as much as he needed to see.

She drove him back to his hotel and gave him her card, told him to telephone her at home, if necessary, if he wanted to see any further houses or wanted to revisit any of those he'd looked at. He thanked her warmly. Shook her hand. Upstairs in his hotel room he ripped her card into several swift pieces and dropped them into the wastebasket.

He went to bed and slept for fifteen hours straight. Woke feeling wonderfully refreshed, suffused with a curious tender strength. Where was he? Why had he come here? What powers were given him? So close to extinction, to move an inch was to move a thousand miles.

THE KNIFE

She was a religious woman, mildly—the aftermath of a rural Methodist upbringing. But that was some time ago and she rarely gave a thought to religion now, or to what's called God. Certainly she wasn't superstitious. If her dreams of the previous night had brought her a premonition of disaster, she didn't recall it and would have discounted it in any case; she was always edgy, though not necessarily unhappy, when her husband was away. She rather liked, she said, spending a day or two alone with her daughter. It was like old times, she said. Meaning a few years ago when Bonnie was a baby.

The night before, Bonnie had showed Harriet a glossy reproduction of a Chagall painting—the one in which a startled woman is being kissed by a floating, sinuous lover, a dream transmuted into colors so audacious you couldn't help smiling as if in recognition—and when Bonnie said with her new skepticism, "Nobody can do *this*, can they!" Harriet said, "Oh, people can do anything, sometimes." The answer was meant to be fanciful: Bonnie was of an age now—eight, nearly nine—when the most subtle intonations and nuances in adults' voices registered with her, like music. Harriet sometimes wondered if she and her husband were training their daughter in the ambiguities of life and not its stark primary colorations.

That day, a day in late spring, had been unusually warm but by evening the temperature had dropped twenty degrees. A sudden fierce wind was blowing up so Harriet went about closing windows; she was straining to close a window in the rear room—a handsome converted porch, mostly glass, her husband used as his study at home—when she saw a movement, the fleet afterimage of a movement, somewhere behind her, reflected in the glass. And she knew. She knew: the height of the figure, its peculiar swiftness, meant it wasn't Bonnie, and of course it wasn't her husband, who was away at an academic conference. She knew, she knew, yet she continued tugging at the window even as her heart beat rapidly and a wave of terror washed over her. She thought, I can get out the back door, I can run for help, but she knew she'd never leave Bonnie behind; Bonnie was upstairs in her room.

She had left a door unlocked, the door leading into the garage. She knew at once that was it. Everyone in the neighborhood kept doors unlocked during the day, children were always trailing in and out of houses, why had hers been singled out? She could have wept for the mistake she'd made she could not now undo.

She saw by the digital clock on her husband's desk that it was 7:40. She thought, I must remember that time.

She was behaving, still, as if nothing were wrong. Dreamy and shivering. Walking a little slower and more stiffly than usual. Even as she reentered the house knowing how the air was disturbed by their presence, smelling them, something acrid and sweaty and excited, sensing their very weight on the floorboards, she was consciously behaving as if nothing were wrong. As if, observing her, taking pity on her, they might yet relent and go away. She found herself staring at the dining room clock, but this time the hour didn't register.

Someone said loudly, "Lady!" and she turned to see two youngish men advancing toward her, two strangers, both in jeans, T-shirts: one of them with a flattened nose and oddly appealing eyes, the other tall, rangy, weedy, with long lank faded red hair, jutting ears, a light dusting of freckles on his face. He was the one carrying the knife.

They were high, nerved up, staring at her and grinning, both talking at once. "We're not going to hurt you, lady! Just stay cool! Stay cool!"—she would think afterward that they spoke like hoodlums on television or in the movies, for how otherwise would they speak?—"Got some cash in here? Find us some cash, lady! Where's your purse, lady? C'mon, lady, nobody's going to get hurt! Get your ass moving and nobody's going to get hurt!"

Her heartbeat was so hard and rapid she thought she was going to faint, and afterward she would realize with a stab of angry regret that had she fainted at that moment, had she simply fallen, limp and helpless, crashing to the floor, they would probably have fled the house: grabbed a few things, whatever was handy, and fled. But, no: she made an effort to keep from fainting as if out of courtesy! And it was pride too, for she thought of herself as a woman who took control of situations, a woman who was mature, responsible, not hysterical—a woman with a steady level gaze whom you could trust.

That was what she wanted the men to think, wasn't it—that they could trust her—for wasn't she cooperative, wasn't she calm and even in a way gracious, leading them into the kitchen where she'd left her purse (except it wasn't there: where was it?) and speaking quietly to them, saying, "You don't want to do this, really; my husband will be home in a few minutes—he'll be back before eight o'clock"; saying, "That knife makes me nervous, why don't you put it away, it isn't necessary, really"; not quite pleading: "My daughter is upstairs, she's only eight years old, please don't frighten her—please go away before you frighten her." But where was her purse? Why couldn't she find her purse? Her teeth had begun to chatter and her hands and knees were shaking uncontrollably.

They were her age, perhaps a year or two younger. Mature men in their early thirties but loud, loutish, deliberately clumsy, it almost seemed, like teenagers. Scared of what they were doing but exhilarated by it too—showing off, Harriet saw, for each other's benefit. And, seeing that she was an attractive woman, a small-boned terrified woman, no match for them, perhaps for her benefit as well.

They gave her orders in high breathless voices, telling her to get some cash and where's the silverware and nobody's going to get hurt if she did what they said. "Move your ass, lady! C'mon, lady!" the man with the knife said repeatedly in a boyish sniggering tone as if Harriet were a dumb creature in need of prodding. So naturally Bonnie heard them—how could the child have failed to hear them?—and started downstairs, and Harriet, her hands shaking even more violently, pulling open a drawer to show the men her silverware in its worn chamois-lined tray—what remained of an elegant sterling set belonging to her grandmother, rarely used now and badly tarnished—thought she would never hear anything again in her life so wrenching, so unspeakably terrible, as her daughter's running footsteps on the stairs and her daughter's lifted voice, inquisitive rather than alarmed, "Mommy? Mommy?"

"Don't come in here, honey," Harriet called out. "Bonnie? Go back upstairs, please," keeping her voice level and taking pride in the fact: yes, her voice *is* level, Mommy *is* calm, Bonnie will remember when it's over.

For she was thinking, even then, even as Bonnie ran into the kitchen, that this wasn't happening to her alone, this was happening to Bonnie as well and she must behave in a way that reflected the fact. And she was thinking that the men would be yet more impressed, how could they not be impressed—a woman behaving so rationally so cooperatively you might even say so sweetly under these emergency circumstances; surely they would feel admiration for her? sympathy for her? Surely they would go away quickly with whatever she could give them and would not injure her or her daughter—wouldn't they?

Harriet saw that the men were nearly as frightened of Bonnie as Bonnie was frightened of them; they were so high, so stoned, they hadn't seemed to have counted on a child. She said calmly, "Let her go up to her room, please"—she didn't want to plead or beg, she hoped simply to sound reasonable—"she's just a little girl, let her go up to her room, please," as Bonnie, whimpering and sobbing, hid behind her, clutching at her legs. The child was small-boned like her mother, with her mother's pale silvery-blond hair, her wide-spaced brown eyes. Her cheeks were babyish, plump, streaked now with tears. How quickly, Harriet thought, children cry . . . as if the tears are always there, in readiness. "Let her go upstairs, please," Harriet told the men with as much an air of authority, maternal authority, as she could simulate. "Don't frighten her like this—have some compassion!" The man with the flattened nose seemed confused by her words and shrugged OK, but the one with the knife said no—"Hell, no, lady"—his mouth stretching like a rubber band in a fond leering smile as if he knew Harriet intended to trick him and he was too smart for her. When he smiled his cheeks dimpled.

"She'd call the police or something. You think we're assholes? She don't need to go anywhere."

They were examining the silverware, they were going to dump it into a grocery bag they'd found in one of the cupboards, but the man with the flattened nose said nervously he didn't think it looked like anything much and the man with the knife, the lanky red-haired grinning man, said in derision, "That's *tarnish*, asshole, that's how you know it's the real thing!"

Harriet said desperately, "Please take it. It's good silver, really. It's worth money."

"OK, lady, and where's your purse?" the man with the knife said. "Where's your purse you said was out here?"

"I think it must be in the bedroom—"

"You said it was out here, lady."

"I don't know where it is. I don't think there's much money in it—"

"Shut up! Find it! Get a move on!"

"My husband will be home in a few minutes. He—"

"Fuck 'my husband'! Fuck that shit! Who you think you're jiving? *Get a move on!*"

He was furious suddenly, shouting in her face. Bonnie began screaming "Mommy! Mommy! Mommy!" She was pawing at Harriet as if she were crazed and Harriet had all she could do to subdue her, pinion her arms, clutch her tight. She could feel her daughter's heart beating wildly inside her small rib cage. How fragile, she thought, how easily smashed. . . . "Bonnie," she whispered, "Bonnie—it's all right, it's all right, really," saying the same words over and over like an incantation. To the men she said, "Let me put her in the bathroom, at least—there's a bathroom downstairs. Let me get her out of the way, please." She was pleading now, her voice rising: "My daughter can't help you, she has nothing to do with this—*please!*"

The man with the knife was still suspicious but his friend said, "Yeah, OK—good idea," and that seemed to be it. Bonnie was making them both very nervous. Harriet half carried her daughter to the bathroom in the hall, whispering to her to be a good girl, to be quiet, it would all be over in a few minutes, please please be quiet, could she promise? Lock the door and don't unlock it until Mommy tells her to: promise? "What if the kid climbs out the fucking window?" the man with the knife was saying in an aggrieved voice. His friend said, "She ain't going to climb out no window, it's too high. Get cool."

So Harriet hugged Bonnie a final time and shut her up in the closet-sized prettily decorated guest bathroom that always smelled of lemon-scented soap no one, even guests, ever used, and she thought, Now it will be all right, telling herself, Now it will be all right, even as she turned back to the men and saw the light around their heads blotch and darken as if it were about to go out. She was panicked, swaying, on the verge of fainting again, and again she willed herself to recover: head lowered, blood rushing into the arteries with a terrible percussive force. One of the men grabbed her by the shoulder and gave her a furious shake. "C'mon, lady! Cut that shit! *C'mon!*"

They shoved Harriet forward. They carried the silverware loose in the paper bag, and in the dining room she showed them the brass candlesticks on the mantel and they took those too, "They're expensive, they're worth money," Harriet said, and she led them into her husband's study where his newly purchased German-made camera was kept on a shelf, "There—that's worth at least a thousand dollars," she said, absurdly gratified when the man with the flattened nose snatched the camera up like a prize, though she knew it wasn't worth $1,000 or half that much. "You can sell all these things," she said. "They're worth money."

She could hear Bonnie crying in the rear of the house.

She said, still in her reasonable voice, "Why don't you leave now? If you leave now I won't call the police. You can have those things. I promise I won't call the police."

They were in the living room, which ran nearly the length of the front of the house. Its pretensions of understated taste, elegance— nubby tweed sofa, matching chairs, glass-topped coffee table, wall-to-wall beige carpeting, above all the glossy-leafed plants in their earthenware pots—struck Harriet as comical. She wondered that the men, hands on their hips, staring, assessing, did not laugh aloud.

They asked where was the TV and when Harriet said it was kept in another room one of them said, "OK, show me," and the other said derisively, "Who's going to carry a TV?" so that was dropped. They were going to go upstairs but one of them changed his mind, suddenly gripping Harriet by the back of the neck—it was this gesture that made her understand she was in trouble, seriously in trouble: the abrupt contact, the hard canny fingers closing on her flesh stopping her cold as a dog is stopped by his collar—and said in a triumphant voice, "Just a minute lady, *take that down*"—indicating of all things an oil painting, an unframed abstract canvas done by one of Harriet's friends, on the wall behind the sofa.

"Take it down? Why?"

"Let's just see what's behind it!"

"Behind it?"

Then she realized: he thought there might be a wall safe hidden behind the painting.

She said, "I'm afraid you have the wrong idea about this household," actually trying to laugh, to make a sound like laughter, faint and breathless, incredulous. She said, "Do you think we're wealthy people? This isn't a wealthy neighborhood—can't you tell?" She added, not wanting to insult them, "I'm just trying to save you time."

One of the men pushed her forward, the flat of his hand between her shoulder blades in a rude shove. "Do what I *say*, lady!" It was the young man with the knife: his dull-red hair had fallen into his face; he gave off a fierce hot odor of sweat and indignation. "Do what I *say* and you won't get hurt."

They were on the stairs when for no reason Harriet could determine the man with the flattened nose changed his mind: he was leaving.

He'd had it, he said, he was getting the hell out, and he and his friend argued briefly on the stairway landing but he had his way and ran back downstairs. He was carrying the bulky grocery bag with its mismatched rattling contents.

Harriet felt her heart clench, knowing it would be worse now.

(It would turn out that the first man to leave the house left by the front door—bold, brash, stupid, unthinking—and no one in the neighborhood saw him, or reported having seen him. The second man was to leave, a half hour later, by the door to the garage, as he'd come in.)

He was angry now, angrier, because of his "asshole" friend and Harriet "wasting his time like she was"—pushing her along the darkened hall to the bedroom where her purse had to be; it couldn't be any other place, Harriet was thinking, biting her lower lip and praying; it can't be any other place: and when she switched on the bedroom light there it was, there, on the bureau where of course she'd left it. She could have wept with gratitude.

She would have handed her purse over to the man but he snatched it up eagerly, opened it, drew out the wallet, letting the purse fall to the floor, his own hands trembling as if with a faint palsy. Harriet saw that his knuckles were oddly big-boned, scraped-looking. His fingernails were edged with dirt.

She said apologetically, "I'm afraid there isn't much."

He was counting out bills, breathing hard. Harriet's eye darted about the bedroom hopeful of things—anything—she might offer. Her jewelry, of course, a few heirlooms but they were inexpensive; the rings she was wearing; and her watch—not really expensive items but could he tell the difference? She was thinking that the bedroom was so quietly attractive a room, neat, clean, the bed made (of course: Harriet had been trained from the age of nine to make any bed she slept in within a few seconds of rising from it), the mahogany furniture polished, lovely pale silky curtains, and the rest—the evidence of lives intelligently but not extravagantly lived. Surely the man with the knife could *see?* And would not want to hurt her, for so little reason?

(Bonnie had stopped crying. Or, more likely, Harriet couldn't hear her any longer. The house was unnaturally quiet: no radio, no television, no voices. Harriet would have liked to think that Bonnie had disobeyed her and left the bathroom—was now running, running for her life, next door to get help—but she knew this couldn't be: Bonnie would never have disobeyed her under these extreme circumstances. She would not unlock the door until Mommy gave her permission.)

The man with the knife counted out 73 dollars and some change and didn't look very happy, and Harriet said quickly, "I just went shopping today, that's why there isn't—" He raised his eyes to hers: blood-threaded, glassy, the irises so dark they couldn't be distinguished from the pupils. The eyes seemed too loose in their sockets and Harriet could see, close up, scar tissue above each eye, tiny stitchlike marks in the skin.

He said, slyly, "OK, where's the rest?"

"The rest?"

"Hidden somewhere? In a drawer? Underneath something?"

"I don't have any more money," Harriet said. "This is all I have."

"Come off it!"

"Please, you promised—"

"Where's the money? Where's the *real* money?"

He was getting excited, waving the knife, gesturing with it, giving off a frantic hot scent like rancid grease. His facial skin was now the color and texture of curdled milk. The freckles stood out like dirty rain spots. "Just don't you lie to me, lady," he said, "nobody lies to me, lady." He stuffed the bills in his jeans pocket, taking no notice of the coins that fell to the floor. "Nobody lies to *me*."

Harriet said, stammering, "But we don't keep money in the house. We don't keep cash. I have a checkbook—"

"A checkbook! You going to write me a check, lady?"

"I have some jewelry—that's all I have—in this drawer here—"

He shoved her aside and yanked open the drawer, pawing through Harriet's things. She had costume jewelry mainly, dozens of pairs of earrings, glass beads, Indian necklaces, brooches she rarely wore, but in her little red jewelry box—a gift from her parents for her sixteenth birthday—there were a string of good cultured pearls and an old diamond-and-emerald bracelet of her grandmother's and several rings of varying degrees of worth, and these things the man with the knife scooped up, greedy yet embittered, as if knowing they were worth very little, really: he was being cheated.

"My watch," Harriet said, slipping it off, handing it over. "It might be worth something." He examined it skeptically (and he had a right to be skeptical; it was only a moderately priced watch classily styled, with miniature facets in the white gold framing the timepiece that winked and glittered in a simulation of diamonds). "That's all I have. I don't have anything else—please believe me," Harriet said.

He ignored her, didn't hear her, rifling through the bureau drawers in search of cash—and there was no cash—tossing clothing to the floor: Harriet's underwear, Harriet's panty hose, her husband's socks, shorts, undershirts. He found several pairs of cuff links and tried to stuff them in a pocket and when they slipped through his fingers he didn't trouble to pick them up. Next he went to the clothes closet and pawed furiously through Harriet's and her husband's clothes, cursing in a loud whining voice like a small child. His breath came so harshly now Harriet could hear him across the room.

Why was he staying on so long, risking so much? He should have been eager, like his friend, to escape.

Why was he talking to himself, behaving with such self-conscious bravado? Was it for Harriet's benefit?

Her initial shock had subsided. Like a powerful shot of adrenaline, it had been; now it was gone. She was left with a chill desperate calm, thinking, I am trapped, and Bonnie is trapped, until this is over.

"My husband—" she began, and broke down.

"If you leave now—" she began.

"I don't have anything more. We don't—"

The man with the knife approached her and stood with his hands on his hips, smiling his sly little smile. "OK, lady, cut the shit," he said flatly.

Harriet didn't want to think that she knew, even before he knew, what he would do. She didn't want to think that.

She would wonder afterward when it first occurred to him: after he'd counted out the money in her wallet, seen how little there was, how little the break-in was going to net him—so much energy expended, so much risk, for so little? Or had it been when he'd first glimpsed her, downstairs, tugging at the window in her husband's study? But perhaps it had been his plan, his intention, all along, before he'd ever stepped into her house: any woman, any female, helpless, and available to him . . . ?

He said, not meanly, "You think you're hot shit, don't you? People like you."

"What? Why?"

"Living up here. People like you."

"What do you mean?" Harriet asked, though she knew what he meant. Her voice sounded weak, guilty.

"What's your husband do?"

"He teaches history at the university."

He laughed to show he didn't think much of it, history at the university.

They were standing quite close together and might have been having an ordinary if rather intense conversation. Until this moment Harriet had not really looked at the knife. She had seen it, she'd known what it was but had not wanted to look. Now she saw that it was about eight inches long and there was something strange about it—a sporty, chunky look to it—a fat two-edged blade. Two-edged? The handle was unnaturally long, simulated carved wood, probably plastic, black. She thought, He won't really hurt me. He doesn't intend to hurt me.

She thought, I could run.

The knife held conspicuously, he brushed his long damp hair out of his face with both hands in a deft, practiced gesture. He liked himself and he liked her watching him, and Harriet thought of a mass murderer who'd been quoted in the newspaper the previous year, a man who'd killed forty women including a twelve-year-old girl, and he'd said arrogantly, rhetorically, "Who has seen the past? Who has touched the past?" He was an intelligent man, an educated man, a lawyer in fact; he'd been eloquent enough, saying, "The past? The past is a mist. The past doesn't exist."

And a woman had consented to marry him, after his conviction: borne him a child, a little girl.

Harriet thought, These things can't be.

Harriet thought, How can God let such things happen?

The red-haired young man with the knife was pulling back the bedspread—an odd, even quaint, sense of decorum. He said, "Get down."

Harriet stood frozen. She said, "You promised you wouldn't hurt me."

"I'm not going to hurt you," he said. "Just get down."

"My daughter is downstairs—"

"C'mon. Now. Do it. Get *down*."

"I can't," Harriet said, her voice breaking. "I can't do it." She began to cry. She said, "My husband—"

"You're somebody's wife!" the man said. He spoke with an air of angry incredulity as if Harriet were trying to trick him again. "You fuck all the time! You had a kid! What the hell! It's nothing! Don't tell *me*!"

Harriet said desperately, "No. Please. You promised. You said you wouldn't—"

"Nobody's going to hurt you, for Christ's sake," the man said. "Just get down here," he said, shoving her onto the bed, "and shut *up*."

"My daughter—"

"You want to see her again? Your daughter? Do you? You want to see her again?" he said.

He rapped her across the mouth with his knuckles. Harriet drew breath to scream but knew she should not scream—should not scream—not now: he was standing over her, panting, big-eyed, the knife in his hand.

She said, "You promised you wouldn't hurt me. I'm afraid of the knife."

"I'm not going to use the knife."

"Yes, but I'm afraid of it."

He was fumbling with his pants, flush-faced, excited. Harriet shut her eyes to a flurry of lights, something hot and crackling behind her eyelids; she shut her eyes and forced herself to open them again, to speak clearly, coherently, even now. "I'm afraid of the knife. Please put away the knife."

"You want to hold it? You can hold it," he said, crouching over her. "Go ahead, hold it. *Take* it." He was smiling his hard tight clenched smile. Harriet thought, He's crazy. Then she thought, He's trying to be a gentleman—is that it?

He pressed the knife into her fingers and it fell onto the bed. He picked it up and pressed it again into her fingers, closed her fingers around it. He said, "You're nice. You're pretty. You owe me money. You owe me fucking *something*, and you know it. Just lay still."

Harriet held the knife; Harriet was holding it, her arm bent awkwardly at the elbow. Her wrist was so weak it might have snapped like dried kindling.

Is this rape? she thought. *This?*—as the man pried her legs apart, poked himself against her. Rivulets of sweat ran down his face; his tongue appeared between his teeth in a parody of intense childlike concentration. Again he said he wouldn't hurt her, "This won't hurt, lady, just lay still," and Harriet was pinned beneath him rigid and disbelieving, thinking even now, This can't be happening, this can't, can't be happening—her legs spread wide, sweat-slick and clumsy, knees high as if she were on an examination table, feet caught in stirrups. The knife had slipped again from her fingers and she could not keep from crying out, a series of high little screams, she could not keep from fighting, threshing—

"Just lay still."

As a child of four Harriet had fallen from a porch on the second floor of her parents' Cape Cod summer house; she'd leaned against a railing that was badly rotted and gave way beneath her weight. Very likely she would have been killed or severely injured if it hadn't been for an overgrown evergreen shrub that broke her fall.

But she wasn't killed, wasn't even injured except for scratches and bruises and the shock of the accident. And forever afterward it was a legend of the family, one of those happy legends that spring up and thrive and are never forgotten in families, that Harriet was blessed with luck: fool's luck, perhaps, but luck nonetheless.

So now, returning to consciousness, alone in her bed, alone in her bedroom, alive, throbbing with pain but alive, she thought only, It's over.

In that first instant, before the pain really hit, and the disbelief, the loathing, the nausea—before, even, she began to call her daughter's name—she thought only, It's over. We're safe.

She telephoned the police first, and then her husband who was in Chicago, and she spoke evenly and carefully, keeping her voice low, calm, modulated; she was determined to demonstrate that she wasn't all that upset, she certainly wasn't hysterical: only a robbery after all, and they hadn't taken very much.

The police arrived within minutes and questioned her for about an hour. They asked for descriptions of the men and they asked if she recognized either or both of the men and they asked were the men armed, and Harriet said hesitantly, "Well—yes. I think one of them had a knife."

Bonnie was upstairs in bed by this time, Bonnie would have no part in the interrogation, perhaps Bonnie had not even seen the knife? Harriet was saying carefully, "I think one of them had a knife he kept in his pocket, you know, sort of threatening, in his pocket—"

"A knife? Not a gun?"

"Oh, no, not a gun. A knife, I think—"

"Did you see it?"

"I think I did, yes, actually—"

"Did he threaten you with it?"

"He did, yes, in a way, but not—"

"He didn't touch you with it?"

"Oh, no. No, he didn't touch me with it," she said emphatically. "He wasn't the kind—I mean, he didn't do that."

"Did either of them touch you?"

"Yes, but not—"

"Not roughly?"

She began to speak quickly. "I don't know, really. It was all so frightening and confused and I was worried mainly about my daughter. I mean—as soon as I thought she'd be safe it was only a matter of time, giving them some money, not much but all I had: seventy-three dollars, it was, and some jewelry, and my husband's camera, and a few other things, I've forgotten exactly; we don't have much that's valuable and I offered them what we had, I didn't protest or try to resist, I didn't think it was worth it, after all—not with my daughter here."

Which was of course—wasn't it?—the wisest thing to have done.

As the police told her. And others were to tell her, admiringly: the wisest thing to have done—to save your and Bonnie's lives.

She told the police about the robbery in as much detail as she could recall—she was to remember more the next morning and more, by degrees, in the days following—but she did not tell them about the rape because perhaps it had not been a rape? She'd held the knife in her fingers, after all, and had not used it.

And he had not hurt her—much. Not so much as he might have.

I think he liked me, she thought.

He didn't really want to hurt me, she thought.

I left the door unlocked and wasn't that an invitation to—
something?

And the shame. And the public humiliation.

And her husband. "I can't do that to him," she said aloud. She
was angry, not despairing, as if she were arguing with someone.

The police believed her, or seemed to. Her husband believed
her. Or seemed to. (But she wasn't sure. Those much-repeated questions, questions: Did they threaten you physically? Did they touch
you? What kind of knife was it—how close did he come to using it
on you?) The men were to be apprehended within two weeks, but
it was only a few days later that Harriet was standing at a window
in Bonnie's room—headachy, groggy from a powerful dose of co-
deine—watching steamy air rise from grass, sidewalks, the roofs of
neighboring houses. It was a prematurely warm day, the sun seemed
unnaturally bright though the sky was massed with rain clouds, and
Harriet glanced up and saw a human figure—an angel?—contorted
and struggling like a swimmer in the clouds: angular, sculpted, purely
white, beautiful as living marble. What was it? Was she going mad?
She fell to her knees as her parents had done in the little Methodist
church in the country long ago and she cried aloud, "God, don't let
me turn into a religious lunatic!" and when she looked up again of
course the figure was gone. Just oddly shaped clouds, rain-swollen,
turbulent, an El Greco sky.

That evening she would tell her husband about the rape. And
what would happen, as a consequence, would happen.

THE HAIR

The couples fell in love but not at the same time, and not evenly. There was perceived to be, from the start, an imbalance of power. The less dominant couple, the Carsons, feared social disadvantage. They feared being hopeful of a friendship that would dissolve before consummation. They feared seeming eager.

Said Charlotte Carson, hanging up the phone, "The Riegels have invited us for dinner on New Year's," her voice level, revealing none of the childlike exultation she felt, nor did she look up to see the expression on her husband's face as he murmured, "Who? The Riegels?" pausing before adding, "That's very nice of them."

Once or twice, the Carsons had invited the Riegels to their home, but for one or another reason the Riegels had declined the invitation.

New Year's Eve went very well indeed and shortly thereafter—though not too shortly—Charlotte Carson telephoned to invite the Riegels back.

The friendship between the couples blossomed. In a relatively small community like the one in which the couples lived, such a new, quick, galloping sort of alliance cannot go unnoticed.

So it was noted by mutual friends who felt some surprise, and perhaps some envy. For the Riegels were a golden couple, newcomers to the area who, not employed locally, had about them the glamour of temporary visitors.

In high school, Charlotte Carson thought with a stab of satisfaction, the Riegels would have snubbed me.

Old friends and acquaintances of the Carsons began to observe
that Charlotte and Barry were often busy on Saturday evenings, their
calendar seemingly marked for weeks in advance. And when a date
did not appear to be explicitly set Charlotte would so clearly—in-
sultingly—hesitate, not wanting to surrender a prime weekend evening only to discover belatedly that the Riegels would call them at
the last minute and ask them over. Charlotte Carson, gentlest, most
tactful of women, in her mid-thirties, shy at times as a schoolgirl of
another era, was forced repeatedly to say, "I'm sorry—I'm afraid we
can't." And insincerely.

Paul Riegel, whose name everyone knew, was in his early forties:
he was a travel writer; he had adventures of a public sort. He published articles and books, he was often to be seen on television, he
was tall, handsome, tanned, gregarious, his graying hair springy at
the sides of his head and retreating rather wistfully at the crown of
his head. "Your husband seems to bear the gift of happiness," Charlotte Carson told Ceci Riegel. Charlotte sometimes spoke too emo-
tionally and wondered now if she had too clearly exposed her heart.
But Ceci simply smiled one of her mysterious smiles. "Yes. He tries."

In any social gathering the Riegels were likely to be, without
visible effort, the cynosure of attention. When Paul Riegel strode
into a crowded room wearing one of his bright ties, or his familiar
sports-coat-sports-shirt-open-collar with well-laundered jeans, people looked immediately to him and smiled. There's Paul Riegel! He
bore his minor celebrity with grace and even a kind of aristocratic
humility, shrugging off questions in pursuit of the public side of his
life. If, from time to time, having had a few drinks, he told wildly
amusing exaggerated tales, even, riskily, outrageous ethnic or dialect
jokes, he told them with such zest and childlike self-delight his listeners were convulsed with laughter.

Never, or almost never, did he forget names.

And his wife, Ceci—petite, ash-blond, impeccably dressed, with
a delicate classically proportioned face like an old-fashioned cameo—
was surely his ideal mate. She was inclined at times to be fey but
she was really very smart. She had a lovely whitely glistening smile
as dazzling as her husband's and as seemingly sincere. For years she
had been an interior designer in New York City and since moving
to the country was a consultant to her former firm; it was rumored

that her family had money and that she had either inherited a small fortune or spurned a small fortune at about the time of her marriage to Paul Riegel.

It was rumored too that the Riegels ran through people quickly, used up friends. That they had affairs.

Or perhaps it was only Paul who had affairs.

Or Ceci.

Imperceptibly, it seemed, the Carsons and the Riegels passed from being friendly acquaintances who saw each other once or twice a month to being friends who saw each other every week, or more. There were formal dinners, and there were cocktail parties, and there were Sunday brunches—the social staples of suburban life. There were newly acquired favorite restaurants to patronize and, under Ceci's guidance, outings to New York City to see plays, ballet, opera. There were even picnics from which bicycle rides and canoe excursions were launched—not without comical misadventures. In August when the Riegels rented a house on Nantucket Island they invited the Carsons to visit; when the Riegels had houseguests the Carsons were almost always invited to meet them; soon the men were playing squash together on a regular basis. (Paul won three games out of five, which seemed just right. But he did not win easily.) In time Charlotte Carson overcame her shyness about telephoning Ceci as if on the spur of the moment—"Just to say hello!"

Ceci Riegel had no such scruples, nor did Paul, who thought nothing of telephoning friends—everywhere in the world; he knew so many people—at virtually any time of the day or night, simply to say hello.

The confidence born of never having been rejected.

Late one evening the Carsons were delighted to hear from Paul in Bangkok, of all places, where he was on assignment with a *Life* photographer.

Another time, sounding dazed and not quite himself, he telephoned them at 7:30 A.M. from John F. Kennedy Airport, newly arrived in the States and homesick for the sound of "familiar" voices. He hadn't been able to get hold of Ceci, he complained, but they were next on his list.

Which was enormously flattering.

Sometimes when Paul was away on one of his extended trips,

Ceci was, as she said, morbidly lonely, so the three of them went out for Chinese food and a movie or watched videos late into the night; or impulsively, rather recklessly, Ceci got on the phone and invited a dozen friends over, and neighbors too, though always, first, Charlotte and Barry—"Just to feel I *exist*."

The couples were each childless.

Barry had not had a male friend whom he saw so regularly since college, and the nature of his work—he was an executive with Bell Labs—seemed to preclude camaraderie. Charlotte was his closest friend but he rarely confided in her all that was in his heart: this wasn't his nature.

Unlike his friend Paul he preferred the ragged edges of gatherings, not their quicksilver centers. He was big-boned with heavy-lidded quizzical eyes, a shadowy beard like shot, deep in the pores of his skin, wide nostrils, a handsome sensual mouth. He'd been an all-A student once and carried still that air of tension and precariousness strung tight as a bow. Did he take himself too seriously? Or not seriously enough? Wild moods swung in him, rarely surfacing. When his wife asked him why was he so quiet, what was he thinking, he replied, smiling, "Nothing important, honey," though resenting the question, the intrusion. The implied assertion: *I have a right to your secrets*.

His heart pained him when Ceci Riegel greeted him with a hearty little spasm of an embrace and a perfumy kiss alongside his cheek, but he was not the kind of man to fall sentimentally in love with a friend's wife. Nor was he the kind of man, aged forty and wondering when his life would begin, to fall in love with his friend.

The men played squash daily when Paul was in town. Sometimes, afterward, they had lunch together, and a few beers, and talked about their families: their fathers, mainly. Barry drifted back to his office pale and shaken and that evening might complain vaguely to Charlotte that Paul Riegel came on a little too strong for him, "As if it's always the squash court, and he's always the star."

Charlotte said quickly, "He means well. And so does Ceci. But they're aggressive people." She paused, wondering what she was saying. "Not like us."

When Barry and Paul played doubles with other friends, other men, they nearly always won. Which pleased Barry more than he would have wished anyone to know.

And Paul's praise: it burned in his heart with a luminosity that endured for hours and days and all in secret.

The Carsons were childless but had two cats. The Riegels were childless but had a red setter bitch, no longer young.

The Carsons lived in a small mock-Georgian house in town; the Riegels lived in a glass, stone, and redwood house, custom-designed, three miles out in the country. The Carsons' house was one of many attractive houses of its kind in their quiet residential neighborhood and had no distinctive features except an aged enormous plane tree in the front which would probably have to be dismantled soon—"It will break our hearts," Charlotte said. The Carsons' house was fully exposed to the street; the Riegels' house was hidden from the narrow gravel road that ran past it by a seemingly untended meadow of juniper pines, weeping willows, grasses, wildflowers.

Early on in their friendship, a tall cool summer drink in hand, Barry Carson almost walked through a plate glass door at the Riegels'—beyond it was the redwood deck, Ceci in a silk floral-printed dress with numberless pleats.

Ceci was happy and buoyant and confident always. For a petite woman—size five, it was more than once announced—she had a shapely body, breasts, hips, strong-calved legs. When she and Charlotte Carson played tennis, Ceci was all over the court, laughing and exclaiming, while slow-moving premeditated Charlotte, poor Charlotte, who felt, in her friend's company, ostrich-tall and ungainly, missed all but the easy shots. "You need to be more aggressive, Char!" Paul Riegel called out. "Need to be *murderous!*"

The late-night drive back to town from the Riegels' along narrow twisty country roads, Barry behind the wheel, sleepy with drink yet excited too, vaguely sweetly aching, Charlotte yawning and sighing, and there was the danger of white-tailed deer so plentiful in this part of the state leaping in front of the car; but they returned home safely, suddenly they were home, and, inside, one of them would observe that their house was so lacking in imagination, wasn't it? So exposed to the neighbors? "Yes, but you wanted this house." "No, you were the one who wanted this house." "Not *this* house—but this was the

most feasible." Though sometimes one would observe that the Riegels' house had flaws: so much glass and it's drafty in the winter, so
many queer elevated decks and flights of stairs, wall-less rooms,
sparsely furnished rooms like designers' showcases, and the cool
chaste neutral colors that Ceci evidently favored: "It's beautiful, yes,
but a bit sterile."

In bed exhausted they would drift to sleep, separately wandering
the corridors of an unknown building, opening one door after another in dread and fascination. Charlotte, who should not have had
more than two or three glasses of wine—but it was an anniversary
of the Riegels: they'd uncorked bottles of champagne—slept fitfully,
waking often dry-mouthed and frightened not knowing where she
was. A flood of hypnagogic images raced in her brain; the faces of
strangers never before glimpsed by her thrummed beneath her eyelids. In that state of consciousness that is neither sleep nor waking
Charlotte had the volition to will, ah, how passionately, how de-
spairingly, that Paul Riegel would comfort her: slip his arm around
her shoulders, nudge his jaw against her cheek, whisper in her ear
as he'd done once or twice that evening in play but now in serious-
ness. Beside her someone stirred and groaned in his sleep and kicked
at the covers.

Paul Riegel entranced listeners with lurid tales of starving Cam-
bodian refugees, starving Ethiopian children, starving Mexican beg-
gars. His eyes shone with angry tears one moment and with mischief
the next, for he could not resist mocking his own sobriety. The
laughter he aroused at such times had an air of bafflement, shock.

Ceci came to him to slip an arm through his as if to comfort or
to quiet, and there were times when quite perceptibly Paul shook
off her arm, stepped away, stared down at her with a look as if he'd
never seen the woman before.

When the Carsons did not see or hear from the Riegels for several
days their loneliness was almost palpable: a thickness in the chest, a
density of being, to which either might allude knowing the other
would immediately understand. If the Riegels were actually away
that made the separation oddly more bearable than if they were in
fact in their house amid the trees but not seeing the Carsons that
weekend or mysteriously incommunicado with their telephone answering tape switched on. When Charlotte called, got the tape, heard

the familiar static-y overture, then Paul Riegel's cool almost hostile voice that did not identify itself but merely stated *No one is here right now; should you like to leave a message please wait for the sound of the bleep*, she felt a loss too profound to be named and often hung up in silence.

It had happened as the Carsons feared—the Riegels were dominant. So fully in control.

For there was a terrible period, several months in all, when for no reason the Carsons could discover—and they discussed the subject endlessly, obsessively—the Riegels seemed to have little time for them. Or saw them with batches of others in which their particular friendship could not be readily discerned. Paul was a man of quick enthusiasms, and Ceci was a woman of abrupt shifts of allegiance; thus there was logic of sorts to their cruelty in elevating for a while a new couple in the area who were both theoretical mathematicians, and a neighbor's houseguest who'd known Paul in college and was now in the diplomatic service, and a cousin of Ceci's, a male model in his late twenties who was staying with the Riegels for weeks and weeks and weeks, taking up every spare minute of their time, it seemed, so when Charlotte called, baffled and hurt, Ceci murmured in an undertone, "I can't talk now, can I call you back in the morning?" and failed to call for days, days, days.

One night when Charlotte would have thought Barry was asleep he shocked her by saying, "I never liked her, much. Hot-shit little Ceci." She had never heard her husband utter such words before and did not know how to reply.

They went away on a trip. Three weeks in the Caribbean, and only in the third week did Charlotte scribble a postcard for the Riegels—a quick scribbled little note as if one of many.

One night she said, "*He's* the dangerous one. He always tries to get people to drink too much, to keep him company."

They came back, and not long afterward Ceci called, and the friendship was resumed precisely as it had been—the same breathless pace, the same dazzling intensity—though now Paul had a new book coming out and there were parties in the city, book signings at bookstores, an interview on a morning news program. The Carsons gave a party for him, inviting virtually everyone they knew locally, and the party was a great success and in a corner of the house Paul Riegel hugged Charlotte Carson so hard she laughed, protesting her ribs would crack, but when she drew back to look at her friend's face she saw it was damp with tears.

Later, Paul told a joke about Reverend Jesse Jackson that was a masterpiece of mimicry though possibly in questionable taste. In the general hilarity no one noticed, or at least objected. In any case there were no blacks present.

The Riegels were childless but would not have defined their condition in those terms: as a lack, a loss, a negative. Before marrying they had discussed the subject of children thoroughly, Paul said, and came to the conclusion *no*.

The Carsons too were childless but would perhaps have defined their condition in those terms, in weak moods at least. Hearing Paul speak so indifferently of children, the Carsons exchanged a glance almost of embarrassment.

Each hoped the other would not disclose any intimacy.

Ceci sipped at her drink and said, "I'd have been willing."

Paul said, "*I* wouldn't."

There was a brief nervous pause. The couples were sitting on the Riegels' redwood deck in the gathering dusk.

Paul then astonished the Carsons by speaking in a bitter impassioned voice of families, children, parents, the "politics" of intimacy. In any intimate group, he said, the struggle to be independent, to define oneself as an individual, is so fierce it creates terrible waves of tension, a field of psychic warfare. He'd endured it as a child and young adolescent in his parents' home, and as an adult he didn't think he could bear to bring up a child—"especially a son"—knowing of the doubleness and secrecy of the child's life.

"There is the group life, which is presumably open and observable," he said, "and there is the secret inner real life no one can penetrate." He spoke with such uncharacteristic vehemence that neither of the Carsons would have dared to challenge him or even to question him in the usual conversational vein.

Ceci sat silent, drink in hand, staring impassively out into the shadows.

After a while conversation resumed again and they spoke softly, laughed softly. The handsome white wrought-iron furniture on which they were sitting took on an eerie solidity even as the human figures seemed to fade: losing outline and contour, blending into the night and into one another.

Charlotte Carson lifted her hand, registering a small chill spasm of fear that she was dissolving, but it was only a drunken notion of course.

For days afterward Paul Riegel's disquieting words echoed in her head. She tasted something black, and her heart beat in anger like a cheated child's. *Don't you love me then? Don't any of us love any of us?* To Barry she said, "That was certainly an awkward moment, wasn't it? When Paul started his monologue about family life, intimacy, all that. What did you make of it?"

Barry murmured something evasive and backed off.

The Carsons owned two beautiful Siamese cats, neutered male and neutered female, and the Riegels owned a skittish Irish setter named Rusty. When the Riegels came to visit Ceci always made a fuss over one or the other of the cats, insisting it sit in her lap, sometimes even at the dinner table, where she'd feed it on the sly. When the Carsons came to visit, the damned dog as Barry spoke of it went into a frenzy of barking and greeted them at the front door as if it had never seen them before. "Nice dog! Good dog! Sweet Rusty!" the Carsons would cry in unison.

The setter was rheumy-eyed and thick-bodied and arthritic. If every year of a dog's age is approximately seven years in human terms, poor Rusty was almost eighty years old. She managed to shuffle to the front door to bark at visitors but then lacked the strength or motor coordination to reverse herself and return to the interior of the house so Paul had to carry her, one arm under her bony chest and forelegs, the other firmly under her hindquarters, an expression of vexed tenderness in his face.

Dryly he said, "I hope someone will do as much for me someday."

One rainy May afternoon when Paul was in Berlin and Barry was in Virginia visiting his family, Ceci impulsively invited Charlotte to come for a drink and meet her friend Nils Larson—or was the name Lasson? Lawson?—an old old dear friend. Nils was short, squat-bodied, energetic, with a gnomish head and bright malicious eyes, linked to Ceci, it appeared, in a way that allowed him to be both slavish and condescending. He was a "theater person"; his bubbly talk was studded with names of the famous and near-famous. Never once did he mention Paul Riegel's name, though certain of his mannerisms—head thrown back in laughter, hands gesticulating as he spoke—reminded Charlotte of certain of Paul's mannerisms. The man was Paul's elder by perhaps a decade.

Charlotte stayed only an hour, then made her excuses and slipped away. She had seen Ceci's friend draw his pudgy forefinger across the nape of Ceci's neck in a gesture that signaled intimacy or the arrogant pretense of intimacy, and the sight offended her. But she never told Barry and resolved not to think of it and of whether Nils spent the night at the Riegels' and whether Paul knew anything of him or of the visit. Nor did Ceci ask Charlotte what she had thought of Nils Larson—Lasson? Lawson?—the next time the women spoke.

Barry returned from Virginia with droll tales of family squabbling: his brother and his sister-in-law, their children, the network of aunts, uncles, nieces, nephews, grandparents, ailing elderly relatives whose savings were being eaten up—invariably the expression was "eaten up"—by hospital and nursing home expenses. Barry's father, severely crippled from a stroke, was himself in a nursing home from which he would never be discharged, and all his conversation turned upon this fact, which others systematically denied, including, in the exigency of the moment, Barry. He had not, he said, really recognized his father. It was as if another man—aged, shrunken, querulous, sly—had taken his place.

The elderly Mr. Carson had affixed to a wall of his room a small white card on which he'd written some Greek symbols, an inscription he claimed to have treasured all his life. Barry asked what the Greek meant and was told, *When my ship sank, the others sailed on.*

Paul Riegel returned from Berlin exhausted and depressed despite the fact, a happy one to his wife and friends, that a book of his was on the paperback bestseller list published by *The New York Times.* When Charlotte Carson suggested with uncharacteristic gaiety that they celebrate, Paul looked at her with a mild quizzical smile and asked, "Why, exactly?"

The men played squash, the women played tennis.

The Carsons had other friends, of course. Older and more reliable friends. They did not need the Riegels. Except they were in love with the Riegels.

Did the Riegels love them? Ceci telephoned one evening and

Barry happened to answer and they talked together for an hour, and afterward, when Charlotte asked Barry what they'd talked about, careful to keep all signs of jealousy and excitement out of her voice, Barry said evasively, "A friend of theirs is dying. Of AIDS. Ceci says he weighs only ninety pounds and has withdrawn from everyone: 'slunk off to die like a sick animal.' And Paul doesn't care. Or won't talk about it." Barry paused, aware that Charlotte was looking at him closely. A light film of perspiration covered his face; his nostrils appeared unusually dark, dilated. "He's no one we know, honey. The dying man, I mean."

When Paul Riegel emerged from a sustained bout of writing the first people he wanted to see were the Carsons of course, so the couples went out for Chinese food—"a banquet, no less!"—at their favorite Chinese restaurant in a shopping mall. The Dragon Inn had no liquor license so they brought bottles of wine and six-packs of beer. They were the last customers to leave, and by the end waiters and kitchen help were standing around or prowling restlessly at the rear of the restaurant. There was a minor disagreement over the check, which Paul Riegel insisted had not been added up "strictly correctly." He and the manager discussed the problem and since the others were within earshot he couldn't resist clowning for their amusement, slipping into a comical Chinese (unless it was Japanese?) accent. In the parking lot the couples laughed helplessly, gasping for breath and bent double, and in the car driving home—Barry drove: they'd taken the Carsons' Honda Accord, and Barry was seemingly the most sober of the four of them—they kept bursting into peals of laughter like naughty children.

They never returned to the Dragon Inn.

The men played squash together but their most rewarding games were doubles in which they played, and routed, another pair of men.

As if grudgingly, Paul Riegel would tell Barry Carson he was a "damned good player." To Charlotte he would say, "Your husband is a damned good player but if only he could be a bit more *murderous!*"

Barry Carson's handsome heavy face darkened with pleasure when he heard such praise, exaggerated as it was. Though afterward, regarding himself in a mirror, he felt shame: he was forty years old, he had a very good job in a highly competitive field, he had a very good marriage with a woman he both loved and respected, he be-

lieved he was leading, on the whole, a very good life, yet none of
this meant as much to him as Paul Riegel carelessly complimenting
him on his squash game.

How has my life come to this?

Rusty developed cataracts on both eyes and then tumorous
growths in her neck. The Riegels took her to the vet and had her
put to sleep, and Ceci had what was reported to the Carsons as a
breakdown of a kind: wept and wept and wept. Paul too was shaken
by the ordeal but managed to joke over the phone about the dog's
ashes. When Charlotte told Barry of the dog's death she saw Barry's
eyes narrow as he resisted saying Thank God! and said instead,
gravely, as if it would be a problem of his own, "Poor Ceci will be
inconsolable."

For weeks it wasn't clear to the Carsons that they would be invited
to visit the Riegels on Nantucket; then, shortly before the Riegels
left, Ceci said as if casually, "We did set a date, didn't we? For you
two to come visit?"

On their way up—it was a seven-hour drive to the ferry at Woods
Hole—Charlotte said to Barry, "Promise you won't drink so much
this year." Offended, Barry said, "I won't monitor your behavior,
honey, if you won't monitor mine."

From the first, the Nantucket visit went awkwardly. Paul wasn't
home and his whereabouts weren't explained, though Ceci chattered
brightly and effusively, carrying her drink with her as she escorted
the Carsons to their room and watched them unpack. Her shoulder-
length hair was graying and disheveled; her face was heavily made
up, especially about the eyes. Several times she said, "Paul will be
so happy to see you," as if Paul had not known they were invited;
or, knowing, like Ceci herself, had perhaps forgotten. An east wind
fanned drizzle and soft gray mist against the windows.

Paul returned looking fit and tanned and startled about the eyes;
in his walnut-brown face the whites glared. Toward dusk the sky
lightened and the couples sat on the beach with their drinks. Ceci
continued to chatter while Paul smiled, vague and distracted, looking
out at the surf. The air was chilly and damp but wonderfully fresh.
The Carsons drew deep breaths and spoke admiringly of the view.
And the house. And the location. They were wondering had the

Riegels been quarreling? Was something wrong? Had they themselves come on the wrong day or at the wrong time? Paul had been effusive too in his greetings but had not seemed to see them and had scarcely looked at them since.

Before they sat down to dinner the telephone began to ring. Ceci in the kitchen (with Charlotte who was helping her) and Paul in the living room (with Barry; the men were watching a televised tennis tournament) made no move to answer it. The ringing continued for what seemed like a long time, then stopped and resumed again while they were having dinner, and again neither of the Riegels made a move to answer it. Paul grinned, running both hands roughly through the bushy patches of hair at the sides of his head, and said, "When the world beats a path to your doorstep, beat it back, friends! *Beat it back for fuck's sake!*"

His extravagant words were meant to be funny of course but would have required another atmosphere altogether to be so. As it was, the Carsons could only stare and smile in embarrassment.

Ceci filled the silence by saying loudly, "Life's little ironies! You spend a lifetime making yourself famous, then you try to back off and dismantle it. But it won't dismantle! It's a mummy and you're inside it!"

"Not *in* a mummy," Paul said, staring smiling at the lobster on his plate, which he'd barely eaten, "you *are* a mummy." He had been drinking steadily, Scotch on the rocks and now wine, since arriving home.

Ceci laughed sharply. " 'In,' 'are,' what's the difference?" she said, appealing to the Carsons. She reached out to squeeze Barry's hand, hard. "In any case you're a goner, right?"

Paul said, "No, *you're* a goner."

The evening continued in this vein. The Carsons sent despairing glances at each other.

The telephone began to ring, and this time Paul rose to answer it. He walked stiffly and took his glass of wine with him. He took the call not in the kitchen but in another room at the rear of the house, and he was gone so long that Charlotte felt moved to ask if something was wrong. Ceci Riegel stared at her coldly. The whites of Ceci's eyes too showed above the rims of the iris, giving her a fey festive party look at odds with her carelessly combed hair and the tiredness deep in her face. "With the meal?" she asked. "With the house? With us? With *you?* I don't know of anything wrong."

Charlotte had never been so rebuffed in her adult life. Barry too felt the force of the insult. After a long stunned moment Charlotte murmured an apology, and Barry too murmured something vague, placating, embarrassed.

They sat in suspension, not speaking, scarcely moving, until at last Paul returned. His cheeks were ruddy as if they'd been heartily slapped and his eyes were bright. He carried a bottle of his favorite Napa Valley wine, which he'd been saving, he said, just for tonight. "This is a truly special occasion! We've really missed you guys!"

They were up until two, drinking. Repeatedly Paul used the odd expression "guys" as if its sound, its grating musicality, had imprinted itself in his brain. "OK, guys, how's about another drink?" he would say, rubbing his hands together. "OK, guys, how the hell have you been?"

Next morning, a brilliantly sunny morning, no one was up before eleven. Paul appeared in swimming trunks and T-shirt in the kitchen around noon, boisterous, swaggering, unshaven, in much the mood of the night before—remarkable! The Riegels had hired a local handyman to shore up some rotting steps and the handyman was an oldish gray-grizzled black and after the man was paid and departed Paul spoke in an exaggerated comical black accent, hugging Ceci and Charlotte around their waists until Charlotte pushed him away stiffly, saying, "I don't think you're being funny, Paul." There was a moment's startled silence; then she repeated, vehemently, "*I don't think that's funny, Paul.*"

As if on cue Ceci turned on her heel and walked out of the room.

But Paul continued his clowning. He blundered about in the kitchen, pleading with "white missus": bowing, shuffling, tugging what remained of his forelock, kneeling to pluck at Charlotte's denim skirt. His flushed face seemed to have turned to rubber, his lips red, moist, turned obscenely inside out. "Beg pardon, white missus! Oh, white missus, beg pardon!"

Charlotte said, "I think we should leave."

Barry, who had been staring appalled at his friend, as if he'd never seen him before, said quickly, "Yes. I think we should leave."

They went to their room at the rear of the house, leaving Paul behind, and in a numbed stricken silence packed their things, each of them badly trembling. They anticipated one or both of the Riegels following them but neither did, and as Charlotte yanked sheets off the bed, towels off the towel rack in the bathroom, to fold and pile them neatly at the foot of the bed, she could not believe that their friends would allow them to leave without protest.

With a wad of toilet paper she cleaned the bathroom sink as Barry called to her to please hurry. She examined the claw-footed tub—she and Barry had each showered that morning—and saw near the drain a tiny curly dark hair, hers or Barry's, indistinguishable, and this hair she leaned over to snatch up but her fingers closed in air and she tried another time, still failing to grasp it, then finally she picked it up and flushed it down the toilet. Her face was burning and her heart knocking so hard in her chest she could scarcely breathe.

The Carsons left the Riegels' cottage in Nantucket shortly after noon of the day following their arrival.

They drove seven hours back to their home with a single stop, silent much of the time but excited, nervously elated. When he drove Barry kept glancing in the rearview mirror. One of his eyelids had developed a tic.

He said, "We should have done this long ago."

"Yes," Charlotte said, staring ahead at dry sunlit rushing pavement. "Long ago."

That night in their own bed they made love for the first time in weeks, or months. "I love you," Barry murmured, as if making a vow. "No one but you."

Tears started out of the corners of Charlotte's tightly shut eyes.

Afterward Barry slept heavily, sweating through the night. From time to time he kicked at the covers, but he never woke. Beside him Charlotte lay staring into the dark. What would become of them now? Something tickled her lips, a bit of lint, a hair, and though she brushed it irritably away the tingling sensation remained. What would become of them, now?

SHOPPING

An old ritual, Saturday morning shopping. Mother and daughter. Mrs. Dietrich and Nola. Shops in the village, stores and boutiques at the splendid Livingstone Mall on Route 12: Bloomingdale's, Saks, Lord & Taylor, Bonwit's, Neiman-Marcus, and the rest. Mrs. Dietrich would know her way around the stores blindfolded but there is always the surprise of lavish seasonal displays, extraordinary holiday sales, the openings of new stores at the mall like Laura Ashley, Paraphernalia. On one of their mall days Mrs. Dietrich and Nola would try to get there at midmorning, have lunch around 1 P.M. at one or another of their favorite restaurants, shop for perhaps an hour after lunch, then come home. Sometimes the shopping trips were more successful than at other times, but you have to have faith, Mrs. Dietrich tells herself. Her interior voice is calm, neutral, free of irony. Even since her divorce her interior voice has been free of irony. You have to have faith.

Tomorrow morning Nola returns to school in Maine; today will be spent at the mall. Mrs. Dietrich has planned it for days—there are numerous things Nola needs, mainly clothes, a pair of good shoes; Mrs. Dietrich must buy a birthday present for one of her aunts; mother and daughter need the time together. At the mall, in such crowds of shoppers, moments of intimacy are possible as they rarely are at home. (Seventeen-year-old Nola, home on spring break for a brief eight days, seems always to be *busy*, always out with her *friends*, the trip to the mall has been postponed twice.) But Saturday, 10:30

54

A.M., they are in the car at last headed south on Route 12, a bleak March morning following a night of freezing rain; there's a metallic cast to the air and no sun anywhere in the sky but the light hurts Mrs. Dietrich's eyes just the same. "Does it seem as if spring will ever come? It must be twenty degrees colder up in Maine," she says. Driving in heavy traffic always makes Mrs. Dietrich nervous and she is overly sensitive to her daughter's silence, which seems deliberate, perverse, when they have so little time remaining together—not even a full day.

Nola asks politely if Mrs. Dietrich would like her to drive and Mrs. Dietrich says no, of course not, she's fine, it's only a few more miles and maybe traffic will lighten. Nola seems about to say something more, then thinks better of it. So much between them is precarious, chancy—but they've been kind to each other these past seven days. Nola's secrets remain her own and Mrs. Dietrich isn't going to pry; she's beyond that. She loves Nola with a fierce unreasoned passion stronger than any she felt for the man who had been her husband for thirteen years, certainly far stronger than any she ever felt for her own mother. Sometimes in weak despondent moods, alone, lonely, self-pitying, when she has had too much to drink, Mrs. Dietrich thinks she is in love with her daughter, but this is a thought she can't contemplate for long. And how Nola would snort in amused contempt, incredulous, mocking—"Oh, *Mother!*"—if she were told.

("Why do you make so much of things? Of people who don't seem to care about you?" Mr. Dietrich once asked. He had been speaking of one or another of their Livingstone friends, a woman in Mrs. Dietrich's circle; he hadn't meant to be insulting but Mrs. Dietrich was stung as if he'd slapped her.)

Mrs. Dietrich tries to engage her daughter in conversation of a harmless sort but Nola answers in monosyllables; Nola is rather tired from so many nights of partying with her friends, some of whom attend the local high school, some of whom are home for spring break from prep schools—Exeter, Lawrenceville, Concord, Andover, Portland. Late nights, but Mrs. Dietrich doesn't consciously lie awake waiting for Nola to come home; they've been through all that before. Now Nola sits beside her mother looking wan, subdued, rather melancholy. Thinking her private thoughts. She is wearing a bulky quilted jacket Mrs. Dietrich has never liked, the usual blue jeans, black calfskin boots zippered tightly to mid-calf. Her delicate profile, thick-lashed eyes. Mrs. Dietrich must resist the temptation to ask, Why are you so quiet, Nola? What are you thinking? They've been through all that before.

Route 12 has become a jumble of small industrial parks, high-rise office and apartment buildings, torn-up landscapes: mountains of raw earth, uprooted trees, ruts and ditches filled with muddy water. Everywhere are yellow bulldozers, earthmovers, construction workers operating cranes, ACREAGE FOR SALE signs. When Mr. and Mrs. Dietrich first moved out to Livingstone from the city sixteen years ago this stretch along Route 12 was quite attractive, mainly farmland, woods, a scattering of small suburban houses; now it has nearly all been developed. There is no natural sequence to what you see— buildings, construction work, leveled woods, the lavish grounds owned by Squibb. Though she has driven this route countless times, Mrs. Dietrich is never quite certain where the mall is and must be prepared for a sudden exit. She remembers getting lost the first several times, remembers the excitement she and her friends felt about the grand opening of the mall, stores worthy of serious shopping at last. Today is much the same. No, today is worse. Like Christmas when she was a small child, Mrs. Dietrich thinks. She'd hoped so badly to be happy she'd felt actual pain, a constriction in her throat like crying.

"*Are* you all right, Nola? You've been so quiet all morning," Mrs. Dietrich asks, half scolding. Nola stirs from her reverie, says she's fine, a just perceptible edge to her reply, and for the remainder of the drive there's some stiffness between them. Mrs. Dietrich chooses to ignore it. In any case she is fully absorbed in driving—negotiating a tricky exit across two lanes of traffic, then the hairpin curve of the ramp, the numerous looping drives of the mall. Then the enormous parking lot, daunting to the inexperienced, but Mrs. Dietrich always heads for the area behind Lord & Taylor on the far side of the mall, Lot D; her luck holds and she finds a space close in. "Well, we made it," she says, smiling happily at Nola. Nola laughs in reply—what does a seventeen-year-old's laughter *mean?*—but she remembers, getting out, to lock both doors on her side of the car. Even here at the Livingstone Mall unattended cars are no longer safe. The smile Nola gives Mrs. Dietrich across the car's roof is careless and beautiful and takes Mrs. Dietrich's breath away.

The March morning tastes of grit with an undercurrent of something acrid, chemical; inside the mall, beneath the first of the elegant brass-buttressed glass domes, the air is fresh and tonic, circulating from invisible vents. The mall is crowded, rather noisy—it *is* Saturday morning—but a feast for the eyes after that long trip on Route 12. Tall slender trees grow out of the mosaic-tiled pavement; there are beds of Easter lilies, daffodils, jonquils, tulips of all colors. There are cobblestone walkways, fountains illuminated from within, wide promenades as in an Old World setting. Mrs. Dietrich smiles with relief. She senses that Nola too is relieved, cheered. It's like coming home.

The shopping excursions began when Nola was a small child but did not acquire their special significance until she was twelve or thirteen years old and capable of serious, sustained shopping with her mother. Sometimes Mrs. Dietrich and Nola would shop with friends, another mother and daughter perhaps, sometimes Mrs. Dietrich invited one or two of Nola's school friends to join them, but she preferred to be alone with Nola and she believed Nola preferred to be alone with her. This was about the time when Mr. Dietrich moved out of the house and back into their old apartment building in the city—a separation, he'd called it initially, to give them perspective, though Mrs. Dietrich had no illusions about what "perspective" would turn out to entail—so the shopping trips were all the more significant. Not that Mrs. Dietrich and Nola spent very much money; they really didn't, *really* they didn't, when compared to friends and neighbors. And Mr. Dietrich rarely objected: the financial arrangement he made with Mrs. Dietrich was surprisingly generous.

At seventeen Nola is shrewd and discerning as a shopper, not easy to please, knowledgeable as a mature woman about certain aspects of fashion, quality merchandise, good stores. She studies advertisements, she shops for bargains. Her closets, like Mrs. Dietrich's, are crammed, but she rarely buys anything that Mrs. Dietrich thinks shoddy or merely faddish. Up in Portland, at the academy, she hasn't as much time to shop, but when she is home in Livingstone it isn't unusual for her and her girlfriends to shop nearly every day. Sometimes she shops at the mall with a boyfriend—but she prefers girls. Like all her friends she has charge accounts at the better stores, her own credit cards, a reasonable allowance. At the time of their settlement Mr. Dietrich said guiltily that it was the least he could do for them: if Mrs. Dietrich wanted to work part-time, she could (she was trained, more or less, in public relations of a small-scale sort); if not, not. Mrs. Dietrich thought, It's the most you can do for us too.

Near Baumgarten's entrance mother and daughter see a disheveled woman sitting by herself on one of the benches. Without seeming to look at her, shoppers are making a discreet berth around her, a stream following a natural course. Nola, taken by surprise, stares. Mrs. Dietrich has seen the woman from time to time at the mall, always alone, smirking and talking to herself, frizzed gray hair in a tangle, puckered mouth. Always wearing the same black wool coat, a garment of fairly good quality but shapeless, rumpled, stained, as if she sleeps in it. She might be anywhere from forty to sixty years of age. Once Mrs. Dietrich saw her make menacing gestures at children who were teasing her, another time she'd seen the woman staring belligerently at *her*. A white paste had gathered in the corners of her mouth.

"My God, that poor woman," Nola says. "I didn't think there were people like her here—I mean, I didn't think they would allow it."

"She doesn't seem to cause any disturbance," Mrs. Dietrich says. "She just sits. Don't stare, Nola, she'll see you."

"You've seen her here before? Here?"

"A few times this winter."

"Is she always like that?"

"I'm sure she's harmless, Nola. She just *sits*."

Nola is incensed, her pale blue eyes like washed glass. "I'm sure *she's* harmless, Mother. It's the harm the poor woman has to endure that is the tragedy."

Mrs. Dietrich is surprised and a little offended by her daughter's passionate tone but she knows enough not to argue. They enter

Baumgarten's, taking their habitual route. So many shoppers! So much merchandise! Dazzling displays of tulips, chrome, neon, winking lights, enormous painted Easter eggs in wicker baskets. Nola speaks of the tragedy of women like that woman—the tragedy of the homeless, the mentally disturbed: bag ladies out on the street, outcasts of an affluent society—but she's soon distracted by the busyness on all sides, the attractive items for sale. They take the escalator up to the third floor, to the Clubhouse Juniors department, where Nola often buys things. From there they will move on to Young Collector, then to Act IV, then to Petite Corner, then one or another boutique and designer—Liz Claiborne, Christian Dior, Calvin Klein, Carlos Falchi, and the rest. And after Baumgarten's the other stores await, to be visited each in turn. Mrs. Dietrich checks her watch and sees with satisfaction that there's just enough time before lunch but not *too* much time. She gets ravenously hungry, shopping at the mall.

Nola is efficient and matter-of-fact about shopping, though she acts solely upon instinct. Mrs. Dietrich likes to watch her at a short distance, holding items of clothing up to herself in the three-way mirrors, modeling things she thinks especially promising. A twill blazer, a dress with rounded shoulders and blouson jacket, a funky zippered jumpsuit in white sailcloth, a pair of straight-leg Evan Picone pants, a green leather vest: Mrs. Dietrich watches her covertly. At such times Nola is perfectly content, fully absorbed in the task at hand; Mrs. Dietrich knows she isn't thinking about anything that would distress her. (Like Mr. Dietrich's betrayal. Like Nola's difficulties with her friends. Like her difficulties at school—as much as Mrs. Dietrich knows of them.) When Nola glances in her mother's direction Mrs. Dietrich pretends to be examining clothes for her own purposes. As if she's hardly aware of Nola. Once, at the mall, perhaps in this very store in this very department, Nola saw Mrs. Dietrich watching her and walked away angrily, and when Mrs. Dietrich caught up with her she said, "I can't stand it, Mother." Her voice was choked and harsh, a vein prominent in her forehead. "Let me go. For Christ's sake will you let me go." Mrs. Dietrich didn't dare touch her though she could see Nola was trembling. For a long terrible moment mother and daughter stood side by side near a display of bright brash Catalina beachwear while Nola whispered, "Let me go. *Let me go.*" How the

scene ended Mrs. Dietrich can't recall—it erupts in an explosion of
light, like a bad dream—but she knows better than to risk it again.

Difficult to believe that girl standing so poised and self-assured
in front of the three-way mirror was once a plain, rather chunky,
unhappy child. She'd been unpopular at school. Overly serious. Anxious. Quick to tears. Aged eleven she hid herself away in her room
for hours at a time, reading, drawing pictures, writing little stories
she could sometimes be prevailed upon to read aloud to her mother,
sometimes even to her father, though she dreaded his judgment.
She went through a "scientific" phase a little later; Mrs. Dietrich
remembers an ambitious bas-relief map of North America, meticu-
lous illustrations for "photosynthesis," a pastel drawing of an eerie
ball of fire labeled RED GIANT (a dying star?), which won a prize in
a state competition for junior high students. Then for a season it was
stray facts Nola confronted them with, often at the dinner table.
Interrupting her parents' conversation to say brightly, "Did you know
that Nero's favorite color was green? He carried a giant emerald and
held it up to his eye to watch Christians being devoured by lions."
And, "Did you ever hear of the raving ghosts of Siberia, with their
mouths always open, starving for food, screaming?" And once at a
large family gathering, "Did you all know that last week downtown
a little baby's nose was chewed off by rats in his crib—a little *black*
baby?" Nola meant only to call attention to herself, but you couldn't
blame her listeners for being offended. They stared at her, not knowing what to say. What a strange child! What queer glassy-pale eyes!
Mr. Dietrich told her curtly to leave the table; he'd had enough of
the game she was playing and so had everyone else.
Nola stared at him, her eyes filling with tears. Game?
When they were alone Mr. Dietrich said angrily to Mrs. Dietrich,
"Can't you control her in front of other people, at least?" Mrs. Dietrich was angry, too, and frightened. She said, "I *try*."

They sent her off aged fourteen to the Portland Academy up in
Maine, and without their help she matured into a girl of considerable
beauty. A heart-shaped face, delicate features, glossy red-brown hair
scissor-cut to her shoulders. Five feet seven inches tall weighing less
than one hundred pounds, the result of constant savage dieting. (Mrs.

Dietrich, who has weight problems herself, doesn't dare inquire as to details. They've been through that already.) All the girls sport flat bellies, flat buttocks, jutting pelvic bones. Many, like Nola, are wound tight, high-strung as pedigreed dogs, whippets for instance, the breed that lives for running. Thirty days after they'd left her at the Portland Academy, Nola telephoned home at 11 P.M. one Sunday giggly and high, telling Mrs. Dietrich she adored the school she adored her suitemates she adored most of her teachers particularly her riding instructor Terri, Terri the Terrier they called the woman because she was so fierce, such a character, eyes that bore right through your skull, wore belts with the most amazing silver buckles! Nola loved Terri but she wasn't *in* love—there's a difference!

Mrs. Dietrich broke down weeping, *that* time.

Now of course Nola has boyfriends. Mrs. Dietrich has long since given up trying to keep track of their names. And, in any case, the Paul of this spring isn't necessarily the Paul of last November, nor are all the boys necessarily students at the academy. There is even one "boy"—or young man—who seems to be married: who seems to be, in fact, one of the junior instructors at the school. (Mrs. Dietrich does not eavesdrop on her daughter's telephone conversations but there are things she cannot help overhearing.) Is your daughter on the pill? the women in Mrs. Dietrich's circle asked one another for a while, guiltily, surreptitiously. Now they no longer ask.

But Nola has announced recently that she loathes boys—she's fed up.

She's never going to get married. She'll study languages in college, French, Italian, something exotic like Arabic, go to work for the American foreign service. Unless she drops out of school altogether to become a model.

"Do you think I'm too fat, Mother?" she asks frequently, worriedly, standing in front of the mirror, twisted at the waist to reveal her small round belly which, it seems, can't help being round: she bloats herself on diet Cokes all day long. "Do you think it *shows?*"

When Mrs. Dietrich was pregnant with Nola she'd been twenty-nine years old and she and Mr. Dietrich had tried to have a baby for nearly five years. She'd lost hope, begun to despise herself; then suddenly it happened: like grace. Like happiness swelling so powerfully it can barely be contained. I can hear its heartbeat! her husband exclaimed. He'd been her lover then, young, vigorous, dreamy. Caressing the rock-hard belly, splendid white tight-stretched skin, that roundness like a warm pulsing melon. Never before so happy, and never since. Husband and wife. One flesh. Mr. Dietrich gave Mrs. Dietrich a reproduction on stiff glossy paper of Dante Gabriel Rossetti's *Beata Beatrix*, embarrassed, apologetic, knowing it was sentimental and perhaps a little silly but that was how he thought of her—so beautiful, rapturous, pregnant with their child. Her features were ordinarily pretty, her wavy brown hair cut short; Mrs. Dietrich looked nothing like the extraordinary woman in Rossetti's painting in her transport of ecstasy but she was immensely flattered and moved by her husband's gift, knowing herself adored, worthy of adoration. She told no one, but she knew the baby was to be a girl. It would be herself again, reborn and this time perfect.

Not until years later did she learn by chance that the woman in Rossetti's painting was in fact his dead wife Lizzy Siddal, who had killed herself with an overdose of laudanum after the stillbirth of their only child.

"Oh, Mother, isn't it *beautiful*!" Nola exclaims.

It is past noon. Past twelve-thirty. Mrs. Dietrich and Nola have made the rounds of a half dozen stores, traveled countless escalators, one clothing department has blended into the next and the chic smiling saleswomen have become indistinguishable, and Mrs. Dietrich is beginning to feel the urgent need for a glass of white wine. Just a glass. "Isn't it beautiful? It's *perfect*," Nola says. Her eyes glow with pleasure, her smooth skin is radiant. Modeling in the three-way mirror a queer little yellow-and-black striped sweater with a ribbed waist, punk style, mock cheap (though the sweater by Sergio Valente, even "drastically reduced," is certainly not cheap), Mrs. Dietrich feels the motherly obligation to register a mild protest, knowing Nola will not hear. She must have it and will have it. She'll wear it a few times, then retire it to the bottom of a drawer with so many other novelty sweaters, accumulated since sixth grade. (She's like her mother in that regard—can't bear to throw anything away. Clothes, shoes, cosmetics, records; once bought by Nola Dietrich they are hers forever, crammed in drawers and closets.)

"*Isn't* it beautiful?" Nola demands, studying her reflection in the mirror.

Mrs. Dietrich pays for the sweater on her charge account.

Next they buy Nola a good pair of shoes. And a handbag to go with them. In Paraphernalia where rock music blasts overhead and Mrs. Dietrich stands to one side, rather miserable, Nola chats companionably with two girls—tall, pretty, cutely made up—she'd gone to public school in Livingstone with, says afterward with an upward rolling of her eyes, "God, I was afraid they'd latch onto us!" Mrs. Dietrich has seen women friends and acquaintances of her own in the mall this morning but has shrunk from being noticed, not wanting to share her daughter with anyone. She has a sense of time passing ever more swiftly, cruelly.

Nola wants to try on an outfit in Paraphernalia, just for fun, a boxy khaki-colored jacket with matching pants, fly front, zippers, oversized buttons, so aggressively ugly it must be chic, yes of course it *is* chic, "drastically reduced" from $245 to $219. An import by Julio Vicente and Mrs. Dietrich can't reasonably disapprove of Julio Vicente, can she. She watches Nola preening in the mirror, watches other shoppers watching her. My daughter. Mine. But of course there is no connection between them, they don't even resemble each other. A seventeen-year-old, a forty-seven-year-old. When Nola is away she seems to forget her mother entirely—doesn't telephone, certainly doesn't write. It's the way all their daughters are, Mrs. Dietrich's friends tell her. It doesn't *mean* anything. Mrs. Dietrich thinks how when she was carrying Nola, those nine long months, they'd been completely happy—not an instant's doubt or hesitation. The singular weight of the body. A state like trance you are tempted to mistake for happiness because the body is incapable of thinking, therefore incapable of anticipating change. Hot rhythmic blood, organs packed tight and moist, the baby upside down in her sac in her mother's belly, always present tense, always *now*. It was a shock when the end came so abruptly, but everyone told Mrs. Dietrich she was a natural mother, praised and pampered her. For a while. Then of course she'd had her baby, her Nola. Even now Mrs. Dietrich can't really comprehend the experience. *Giving birth. Had a baby. Was born.* Mere words, absurdly inadequate. She knows no more of how love ends than she knew as a child, she knows only of how love begins—in the belly, in the womb, where it is always present tense.

The morning's shopping has been quite successful, but lunch at La Crêperie doesn't go well. For some reason—surely there can be no reason?—lunch doesn't go well at all.

La Crêperie is Nola's favorite mall restaurant, always amiably crowded, bustling, a simulated sidewalk café with red-striped umbrellas, wrought-iron tables and chairs, menus in French, music piped in overhead. Mrs. Dietrich's nerves are chafed by the pretense of gaiety, the noise, the openness onto one of the mall's busy promenades where at any minute a familiar face might emerge, but she is grateful for her glass of chilled white wine—isn't it red wine that gives you headaches, hangovers?—white wine is safe. She orders a small tossed salad and a creamed chicken crêpe and devours it hungrily—she *is* hungry—while Nola picks at her seafood crêpe with a disdainful look. A familiar scene: mother watching while daughter pushes food around on her plate. Suddenly Nola is tense, moody, corners of her mouth downturned. Mrs. Dietrich wants to ask, What's wrong? She wants to ask, Why are you unhappy? She wants to smooth Nola's hair back from her forehead, check to see if her forehead is overly warm, wants to hug her close, hard. Why, why? What did I do wrong? Why do you hate me?

Calling the Portland Academy a few weeks ago Mrs. Dietrich suddenly lost control, began crying. She hadn't been drinking and she hadn't known she was upset. A girl unknown to her, one of Nola's suitemates, was saying, "Please, Mrs. Dietrich, it's all right, I'm sure Nola will call you back later tonight—or tomorrow, Mrs. Dietrich? I'll tell her you called, all right, Mrs. Dietrich?" as embarrassed as if Mrs. Dietrich had been her own mother.

How love begins. How love ends.

Mrs. Dietrich orders a third glass of wine. This is a celebration of sorts, isn't it? Their last shopping trip for a long time. But Nola resists, Nola isn't sentimental. In casual defiance of Mrs. Dietrich she lights up a cigarette—yes, Mother, Nola has said ironically, since *you* stopped smoking *everybody* is supposed to stop—and sits with her arms crossed, watching streams of shoppers pass. Mrs. Dietrich speaks lightly of practical matters, tomorrow morning's drive to the airport and will Nola telephone when she gets to Portland to let Mrs. Dietrich know she has arrived safely? La Crêperie opens onto an atrium three stories high, vast, airy, lit with artificial sunlight, tastefully decorated with trees, potted spring flowers, a fountain, a gigantic white Easter bunny, cleverly mechanized, atop a nest of brightly painted wooden eggs. The bunny has an animated tail, an animated nose; paws, ears, eyes that move. Children stand watching it, screaming with excitement, delight. Mrs. Dietrich notes that Nola's expression is one of faint contempt and says, "It *is* noisy here, isn't it?"

"Little kids have all the fun," Nola says.

Then with no warning—though of course she'd been planning this all along—Nola brings up the subject of a semester in France, in Paris and Rouen, the fall semester of her senior year it would be; she has put in her application, she says, and is waiting to hear if she's been accepted. She smokes her cigarette calmly, expelling smoke from her nostrils in a way Mrs. Dietrich thinks particularly coarse. Mrs. Dietrich, who believed that particular topic was finished, takes care to speak without emotion. "I just don't think it's a very practical idea right now, Nola," she says. "We've been through it, haven't we? I—"

"I'm going," Nola says.

"The extra expense, for one thing. Your father—"

"If I get accepted, I'm going."

"Your father—"

"The hell with him too."

Mrs. Dietrich would like to slap her daughter's face. Bring tears to those steely eyes. But she sits stiff, turning her wineglass between her fingers, patient, calm; she's heard all this before; she says, "Surely this isn't the best time to discuss it, Nola."

Mrs. Dietrich is afraid her daughter will leave the restaurant, simply walk away; that has happened before and if it happens today she doesn't know what she will do. But Nola sits unmoving, her face closed, impassive. Mrs. Dietrich feels her quickened heartbeat. It's like seeing your own life whirling in a sink, in a drain, one of those terrible dreams in which you're paralyzed—the terror of losing her daughter. Once after one of their quarrels Mrs. Dietrich told a friend of hers, the mother too of a teenaged daughter, "I just don't know her any longer; how can you keep living with someone you don't know?" and the woman said, "Eventually you can't."

Nola says, not looking at Mrs. Dietrich, "Why don't we talk about it, Mother."

"Talk about what?" Mrs. Dietrich asks.

"You know."

"The semester in France? Again?"

"No."

"What, then?"

"You *know*."

"I don't know, really. Really!" Mrs. Dietrich smiles, baffled. She feels the corners of her eyes pucker white with strain.

Nola says, sighing, "How exhausting it is."

"How *what*?"

"How exhausting it is."

"What is?"

"You and me."

"What?"

"Being together."

"Being together how?"

"The two of us, like this—"

"But we're hardly ever together, Nola," Mrs. Dietrich says.

Her expression is calm but her voice is shaking. Nola turns away, covering her face with a hand; for a moment she looks years older than her age—in fact exhausted. Mrs. Dietrich sees with pity that her daughter's skin is fair and thin and dry—unlike her own, which tends to be oily—it will wear out before she's forty. Mrs. Dietrich reaches over to squeeze her hand. The fingers are limp, ungiving. "You're going back to school tomorrow, Nola," she says. "You won't come home again until June twelfth. And you probably will go to France—if your father consents."

Nola gets to her feet, drops her cigarette to the flagstone terrace, and grinds it out beneath her boot. A dirty thing to do, Mrs. Dietrich thinks, considering there's an ashtray right on the table, but she says nothing. She dislikes La Crêperie anyway.

Nola laughs, showing her lovely white teeth. "Oh, the hell with him," she says. "Fuck Daddy, right?"

———

They separate for an hour, Mrs. Dietrich to Neiman-Marcus to buy a birthday gift for her elderly aunt, Nola to the trendy new boutique Pour Vous. By the time Mrs. Dietrich rejoins her daughter she's quite angry, blood beating hot and hard and measured in resentment; she has had time to relive old quarrels between them, old exchanges, stray humiliating memories of her marriage as well; these last-hour disagreements are the cruelest and they are Nola's specialty. She locates Nola in the rear of the boutique amid blaring rock music, flashing neon lights, chrome-edged mirrors, her face still hard, closed, prim, pale. She stands beside another teenaged girl, looking in a desultory way through a rack of blouses, shoving the hangers roughly along, taking no care when a blouse falls to the floor. Mrs. Dietrich remembers seeing Nola slip a pair of panty hose into her purse in a village shop because, she said afterward, the saleswoman was so damned slow coming to wait on her; fortunately Mrs. Dietrich was there, took the panty hose right out, and replaced it on the counter. No big deal, Mother, Nola said, don't have a stroke or something. Seeing Nola now, Mrs. Dietrich is charged with hurt, rage; the injustice of it, she thinks, the cruelty of it, and why, and why? And as Nola glances up, startled, not prepared to see her mother in front of her, their eyes lock for an instant and Mrs. Dietrich stares at her with hatred. Cold calm clear unmistakable hatred. She is thinking, Who are *you*? What have I to do with *you*? I don't know *you*, I don't love *you*, why should I?

Has Nola seen, heard? She turns aside as if wincing, gives the blouses a final dismissive shove. Her eyes look tired, the corners of her mouth downturned. Anxious, immediately repentant, Mrs. Dietrich asks if she has found anything worth trying on. Nola says with a shrug, "Not a thing, Mother."

On their way out of the mall Mrs. Dietrich and Nola see the disheveled woman in the black coat again, this time sitting prominently on a concrete ledge in front of Lord & Taylor's busy main entrance, shopping bag at her feet, shabby purse on the ledge beside her. She is shaking her head in a series of annoyed twitches as if arguing with someone but her hands are loose, palms up, in her lap. Her posture is unfortunate—she sits with her knees parted, inner thighs revealed, fatty, dead white, the tops of cotton stockings rolled tight cutting into the flesh. Again, streams of shoppers are making a careful berth around her. Alone among them Nola hesitates, seems about to approach the woman—Please don't, Nola, please! Mrs. Dietrich thinks—then changes her mind and keeps on walking. Mrs. Dietrich murmurs, "Isn't it a pity, poor thing, don't you wonder where she lives, who her family is?" but Nola doesn't reply. Her pace through the first floor of Lord & Taylor is so rapid that Mrs. Dietrich can barely keep up.

But she's upset. Strangely upset. As soon as they are in the car, packages and bags in the back seat, she begins crying.

It's childish helpless crying, as though her heart is broken. But Mrs. Dietrich knows it isn't broken; she has heard these very sobs before. Many times before. Still she comforts her daughter, embraces her, hugs her hard, hard. A sudden fierce passion. Vehemence. "Nola honey, Nola dear, what's wrong, dear? everything will be all right, dear," she says, close to weeping herself. She would embrace Nola even more tightly except for the girl's quilted jacket, that bulky L. L. Bean thing she has never liked, and Nola's stubborn lowered head. Nola has always been ashamed, crying, frantic to hide her face. Strangers are passing close by the car, curious, staring. Mrs. Dietrich wishes she had a cloak to draw over her daughter and herself, so that no one would see.

THE BOYFRIEND

She hadn't made any mistakes, at least any serious mistakes, in quite a while. So she'd become complacent.

Her name was Miriam, she was thirty-six years old, tall, long-legged, good-looking, with a pale smooth freckled skin and honey-brown eyes set sly and slanted in her face, as if in irony. When she smiled the corners of her mouth turned tartly, sometimes provocatively, downward.

She'd spent most of her adolescent and adult life in love but now, rather wonderfully, she wasn't in love with anyone, not even with the idea of love. It was exhilarating how, these days, her thinking swung free and wide and wild—she saw a scythe flashing in the sun, swinging and cutting, loosed to the world. What joy in it: loosed to the world! She smiled, seeing it. Her mouth turned downward in irony.

The year before, Miriam had become involved a little too seriously with a man named Swanger. She had liked him enormously but they'd had a misunderstanding and he'd waited too long to telephone her; when he did, Miriam had been abrupt with him, perhaps rude, and he hadn't called back. She rarely thought of him now except in weak, deplenished moods, when she was depressed about her job or worried about the future. (But what after all *was* the future? She imagined it as grainy and achromatic, a region inhabited by people she didn't know.) Like Miriam, Swanger had been married a long time ago. Unlike Miriam he'd never troubled to get a divorce. He had a wife he hadn't seen in five years, two children he rarely saw and never talked about. The only anecdote he told of his former domestic life was about a cat they'd owned named Sheba: an alley cat but very beautiful, Swanger said, gray, long-haired, with tawny eyes, "almost unnaturally sweet-tempered." One morning when he let Sheba in the house she'd been frantic to snuggle against him, burrow into his armpit; she'd made spasmodic attempts to knead her paws against him, as if nursing, but she'd been oddly silent and it was only then that Swanger discovered her crushed backbone, the useless back legs—the poor creature must have been struck by a car, dragged herself to the kitchen door, waited to be let in. She convulsed and died in his hands; there was nothing he could do.

Relating the story, Swanger held out his hands as if to examine the fingers, with an air of faint and even bemused incredulity. Miriam had stared at them too, not knowing what to say. A sad story but what do you say?

One night recently she'd dreamt of Swanger, or of someone meant to be Swanger; the figure in the dream had only approximated the real man. She dreamt he was dead and perfectly at peace; she herself had felt little grief; it was one of those thin, fleeting dreams as if you're swimming swiftly in an element like water, lightly skimming the surface of the water—now beneath it, now above, now asleep and now awake and now asleep again—and all of it fleeting, inconsequential. So that's it, Miriam thought.

"Are you alone?" this man McCurdy asked, and Miriam shrugged and said, "Evidently." He was a friend of a friend of Swanger's, or maybe only an acquaintance of an acquaintance of Swanger's, but in any case harmless seeming. Upbeat and smiling and no one to take seriously but, yes, why not? Miriam was bored with the conversations she'd been having, why not? They were in the twilit Hacienda Lounge of the newly opened Marriott Inn one Friday evening in March. McCurdy drifted over to Miriam and her friends and began talking with her: Bill McCurdy was his name, he identified himself as a computer consultant and seemed to know that Miriam had a Ph.D., called her, jokingly, "Dr. Carey." (Miriam's degree was in economics and city planning. She worked for the city at a salary just slightly higher than she'd been earning as an untenured assistant professor at one of the upstate SUNY campuses.) She let McCurdy buy her a drink, and then she let him buy her another. His eyes were damp, shiny, hopeful; his mustache was neat and delicate as if it had been penciled in. His fine-spun hair was seriously thinning at the crown of his head and Miriam supposed this greatly disturbed him—he couldn't have been much over thirty. As he spoke he touched Miriam's arm repeatedly; he was so warm, sympathetic, eager to please— the kind of kid, Miriam thought cruelly, who runs for class office every year in high school and never wins.

They left the Hacienda and went to another cocktail lounge, then to a popular tavern, the Belvedere, on the outskirts of the city. Then, not quite drunk but feeling expansive, ebullient, McCurdy suggested they drive to Kingston to a really good restaurant, a steak house famous in the area and famously expensive. If it wasn't too late when they finished dinner, McCurdy said, they could drop in at the sports arena close by where there was boxing that evening; a junior division title bout was the main feature, would Miriam be interested? Absolutely not, Miriam thought, but heard herself say aloud, "Why not?" She'd gone to the steak house with Swanger a few times, and she'd even gone to the sports arena once to see some boxing, with Swanger and a group of friends; her memory of the evening was vague but good: she'd had a good enough time, why not? Living alone is living in perpetual irony and thinking, more and more frequently, Why not?

She saw the scythe moving, swinging, flashing. Exuberance in its energies, and she'd mistaken it for her own.

They drove twenty-five miles to Kingston in McCurdy's flashy little red MG and, as Miriam might have foreseen, were unable to get into the steak house; there was an hour's wait. So they settled for an Italian restaurant, overpriced too, and crowded, and McCurdy ate unnervingly fast and Miriam wasn't hungry but had a good deal of chianti. Then there was the boxing match, about which McCurdy was deadly serious. As soon as they entered the sports arena Miriam knew it was a mistake: the noise, the smells, the near-naked sweating men in the ring. McCurdy had even bought tickets for ringside, third row; the time Swanger had brought Miriam here they and their friends had sat farther back. The mood then had been light, free, rowdy; they'd passed joints and pint bottles of whiskey back and forth like kids at a football game. When action in the ring got rough Swanger had gripped Miriam's hand hard, to protect her or to console her, she'd thought at first; then it was clear he'd done it unconsciously. The third row, with McCurdy, was far too close, and within five minutes Miriam stopped watching. She swallowed hard and shut her eyes, didn't see the knockout sequence though the crowd had gone wild. Didn't open her eyes until she heard a gong loudly ringing, signaling the end—even then she regretted opening them.

"Christ! Wasn't that something!" McCurdy said, wiping his face with a tissue.

Afterward, in Miriam's living room, McCurdy tried to demonstrate for her the ingenious way in which the twenty-three-year-old black challenger had knocked out the twenty-eight-year-old black champion in the eighth round. The challenger's name was Lightning Smith and Jesus he *had* been quick as lightning, and powerful too, and McCurdy insisted he'd never seen anything like it. Weren't they lucky, to have gotten seats in the third row! McCurdy's color was high, his eyes dilated, an almost palpable excitement about him like a nimbus. He smelled of cologne, wine, perspiration. It was nearly 1:30 A.M. and Miriam dutifully offered him a drink but had nothing herself, waiting for him to go home. He regarded her with worried eyes. "You didn't enjoy the fight, did you," he said suddenly. Miriam said she'd enjoyed it well enough. "No," McCurdy said, hurt, embarrassed. "You didn't really enjoy it. I can tell." He sat on her sofa silent and brooding for some minutes, and Miriam thought, Go home, go home, but he merely looked at her with his hurt damp eyes and said, "Didn't you tell me you liked boxing, you'd gone to lots of matches? Didn't you tell me that?" Miriam said he must have misunderstood; she'd gone to only one other boxing match in her life. "With Swanger, wasn't it?" McCurdy said. He smiled bitterly, sipped at his drink. "Let's drop the subject," he said. He spoke abruptly but his tone was agreeable.

For what seemed a very long time then he talked about his job, his past, his plans for the future. Miriam didn't trouble to follow and after a while didn't trouble to give the impression of following. She was looking around her tiny living room and thinking it was time for her to leave this house, time to leave this city, time to leave her job. She deserved better. In college and in graduate school Miriam had been generously praised for the high quality of her work and for a certain determinedness in her manner—a "professional attitude," it might be called. She'd been feared too, and resented, for her outspokenness; her sense, sometimes barely contained, that *she* should be first because *she* was best. But things had changed in recent years. She had chosen the wrong job as a young Ph.D. when she'd had her pick of a dozen excellent jobs and now things had changed: she'd lost her old competitive edge, her sense of herself was blunted, numbed. Out of habit she scanned the help wanted section of any newspaper she came across, no matter how distant or improbable the city. She studied rental columns, even property-for-sale columns, waiting for something, the right, magical thing, to strike her eye. (She rented a four-room house, a "bungalow" as the real estate listing had described it, in a fraying residential neighborhood of similar wood-frame and stucco houses. She'd lived here now for four years but thought of it as temporary.) She had a wide loose circle of friends rather like herself, men and women both, unattached, once-married, no longer young yet still waiting for their lives to begin, to take hold. Their real lives.

McCurdy asked Miriam did she mind if he poured himself a little more Scotch? One for the road. On his feet, restless, drink in hand, he stood over her and began to ask about her marriage, hadn't someone told him she *had* been married?—but hadn't any children, of course—and Miriam said, annoyed, they could talk about it another time. McCurdy persisted, missing the edge in her voice or misinterpreting it for coyness. Had she been badly hurt? he asked. Was she bitter? Disillusioned? *He* had had a few "class-A" disappointments in his life which he wouldn't go into, they were too depressing. He said, "I suppose there are always emotional scars after, you know, a divorce," and Miriam, provoked, said with a harsh little laugh that it had all happened so long ago she'd forgotten the details. "There's a point where a husband becomes just another boyfriend," she said dismissively. "All that remains of him is the outline."

McCurdy laughed, startled. As if Miriam had said something wittily obscene.

———

By two-thirty it was clear McCurdy had no intention of leaving and that Miriam was in trouble.

He'd grown belligerent, nasty—the transition was so swift Miriam was taken completely by surprise. He was asking her about Swanger and his friends but mainly about Swanger—what kind of a man was he; what kind of, you know, *man* was he?—and when Miriam said that was none of his business he said, smiling, his voice mocking, "Then whose business is it?" He laughed as if he'd said something witty.

Miriam said he was drunk and McCurdy said he'd be the judge of that. He accused her of "exploiting" him. He accused her of "never looking him in the eye." He accused her of trying to put words in his mouth to make him into a "puppet." His boyish face was flushed and his eyes glassy and heavy-lidded as if he were doing a crude imitation of a drunk. The corners of his mouth, Miriam saw, were wet with saliva.

"I think you'd better go home," she said. She'd forgotten his first name and didn't want to risk guessing.

McCurdy bounced to his feet as if he'd been waiting for this. Miriam got up quickly, backing away. It was a familiar scene, Miriam thought, dazed, though in fact it had never happened to her before—not in this house: McCurdy advancing upon her, swaying and fool-ishly menacing, mimicking her in a falsetto voice, " 'I think you'd better go home! I think you'd better go home!' "

"I'll call the police—"

" 'I'll call the police!' "

"Look—"

" 'Look! Oh, look! Look!' "

McCurdy was clearly enjoying himself and Miriam, still backing away, didn't know what to do. If she screamed, if they began shouting at each other, maybe the neighbors would hear and call the police, but probably not. It was a neighborhood in which, now and then, quarrels erupted out into front yards, into the street. She didn't know her neighbors well and understood that, on both sides, they didn't quite approve of her. And it would be impossible for her to get to a telephone herself, with McCurdy stalking her.

McCurdy was now emotional, accusing Miriam of having tried to manipulate him all evening. She'd drawn him to her with her eyes and then she'd pretended it was all innocent, accidental. She'd lied to him about boxing, led him on. She was like Swanger—leading people on. "I know about women like you," he said. "I know about *you*, Dr. Carey." With balled fists he feinted at her head, laughed as she screamed and ducked. He advanced upon her, until she felt something against her back: the edge of a table. "What are you afraid of now?" he said, jeering. "Why'd you invite me here if you're afraid of it?"

Miriam said, pleading, "Don't. Please."

"*I know all about you*," McCurdy said.

Then, to Miriam's relief, he relented.

He backed away, talking, chuckling angrily to himself. He poured the rest of the Scotch into his glass and drank it down and wandered out of the room, down the hall; was he headed for the bathroom? The bedroom? Miriam heard a crashing sound; Miriam heard him laughing to himself. After a minute she went to investigate and there he was, the son of a bitch, the arrogant bastard, sprawled atop her bed. Drink and all! He'd splashed whiskey on the bedspread, lay there panting and grunting like a pig. As Miriam stood in the doorway McCurdy peeked up at her, gave her a weird wet toothy grin. Wasn't he a naughty boy, burrowing into her bedclothes, kicking, squirming, thrashing around so that the bedsprings creaked and the floor trembled? He wasn't leaving, he said. He was fucking tired and he wasn't leaving and Miriam could crawl in with him—take off her clothes, and his—or Miriam could sleep on the sofa or on the floor or she could fuck herself, fucking slut, cunt, didn't give a shit what she did, *he* was going to sleep. He shut his eyes and made loud mock snoring noises.

Miriam told him the joke had gone far enough. Miriam told him she wouldn't call the police if he left now; she began to slap at him, scream at him, but he seemed hardly to hear. His eyes were closed, his mouth slack and wet. When Miriam clawed at his legs, meaning to pull him off the bed, he kicked her in the stomach—kicked her hard—and she let go. It took her perhaps five minutes to recover from the blow and by then McCurdy was asleep, deeply asleep, snoring in earnest, Miriam's bedspread twisted around him.

Though Miriam was fully sober now she couldn't seem to think what to do. She dialed the police emergency number taped to the wall beside her kitchen phone but hung up before anyone answered. She didn't want police, strangers, in her house, didn't want anyone to know about McCurdy. A patrol car, lights and sirens, neighbors looking out of their windows? She grabbed her coat, ran outside.

A damply cold night, late winter, a faint fading moon, and up and down Miriam's street the proper little tacky little houses were darkened; she was alone. She was sobbing angrily, adrenaline still flooding her veins, pumping her heart. McCurdy's car was parked at the curb but of course Miriam's car was in the parking lot at the Marriott Inn; she'd forgotten all about it. "Asshole," she whispered. "*You're* the one."

So she walked. Not to the Marriott but to Swanger's apartment.

It was two miles, she'd walked it several times in the past—the two of them had walked it together, in fact, though not at such a pace, with such ferocity. Now that the danger was past—if there had been any danger—Miriam was shaking with rage, or fear; her heart began to miss beats, a symptom of acute physical distress she hadn't felt in years. Was she going to die? Was it no more than she deserved? She paused, caught her breath, continued on. She was arguing with herself, calling herself names, the usual litany of names she'd called herself since adolescence. She began to wonder if McCurdy might not wake up and get in his car and pursue her—though he wasn't (was he?) the kind of man to *really* hurt a woman, to *really* want revenge.

When a car's headlights appeared behind her, however, she lost control and ran to hide. Waited for the car to pass and, no, it wasn't McCurdy; still she waited, trembling behind an evergreen shrub in a stranger's front yard. How humiliated she'd become, how comical a figure: Miriam Carey, Ph.D.

She walked on. Her heartbeat was calmer but decidedly erratic. She still couldn't recall McCurdy's first name, was it Bill, was it Bob, something short and commonplace and American like his boyish face, earnest manner, that pushy persistent smile. Are you alone? he'd asked, and Miriam should have said, Of course not, I'm with friends. Turned away, frozen him out. She'd made a fool of herself now and very likely everyone would know.

And McCurdy: he'd never forgive her. He would apologize, no doubt, he'd apologize profusely, but he would never forgive her.

He'd nurse his resentment of her, his hatred for her, in secret. "I know the type," Miriam said aloud. She was breathless, oddly exhilarated, still quite shaken.

Swanger lived on the ground floor of a converted Victorian house on a street of similar houses, long past their prime. Miriam had always admired the house, its design—so substantial, so in excess, even, of the substantial—she'd often tried to imagine what life must have been like in it, generations ago. A single family, living in that immense house: three floors, innumerable rooms, steep gabled roofs and bay windows and a front porch trimmed in ornamental fretwork. It was difficult, however, to think of the house in anything but its present state, partitioned into apartments in a shabby slipping-down neighborhood. Swanger lived here because the rent was reasonable and he was paying child support for children he never saw.

Miriam rang the doorbell and waited. He was home; she recognized his car at the curb. He was in bed, the lights were out, but was he alone in bed, was he alone? That was another question.

Swanger switched on the outside light, opened the door, called out, "Yes? What? Who is it?" He had pulled on a pair of trousers and was shirtless, barefoot—staring at Miriam as if he'd never seen her before.

As soon as Miriam saw Swanger she began to lose control. She couldn't speak. Couldn't answer his questions—"Miriam? What is it? What's wrong?" Behind him the room was pitch dark but she knew where the sofa was, she knew the meager rooms in which Swanger lived as if they were her own, which, for a brief while, they'd been, or nearly. The sofa was covered in badly worn green velvet with a cherrywood frieze along its back, she'd helped Swanger pick it out at the Goodwill store downtown, the two of them exhilarated as newlyweds, secure in their conviction that they loved each other and that their love would last. Impossible to so much as imagine it might not last, or that like cruel, fascinated children, they might smash it of their own volition, simply to see if it would smash.

"Hank. Help me. I made a mistake."

"Miriam, of course—come in!"

Miriam started past him for the sofa but her knees buckled; she would have struck the floor like a dead weight if he hadn't caught her. He helped her to the sofa, stone-cold sober, asking what was wrong; had someone hurt her? Miriam drew in a sharp breath, whimpering with pain, a sharp pain in her stomach where she'd been kicked, a pain in her chest where her heart beat so rapidly—and then she was lying down, Swanger was lifting her legs to settle her onto the sofa, and she remembered that the sofa was one of the places they'd made love, so tenderly, those first few months, but only one of the places. She began to cry helplessly, angrily.

Swanger turned on a light and squatted beside her. She saw a look in his face she'd never seen before—a look of sheer astounded wonder.

"Are you ill?—injured? Did someone attack you? Should I call an ambulance?"

He was stroking her forehead, finding it not feverish as perhaps he'd anticipated, but cold, clammy. Miriam took hold of his hand and gripped it for a moment, hard, without speaking.

Miriam was having a tachycardiac seizure: not a severe one, a mild one, she knew the symptoms, she'd had such seizures occasionally since the age of seventeen and knew they were not fatal, or need not be fatal, the heart beats too rapidly for blood to circulate normally through the body, the extremities in particular, thus her toes and fingers had gone icy cold, her skin clammy, like death, like the death that crept up Socrates' legs as he lay dying, but in Miriam's case it was only a simulacrum of death: mock death.

"Shall I call an ambulance?" Swanger asked.

In his fear for her, in his astonishment, he was speaking with an odd formality. The skin of his face too had gone dead white, drained of blood.

"Thank you, no," Miriam whispered.

"Are you sure? You look—" He hesitated, now touching her cheek, drawing his thumb slowly along the line of her jaw.

Miriam tried to laugh. "—like hell?"

"—distressed."

Miriam tried to speak but couldn't get her breath. A sharp pain radiated through her stomach and groin.

She shut her eyes. Swanger was speaking, meaning to console her, assuring her she was safe, she was going to be all right, he would take care of her, if only she would tell him what was wrong, but

Miriam did not know what was wrong; could not give it a name. She pressed the back of her hand over her eyes, not wanting to see her lover's face so open to her, vulnerable as if she'd wakened him from sleep, which in fact she had. There were little tucks and creases in his skin that she hadn't recalled.

Miriam was whispering, "—I'm so ashamed. Forgive me."

"Ashamed? Of what?"

"Hank. Forgive me."

Swanger squatted beside her, stroking her forehead, her hair. Her shoulders. He touched his mouth against her temple lightly as if to comfort her: not knowing how to comfort her—baffled, alarmed. No doubt he smelled her breath, the sweet winey breath, so much of their lovemaking had been a matter of sweet winey breaths exchanged. She recalled, once, in her bed, in that other house, how she'd clutched at him in desperation that, yes, she would die: torn out of herself, she would die—and he'd held her. And what had seemed a very long time had passed, and gradually they'd begun hearing the sounds of Miriam's neighborhood, a dog barking, a car with an aged muffler passing in the street, and the fact of it was, is, you don't die, quite like that.

Swanger asked, a new note in his voice, "Did somebody hurt you? Who was it?"

Quickly Miriam shook her head. "No."

"Who was it?"

"No one, Hank."

"I said, who?"

"No one," said Miriam, sobbing. "—It was my own fault."

"What was your own fault?"

Miriam was sobbing, and then Miriam was laughing. Demeaning tears leaked from the corners of her eyes.

"I made a mistake. No one's to blame but me. A kick in the stomach—it's what I deserve. Can't blame being a woman, my life, my job, I made mistakes, I can only blame *me*," she said. She was gripping Swanger's hand, holding it tight.

"Jesus, Miriam! Somebody kicked you in the stomach?"

"No one," Miriam said. *"Really."*

She lay very still, her hand over her eyes. She could hear Swanger breathing harshly. He was a man with anger in him, as she was a woman with anger in her: so, she'd known him, and had been afraid.

"Tell me who it is," Swanger said quietly.

"—No one."

After a while Swanger relented; or, maybe, his haunches had begun to ache. He leaned back, balanced on his heels. In silence, brooding, he stared at her. He had seen her naked many times, he had seen her in the aftermath of passion, and now he was thinking, maybe, he had not known her at all. But she'd come to him.

"I'll find out, eventually," Swanger said. He touched her throat where an artery was beating hard, stroked it, wonderingly. As if practiced, he drew his fingers upward against the artery in light deft feathery motions. "Is this what you told me about—some kind of palpitations? Heart?"

Miriam did not remember having told Swanger this.

"If you lie still—you'll be all right? You think so?"

"I think so."

"How about a drink, then, hon?—a little bourbon and water?"

Swanger laughed, a mirthless sort of laugh, meaning, my God, *I* could use a drink, don't deny me.

"No thank you," Miriam said. Then, "Well—yes."

Swanger grunted, straightening. He was a tall man in his late thirties, long-limbed, rangy, a former athlete who inhabited his aging, imperfect body with a look of bemused concentration. A good-looking man, Miriam had thought, the first night they'd met, except he had a habit of smiling too readily, rapaciously. Baring his teeth like a reflex of nerves.

Miriam opened her eyes and Swanger was gone and she felt a sudden rush of panic, seeing nothing above her but a blinding light. She was lying on the green velvet sofa at such an angle that the bare bulb of a light shone directly into her face. Beyond the light where there should have been a ceiling there seemed to be nothing save empty space, and to her horror Miriam saw again the brightly lit boxing ring, the filthy stained canvas, the taut ropes like the ropes of an animal pen, and there, in one corner, demonic in triumph, the winning boxer climbing up the ropes like a child, raising his gloved hands to the ecstatic crowd. The other boxer lay with an arm flung out, his damp chest rising and falling, blood leaking from his nose and mouth. Why? why? Miriam was saying, aloud, terrified, "Oh. Oh, no. Please. I don't want to die. I'm not ready."

Swanger was standing over her, glasses in both hands, a bottle under his arm. He was smiling. "Eventually, I'll find out his name," he said. "But, for now—"

Miriam said, "Yes."

PASSION

They were separated for nearly two years before they were divorced, and they were divorced for nearly five years before one of them died. Dennis heard the news just as he was leaving to pick up his wife's eight-year-old daughter at a children's birthday party.

A mutual acquaintance called, a man Dennis had never known well. He had only secondhand information, there hadn't yet been anything about it in the newspaper, but the facts seemed to be that Rona was dead, had committed suicide—had slashed her wrists with a razor and had died, alone, the previous morning, leaving no note behind, in an apartment in a suburb some thirty miles away. The address was new to Dennis, and at first he seemed not even to recognize the name of the suburb, though he'd been living in this part of the state for fifteen years. What was she doing there? Why *there?* Evidently she'd moved another time without telling him. . . . As he stood pressing the telephone receiver to his ear, beginning to sweat with the force of a blow so hard it seemed to pass through him without touching him, it was this fact he focused upon: that Rona had moved again, the fifth or sixth time since the divorce, and he hadn't known; she'd promised to keep in touch with him and had not; it was like her to forget him, so very like that woman to think of no one but herself.

He stood in his wool-lined trench coat, trembling, angry, very warm, cupping his hand to the telephone receiver so that his wife, in an adjoining room, would not overhear. As, at the start of his second marriage, for a year or two, he'd kept his telephone conversations with Rona secret—for no other reason than that he hadn't wanted Charlotte, whom he loved, to be upset over his concern for an ex-wife whom he no longer loved but for whom he felt some responsibility. Now he was asking why Rona had moved to that particular suburb—was there any logic to it, was there any man involved?—knowing of course that there was, there would have to be. A man, or men. He was asking if Rona had left any note or explanation behind, though he'd already been told it seemed she had not. And who had found her? And where was the body? And what about her family, had they been notified? Was *he* expected to deal with it?

"I can't," he said. "I don't have time. I don't have any more time for her. I have my own life now. In fact I'm on my way out of the house now; I have to pick up my daughter."

He was speaking with such urgency that his wife heard him after all. When he hung up she asked, "What is it? Is it bad news?" and he said, wiping his forehead with a tissue, dazed, half smiling, looking her frankly in the face, "In a way I suppose it's good news—I mean, in a way. I'll explain later."

"Good news? But you seem so—"

"I'll explain later," he said. "I'm late picking up Suzanne."

He was so warm, uncomfortably warm, he had to get out of the house. Out into the windy November evening that smelled of leaves, damp earth, imminent snow. Good news. He was free! His heart pumped hard and fast in the first flush of grief.

Later he would be ashamed, deeply embarrassed, when Charlotte told him what he'd said that day. He had not meant it in the most obvious sense, he told her; he had not meant it at all. "I don't think I actually said 'good' news, did I? I don't remember that." And, still later: "You must have misunderstood. I mean, you heard me wrong."

"That's possible," Charlotte said carefully.

"Also, it was a considerable shock," Dennis said. "Picking up the telephone like that, hearing—what I'd heard. No warning—"

"Yes," said Charlotte. "That must have been it."

The last memory Dennis had of Rona was her lunging at him—
her beautiful, very white, carefully made-up face contorted with an
insane rage. They had stopped for a drink after the final ceremonial
signing of their divorce papers in her attorney's office; they'd been
talking, Dennis had thought, companionably together, even rather
happily; and then with no warning Rona had gone silent, swallowed
a large mouthful of her drink, sat staring at the tessellated top of the
little table in which dull patches of light flashed and glowered. Close
by, suddenly too loud, was a piano being played in mock-ebullient
cocktail style. Rona whispered something Dennis couldn't hear and
when he leaned toward her, cupping a hand to his ear, polite, def-
erential, courtly, she'd lost control and struck at him—slapping and
clawing with her nails. It was so like Rona to take him by surprise,
Dennis hadn't really known, in the shock and confusion of the moment, whether she was lunging at him in a display of exaggerated
affection or in rage. She rose from her seat with such violence that
the little table nearly tipped over; their drinks fell to the floor. In a
choked voice Rona said what sounded like "You! *You!*" Dennis
managed to defend himself by seizing her wrists, forcing her down.
She was a small woman but surprisingly strong, wiry, snakelike, he'd
thought, when fits of temper overcame her; she didn't fight fair, some
childlike voice in him protested, you never knew from which angle
she'd attack, which low blow or cruel remark she'd throw. "Rona,
for God's sake, stop. Rona, please don't do this," he begged. He was
stricken with shame, that others in the cocktail lounge were staring
at them. That his failure as a man was at last being exposed, celebrated, in public.

In these few terrible seconds Rona had become fierce, feverish,
disheveled as a drunken woman—and that would be her excuse, no
doubt, that she *was* drunk; she'd had two quick, highly potent drinks,
on an empty stomach—and Dennis had become totally sober, a man
waking from a dream. Signing the divorce papers had been a relief
to him after years of protracted anxiety; his grief at the breakup of
the marriage, and his loss of Rona, was behind him and, he'd thought,
rapidly retreating, like a scene of devastation viewed from a speeding
car. And now the woman was hot-eyed, murderous, her face drained
white. "I hate you!" she was saying, incredibly. "How could you let
this happen to us?"

How many times in their marriage had Rona turned on him like this, accusing him, blaming him, for things she'd done herself or caused to be done—for what had he ever done, except by way of her desire? She knew how to hurt, she knew what hurt, and he'd never been assured, thinking these exchanges over afterward, brooding upon them for days, weeks, months, that in fact she was wrong. Her fury, the stark simplicity of her words, aroused in her with such terrifying swiftness, seemed to carry a logic and authority of their own. But her insights, if they were insights, came always too late. And that too was part of it, Dennis thought—they came, these killing blows, too late.

"How could you let this happen to us after we loved each other so much?" Rona said, wiping at her face with a napkin. She was quieter now, preparing to leave. She'd assaulted him, hurt him, and now she would leave.

"But why me?"

"A man of character would never have let this happen," Rona said. "A man of passion."

It was an accusation she'd made often in the past; he simply had no defense against it. He wanted to clap his hands over his ears and shut his eyes tight. He wanted to cringe, to writhe in utter physical shame. In his professional life he was a man of infinite tact, intelligence, presence; in his private life, what might be called his emotional life, he had always seemed to himself mysteriously undefined, at once an adult man and a child of perhaps eleven years of age. Even before the breakup of his marriage he'd had a recurrent dream in which he stepped into an elevator as the doors opened, only to find himself in space—terrified, unable to scream for help, flailing and clawing to save his life. The dream struck him as an image of his predicament, yet to have defined that predicament, to have given it a precise vocabulary: this was a task seemingly beyond him.

Rona said nothing more. She simply got to her feet and walked away as Rona always did, and Dennis was left behind to deal with the consequences: pay the bill and pay for the broken glasses and leave a generous tip and apologize, profusely apologize. It was what Dennis always did, and could be relied upon to do, with his usual embarrassed tact.

———

Driving across town to pick up Suzanne, Dennis thought of these things: recalled, with painful, almost hallucinatory vividness, the terrible scene in the cocktail lounge. It was a scene one might interpret as luridly comic or heartrendingly pathetic, depending on one's point of view. He had not thought of it consciously for a very long time; it wasn't, after all, a memory in which he took much pride. And what was odd about it was his inclination to place it earlier in time, to consider it the turning point of his life with Rona, when in fact it had occurred after the formal divorce. It was a coda of sorts, not a climax. And not a resolution.

And now Rona was dead.

And she had killed herself for a man, and he had not been that man.

The children's birthday party was being held in an apartment on the fifth floor of a handsome new building overlooking a park. There was romance in the setting—the parents of Suzanne's classmates were generally well-to-do—and Dennis, no less than Charlotte, was grateful that Suzanne seemed to be taking her place in this world without much effort, as if by entitlement. Both he and Charlotte were from family backgrounds that might have been described as modest, but their backgrounds were no more relevant to their lives now than were old report cards or college transcripts. Dennis was a professor of law at a good, solid, second-level law school and Charlotte was an assistant curator at the local museum of fine arts: an attractive couple, a quintessentially contemporary couple, Dennis thought, both previously married, both serious about their careers without being unrealistically ambitious or more than ordinarily competitive. Dennis liked it that his wife's friends and, so far as he was aware, those parents of Suzanne's classmates they'd become friendly with in the past several years knew him only as Charlotte's husband: not as Rona's former husband. To these people Rona Sorenson had not existed, and her death now would cause no comment or speculation. They would not look at him with curiosity, wondering at the depth of his loss, or his shame.

Dennis climbed the stairs to the seventh floor. How he needed the exertion of his heart and lungs, the wakefulness of physical strain! When he rang the doorbell he was out of breath and perspiring and nervously elated, but Suzanne's classmate's mother seemed not to notice or, if she noticed, gave no sign. Would he like to join her in a drink? The past two hours, she said, had been just a bit harried. "Thank you so much, I can't," Dennis said. "It wouldn't be real," he said vaguely, peering into the brightly lit room in which children were playing some sort of game with cushions and pillows and making a good deal of noise. He hadn't been aware of what he said, exactly, and, in the confusion, his hostess hadn't heard either. There was pretty blond Suzanne in a pink dress with a lace collar—he called her name and felt his heart contract in joy, or was it sheer paternal pride, when the little girl shouted "Daddy!" and ran at him, warm, damp, happy, quivering with excitement. In the elevator and in the car Suzanne chattered to him nonstop about the birthday party, the presents, a prize she herself had won, the cake, ice cream—and Dennis, smiling, numbed, thought, It's as if nothing has happened, then. Nothing has happened.

There was a small obituary in the next morning's paper. No photograph, of course—Rona Sorenson, for all her beauty, her energy and ambition, had had no career of significance. It was something of a shock to Dennis to see, in print, that she'd been thirty-six years old at the time of her death, though he knew her age as well as his own; a shock too to see in print, so stark and without qualification, the summary of the police and coroner's report: self-inflicted death.

Impossible, Dennis thought.

He read and reread the brief obituary. If Rona had really killed herself, as they were claiming, why hadn't she left a note behind? It was as much unlike Rona Sorenson to have failed to leave a note in such dramatic circumstances as to have committed suicide in the first place.

He couldn't sit still, had to walk, pace—not knowing where he went—upstairs, downstairs into the basement: vague, groping, stunned. What was more improbable, that Rona had killed herself in so very flamboyant a way or that she was dead? He was ashamed, baffled. Repeatedly he told Charlotte he simply didn't believe it; he *knew* Rona.

"She may have changed since you saw her last," Charlotte said.

Charlotte had never met Rona but she'd heard a good deal about her over the years, as much from other sources as from Dennis. "After all, you hadn't seen her in a while."

Dennis said, "But she wasn't the sort of woman who changes. . . . I would have sworn to that."

That day, and the following days, Dennis spent a good deal of time on the telephone. He called police headquarters and insisted upon speaking with one of the detectives assigned to Rona Sorenson's case; he tried without success to reach the man who'd done the autopsy. He called old—that is, former—friends and acquaintances, spent hours tracking down people of whom he had not heard or so much as thought in years. They were Rona's people rather than his, and after the divorce he'd drifted away from them, or they from him, with little regret. For a while Rona had acted with a local drama group in semiprofessional productions and had been, Dennis thought, really quite good—it was a mystery to them all, as to Rona, why she'd never received any serious offers to act. And she'd been a model for one of the downtown department stores for a time. And an assistant on a local television interview show. And, at the time of their breakup, she'd been hired by a public relations firm . . . though that wasn't the reason, Dennis recalled with discomfort, for their breakup. In each phase of Rona's life, or what Rona had been in the habit of calling, not without irony, her career, there were people, mainly men, with whom Dennis became acquainted and in some cases friendly; but it was disconcerting, now, how many of them seemed to have vanished. And it was disconcerting in another way, when he did connect with one or another old acquaintance and found himself speaking in a forced, urgent, intimate voice—as if it had been only yesterday they'd seen each other, and had meant to keep in contact. When Dennis heard certain voices he felt a vague resentful surprise that these people were still alive.

The conversations left him weak but exhilarated. He was learning so much!—piecing together so much!—acquiring new names, new numbers, new information. That Rona was actually dead was a fact he could not consider, but he was very much caught up in learning all he could about her in the years following the divorce. He learned, for instance, that she'd been unemployed at the time of her death; that she'd been living with a man for nearly a year, and he'd moved out—at her insistence, one source said; of his own volition, said another—only six weeks before her death. He learned that, since the divorce, Rona had been estranged from her parents. That she often quarreled with friends, was said to have become increasingly unreliable, unstable, "emotional." And that there was a rumor the autopsy had revealed signs of alcohol and drugs.

One evening, when he was between telephone calls, Charlotte came into his study uninvited and laid a hand gently on his shoulder. Dennis had closed his study door to keep both her and Suzanne out, though he'd meant nothing hostile or rude. "Would you like to talk about it?" Charlotte asked.

"Talk about what?"

"You know—her death. The way it happened."

"There's nothing to talk about."

"Isn't there?"

Dennis smiled up at her. "Is this an interrogation?"

"Why don't you talk about it? Since, after all, you're thinking about it so much."

"How do you know I'm thinking about it 'so much'?" Dennis asked, still smiling. Something shifted in him, in his very brain, and he was his lawyerly self, alert, actually elated, thinking *I can do this, this I can do.* "And what do you mean by 'so much'? What, in your opinion, would be 'just enough'?"

He could see how, for the merest fraction of an instant, Charlotte was tempted to give in: to quarrel with him as he so clearly wanted. But she said instead, carefully, "I just meant, you're going through a difficult time. After all . . ."

She was about to say, but did not say, *after all, you loved her.*

". . . the circumstances of the death were so shocking. She must have been very unhappy, the poor woman—"

"Yes," Dennis said quickly, cutting her off.

He saw Charlotte glance at the sheet of paper in front of him which he'd made a half-conscious effort to hide. It was notes, mainly names, telephone numbers, addresses. In the margins, in ornate block letters, were RONA RONA RONA and HECTOR RIVERA HECTOR RIVERA HECTOR RIVERA. "Who is that?" Charlotte asked. "Hector Rivera?"

Dennis tried to keep his voice from showing the annoyance he felt. He said, "Hector Rivera is the name of Rona's last lover."

"Oh. I see. Is he anyone you know?"

"The last known lover, I should say."

"Is he anyone you know?"

"Of course not, Charlotte. Don't be absurd."

"I only meant—"

"I know what you meant. Don't be absurd."

"Maybe if you'd gone to the funeral—"

"Yes," Dennis said coldly. "But I didn't."

Once, many years ago, when Dennis was a young man of twenty-eight or -nine, newly married, very much in love, he happened to see his wife Rona on the street, walking with a mutual acquaintance, a man, and guessed, simply by the way the two were assiduously not touching, not even looking at each other as they talked—their earnest talk punctuated with laughter—that they were lovers. He drew back, not wanting them to see him. He drew back, his heart clenched. Was it so? Could it be so? And why? Seeing that, at this time, Rona did love him—and gave every evidence, physical and otherwise, of loving him.

That evening they went out to dinner with another couple. Dennis asked casually if any of them were familiar with the theory that mankind has invented myths of all kinds—romantic, religious, transcendental, "mystical"—to deny the bleak, unmitigated horror of biological life: that human beings no less than other creatures are simply part of an immense food chain.

Rona laughed and said quickly that she didn't want to hear such a thing—not right now.

"When, then?" Dennis asked.

Rona put her hands over her ears.

"When, then?" Dennis persisted.

Rona put a hand playfully over his mouth. Dennis drew it away, not altogether playfully.

Rona shivered and said, "I hate talk like that, crude cynical speculation. I *hate* it and I'm not going to listen to it." The other couple looked at them, smiling, uneasy. It was clear that something was wrong, and abruptly wrong; but what was it? Rona kissed Dennis on the cheek and slipped out of the booth to go to the rest room and Dennis was left behind, flushed and unable to speak for some minutes, not quite trusting his voice. How the scene, or the evening, ended, he would not recall afterward. He would not even be able to recall what Rona said when she returned or how long she'd been gone. Had she telephoned her lover in the interim? Or had there been no lover, at that time?

Now, after her death, he thought about that theory: that our human myths, our heroic, inflated images of ourselves, the insistent spirituality of our highest beliefs, were all in defiance of the food chain. The food chain! Not very romantic, after all.

He'd heard from a friend that Rona had been cremated. He wondered if it was by her own wish or someone else's.

He dialed the number listed in the directory as Hector Rivera's. Dialed it a dozen times, and no answer. And then one night, very late, when Charlotte and Suzanne were sleeping and he knew himself alone, and secret, and invulnerable, he went into his study and shut the door and, in the dark, dialed the number another time—and a man answered on the first ring.

"Yes? Hello? Who is this?"

Dennis thought, He's the killer.

"Hello? Is someone there?" The voice was sharp, alert, wary. It was past 3 A.M. and Rivera hadn't been sleeping and Dennis knew why but said nothing, not a word, hunched over his desk, staring fascinated at a dull glowering patch of moonlight on the polished mahogany surface. Rivera hung up and Dennis continued to hold the receiver to his ear, Yes, he's the one, obviously he's the one; she couldn't have done such a terrible thing to herself, never.

Next day, purely by chance, two events occurred: Dennis drove out to the suburb in which Rona had lived in order to see what her apartment building looked like and to drive past—in fact, several times past—the address listed as Hector Rivera's (Rona's apartment was in a five-story building of no particular distinction, postwar granite-and-stucco on a busy suburban street; Rivera lived in a newer, taller, but rather cheaply flashy building that boasted LUXURY APTS— 2 | 3 BEDROOMS STILL RENTING); and, when he returned to his office at the law school, he received a telephone call from a man who lived in Rona's very building—the fellow tenant of Rona's, a man named

Courtney, who had talked the building's manager into unlocking her door after he'd failed to see her for several days. This Courtney, soft-spoken, seemingly shy, now introduced himself over the telephone as a friend of the late Rona Sorenson, "your former wife," who had volunteered to help clean her apartment. He thought Dennis might like to know that there were items belonging to him among the possessions of the late Rona Sorenson.

"What do you mean? What kind of items?" Dennis asked.

"Papers. Letters, I guess," Courtney said. "There's some boxes I'm going through—your name's on some of the things."

"I'll be right there," Dennis said. "What's the address, exactly?"

When Dennis arrived he found Courtney—a slight man, youngish, sallow-skinned, with watery eyes and a self-deprecatory manner—waiting for him in the third-floor corridor outside Rona's apartment. There was something less than wholesome about him, but Dennis shook hands vigorously and with gratitude. Here was his way in, the man who could answer all his questions.

"I was just a neighbor friend of Rona's," Courtney said with exaggerated care. "Not, you know, one of her man friends. I mean, not"—he gestured vaguely, sadly—"not one of her lovers."

"Did she have many lovers?" Dennis asked casually.

"Too many."

It was an odd, wistful answer. As Courtney led Dennis into the apartment he exchanged a glance with him that was meant to be meaningful, perhaps conspiratorial. He sighed, wriggled his thin shoulders in a mild shrug. "Though not in the past year," he said. "With Rivera she was making an effort to be monogamous."

"Rivera?"

"Hector Rivera. Hadn't you heard? He used to live here, with her. He was the current boyfriend—the last."

"Where is he now?"

"Oh, around. He was pretty broken up by it—what happened." Courtney sighed again and glanced at Dennis. "So was I. I bet you were too. I *liked* her, you know. I mean, she could be terrible, just so terribly self-centered and demanding, but she could be so sweet too. Just the *sweetest*."

"Yes," Dennis said, swallowing hard, looking around the living room. "That's right."

"I mean, you could forgive that woman *anything*. Or almost."

Dennis found it hard to concentrate on the man's chatter. He was beginning to feel faint, sick. So this was where Rona, whom he'd once loved so desperately, had ended her days: in this ordinary, shabby, not very clean apartment with its windows fronting on a busy street. Not that it was squalid, or even particularly dirty; it was merely ordinary. He recognized a well-worn leather sling chair from the days of their marriage, and a wall mirror with a wide mother-of-pearl frame, and, in the narrow dining room alcove, the very dining room table and chairs they'd bought together: austere, graceful, perhaps rather pretentious Danish modern. With no warning Dennis began crying. He cried in great gulping sobs, turned away from Courtney, helpless.

After a minute Courtney said, seemingly embarrassed but pleased as well, "Hey, look, Dennis—can I call you Dennis?—it's OK. I've been crying a lot too. I mean, I keep thinking I could have saved her. You know—knocked on her door at the right moment, invited her in for a drink or to watch a tape on my VCR; we used to do that, sometimes, after Rivera moved out. She was lonely, you know, really I think desperately lonely, but didn't want to let on. She had her pride, you know? I guess you knew her better than I ever could." He let his hand fall on Dennis's shoulder. "She talked about you, sometimes. She thought the world of you, you know."

Dennis blew his nose. He said, "I don't know if I want to hear that."

"Well, yeah. OK. I'm just telling you."

Courtney led Dennis along a narrow hallway in the direction of the bedroom. He indicated the bathroom—the door was closed—where they'd found Rona, partly dressed, lying in a pool of blood. "The most . . . the *most* terrifying thing I have ever seen," Courtney said, shuddering. "The saddest, too. And the most *unnecessary*."

Dennis pushed open the bathroom door; the catch gave way easily. It was a small room with a tiny window, crank operated, so very like the bathroom, long forgotten, in the first apartment he and Rona had rented together in Ann Arbor that Dennis felt a thrill of recognition. But the gold-spangled shower curtain was badly stained, the walls blistered and peeling, the tile floor discolored. "She couldn't have done it to herself," Dennis said quietly. "She wasn't that kind of person."

Courtney closed the door quickly. "No point in dwelling on it," he said.

"She wouldn't have had the physical courage. Anyone who knew her would—"

Courtney murmured something Dennis couldn't hear. He wriggled his shoulders in a fastidious little shudder.

"—would *know*. Whatever the police have said."

"Pointless to dwell on it," Courtney said. "My first and final statement."

Though it was small and had only a single window, the bedroom was a much more attractive room than the others. Dennis recognized Rona's touch here: over the bed the framed photograph of a snow-covered peak in the Rockies that Dennis had taken on their sole trip west and Rona liked so much she'd had enlarged; the bed itself, an "antique" four-poster they'd bought in a discount furniture store. Other items were new and strange—purple-satiny drapes that were too wide and too dramatic for the narrow window; excessively plush, rather cheap-looking throw rugs; an exercise bicycle with a fuzzy white seat—but Dennis recognized his wife's touch in these too. He wiped his eyes, trying to smile. What was funny? *Was* something funny? Courtney was watching him closely out of the corners of his deep-sunken eyes.

"Are you feeling strong enough to proceed?" he asked.

Still quietly, Dennis said, "You know she must have been murdered. It can't have been suicide." He wanted to seize the man by his shoulders to make him listen. "She simply couldn't have done it: taken a razor and—"

Courtney made a childish face of revulsion and disdain. "Please," he said. "You needn't go into it."

"She wouldn't have had the physical strength. Someone else must have done it."

When Courtney made no reply Dennis said, in a slightly more aggressive voice, "Are you a friend of his, this Rivera?"

"No."

"But you seem to be protecting him."

"*No.*"

"Why did the police—"

"Don't ask me about the police! Please. I am hardly a spokesman for the police."

"You were Rona's friend, I thought."

"I was Rona's friend *to a degree*. She snubbed me when life went well for her and rapped on my door when it didn't. I'd like to say I didn't mind, but perhaps I did, just as you would—or perhaps did?" He paused, looking at Dennis. "In a way—in my way—I adored her. In another way I disliked her intensely for the very ease with which she manipulated me; *my* weakness was *her* strength, as she well knew! I was on hand to take care of her when she was in one of her states, or coming down from a high; I was there to listen to her side of it, with what's-his-name—indeed, yes. And once or twice, such was my bad luck, I listened to *his* side of it too."

"What is he like?"

Courtney ignored the question. "She was a woman of passion, and she evoked passion in certain parties—there's the gist of it. *You* must know; you were married to her."

"What sort of states was she in? What sort of highs?"

"Oh, various things," Courtney said vaguely. "I don't find it an agreeable prospect, to tattle on the dead. This box here—"

Dennis said excitedly, "In the paper it was mentioned in passing that the police picked up Rivera and questioned him, then let him go. Evidently there were witnesses, friends of his, who claimed he was with them when—"

Courtney made a fluttery gesture, clapping his hands over his ears. "The coroner's autopsy is final, and so is the police decision, Dennis, so please. Just—please."

"Cases can be reopened."

"Just—*please*."

"What kind of man is Rivera?"

"You've asked me that! I don't know! He's a small-time businessman or something; who can account for Rona's taste? I think he's married, I wouldn't doubt but there's a wife somewhere, that's along the lines of what Rona herself suspected, but who knows? I can say, Dennis," Courtney said, half closing his eyes as if in fatigue, "the poor man *is* suffering over all this, one way or another. He *did* love her; and maybe, Dennis, just *maybe*, Rona wanted it done. I mean in a way. In a way some women do. Some women and some men, when they've had enough."

"What are you saying?" Dennis asked. Then: "It's a tragedy."

"It always is."

"I suppose they couldn't prove he had been involved? I suppose they searched the apartment, dusted for fingerprints, that sort of thing, talked to witnesses—"

"There were no witnesses, Dennis. *I* wasn't even home that weekend."

"She would have left a note if she had done it. She wasn't the kind of person to have not left a note."

Courtney lowered his voice again. "There was a Bible on the bed, here. *In* the bed, I should say; the bed wasn't made. A Bible face down on the bed, of all grotesque things!"

"What do you mean? Why was it grotesque?"

"*Rona*—with a Bible? Please don't make me laugh. There was never a Bible in this apartment, and she never once spoke in my presence of anything remotely biblical or religious; she was utterly, utterly untouched by that sort of thing. Not a superstitious bone in her body."

"Then whose Bible was it? Why was it there?"

"Well, we just don't know, do we. We will just have to live with that little mystery, won't we." Courtney drew his fingers rapidly through his hair and expelled his breath in a long theatrical sigh. He smiled, or smirked, at Dennis. "Seeing that there were no fingerprints other than hers."

He overturned a small cardboard box, and a number of papers, mainly letters, spilled out onto the bed. As Dennis stared he said in a lowered, casual voice, "I *don't* know why we're talking like this. I mean, I *really* don't know; it's such a waste of breath, and upsetting to the adrenal system. I mean it really *is*. Can't you just feel your pulse racing? And sweat! I don't like to sweat if I can avoid it—at least not in my clothes.

"These letters," Courtney continued, "might be of interest to you. I'm a sentimental man myself and simply could not bear to throw away love letters—I mean, I saw at once what they were and wasn't required to read them in any detail. All I did, Dennis, I swear, was glance through them to establish their general tone, and here's your signature—it *is* yours, of course?"

Dennis took one of the letters from him with a sensation of dread: two sheets of creased and wrinkled stationery, covered in faded ink, a handwriting that very much resembled his own. The letter was dated *Tuesday, November 16*—but what year? He handed it back to Courtney, shutting his eyes. "I don't think I want to see this," he said.

"There are about fifteen of them—from you, I mean," Courtney said briskly. "Of course, being Rona, she had other letters as well—from men. But yours are the only ones I could identify—knowing, of course, that *Dennis* would have to be you since you were married to her. The others," he said, sighing, with an airy wave of his hand, "are just first names, forever assigned to oblivion. *Requiescat in pace.*"

Dennis stared at the little pile of letters but could not bring himself to touch them. Why had Rona kept them? What possible significance had they had to her? She had cut him out of her life with such careless abruptness; she'd been unfaithful to him—how many times?—feeling no guilt afterward except at guilt's very absence. "Why don't I feel it more strongly, that I've hurt you?" she had actually asked him once. "The person I love most in the world," she'd added, as if as an afterthought. A pulse in Dennis's head began to beat, hard, hard. He hated the woman, that she'd done this to him.

Courtney was saying in a softened voice, "She kept clippings of you too. Not many—I mean, not many that I came across. I don't know what I did with them unless they're in the box with the other things, the snapshots. That box there. An interview in the paper on the occasion of something or other."

Dennis saw that Rona had saved not only his letters but in some cases the envelopes they'd come in. Because of the stamps, he supposed; it had been a custom of his to use special stamps when he wrote to her, in reference to one or another "special" thing between them. He'd forgotten he had taken such pains . . . just as he'd forgotten what the letters contained. It was a terrifying fact that, should he make the effort, should he give himself up to it, each of those faded stamps might be decoded. Each of those letters would

open up an small epoch in his life, long forgotten, when he'd written
to Rona, whom he imagined, as he wrote, watching him, watching
him with love, her dark eyes intent upon him, her skin smooth,
rather pale, and the small perfect features, the perfectly shaped lips,
perfect ears he'd kissed, memorized, the waxy-pale whorls of the
ears, every part of her body, every inch, memorized, luminous with
love—his love, that is; his desire, for her. As a young man he'd been
lost in the contemplation of first love, entranced by the erotic physical
connection, the seemingly incredible fact that, for protracted delirious minutes, he could actually sink himself in another's body, in *her*
body, in another's pliant flesh: tight, blood-heated, pulsing with its
own interior rhythms. He had not really known Rona Sorenson, but
he'd believed he had. He'd believed that his love for her somehow
contained her, possessed her, held her still: she was his lover, and
then his wife. His.

That it was all a kind of dream or illusion he'd understood afterward—but hadn't believed. "I suppose I just don't love you that
way any more," Rona had said thoughtfully, at the end. "I'm not sure
that I ever did."

"I can't find the clippings but they're in here, I'm sure," Courtney
was saying. "Rona saved all sorts of odd little things, I would say out
of a kind of terror of losing them—*not* saving them. After all, you
are only young once, only young and newly married once, whatever
comes later. There *is* an incontestable logic in that, don't you think?"
He straightened, looking at Dennis. "But you *are* going to take them,
I hope?"

"Yes. All right."

Dennis picked up the letters carefully, folded them without reading so much as a line, put them in his pockets. There were so many
he needed two pockets. He'd throw them away, he thought, as soon
as he was out of this terrible man's company.

"You *are* going to read them?" Courtney persisted.

"Yes. Of course."

"Why don't you sort through the snapshots—and take the ones
you want?"

"Yes," Dennis said numbly, "but not today."

Courtney glanced at him and said, relenting, "Well, I suppose
this is hard on you. If another time, though, it will have to be another

time soon. Her things have to be cleared out by the end of the week."

"The end of the week?"

"That's when the rent runs out. The month's rent." Courtney hesitated. "*He* was paying for it—Rivera, I mean. The apartment is in his name. The lease."

"I see," Dennis said.

"He won't so much as step into the apartment, and the Sorensons—her family—they won't either. They've told the landlord they don't want *any*thing, he can do whatever with it he wants. I get so upset thinking how small-minded and cruel people can be, unless—well, *you* must know them—this is the only defense they can erect against what has happened, or what they *think* has happened."

"Yes," Dennis said, suddenly exhausted. He had no idea what Courtney was talking about. "That's so."

Sunlight was falling in a narrow shaft through the window, giving a gauzy, hazy edge to the drapes, illuminating, rather too vividly, the dust and surface grime on the windowsill, the tops of the bed's carved posters, the jaunty curved handles of the exercise bicycle. There were dust balls, pale and puffy as dandelion seed, in the corners of the room, and, on the window ledge, the shadowy darting shapes of pigeons. . . . If Rona could be here with them, Dennis thought, standing where he stood, seeing what he saw—the contours and surfaces of the physical world she'd left, lit by the winter sun yet ordinary, in no way romantic or mysterious—perhaps she would not have left it, by her own wish or another's.

At the door Courtney shook Dennis's hand with surprising vigor and said, shyly, "Goodbye, Dennis. We'll see each other again, I hope?"

"Yes," Dennis said. "I hope."

If the gesture hadn't been too extreme he would have thrown the letters away immediately, in a trash can on the street. But he decided to keep them, for a while. In his office at the law school where Charlotte wasn't likely to find them.

He would never read them—the very thought filled him with dread. But he'd keep them, for a while.

Late that night, in his study, in the dark, he dialed Hector Rivera's number again. No answer. He waited a few minutes, then tried again. I know you're there and I know who you are, he thought. I can wait a long, long time.

One evening shortly before Christmas as they were undressing in their bedroom, Charlotte said suddenly, "I think something is happening to us, Dennis. I'm afraid."

Dennis said nothing at first. Then: "It isn't happening to you. It has nothing to do with you."

"That's it," Charlotte said. "It has nothing to do with me. Or with Suzanne. Does it?"

Dennis didn't speak. He was turned from her, reluctant to face her. There was a heaviness in the air between them that made it difficult to breathe. "People kill themselves, women kill themselves," Charlotte said, her voice rising, "all the time. Read the newspaper, Dennis—the suicide rate is rising."

"What on earth are you talking about?"

"Read the newspaper!"

Then, suddenly, they were shouting at each other. Charlotte rushed at him and Dennis ducked away, pushed her aside. She came at him again as if to slap or claw, and he seized her wrists and forced her down clumsily. They were both panting, trembling badly. "I hate you," Charlotte whispered. "For what you're doing to us."

"Don't be ridiculous," he said, frightened. "I'm not doing anything to us."

"You're still in love with her."

"I'm not in love with anyone." Then, hearing what he'd said: "I mean—I'm not in love with *her*. You know better."

Charlotte turned from him, sobbing angrily. Dennis stood over her helpless. He wanted to touch her, comfort her, yet couldn't bring himself to touch her.

"Don't be ridiculous," he said again, guiltily. "This isn't like you."

It frightened him, the emotion he felt—its crudeness, violence. He wondered was it passion. He wondered was it anything to which he might give a name.

MORNING

The evening of the day her lover first took her to see his farm nine miles out in the country, an insect resembling a tiny spider, but less quick-witted than a spider, appeared seemingly out of nowhere on Lydia Freeman's back, between her shoulder blades, crawling in the direction of her bare neck. "What's this?" her husband said, picking the insect carefully off. "What is it?" Lydia asked, twisting and cringing like a guilty child. "It looks like a spider," Meredith said. He held the creature aloft between his clean bitten-down fingernails. It was a tick: Lydia's lover had discovered one on his bare leg, a tiny black spot like a mole on his fair fuzzy leg as, awkwardly, with deliberate clownishness, he'd stumbled about hauling up his trousers. They were in an upstairs room of the old derelict house. He'd picked the insect off his leg and held it as Meredith was doing to show Lydia; most ticks were harmless, he said, but some were infected and carried serious diseases. "A spider," Lydia said, taking the insect from her husband and running off to flush it down the toilet.

Her lover had told her the tick is such a hardy creature, flushing it down a toilet is about all you can do to get rid of it. That, or setting it on fire.

It was an adventure of the early sixties, that time of innocence. She was twenty-six, married, a graduate student in philosophy at

---

101

a midwestern land-grant university of some distinction, and a Pla-
tonist. She had come to Platonism late but with ferocity, a passion
for truth licking about her like erotic flames. *I want to learn! I want
to know! I want, want!*

Those days, in her philosophy seminars, she was brilliant. A handsome young woman with a solid, supple body, back straight, neck a
fine pale stalk, eyes very dark, bright, suspicious, her brown hair
already streaked with gray like spikes, a horsy sort of hair, crackling
as if with static electricity about her head. Contentious, easily excitable and easily wounded, but on the whole brilliant. One or two of
her professors were in love with her—with the idea of her, that is.

In each generation of graduate students in philosophy there were
roles, as if by Platonic decree, to be filled. The brilliant young man.
The brilliant young woman. The troubled young man. The neurotic
young woman. The young man in-over-his-head, the young woman
desperate-to-please. Lydia Freeman, née Sebera, was the brilliant but
temperamental young woman.

It had not occurred to her—it would not occur to her for years—
that, for all her brains and passion, professional philosophy was no
field for a woman. None of the texts were by women. None of the
important commentaries were by women. None of her professors
were women. Lydia could be only a ministering angel, a sainted
drudge, a Nightingale of the trenches, bringing life and healing to
others while remaining incomplete and tainted herself. When, speaking of other things, her lover happened to inquire, "Isn't it difficult
for a woman, in philosophy?" Lydia did not seem to hear. She said
carelessly, "I'm not a woman when I'm doing philosophy!"

This led naturally to a spate of kisses, embracing and cuddling
and cozying of the kind that frequently inspires lovers to observe,
What a good, happy world it is! For all lovers' talk leads to a single
rush of a conclusion, like great rivers emptying themselves in the
ocean.

And Lydia's lover Scott, a long-married man and a father several
times over, was by both nature and practice so comfortable in his
physicality, so instinctive in ways of demonstrating love, it scarcely
mattered what "subject" the two of them discussed—it led to a single
conclusion.

———

Those were years when for hours each day, day following day, Lydia Freeman dwelt inside a skull.

Her work was reading, thinking, writing: a buzzing hive of ideas, propositions, syllogisms, symbols, words. In the bowels of the university library where it was neither day nor night she lost herself in the text before her, fluorescent-lit, framed by her grasping hands. A head upon a stalk, a brain inside a skull—what need of a body?

Form precedes content. Essence precedes existence. The phenomenal world is a sort of skeleton upon which things, actual *things* in their *thingness*, are draped. If you know the skeleton, the outer appearances become transparent, invisible. You can look right through them.

It was a way for Lydia to be religious again without being religious. She'd left her working-class Methodism behind when she left her family behind, aged eighteen. A lifetime ago.

Denying her womanliness for so many hours of the day, she almost dreaded the violence of its return. *Passion is faceless and mere blindness of will*—thus Schopenhauer. But she was newly in love and did not heed. When the university library closed she walked swiftly, half ran, a mile across the darkened campus to the warren of prefabricated housing for married students known as the Barracks in which she and her thirty-year-old husband, Meredith Freeman, a graduate student in economics, lived in a duplex apartment. (Rarely, that first year, did Lydia meet her lover in the evenings—a family man finds it difficult to get away after dinner.) How her heart pounded with joy, with dread and guilt! How happy she was! She saw her lover, when she saw him, late afternoons; spoke with him, when she spoke with him, at unpredictable hours of the day. Then there was the long chaste stretch of evening. And night. And awaiting her, in duplex 9-B, her husband, Meredith, who would be working at the kitchen table on his dissertation, books and papers spread before him, manual typewriter, hand calculator, pencils, coffeepot and cup, ashtray, cigarettes: Meredith with his monkish Dürer face, bare bony toes twined around the legs of his chair, ambitious and hard-working and "brilliant" too. Meredith's moods rose and fell with abrupt seismic shifts in his assessment of himself, and Lydia could not predict if he might greet her with a distracted peck of a kiss (if she bent her cheek to him) or with his cool smile and voice faint, querulously lifted: "Lydia? So soon? Is it that late?"

Still, when Lydia approached their duplex apartment, hurrying across the barren toy-littered yards, hearing the raised voices of their neighbors, radios, crying babies, and smelling the familiar odors of grease and diapers, she knew herself happy. The world was a good place! Her nostrils widened with desire, her mouth watered. *I want, I want, I want.*

In her paperback copy of Spinoza's *Ethics*, Lydia underlined *He who repents is twice unhappy and doubly weak.*

At the time she fell in love with another woman's husband, she and her own husband had been married five years.

Five years: she could not decide if that was a brief space of time or a small eternity.

Meredith Freeman was a tall, angular, self-conscious young man with a boy's face, thinning pale hair, shrewd ghostly eyes. His forehead creased frequently with currents of dissatisfaction: he saw much in the world that fell short of his standards. He had insisted upon marriage immediately after Lydia graduated from the small church-related liberal arts college in Michigan where they'd met—Meredith had been an instructor in economics and political science. He loved her, he'd said, but he was no romantic: he valued women for depth of character and intelligence; he wanted someone as career-minded as himself. By his mid-twenties he had plotted the trajectory of his life: the Ph.D. written under a famous economist; the subsequent move to the East, to one of the Ivy League universities or their equivalent; eventually, perhaps, to Washington.

In due time, Meredith said, they'd start a family.

It had been he who'd guided their joint move from Michigan— the acquisition of their graduate fellowships—to this university. On her own, where might Lydia have gone? She'd discovered she loved philosophy—she loved the life of the mind, the life of books—but she was too vague about specifics to have chosen well. One day three years ago Meredith had said, "Here, Lydia, look through this." He'd brought home a graduate school catalog and application forms. That night, they'd made them out together like children doing homework.

Lydia, brainy and absentminded, took to housewifery with unexpected fervor. She did most of the meal preparation and most of the kitchen cleanup; she vacuumed, dusted, scrubbed. At such times, her hands usefully occupied, her mind was free to apply itself to philosophic abstractions. Her short-term memory was so acute she could envision columns of print; could deftly proofread and revise her own knotty papers; while washing dishes or sponging clean the sticky linoleum floor she rehearsed razor-sharp arguments for her seminars, coruscating queries to be brought to bear upon vulnerable propositions of Aristotle, Kant, Schopenhauer, Berkeley. Meredith, whose nerves were sensitive, sometimes pointedly asked her to stop her housework, to sit down or go to the library: just be *still*.

"Your energy wears me out," he complained.

He complained, laughingly, "Do you do it on purpose, Lydia?"

Lydia had married at the age of twenty-one: too young.

And knowing virtually nothing about marriage, "marital relations"; acute embarrassment shrouded such matters in her family. (As in her husband's family: Meredith's father was pastor of a Lutheran church in a small city in Minnesota.) Not only had Lydia Sebera no one from whom she might ask advice, she would not have known to ask advice, trusting to mere good intentions, mutual respect and affection and "love." For, as Meredith promised, things would work out in due time.

For the first year or two they worried Lydia might get pregnant, despite Meredith's fussy precautions, but with the passage of time, and fairly quickly, that ceased to be an issue. Early in the marriage they'd often lain wordless together, in bed, like hungry children, eager to suck life and solace from the other's body. If Meredith were sexually attentive and if Lydia warmly responded, the next day, and the days following, he would seem to avoid her: staying up late to work as she slept, slipping out of bed early in the morning as she slept. Meredith had his own life, his interior passions, and Lydia must not interfere! She felt rebuffed, of course, but also relieved. For his behavior exempted her from the obligation of being a wife, a woman, a physical being. She told herself that wasn't her, really. Her body, perhaps, but not *her*.

Then she fell in love with Scott Chaudry, and it seemed to her an impersonal event: fated, inevitable.

As one might think, transported to the moon, *So—this is how it is!*

When they were first alone together in Chaudry's office at the university (the door locked, the overhead lights off, pellets of snow blowing frantically against the windows), Chaudry gripped her shoulders and asked hesitantly, "Are you certain you want to . . . ?" His voice, kindly at even this passionate moment, lifted quizzically. "Lydia. Dear. Are you absolutely certain?" He meant was she certain she wanted to risk her marriage for him: for this.

Her face shone with tears. She could only plead, "Oh, I can't help it; I love *you*."

That was the first of many times the two were to meet in Scott's office at the dead time of day, late afternoon easing to dusk when no one was around. Together, breathless and nimble as gymnasts, they lay on the braided thrift-basement rug to make love; Lydia imagined nothing surrounding them beyond the room's four concrete-block walls but the midwestern plains, a *nothingness* palpable as any substance. Where lovemaking with Meredith was stark and unadorned and usually wordless, lovemaking with Scott Chaudry had always its element of playful discourse, of talk. Was not making love with someone you loved another form of talk, an extension of talk? Scott was a man who liked to laugh and in his company you laughed a good deal, so Lydia learned. And how quickly they were cozily compatible, tender, daring, passionate, rapt with love. Wasn't it love? Lydia had never felt anything like it; she shut her eyes, bit her lips to keep from crying out.

She saw herself illuminated, veins and arteries, skeleton, like a Christmas tree.

Scott Chaudry made no secret of the fact that he was forty-three years old. And married, as he said, one year short of half his life. Could Lydia guess what that might mean?

No, Lydia confessed, she could not. Her marriage with Meredith Freeman felt, now, like yesterday. That brief and that shallow.

"You're like two trees growing side by side," Scott said, resting his elbows on his desk, lightly flexing his fists. "Not touching. But underground your roots are inextricably tangled together."

Lydia stared. What was he telling her? Warning her?

"I realize it sounds corny," Scott said, laughing. "But, dear, it happens to be true: *tangledness* as the primary fact of life."

Lydia said, hurt, "It doesn't sound corny."

Scott Chaudry and his wife had four children, the eldest sixteen, the youngest seven. Showing Lydia snapshots in his wallet he smiled with pleasure, with love, the clearest sort of familial pride. Lydia stared, and swallowed, and pronounced the children beautiful, which was true. Her lover did not show her, nor did she ask to see, snapshots of the wife.

American philosophy was not formally taken up in the graduate seminars offered by Lydia's department, so she audited a course taught by a popular history lecturer named Chaudry of whom she had not previously heard: the course was Intellectual Currents in American History: Emerson, William James, Charles Peirce, John Dewey, Santayana, among others. When Lydia first sought Chaudry out, knocking hesitantly at the door of his office, she thought, Do I want to do this? But what am I doing?

Eventually, she would translate it all into fate: that which could not not be, like Spinoza's closed universe.

It seemed that marriage had made her reckless. She had a vague unarticulated sense that, since she was no longer a virgin, and since she had been a virgin up to the moment of her painful and punctilious deflowering by her bridegroom, it did not matter greatly what she did with that part of her body designated as "sexual."

Scott Chaudry was a historian of no scholarly ambitions but a superb teacher. He was affable, witty, good-hearted, keenly attuned to his students' moods. (Two hundred students were enrolled in his course; the lecture hall was filled.) Lydia had guessed his age as older than forty-three: he was of moderate height and build, beginning to thicken at the waist, with dense wiry hair that had gone completely gray, a broad freckled face, sweet, open, frank as a sunflower, etched with tiny dents and creases. How authoritatively, Lydia thought, he inhabited his body.

And if he had a reputation for attracting the interest of young women students, Lydia did not know of it and did not wish to know.

Later, he told Lydia that he'd had no idea she was married, at
first. And that that might have made a considerable difference. At
first.

It wasn't until the spring—May, prematurely warm, fragrant, and
damply lush—that Scott Chaudry took Lydia Freeman to see his farm
out in the country. He'd been talking of it quite a bit; he'd bought
the property at a bankruptcy auction years ago. Lydia noted that
whenever he spoke of the farm—"my place out in the country"—
his tone became subtly defensive.

"Is it a working farm?" Lydia asked.

"Hardly," Scott said. "It's a"—he paused, seeking the precise
term—"a place. A state of being."

So in Scott's station wagon they drove out into the township of
Merced, taking a circumlocutory route to get out of the university
town unseen. Lydia said laughingly, "Would you like me to hunch
down? Hide in the back seat, maybe?" Scott winced and did not
reply.

The farm was nine miles out in the country; the drive was achingly
beautiful; Lydia wanted it never to end. This was the first time she'd
ever been in Scott Chaudry's car. Evidence of children, family life,
domesticity—what envy she felt! Scott was speaking animatedly of
the farm, which consisted of twelve acres of land and a broken-down
old house, a barn, several outbuildings, rusted farm equipment, an
aged orchard: he'd grown up in Chicago, spent his entire life in urban
areas, wanted with all his heart to live in the country, in the real
country—"Though I know it's absurdly romantic." He had planned
to renovate the house so they could come out on weekends at least,
eventually live there, but somehow there was never money for it,
or it wasn't the right time, or the children were the wrong ages or
not so interested as they'd once been, or Vivian wasn't well, or—
one thing or another. For a while, Scott said, his wife urged him to
sell it but lately she seemed to have forgotten about it, as if, being
his, his folly so exclusively, it had passed out of her consciousness
altogether. He paused. He said, "I wonder what you'll think of it,
Lydia."

Lydia thought, I will fall in love with it.

Lydia came from a rural town in western Michigan. Her earliest memories were of her grandparents' farm, of the crude hearty smells of the barnyard, the tall rows of corn, bees buzzing treacherously around fallen, rotting pears, her German-speaking grandfather laughing and cursing as he sheared a bleating sheep's filthy wool.

To her relief Scott's farm was beautiful, though shabbier, more remote and overgrown than she had imagined.

It was at the end of a badly rutted lane that descended to a sort of shallow, like an old glacier lake. The house and outbuildings were close together; fences were fallen or hidden in weeds; it looked as if pastureland had run up to the house itself, virtually to the windows. The barn was partly collapsed, the corncrib had gone skeletal. In the near distance, in bright sunshine, tall grasses, yellow wildflowers, and thistles grew lushly, undulating in the wind like coarse hair. And there was the house.

Lydia stared. It was like many farmhouses out of her childhood, empty, going to ruin. She felt both a shiver of dread and a sense of coming home.

Scott sighed with pleasure. "Well: my dream house!"

The house was made of wood, foursquare, modest, with a look of having contracted in upon itself. The date 1871 had been etched in its stone foundation. There was a sloping veranda; there were antiquated lightning rods atop the highest peak of the roof; patches of lurid mossy green grew on the shingle boards. The windows had been neatly boarded up, and a NO TRESPASSING notice (peppered with gunshot) had been posted prominently on the front door. Lydia exclaimed, "But it's beautiful!"

She was thinking that, like most abandoned houses, it had a look of being occupied. Though knowing better, she began to feel nervous about going in.

The only sound was from crows, noisily cawing as they circled overhead.

Scott had a key for the side door and they stepped inside. He was saying, "I always have this eerie feeling, every time I come here, that I'm intruding . . . that someone is here."

Lydia said nervously, gripping his arm, "Oh, but not really. The house is *yours*."

"Yes. But it wasn't always."

Inside there was broken glass underfoot, and the wallpaper hung in shreds. Gauzy slatted sunlight fell through the windows.

Holding hands like adventuresome children, they walked through the house. Rain-soaked sofa, broken-backed chairs, exposed wiring, sagging floorboards, a steep staircase to the second floor, and, there, filthy mattresses, cobwebs brushing against their faces, mouse droppings, the husks of dead insects underfoot, a rich sweetish odor of dirt and rot. Lydia was thinking with a peculiar sort of satisfaction, No other woman has been here, like this. Though she knew that Scott's wife had certainly been here, and had passed judgment, and had withdrawn. Still, she thought, no other woman has been here. Like this.

Scott talked excitedly, rather boyishly. He still had hopes for the farm! He wasn't totally disillusioned, or discouraged!

Lydia knew by his keyed-up mood that they would make love. She cast her eyes about, seeking the least uncomfortable and demeaning of spots. That filthy mattress?

But if she didn't remove most of her clothing, why not?

Afterward, there was the incident of the tick, already embedded in Scott's leg just below the knee. He'd picked it off with his fingernails, a look of distaste contorting his face. "Filthy little bugger," he said.

He told Lydia that the elderly owners of the farm had sold off most of its acreage over the years. The original homestead had consisted of more than one hundred acres, but by degrees it had been whittled away to the few he'd bought, these the least farmable, he supposed: hilly fields studded with rock, woods, shallows, swampy soil. Evidently there were no children to inherit; the family was dying out. The old man, suffering from senile dementia, had hoped to subvert fate so he shot himself with his twelve-gauge shotgun in a way meant to be considerate to his wife and others; he'd lain in a shallow creek bed, head downstream, and manipulated the trigger with his toe.

His wife had died within a week or two. She'd never recovered from the shock of finding him.

Lydia said, shivering, "They loved each other."

Scott said lightly, "A good argument, then, for not falling in love."

They straightened their clothes and walked out into the sunshine, blinking in surprise. Was it still daylight? Still so bright? Their love-making took them so far.

Lydia ran in the grass, following the vague trampled path of a deer trail. Fat horseflies buzzed about her head, airborne, glittering. The grass was damp beneath, dry and acrid-smelling above, so tall, so coarse, so twined, flattened, she felt she could swim in it! She could walk on top of it! Scott called to her, laughing.

They investigated the hay barn. The old, old smells made her nostrils pinch: ammoniac, hay-warm, manure and dirt and rotting wood. Lydia said softly, laying her head on Scott's shoulder, "I love it here. This—" She did not know what she said or meant to say; words tumbled from her like her heart's blood pumping out of her body to soak in the filthy floor. "This place you've brought me to."

Scott said quietly, "I love it too."

There are cultures that make a fetish of history, honoring the departed as if the very point of life were posthumous renown, like the ancient Romans; there are cultures with no history at all, no memory, desperate to live in a continual present, out of a horror of duration—the so-called savage cultures. Lydia Freeman read of such things and felt the sharp deflating pang of recognition.

Yes, she thought, if you're a savage you can't bear to contemplate predecessors. About who got there first, and what's to come.

Passion is faceless and mere blindness of will so there were nights when Lydia made love with the man who was her husband and took a harsh sort of pleasure from the act, greedy, desperate, afterward ashamed. She did not even think of Scott; the effort was purely genital, a matter of precision timing like, say, diving from a high board, executing a flawless plunge. With Scott, lovemaking was often too emotional. She clutched at his body as if clutching to keep from sinking, drowning.

She thought, It's a mistake.

She thought, I will die if he stops loving me.

She was waiting for him to say that they must tell the others: her husband, his wife. She rehearsed the words with which she would greet his words.

But rarely did he speak of his wife. And never of her husband.

So, sometimes, she made love with Meredith, never initiating the brief wordless act but not resisting it either. And afterward they lay apart, sweaty, panting, subdued, like swimmers collapsed on the same beach. Comrades of a sort: sister, brother.

Meredith Freeman, alert to atmospheric changes, sensed in Lydia what he could not have named or would not in his Lutheran pride have wished to name. As if making an observation about a third party held in no great esteem by either of them, he remarked to Lydia, "*You're* in odd moods these days. You don't seem to know if you're ecstatic or depressed."

To which Lydia had only a vague stammering reply, conciliatory words that trailed off into silence as if losing momentum, or purpose. She said she was sorry. She said it was her work: reading Croce, Peirce, Kant's *Metaphysics of Morals* in nightmare juxtaposition. She said it was the pressure. She avoided the apartment for as many hours as she dared; and several times, returning late, dreading that calm sardonic smile of her husband's, that "Hello, Lydia!" of nominal courtesy, she was surprised to see that the apartment was empty: a kitchen light burning, a radio bristling with voices, mere cautionary ploys Meredith's father had trained him to observe whenever he left home, to discourage burglars.

Some meals they ate together. Some they ate apart: the Freemans meeting for supper in the student union cafeteria, sitting together but not by design.

When Lydia's head was about to burst with too much abstraction, she fled the library and walked into the night: walked swiftly, broke into a run, purposeless and headlong as she'd been as a child, enraptured by the phenomenon of motion, the legs' unthinking strength, the canny muscles. *I do what I want to do, therefore what I do is what I want. Isn't it?* Without intending it she found herself standing in the shadows of a residential street staring at the house in which the man who was her lover lived with wife, sons, young daughter. The house was a trim decent colonial in no way distinguished from its neighbors. Windows were warm rectangles of light, the blinds discreetly drawn. Were she primitive enough for such nonsense she would have willed him to leave that interior coziness to come to *her*.

That afternoon after love they'd set their watches in tandem.

It was summer and there was a rumor that Professor Chaudry's wife was "unwell" but Lydia knew nothing of it; her intimacy with the man excluded certain points of information.

They began to argue, as if arguing were the next logical step. Scott's philosophy of history was, he said, quite simple: things happen, or they don't happen. He knew, yes, that men made their reputations hammering away at "precipitating factors" and amassing great quantities of data to support their hypotheses, certainly he knew; he'd gone through such stages himself, and eventually he'd come to the conclusion that each event had a thousand thousand causes or, conversely, none at all: "Call it God, call it fate." Lydia was incensed; Lydia was baffled. She accused him of taking ideas too lightly just because he had a settled position in life, a full professorship with tenure. In turn he accused her of taking ideas too seriously. "You remind me," he said, smiling at her with the fondness of watching a child clambering about in its bath, "of myself at your age." Lydia, smarting, insulted, but smiling too, said, "So that diminishes us both!"

It was the peak of their physical passion for each other, however, and very little else seemed really to matter. Chaudry was so thoroughly husband and father and lover there was nothing he might not do, no ardor of which, puppylike, stallionlike, he was not capable: loving her with hands, mouth, tongue, penis, burrowing into her, pumping his life into her, prodigious and wasteful. He was a big-boned man gone soft around the waist but heavy with muscle elsewhere, the torso and thighs particularly. Again and again Lydia heard herself cry *I love you, I love, love you*, the words senseless, mere anguished sound. Again and again she was shaken by the power of the sensations Chaudry caused her to feel, as if such sensations were in fact impersonal, marauding, violating her deepest self, the *I, I, I*.

On the eve of Scott's departure for an August vacation with his children in Colorado (the wife, the mysterious wife, preferred to remain home alone) they were in a motel room five miles from town and it had become late suddenly; they'd slept and woke and it was nearly seven o'clock and Lydia in a panic telephoned Meredith (the Freemans were going out that evening, or had planned to—a rare evening with another couple) to say he should go on without her, she'd meet him and their friends at the restaurant, and Meredith sounded frightened, as if finally things had gone too far, beyond mending. What was wrong? he asked, had he done something wrong? he begged, and Lydia said no, no, she would explain later it had nothing to do with him he should simply go to the restaurant without her and she'd meet him there, and Scott had come up behind her and begun playfully to run his hands over her as, naked, her hair in her face, her voice pleading, she spoke with Meredith, who no longer sounded like Meredith but like a young aggrieved husband who did not understand what was happening to his marriage and was begging to know. Scott buried his face in Lydia's neck, prodded himself against her buttocks, poked and pushed and, growing hard again, eased himself into her, where she was wet, dilated, open; yet Lydia could not put the telephone receiver down, she could not break the connection with Meredith, trying to talk, to give comfort of a kind, to murmur words of assent or promise, as Meredith asked What was it? Where was she? Who was she with? When was she coming home? What had he done wrong? Had he offended her that morning, had he hurt her, had he said the wrong thing? Would she forgive him?

The receiver slipped from Lydia's hand and fell to the carpet and she did not retrieve it.

They sat on the rear steps drinking beer from cans, the long slow night hours shifting to dawn.

"But *why* . . . ?"

"I don't know why."

"You don't love him?"

"It isn't that."

"You *do* love him?"

"No. It isn't that."

"But you either love him or you don't." Meredith paused. All this was new to him; he was a man picking his way with infinite care across a terrain of incalculable danger. Drinking too, in such excess, was new to him. "You either love me or you don't."

"It isn't that."

Lydia jammed her knuckles against her mouth. She was thinking, Aristotle's logic! How old, how dull and discredited, how dead!

Meredith spoke slowly to avoid slurring his words. "You either want the marriage to continue or you don't. I see no other possibility."

"I do. I do want it to continue."

"And what about him? You either love him . . . or you don't."

"There are degrees of loving. You must know."

"Not when marriage is involved."

"Especially when marriage is involved."

"How long has this been going on? At first you said—"

"It doesn't matter. For God's sake."

"Yes, it matters. It matters to me."

"To your pride!"

"Yes. To my pride."

Lydia wept. As if weeping were a way of being forgiven. Or an exorcism. Or a plea for repudiation. *Now he will raise his hand and strike me.*

After a moment's hesitation Meredith laid his arm across her shoulders, to comfort her. They were both breathing quickly; they were both very warm. She heard herself say, choking, "I love you. Oh, God, I'm sick with the thought of having hurt you."

Was it true? Meredith decided to believe. "Are you, Lydia? Are you really?" The childlike lift of his voice.

How tender he was, suddenly, her young husband! As if broken open. Holding Lydia in both his arms and gallant enough not to notice how, as if involuntarily, she stiffened against him.

So it went. The hours that night, and the following day, and the following. Each of their exchanges was about their new terrible subject, a light burning fiercely in their faces, even when they were speaking of other things: What would Meredith like for dinner? Should Lydia do the laundry this morning or Saturday? As if the element in which husband and wife dwelled, the very air of the cramped apartment that constituted "home," had been subtly and irrevocably altered, thickened. They had to push themselves through it; it offered some natural resistance, like water.

Never did Meredith ask the name of Lydia's lover.

His shrewd logic being: since Lydia assured him she was finished with the man should he not be finished with the man too? Meredith knew only that X was married, had children, was a good kind likable man, an easygoing sort of man, not a seducer. Not one of Lydia's professors. No one Meredith knew or was required to know.

Instead of typing out a draft for her dissertation Lydia composed an eight-page letter, a masterpiece of a letter, for Scott Chaudry. Affirming her love for him—for otherwise wouldn't she be a hypocrite? a liar? a fool?—while simultaneously informing him that she could not see him again when he returned in September.

She hadn't left the apartment for days. She was pale, subdued, repentant. She felt herself cleansed—no, more than cleansed, *scoured*. As if with a pad of crinkly steel wool.

Lydia rather liked the sensation, for once. Meredith liked it in her, too.

It was September, and Scott Chaudry had returned, and if he'd received and read Lydia's letter he gave no sign; he did not call. So, chagrined, she understood that he too had wanted it to end, though at their last meeting he'd seemed to love her so, and had spoken of hating to leave her.

And then finally he called—there'd been a domestic crisis, he said, but did not further explain, though he sounded sincere enough, and shaken—and Lydia was overcome with rage, saying, "You don't love me so why keep up the pretense? You never did, did you! I know what you are! I know! I hate you! I wish we were both dead!" So naturally they had to meet, a final time.

It was a lovely autumn day, one of those heartbreak days when you realize you must die though you want to live forever: so Lydia saw, and wept. She was unpracticed in adult weeping and surely looked ugly, but still her lover saw her as beautiful and she in turn saw it in his face, his love for her: his desire.

"My God. I've missed you."

"I've missed *you*."

He was hurriedly undressing, his penis erect from a tangle of silvery glinting hair. He had the look of a creature impaled upon its own flesh.

Afterward they lay together on the rug, the familiar braided rug, like swimmers collapsed on the sand. Oh, they were comrades, conspirators: Scott kissing her damp eyelids, stroking her body, comforting her. "But I do love you, Lydia. My darling. My dear one. How could you ever doubt me?"

Meredith Freeman was trying to do the right thing so years later he might tell himself, reflecting, *I did the right thing.* He was a minister's son after all, and though he no longer believed in the revealed truths of Christianity there lingered in him the urge, perhaps the need, to forgive: to be charitable and not-sinning and martyrish, thereby superior. Yes, and to punish too. In the end when forgiveness ran its course there would have to be some punishing too.

The dishes left all day in the sink, for instance. The toilet left unflushed.

Lydia knew the import of these clues. She had lied persuasively to Meredith and she could not think that he did not believe her yet she knew the import of these clues, though breezing over them as mere accidents, aberrations. She was reading in anthropology: Mead, Bateson, Lévi-Strauss. These names her philosophy professors scarcely knew, or knew only to deride. But here was Lévi-Strauss: newly translated, smart laminated paperback editions, the critical imprimatur of the eastern establishment press. Lydia was growing out of Platonism, not understanding that in fact she was moving into a new species of Platonism, but this had at least the weight of scientific evidence, or seemingly. So much data amassed "in the field" to be hung upon structure's skeleton!

Thus she learned of manners, the significance of manners. What are manners but devices to control and calibrate impurity, strategies of protecting oneself from others and protecting others from oneself? The breakdown in a culture is signaled by, and in turn signals, a breakdown in ordinary manners. For instance the dirty dishes in the sink, not even soaking in water. The scattered pages of the newspaper, the soiled socks and towels, heaping ashtrays, the shockingly unflushed toilet. Lydia tried to transform it into something light, anecdotal, telling Scott, "My husband is turning savage!" Though for a long time she said nothing to Meredith. Not a word!

Then one day, unable to bear it any longer, she confronted him with, "Please don't."

Immediately Meredith said, "Don't what?" His voice uninflected, innocent.

"The toilet, for one thing."

"What? What about the toilet?"

"It isn't like you, Meredith, so why do it?"

"Why do what?"

"Oh, for God's sake, you *know*!"

And suddenly they were shouting. Walls in the Barracks were famously thin but what did the Freemans care, empowered by rage, mutual loathing? In the end Meredith was laughing as if drunk, thoroughly enjoying himself as Lydia had never before witnessed. His face was slit as with a jack-o'-lantern's grin. He said, "What's the difference? Why so sensitive? Do you think my shit is any different from his, sweetheart? From *yours*?"

So it went.

Lydia knew herself watched. Nowhere in this place could she move among people who knew her—along certain sidewalks, into certain buildings, through the maze of carrels on B-level of the library—without being observed, assessed, commented upon, judged. *There she is. That's the one. See her? Lydia Freeman.* Her professors who had such hopes for her, or who'd once had such hopes for her: they now looked upon her with fastidious disdain or ribald interest.

Scott assured her she was imagining things. Scott, nervous himself, insisted she was imagining things, "Exaggerating it all."

She walked a good deal, those weeks. Along the margins of muddy playing fields, in scrubby land along the river, miles from the campus in neighborhoods unknown to her: warehouses, slum tenements, railroad yards. Sometimes she stood for long minutes as if she'd lost all volition or awareness, a stroke victim yet still on her feet. What had she done, and why? She could not remember.

What had she done, what had been the actual sequence of events, actions, beginning with that knock on Scott Chaudry's office door? She could not remember.

Shortly before Christmas, Vivian Chaudry had an automobile accident: she who by her husband's account never drove a car any longer, had deliberately allowed her license to expire, went out with their daughter in the station wagon, drove too fast on pavement slick with ice, and crashed into a barrier. The front of the station wagon was crushed like an accordion but Mrs. Chaudry and the child were only banged up a little, as Scott called it; thank God there'd been no serious injuries, just the shock, the terrible shock of the experience. A few days later Scott Chaudry moved out of his home to take up temporary residence in a motel.

He telephoned Lydia and told her. He asked her to come to him so they could talk.

He would not speak of his wife these days but he spoke of his children—obsessively. He loved them, he said. He did not want to hurt them, he said. He loved Lydia, and he loved his children. *He did not want to hurt anyone.*

He was drinking, and Lydia drank too. She saw that her lover was a middle-aged man. He looked in fact a decade older than his age: eyes ringed with exhaustion, graying whiskers on his jaws. He had developed a nervous tic in one eye, and his old easy affable smile had become a sort of tic too. It frightened Lydia that the relationship between them seemed to have changed as if by a malevolent magic. She thought, I don't know this person. There is some mistake.

Scott Chaudry loved his children, but in the end it seemed he loved Lydia Freeman more. Or maybe his children were sick of him, had been turned against him by their mother. But, no: he loved Lydia more. His girl, his darling, his life. You won't leave me? he was begging. You won't leave me?

She would not leave him, she wasn't that kind of person. And of course she loved him.

She comforted him in the old inevitable ways.

He was working with a local carpenter, intent upon renovating the farmhouse out in Merced Township.

Lydia lived alone now. Meredith had moved out quietly. He was thirty-one years old and suddenly an adult. Though losing his hair, susceptible to stomach upsets and fits of coughing, embarrassingly vain about his standing amid the pack of other Ph.D. candidates in economics, he had acquired a new steeliness: a new manhood.

He and Lydia spoke frequently over the phone, since they had a good deal to discuss. And, now, almost calmly. Like brother and sister who have aired every grievance and secret mean thing, they now could speak of pragmatic matters, business. Against his family's counsel Meredith was filing for a divorce; he'd already seen a lawyer. He knew what he wanted and how to get it. Lydia admired him. The trajectory of his life without her was shrewdly plotted: his Ph.D. would be wrapped up within a few months, the divorce too, everything local settled so that he could move east without encumbrances. Such challenges were translatable into mere units of time: weeks, months. An economist specializing in statistics, Meredith Freeman did not doubt his capacity for navigating such finitude.

And how mature he'd become: adult enough, even, to apologize.

Adult enough to remark, once, unexpectedly, "You know, Lydia, of the two of us, I wouldn't have thought it would be you who would . . ."

Their minds worked sometimes in the same ways, along the same grooves. Lydia said, "Who would transgress?"

"Yes," Meredith said. " 'Transgress.' " He must have liked the taste of the word, its biblical solemnity; he repeated it: " 'Transgress.' "

They were speaking over the telephone. Lydia had to imagine her husband's expression: his faint perplexed smile, the familiar sheen of his forehead, which looked both bony and unprotected.

Repairs on the farmhouse were not proceeding so smoothly as Scott had hoped. But by mid-March there were at least windows both downstairs and up, and insulation, and a wood-burning stove for the kitchen, even a working toilet. So one weekend they drove out to Merced, through the snowy countryside, with groceries, beer, sleeping bags. An impromptu sort of thing, for the fun of it. Lydia had hesitated at first but quickly came around to looking forward to it, like a small child. It was a holiday of a sort, a small adventure.

And how beautiful, the drive into the hills: the snow-covered fields; the tall leafless trees, many-branched and -veined like bodies in X ray; the farmhouse down in the little hollow. Scott had to do some shoveling, Lydia had to rock the car back and forth to get it free where it was stuck, but eventually they got where they were going. Lydia said, "The world is perfect if you don't set yourself in opposition to it!"

At dusk they lit a kerosene lamp, ate their meal, drank beer from cans, settled in for the night. The wood-burning stove glowed with a rich interior heat that radiated grudgingly, to encompass a space of perhaps five feet in diameter. They laid their sleeping bags side by side in front of it.

Both were tired, and groggy from beer, but they made love, their new kind of love, Lydia thought it: slow, calm, domesticated, patient. These past several weeks, their desperation had lifted. Lydia, who had failed to complete her course work for the previous semester, had decided not to register for the spring semester; she'd given up her fellowship. All that, that part of her life, she would deal with in time. Now she took each day as it came. That seemed the best strategy, for now.

Scott continued with his teaching, of course, in the face of scandal. He was grim, he was stubborn, brazening it out in the community, meeting his classes as if nothing were wrong; perhaps nothing *was*. Things fell into place with a semblance of inevitability: his wife would keep the house for the time being; he could see the older children virtually at will; indeed, there might be less hurt, less heartbreak, than he'd feared. Repeatedly he assured Lydia, who felt such guilt, that none of this was her fault even remotely—he should have moved out months, years ago: "There was no love remaining in my marriage." Lydia said, "I should never have married Meredith. I did wrong, to marry him."

The more frequently these words were uttered, the more convincing they were.

A dozen times a day they said, "I love you." "I love *you*."

They whispered often, as with an old habit of conspiracy.

Lying in Lydia's arms in front of the wood-burning stove, still inside her, stunned with pleasure, Scott said, "*This* is where we belong." Lydia murmured, "Oh, yes."

Scott zipped himself up in his sleeping bag and slept, a heavy sleep, his breath rasping like a fine-notched saw. Lydia, alone, slept less readily. She was exhausted but something seemed to be beating between her eyes. She was damp too and sticky from lovemaking but loath to crawl out of her warm sleeping bag and grope her way to the bathroom, where the air was freezing. Gradually she dropped off to sleep, wakened intermittently by Scott's snoring and by the eerie silence of the country. She had forgotten the strange deep silence of the country in winter.

She woke before dawn, her knuckles jammed against her mouth.

Quietly she wriggled out of the sleeping bag, her limbs aching, a sharp pain in the small of her back. The fire in the stove was a dull mass of embers, giving no heat; Scott had intended to wake to put more wood inside but had forgotten. Lydia's breath steamed in anxious little puffs.

Her companion, slack-jawed, unshaven, sallow-skinned in the ashy light, slept and snored undisturbed. There was a strangeness about him, in the sleeping bag that was like a body bag, positioned on the newspaper-covered floorboards in front of the stove.

Lydia walked quietly, not wanting to wake him. She stood shivering at a window. If it had been a clear morning she would have seen a vista of fields and hills, the skeletal corncrib off to one side, but this morning there was fog, a damp opalescent mist, pressing up against the glass like a mouth. It was the first morning of her new life.

NAKED

She was hiking alone in a suburban wildlife preserve two miles from her home when she heard, behind her, erupting seemingly out of nowhere, children's shouts, squeals, and laughter. She turned to see a small pack of black children running along the wood-chip trail. The eldest, a skinny boy of about eleven, in soiled white T-shirt, oversized pants, and sneakers worn without socks, seemed to be shouting at her and gesticulating urgently with both hands—"Hey! Lady! Hey, *you*!"—though his high-pitched jeering words were not wholly intelligible. It was late in the afternoon, in spring, the first really warm, sunny, pleasurable day in weeks; the air was damply tremulous; the earth exuded a sense of quiveringness, scarcely restrained life. She had been hiking for an hour, pushing herself, walking quickly, enjoying the strain of leg, thigh, arm muscles, and a light film of perspiration had gathered over her, and her thoughts, scattered and inchoate initially, had gradually slowed, steadied, crystallized until they were not thoughts at all so much as simply impressions and gliding wordless images as in a dream. And the children, led by the strangely intense, even angry black boy, surged up like unexpected images in that dream.

"Yes? Are you talking to me?" she asked.

The boy laughed as if in delight and derision. Had he not been so young she might have thought him drunk or high on a drug. He came barely to her shoulder, easing toward her like a wiry little animal out for blood. He addressed her in a stream of soprano sounds

underlaid by contempt, but she could make out none of the words
except perhaps "Lady" or "Where you goin', lady?" and his aggressive
intensions bewildered her rather than frightened her since the children were so young, the youngest no more than eight or nine, and
very small, and there were two or three girls among them. "Yes?
What is it? What do you want?" she asked with a mother's slightly
strained calm. They're only children, she told herself even as, instinctively, she took a step backward.

And in the next instant they were upon her.

Even as it was happening, as the children swarmed over her,
pummeling her with their fists, pounding, kicking, tearing, the eldest
leaping up on her to bring her heavily down, savage and deft as a
predatory animal, even as she struggled with them, flailing her arms,
trying too to strike, punch, kick—for she was a woman of some
strength, very fit, unshrinking, resolute—she was thinking, *This can't
be happening!* and *They're only children!* She'd known from her first
sighting of them that they were not children from the University
Heights area in which she lived but from the ragged edge of the old
industrial city below the bluff, that steep drop to a neighborhood of
row houses, tenements, railroad yards, factories, and condemned
mills on the river she and her family rarely glimpsed except from
the interstate expressway elevated over its ruins, but she was a woman
in no way racially prejudiced who had grown up with blacks, gone
to school with blacks, Chinese, Hispanics, and other minorities, as
they were familiarly called, and she was determined to instill in her
children the identical unjudging uncensorious liberalism her parents
had quite consciously instilled in her. So it did not strike her, as
perhaps it should have, upon occasion at least, that these minorities
might look upon her as conspicuously different from themselves and
that, against the grain of all that was reasonable, charitable, and just,
they might wish to do so and take satisfaction in it. And this demonic
little pack of children who had so totally surprised and overcome
her—who beat her, tore her clothes from her, emptied her pockets,
all the while squealing and laughing as if what they did were only in
play—she simply could not believe they were capable of such a thing:
and with such nightmare quickness.

She was forty-six years old, in very good health, a woman of intelligence and independent character, the mother of two young children and the stepmother of a young teenager, wholly unskilled in physical exertion or prowess, as clumsy in this bizarre struggle as a fish hauled from the water and thrown down upon the ground without ceremony to gasp and thrash about and drown in an alien element. Her screams were breathless and incredulous. Her wild blows found no marks or glanced harmlessly off forearms, shoulders, lunging heads. *They're only children!* she was thinking, and as a mother she did not want to hurt children even had she been capable of doing so. The thought came to her too that if she surrendered, if she submitted, put up no further struggle, they would take what they wanted and leave her alone.

And so it was. When she stopped fighting they stopped hitting her, but in the fierce hilarity of their excitement they stripped her clothes from her, turning her, rolling her, tugging at her jeans, whooping with laughter as they tore away her brassiere and underpants, yanked off by sheer force her running shoes, pulled off her socks. She was too overcome by shock to beg them to stop, and the mad fear struck her that they meant to devour her alive: set upon her like ravenous animals, tear the flesh from her bones with their teeth, and eat. For what was there to stop them?

Then they ran away, and were gone, and she was left alone dazed and sobbing in a place she could not have named. The attack had probably not taken more than two or three minutes but it had seemed interminable, and afterward she lay for what seemed like a very long time not daring to move for fear of discovering that they'd crippled her—for her back and buttocks had been soundly kicked. *This is what you deserve*, a voice meanly consoled her, but she was too weakened, too much in pain, to respond.

She guessed she must be alone in the preserve since no one had come in answer to her calls for help.

So she lay still and tried to gather her strength, tried to think what had happened, what she must do next. Her sobs were erratic and resigned rather than the high breathless sobs of hysteria for she was not a hysterically inclined woman; she was a woman who might quell hysteria in others. *It's all right. You're going to be all right. The worst is over.*

So she spoke frequently to her own children, half chidingly, half in affection.

But her clothes had been taken from her. And her car keys.

And her wallet too, of course, and her wristwatch, and her gold chain—yanked so violently from her neck that the catch snapped and her skin was lacerated as by a wire noose. Only the rings on her left hand remained: one of the children had tugged fiercely at them, so hard she'd felt her finger turn in its socket, but her finger must have been swollen; the rings hadn't budged.

Savages, she thought.

Filthy little animals, she thought.

But why had they hated her so, to beat her as well as rob her, and to humiliate her by stripping her clothes from her?

She sat up. Brushed her hair out of her sweaty face. The thought came to her that there was an emergency telephone she could use near the parking area—but almost in the same instant she knew that the emergency phone she was thinking of, and could see so precisely, so desperately, illuminated by a cool blue light, was on a post behind her office building at the university.

She spent a wretched half hour, or more, looking for her clothes. Every part of her body ached as if she had been thrown from a great height, her bones shaken to the marrow but somehow unbroken, able to bear her weight. Her scalp stung where a clump or two of hair had been torn out. Her nose had been bloodied. Both her eyes were swelling and would surely turn black, and her vision was blurred as if she were under water for one of them had tried to rub dried leaves in her eyes: a playground tactic, she supposed, a nasty playground tactic; probably everything that had been done to her was play of a kind, the moves known in advance, deftly and gracefully orchestrated. But she had not known.

She didn't want to think why the children, strangers to her, had hated her so. Hadn't she been quite cordial to the boy, unalarmed, even trying to smile as he approached her? She was by nature and by training an unfailingly friendly woman; she practiced friendliness as a musician practices an instrument, and with as unquestioned a devotion. And there was the unwanted but undeniable privilege of her white skin, which brought with it a certain responsibility not only to be good and decent and charitable but to be nice in being so.

Walking on the wood-chip trail was not painful but walking into the underbrush hurt her feet; the soles were shockingly tender, softer than the palms of her hands. It was disorienting that in this open, public place, where any stranger might suddenly appear, she should be walking with her breasts loose and exposed and that between her legs air touched her in a space that widened and narrowed as she walked. Her vision blurred in the hazy sunshine as with increasing desperation she searched for her things. Surely the children wouldn't have troubled to carry them far? Surely she would find them tossed into the underbrush? Her jeans, her khaki jacket, her shoes, socks, underwear, however ripped and defiled? But her eyes leapt only upon useless things, teasing shapes: newspapers blown into the brush, banks of white wood anemone, smashed bottles and beer cans winking up out of the shadows. She wept in abject frustration.

She was a woman of generous instincts, but her instinct failed her now. What to do? Where to go? She didn't have her car keys and her car was locked—she'd acquired from her husband, a fastidious man, the habit of always locking her car—so if she had wanted to make her way shyly to the parking lot and sit in the car awaiting discovery and rescue she could not do so.

She felt an attack of faintness. The image of a fleshy cartoon woman came to her, a balloon woman, big breasts and belly and pubic hair, hoisted up into the sky. People, mainly men, gathered to gape, smirk, point their fingers. Aloud she cried, "What am I going to do!"

As if in answer, a car pulled into the graveled parking lot not far away. She heard car doors slamming and men's voices. In a panic she plunged into the shrubs to hide, ran without caring about her bare feet and the branches and prickles that tore against her naked body. Like a hunted creature she squatted and hid even as she knew that she should call for help; she had only to raise her voice calling "Help!" or "Help, please!"—a timid, hopeful, desperate appeal—and the nightmare would be over.

She could even call out to her rescuers—she had no doubt they would be rescuers; nearly everyone who came to the preserve was

connected in some way with the university—that she had been
stripped of her clothing and could they please bring her a blanket
or something with which to cover herself; and she could, assuming
the circumstances were right, insist that she was not hurt and did
not want the incident reported to police, nor did she want, or require,
medical attention.

But she said nothing. She crouched low behind a thick bank of
bushes and flowering dogwood, her sweating forehead pressed
against her knees, her arms gripping her legs in a frantic embrace.
The terror of being discovered naked as she was, battered, bruised,
disheveled as a wild animal, was simply too much for her: she wanted
only to hide and not be seen. Nothing mattered to her but that she
not be seen.

So she hid, and the men's voices quickly faded, for they must
have taken one of the other trails and would not find her. If they
had seen her car in the lot they would probably not have really
noticed or remarked upon it. It's all right, she consoled herself repeatedly, not knowing what she meant.

She was a woman who had married late, by choice, and had had
her children late, also by choice; thus she'd formed habits or practices
of solitude that were closely bound up with, perhaps inextricable
from, her character: her private, secret, abiding self. Her blond sunlit
good looks had never mattered greatly to her except as they buoyed
up her naturally exuberant spirit; she thought it simply a matter of
tact to hide from others, including her husband, the small doubts
and shifts of mood that frequently overcame her. It was a matter of
pride that everyone who knew her should think her unfailingly good-
natured, resilient, happy and confident always; or nearly always.

And now, what to do? How to spare herself further humiliation?
She had fled from the men who might have helped her; thus, what
to do?

She would have forgiven the children their savage assault, she
thought, if only they had left her her clothes.

There seemed to her no alternative that was not hideous, shameful. She would end up crouching in the bushes at the side of the
road and flagging down a car with the hope that whoever was driving
the car might be a person she could trust. A man who was a stranger

would be the worst prospect, yet a man who knew her was scarcely better—might in fact be worse, since then word would be spread of her plight and the sordid incident exaggerated. If it were a woman perhaps she could bear it, but if it were a woman who knew her, or knew of her, from her work in the community or her photograph in the local paper, then too the tale would be spread everywhere at once and the rumor would be that she had been sexually assaulted. Even people who wished her well would repeat the tale and thrill to it; some would wonder why she'd been alone in the wildlife preserve; some might even hint that she'd had it coming to her—independent as she was, married to a well-known department chairman at the university, with an excellent job of her own in the university's development office. So the ugly tale would be told and retold numberless times, out of her control. She would be, simply, the woman who was found naked in the Meadowbrook Wildlife Preserve.

And her children would hear of it at school, her six-year-old daughter and her nine-year-old son; they'd be teased, taunted, made to believe things that weren't true. And her stepson—the boy would be crushed with embarrassment for her. And there was her husband, of whom in this context she could barely think: so ambitious, so caught up in his work, so concerned with his reputation in the community. After his relief passed that she hadn't been seriously hurt, she knew he would feel a kindred humiliation.

And if she sought help there would be police to contend with, probably. It was clear from the sight of her that she'd been beaten. The police would insist on questioning her, and how to tell them that her assailants had been mere children, not teenagers but children? And girls among them? And black? *I am not a racist*, she would tell the police carefully. Excising all emotion from her voice: *I am not a racist*.

"I can't risk it."

As in a waking delirium she saw herself, a naked, spectral figure, floating in directions parallel to but hidden from the roads that led to her home, following a variant of the route she would have taken by car. Those familiar suburban-country roads she drove every day. She was only two miles from home, possibly less: couldn't she make it on foot, alone and unassisted? With no one knowing? She calculated it must be about six-thirty. And since she was often home late,

after dark, delayed at the office or socially or with errands, her family
would not begin to miss her for hours; her husband had lately become
involved in fund raising for the university and he too kept an erratic
schedule: sometimes, arriving home, she'd learn from the girl who
watched the children that her husband had telephoned to say he
would not be home for dinner. And her stepson was in and out of
the house. The girl would feed the smaller children at six-thirty; thus
she had no immediate cause to feel anxiety or guilt about them apart
from the anxiety and guilt she felt at the possibility of their learning
of her humiliation or, worse yet, seeing her in the state she was in.

For then they would never see *her* again, as the person she was.

She said aloud, licking her cracked lips, "I can't risk it."

She waited until the sun slanted through the trees and the western
sky turned bluish orange, mottled like a bruise. Around her birds
were calling to one another with renewed urgency, quickened by
the diminution of light: lovely high-pitched cries like ribbons, wires,
threads of sound; she listened, hearing each note with unnatural
clarity. She had never heard such sounds before.

"I want my home again. My own place."

She had established in her mind's eye a map to guide her through
the woods and back fields:

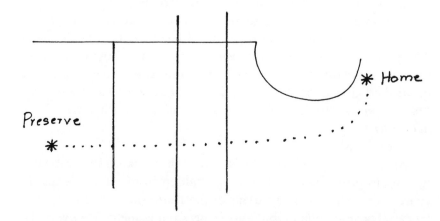

The distance between her present position in the preserve and
her home was approximately two miles. There was no reason she
could not cover it on foot, without being seen! Unavoidably, she

would have to cross three roads, but only the first, bordering the preserve, was large; the others were only residential lanes. It would all be a matter of timing.

Her destination was, not her own front door or even, at least initially, her back door, but the ravine at the rear where she could hide in the shadows and observe the lighted windows of her house: noting the comings and goings of her family, should they be visible. For she did not want them to see her naked, no, not even her husband, not in this debased state of nakedness, with the look of a victim in her face and her body scratched and bruised. Her breasts ached as if the outermost layer of skin had been peeled off; the nipples were hard and puckered in fear. That boy with the mean eyes and jeering mouth had kicked her in the pit of the belly until she'd turned away retching and gasping for breath, but such an outrage would never happen to her again.

Once home, undetected, she could steal away upstairs and revert to herself again. She would bathe, doctor herself up, dress, reappear. If she acted quickly enough, the smaller children would not yet be in bed or asleep. She would prepare a meal, something simple, for her husband and stepson. Or she would join them at the table if they were already eating. She would tell her husband she'd lost her car keys in the woods and had decided to walk home without telephoning him or anyone: no need to fuss; he could drop her off in the morning and she could pick the car up then. It was locked, it was safe. (For the children were surely too young to steal a car!) "You walked home?" her husband would ask, mildly surprised, and she would say, "It wasn't far. I enjoyed the exercise."

Afterward, she would begin the effort of forgetting as resolutely as, years ago, before she was married and living in a fine home, she might have washed a wall of one of her rented apartments preparatory to painting it. *And no one would know.*

None of the children would sense that anything had happened to their mother, for their attention was focused almost exclusively upon themselves: which was only natural and good. Nor would her husband sense anything, for his imagination was absorbed primarily in his own work, his own being; he wasn't a young man any longer but a man at the peak of his powers, or a little beyond: now it was younger men who drew his attention, who fascinated and repelled.

And what in fact would there be for this busy successful well-liked man to notice if she, his wife, his happy confident wife, gave no sign of unease? They rarely had time for love now, in the old, intimate sense. But they were companions and sometimes plotters together, conspirators.

Could you identify the children if you saw them again, Mrs.—?
Yes. I don't know.
What was the color of their skin?
I am not a racist.

How painstakingly she was walking, barefoot! How treacherous the seemingly soft, moist earth, laced with invisible stones and bits of branches! When she left the path, making her way toward the edge of the preserve bordering the road, her feet sank in muck and she had to stifle a scream of panic, for what if this were a bog or even quicksand that might swallow her up without a trace?

But she kept going. There was no other way for her except forward.

She had never noticed how, in the woods, there were so many dead trees: dried lifeless stalks from which dried lifeless leaves, last year's leaves, hung in tatters. And the continuous scurrying of invisible birds, animals. And the continuous wind. On all sides mysterious sounds of rustling, stirring, shifting, as if a gigantic organism were defining itself, never quite rising to consciousness. She felt a thrill of deep calm fear, thinking this thought. It was not one she'd ever had before.

At the road she waited. She was prepared to wait for a long time. In the silence of the countryside the approach of a car and its passing and its subsequent retreat were clearly disparate. If she didn't lose her courage at the last moment and if she didn't step down on something sharp she really should have no difficulty getting across the road and hiding in the wooded area beyond.

A car passed, and another. After an interval another. And then there were several in a row, then what sounded like a diesel truck, heaving and sighing, and then there was silence. She peered excitedly out of the underbrush, seeing nothing but pavement and the farther side of the road. It was nearly dusk but not quite! A figure running across the road, a figure of pale astonishing female nakedness, might be visible for miles.

She was trembling. With oneiric clarity she saw the distance between herself and her home across which she must fly, saw herself crouching in the ravine at the foot of the hill, waiting. She did not trust her family not to stop loving her should they see her; thus they must not be allowed to see her, or to know!

Stooped almost double, she prepared to run. Drew a deep breath as years ago as a girl she would prepare to dive from the high board, eager not merely to reach the water below but to execute a perfectly calibrated dive, entering the water with the deft grace of a hand slicing a porous surface at a slant, unhesitating. For pride would allow no lesser performance!

She threw herself blindly out of hiding and began to run, her forearms steadying her breasts from beneath, and no dive or flight or plunge or physical ecstasy in her life had prepared her for this effort, running naked and wincing, gasping for breath through her opened mouth, eyes wide and stark and fixed on the farther side of the road, not daring to look elsewhere. And then almost at once she was there, and safe, seemingly, scrambling through a shallow ditch and into the field beyond. But somehow she had cut her foot. Stepped on glass and cut her right foot at the heel.

It's all right she told herself. *You're all right.*

She told herself impatiently, *The bleeding will wash the dirt away.*

She walked on, limping. She wasn't going to examine her foot. To her left there were no houses within sight, and to her right there was a farmhouse a short distance away but partly screened by trees, and should someone happen to be looking out a window as she passed it would not be evident that she was naked. Despite her wildly pounding heart she felt a surge of hope, almost of elation.

She was, and had always been, a woman of principle: a woman who believed in intelligent, considered, but not overconsidered action. Everyone who knew her respected her; yes, and some who did not know her quite as she knew herself envied her, and that too was good, or at least provided satisfaction. She could not be exposed now and would not be, but she would have to guard against waves of panic and faint-headedness and the possibility of losing her way, going in circles, as, once, not so long ago, she'd become lost in the wildlife preserve, doubling back on her trail and crossing it until she realized her error and returned safely to her car. Now that she had crossed the first and most dangerous of the roads she would have to keep it firmly in her mind's eye perpendicular at her back, envisioning the next road (how far away was it? She did not think it could be far) perpendicular before her.

She would have thought this interior land merely empty, but there was much evidence of human intrusion: piles of trash scattered along a farmer's lane as if people came here regularly by night and by stealth to dump their unwanted things—rotted tires, automobile parts, an upended refrigerator, a scorched mattress. Like a scavenger, and as eagerly, as unreasonably hopeful, she searched amid the trash for something she could wrap around herself, lifting and dropping a strip of canvas stiff with filth, and what appeared to be a child's playsuit, and other items of clothing that were mere shreds, tatters. She was excited yet dreamy too: standing for a long purposeless moment staring at the debris of strangers, wondering at lives so parallel to her own yet unknown to her. Gnats swarmed about her as if attracted by her very nakedness and the sweaty smell about her. Her right foot throbbed with something like pain but she refused to be drawn into examining it. Vaguely she thought that might be a trick, a trap of a kind.

She walked on, limping, until the farmer's lane ended abruptly in a final pile of trash, out of which something scuttled and ran into the underbrush to hide—a rat, judging by its size.

Her head rang with accusations. *How dare you. How dare touch. My skin doesn't define me. My color, my skin.* She was thinking suddenly of her husband and the happiness of his first marriage, of which he would never speak except crudely to deny it. As if mere words *now* might erase what had been *then* and, having *been*, flowed inexorably into what *is*. "You must think I'm a fool." Her voice sounded loudly but did not startle her.

Now: should she continue in a straight line across an open field in which swaths of wild rose with their deathly thorns were growing or should she take, thus risking the loss of her sense of direction (the road perpendicular at her back, the next road perpendicular, or approximately, before her), the edge of the field where it might be safer? She had forgotten the children, or nearly. They had nothing to do with her since they hadn't known her, and they certainly had nothing to do with her now.

She must have made a decision to make her way along the edge of the field but how slowly she was walking, how timidly—both her feet were bleeding now—thinking how, if she bled, the bleeding would wash away the filth and purify the wounds. Wasn't it puncture wounds in such instances that were dangerous?

She was thinking too what a curiosity it was of female life that, bleeding so frequently, bleeding amid cramps and occasional nausea and faintness, a woman had faith nonetheless that the bleeding would not go on and on until she bled to death. And there was the secrecy of the bleeding—well hidden inside the clothes, always well hidden, discreet and not to be spoken of. Yet how real, such doubleness! She had always liked it, really. She would never give it up, no matter that in a few years the cycle of her body would shift, and she would not bleed again in that way.

Beyond the field the lane began again, broader now, less rutted and less painful underfoot. She believed she knew the property— an old, inoperative farm—but she did not know the owners. Unless she was emerging at a place she hadn't calculated?

A chill began to lift from the darkening earth, though the sky was still fairly light, streaked with clouds. And the birds continued to call to one another, more urgently it seemed.

An error now would be fatal.

Not single pains but a wash of pains rose and throbbed in her body. She did not think of them, but increasingly they penetrated her consciousness and left her panting, whimpering. Her eyes—her head—her scalp—her belly, buttocks, spine—her feet. Forever would she walk in this no-man's-land so strangely close to familiar suburban roads yet hidden from them. The undeveloped still-wild countryside, no longer lucrative for farming, not yet sold for residential building, custom-made homes like the one she and her husband lived in—how strange *she* should be *here*. It was a place for death, for nude female bodies: victims of assaults, murders. She was not one of those women.

Yet she might lose her strength and collapse, might faint, and in a day or two or three she would be found comatose, perhaps dead.

A woman's body, it would be reported. *A woman's nude body* would be the initial report. Balloon breasts and fleshy hips and thighs, a patch of pubic hair at the fork of the legs, eyes rolled whitely up into the skull. It happened all the time. Not a person but a body. And all the prior history of her life—her achievement, her winningness, her sunny smile and resolute optimism, and her love for her family and theirs for her—would be summarily erased. She would become a story, a fiction.

Thus buoyed by anger she walked faster. In the growing dusk she could not make out whether, at the road, she would encounter a facing house, but the sound of an occasional car meant that the road was ahead and proof she was not lost.

Then it happened that a dog began barking excitedly close by, and to her horror the animal trotted up the lane as if to attack her, a dun-colored dog the size of a Labrador retriever but of no distinct breed: it barked, it snarled, the hackles on its shoulders were raised, its long clumsy tail thrashed from side to side. She was in terror of dogs since as a young child she'd once been bitten, or so she believed, though her mother had assured her she hadn't actually been bitten, only badly frightened by a German shepherd, and now she was seized with panic, backing off and murmuring to the aroused animal words plaintive and submissive: "No. Please. Go home. Go *home*." The dog approached to within a few yards, then stopped, crouching, barking in such a frenzy she supposed its owner would hear and come out to see what was going on. There was a farmhouse not far away, a hundred yards perhaps from the lane.

As if for her very life she was begging and pleading in an undertone: "Good dog. Nice dog. Go *home*." She wondered if her nakedness excited the dog, if it could smell her fear, the sharp rank animal odor of her helplessness.

She backed off. She picked up a large tree branch, held it threateningly overhead, and backed off. The dog continued to bark but did not follow. Its tail was thrashing energetically. Did that mean it might be friendly? But she could not take a chance, for as much as the prospect of being attacked by the dog, the prospect of having to call for help terrified her.

Some minutes passed. She thought how people would laugh at

her—the dog's owner, if he came out into the lane to investigate. A
disheveled naked woman confronted by a barking dog, trying to
protect herself with a branch. How had her life come to this?

Gradually the dog's barking subsided, and it appeared that a crisis
of a kind had passed. It allowed her to pass by, then trotted as if
indifferently in her wake, nosing about, sniffing at her heels. She felt
its damp cool muzzle against her bare legs and the backs of her
knees.

Its owner did not appear.

She was nearing home. Crossed the second road in a delirium of
a plunge. Running, sliding somewhere, and staggering downhill. A
swampy place. She snatched at bushes to steady her, like a drunken
woman; leaves tore off in her fingers.

She should never have married, she was thinking. She'd been
happiest alone.

The effort of hypocrisy wearied her.

The need to urinate came suddenly and so violently it was like
a knife blade thrust up inside her. She squatted in a place already
soft with mud and released a pungent burning liquid from her bladder, not in a stream but in tentative little spasms. When she was at
last finished she wiped herself awkwardly with a wad of leaves. She
was thinking, *At least no one has seen.*

Her face burned, her hands shook. A memory came to her as if
emerging from a previous lifetime of having as a small child squatted
in the grass to urinate and watching the liquid streaming from her—
the strange helplessness of something happening to her she could
not control. And someone had called to her, to reprimand her. Or
had someone laughed at her?

At least, this time, no one had seen.

The house floated in the darkness.

How many hours had passed she did not know. Or if it were a
single hour, distended as in a dream.

Why did you do such a thing? he was demanding and she said *I
do what I want to do,* though until that instant she had not known
that this was so.

She had had her children after all as she'd determined to have them. She would not have had two children had she not wanted them, for one would have done. Two was incontestable proof.

And the stepson who eyed her with suspicion, liking her sometimes and at other times not at all. For he was in no way hers and could not be cajoled into thinking so.

Inside the floating house indistinct figures moved. Some of the windows were lit, others darkened. *Why on earth did you do such a thing?* he would ask, for it was his right.

There, at the top of the incline, was the house, the rectangular box, in which she lived. She crouched in the underbrush blinking and rubbing her eyes so that she could see clearly, for it was crucial now that she see. Was the house hers? Or had she taken a wrong turn, become confused in the dark? She had never seen her house from such a position of course and would not perhaps have identified it. She saw movement by one of the windows—a figure that must have been that of her husband, though not quite so tall as she would have imagined her husband—and shortly there came another figure to join him, male or female she could not determine; it must have been the stepson, the fourteen-year-old, and how strange that, seeing him, seeing both of them, having wanted so desperately to get home, she felt no emotion at seeing them, or the indistinct shapes she believed must be them—no more than if they were strangers.

I do what I want to do. So in the dark below the house, squatting where no one could see, she waited naked—until such time as it would become known to her why she was waiting.

II

HEAT

I t was midsummer, the heat rippling above the macadam roads, cicadas screaming out of the trees, and the sky like pewter, glaring.

The days were the same day, like the shallow mud-brown river moving always in the same direction but so slow you couldn't see it. Except for Sunday: church in the morning, then the fat Sunday newspaper, the color comics, and newsprint on your fingers.

Rhea and Rhoda Kunkel went flying on their rusted old bicycles, down the long hill toward the railroad yard, Whipple's Ice, the scrubby pastureland where dairy cows grazed. They'd stolen six dollars from their own grandmother who loved them. They were eleven years old; they were identical twins; they basked in their power.

Rhea and Rhoda Kunkel: it was always Rhea-and-Rhoda, never Rhoda-and-Rhea, I couldn't say why. You just wouldn't say the names that way. Not even the teachers at school would say them that way.

We went to see them in the funeral parlor where they were waked; we were made to. The twins in twin caskets, white, smooth, gleaming, perfect as plastic, with white satin lining puckered like the inside of a fancy candy box. And the waxy white lilies, and the smell of talcum powder and perfume. The room was crowded; there was only one way in and out.

Rhea and Rhoda were the same girl; they'd wanted it that way. Only looking from one to the other could you see they were two.

The heat was gauzy; you had to push your way through like swimming. On their bicycles Rhea and Rhoda flew through it hardly

141

noticing, from their grandmother's place on Main Street to the end of South Main where the paved road turned to gravel leaving town. That was the summer before seventh grade, when they died. Death was coming for them, but they didn't know.

They thought the same thoughts sometimes at the same moment, had the same dream and went all day trying to remember it, bringing it back like something you'd be hauling out of the water on a tangled line. We watched them; we were jealous. None of us had a twin. Sometimes they were serious and sometimes, remembering, they shrieked and laughed like they were being killed. They stole things out of desks and lockers but if you caught them they'd hand them right back; it was like a game.

There were three floor fans in the funeral parlor that I could see, tall whirring fans with propeller blades turning fast to keep the warm air moving. Strange little gusts came from all directions, making your eyes water. By this time Roger Whipple was arrested, taken into police custody. No one had hurt him. He would never stand trial; he was ruled mentally unfit and would never be released from confinement.

He died there, in the state psychiatric hospital, years later, and was brought back home to be buried—the body of him, I mean. His earthly remains.

Rhea and Rhoda Kunkel were buried in the same cemetery, the First Methodist. The cemetery is just a field behind the church.

In the caskets the dead girls did not look like anyone we knew, really. They were placed on their backs with their eyes closed, and their mouths, the way you don't always look in life when you're sleeping. Their faces were too small. Every eyelash showed, too perfect. Like angels, everyone was saying, and it was strange it was so. I stared and stared.

What had been done to them, the lower parts of them, didn't show in the caskets.

Roger Whipple worked for his father at Whipple's Ice. In the newspaper it stated he was nineteen. He'd gone to DeWitt Clinton until he was sixteen; my mother's friend Sadie taught there and remembered him from the special education class. A big slow sweet-faced boy with these big hands and feet, thighs like hams. A shy gentle boy with good manners and a hushed voice.

He wasn't simpleminded exactly, like the others in that class. He was watchful, he held back.

Roger Whipple in overalls squatting in the rear of his father's truck, one of his older brothers driving. There would come the sound of the truck in the driveway, the heavy block of ice smelling of cold, ice tongs over his shoulder. He was strong, round-shouldered like an older man. Never staggered or grunted. Never dropped anything. Pale washed-looking eyes lifting out of a big face, a soft mouth wanting to smile. We giggled and looked away. They said he'd never been the kind to hurt even an animal; all the Whipples swore.

Sucking ice, the cold goes straight into your jaws and deep into the bone.

People spoke of them as the Kunkel twins. Mostly nobody tried to tell them apart: homely corkscrew-twisty girls you wouldn't know would turn up so quiet and solemn and almost beautiful, perfect little dolls' faces with the freckles powdered over, touches of rouge on the cheeks and mouths. I was tempted to whisper to them, kneeling by the coffins, *Hey, Rhea! Hey, Rhoda! Wake up!*

They had loud slip-sliding voices that were the same voice. They weren't shy. They were always first in line. One behind you and one in front of you and you'd better be wary of some trick. Flamey-orange hair and the bleached-out skin that goes with it, freckles like dirty raindrops splashed on their faces. Sharp green eyes they'd bug out until you begged them to stop.

Places meant to be serious, Rhea and Rhoda had a hard time sitting still. In church, in school, a sideways glance between them could do it. Jamming their knuckles into their mouths, choking back giggles. Sometimes laughter escaped through their fingers like steam hissing. Sometimes it came out like snorting and then none of us could hold back. The worst time was in assembly, the principal up there telling us that Miss Flagler had died, we would all miss her. Tears shining in the woman's eyes behind her goggle glasses and one of the twins gave a breathless little snort; you could feel it like flames running down the whole row of girls, none of us could hold back.

Sometimes the word "tickle" was enough to get us going, just that word.

I never dreamt about Rhea and Rhoda so strange in their caskets sleeping out in the middle of a room where people could stare at them, shed tears, and pray over them. I never dream about actual things, only things I don't know. Places I've never been, people I've never seen. Sometimes the person I am in the dream isn't me. Who it is, I don't know.

Rhea and Rhoda bounced up the drive on their bicycles behind Whipple's Ice. They were laughing like crazy and didn't mind the potholes jarring their teeth or the clouds of dust. If they'd had the same dream the night before, the hot sunlight erased it entirely.

When death comes for you, you sometimes know and sometimes don't.

Roger Whipple was by himself in the barn, working. Kids went down there to beg him for ice to suck or throw around or they'd tease him, not out of meanness but for something to do. It was slow, the days not changing in the summer, heat sometimes all night long. He was happy with children that age, he was that age himself in his head—sixth-grade learning abilities, as the newspaper stated, though he could add and subtract quickly. Other kinds of arithmetic gave him trouble.

People were saying afterward he'd always been strange. Watchful like he was, those thick soft lips. The Whipples did wrong to let him run loose.

They said he'd always been a good gentle boy, went to Sunday school and sat still there and never gave anybody any trouble. He collected Bible cards; he hid them away under his mattress for safe-keeping. Mr. Whipple started in early disciplining him the way you might discipline a big dog or a horse. Not letting the creature know he has any power to be himself exactly. Not giving him the oppor-tunity to test his will.

Neighbors said the Whipples worked him like a horse, in fact. The older brothers were the most merciless. And why they all wore coveralls, heavy denim and long legs on days so hot, nobody knew. The thermometer above the First Midland Bank read 98 degrees F. on noon of that day, my mother said.

Nights afterward my mother would hug me before I went to bed. Pressing my face hard against her breasts and whispering things I didn't hear, like praying to Jesus to love and protect her little girl and keep her from harm, but I didn't hear; I shut my eyes tight and endured it. Sometimes we prayed together, all of us or just my mother and me kneeling by my bed. Even then I knew she was a good mother, there was this girl she loved as her daughter that was me and loved more than that girl deserved. There was nothing I could do about it.

Mrs. Kunkel would laugh and roll her eyes over the twins. In that house they were "double trouble"—you'd hear it all the time like a joke on the radio that keeps coming back. I wonder did she pray with them too. I wonder would they let her.

In the long night you forget about the day; it's like the other side of the world. Then the sun is there, and the heat. You forget.

We were running through the field behind school, a place where people dumped things sometimes, and there was a dead dog there, a collie with beautiful fur, but his eyes were gone from the sockets and the maggots had got him where somebody tried to lift him with her foot, and when Rhea and Rhoda saw they screamed a single scream and hid their eyes.

They did nice things—gave their friends candy bars, nail polish, some novelty key chains they'd taken from somewhere, movie stars' pictures framed in plastic. In the movies they'd share a box of pop-corn, not noticing where one or the other of them left off and a girl who wasn't any sister of theirs sat.

Once they made me strip off my clothes where we'd crawled under the Kunkels' veranda. This was a large hollowed-out space where the earth dropped away at one end and you could sit without bumping your head; it was cool and smelled of dirt and stone. Rhea said all of a sudden, *Strip!* and Rhoda said at once, *Strip! Come on!* So it happened. They wouldn't let me out unless I took off my clothes, my shirt and shorts, yes, and my panties too. *Come on,* they said, whispering and giggling; they were blocking the way out so I had no choice. I was scared but I was laughing too. This is to show our power over you, they said. But they stripped too just like me.

You have power over others you don't realize until you test it.

Under the Kunkels' veranda we stared at each other but we didn't touch each other. My teeth chattered, because what if somebody saw us, some boy, or Mrs. Kunkel herself? I was scared but I was happy too. Except for our faces, their face and mine, we could all be the same girl.

The Kunkel family lived in one side of a big old clapboard house by the river; you could hear the trucks rattling on the bridge, shifting their noisy gears on the hill. Mrs. Kunkel had eight children. Rhea and Rhoda were the youngest. Our mothers wondered why Mrs. Kunkel had let herself go: she had a moon-shaped pretty face but her hair was frizzed ratty; she must have weighed two hundred pounds, sweated and breathed so hard in the warm weather. They'd known her in school. Mr. Kunkel worked construction for the county. Summer evenings after work he'd be sitting on the veranda drinking beer, flicking cigarette butts out into the yard; you'd be fooled, almost thinking they were fireflies. He went bare-chested in the heat, his upper body dark like stained wood. Flat little purplish nipples inside his chest hair the girls giggled to see. Mr. Kunkel teased us all; he'd mix Rhea and Rhoda up the way he'd mix the rest of us up, like it was too much trouble to keep names straight.

Mr. Kunkel was in police custody; he didn't even come to the wake. Mrs. Kunkel was there in rolls of chin fat that glistened with sweat and tears, the makeup on her face so caked and discolored you were embarrassed to look. It scared me, the way she grabbed me as soon as my parents and I came in, hugging me against her big balloon breasts, sobbing. All the strength went out of me; I couldn't push away.

The police had Mr. Kunkel for his own good, they said. He'd gone to the Whipples, though the murderer had been taken away, saying he would kill anybody he could get his hands on: the old man, the brothers. They were all responsible, he said; his little girls were dead. Tear them apart with his bare hands, he said, but he had a tire iron.

Did it mean anything special, or was it just an accident Rhea and Rhoda had taken six dollars from their grandmother an hour before? Because death was coming for them; it had to happen one way or another.

If you believe in God you believe that. And if you don't believe in God it's obvious.

Their grandmother lived upstairs over a shoe store downtown, an apartment looking out on Main Street. They'd bicycle down there for something to do and she'd give them grape juice or lemonade and try to keep them awhile, a lonely old lady but she was nice, she was always nice to me; it was kind of nasty of Rhea and Rhoda to steal from her but they were like that. One was in the kitchen talking with her and without any plan or anything the other went to use the bathroom, then slipped into her bedroom, got the money out of her purse like it was something she did every day of the week, that easy. On the stairs going down to the street Rhoda whispered to Rhea, What did you *do?* knowing Rhea had done something she hadn't ought to have done but not knowing what it was or anyway how much money it was. They started in poking each other, trying to hold the giggles back until they were safe away.

On their bicycles they stood high on the pedals, coasting, going down the hill but not using their brakes. *What did you do! Oh, what did you do!*

Rhea and Rhoda always said they could never be apart. If one didn't know exactly where the other was that one could die. Or the other could die. Or both.

Once they'd gotten some money from somewhere, they wouldn't say where, and paid for us all to go to the movies. And ice cream afterward too.

You could read the newspaper articles twice through and still not know what he did. Adults talked about it for a long time but not so we could hear. I thought probably he'd used an ice pick. Or maybe I heard somebody guess who didn't know any more than me.

We liked it that Rhea and Rhoda had been killed, and all the stuff in the paper, and everybody talking about it, but we didn't like it that they were dead; we missed them.

Later, in tenth grade, the Kaufmann twins moved into our school district: Doris and Diane. But it wasn't the same thing.

Roger Whipple said he didn't remember any of it. Whatever he did, he didn't remember. At first everybody thought he was lying; then they had to accept it as true, or true in some way: doctors from the state hospital examined him. He said over and over he hadn't done anything and he didn't remember the twins there that afternoon, but he couldn't explain why their bicycles were at the foot of his stairway and he couldn't explain why he'd taken a bath in the middle of the day. The Whipples admitted that wasn't a practice of Roger's or of any of them, ever, a bath in the middle of the day.

Roger Whipple was a clean boy, though. His hands always scrubbed so you actually noticed, swinging the block of ice off the truck and, inside the kitchen, helping to set it in the icebox. They said he'd go crazy if he got bits of straw under his nails from the icehouse or inside his clothes. He'd been taught to shave and he shaved every morning without fail; they said the sight of the beard growing in, the scratchy feel of it, seemed to scare him.

A few years later his sister Linda told us how Roger was built like a horse. She was our age, a lot younger than him; she made a gesture toward her crotch so we'd know what she meant. She'd happened to see him a few times, she said, by accident.

There he was squatting in the dust laughing, his head lowered, watching Rhea and Rhoda circle him on their bicycles. It was a rough game where the twins saw how close they could come to hitting him, brushing him with their bike fenders, and he'd lunge out, not seeming to notice if his fingers hit the spokes; it was all happening so fast you maybe wouldn't feel pain. Out back of the icehouse, the yard blended in with the yard of the old railroad depot next door that wasn't used any more. It was burning hot in the sun; dust rose in clouds behind the girls. Pretty soon they got bored with the game, though Roger Whipple even in his heavy overalls wanted to keep going. He was red-faced with all the excitement; he was a boy who loved to laugh and didn't have much chance. Rhea said she was thirsty, she wanted some ice, so Roger Whipple scrambled right up and went to get a big bag of ice cubes! He hadn't any more sense than that.

They sucked on the ice cubes and fooled around with them. He was panting and lolling his tongue pretending to be a dog, and Rhea and Rhoda cried, Here, doggie! Here, doggie-doggie! tossing ice cubes at Roger Whipple he tried to catch in his mouth. That went on for a while. In the end the twins just dumped the rest of the ice onto the dirt, then Roger Whipple was saying he had some secret things that belonged to his brother Eamon he could show them, hidden under his bed mattress; would they like to see what the things were?

He wasn't one who could tell Rhea from Rhoda or Rhoda from Rhea. There was a way some of us knew: the freckles on Rhea's face were a little darker than Rhoda's, and Rhea's eyes were just a little darker than Rhoda's. But you'd have to see the two side by side with no clowning around to know.

Rhea said OK, she'd like to see the secret things. She let her bike fall where she was straddling it.

Roger Whipple said he could only take one of them upstairs to his room at a time, he didn't say why.

OK, said Rhea. Of the Kunkel twins, Rhea always had to be first. She'd been born first, she said. Weighed a pound or two more.

Roger Whipple's room was in a strange place: on the second floor of the Whipple house above an unheated storage space that had been added after the main part of the house was built. There was a way of getting to the room from the outside, up a flight of rickety wooden stairs. That way Roger could get in and out of his room without going through the rest of the house. People said the Whipples had him live there like some animal, they didn't want him tramping through the house, but they denied it. The room had an inside door too.

Roger Whipple weighed about one hundred ninety pounds that day. In the hospital he swelled up like a balloon, people said, bloated from the drugs; his skin was soft and white as bread dough and his hair fell out. He was an old man when he died aged thirty-one.

Exactly why he died, the Whipples never knew. The hospital just told them his heart had stopped in his sleep.

Rhoda shaded her eyes, watching her sister running up the stairs with Roger Whipple behind her, and felt the first pinch of fear, that something was wrong or was going to be wrong. She called after them in a whining voice that she wanted to come along too, she didn't want to wait down there all alone, but Rhea just called back to her to be quiet and wait her turn, so Rhoda waited, kicking at the ice cubes melting in the dirt, and after a while she got restless and shouted up to them—the door was shut, the shade on the window was drawn—saying she was going home, damn them, she was sick of waiting, she said, and she was going home. But nobody came to the door or looked out the window; it was like the place was empty. Wasps had built one of those nests that look like mud in layers under the eaves, and the only sound was wasps.

Rhoda bicycled toward the road so anybody who was watching would think she was going home; she was thinking she hated Rhea! hated her damn twin sister! wished she was dead and gone, God

damn her! She was going home, and the first thing she'd tell their
mother was that Rhea had stolen six dollars from Grandma: she had
it in her pocket right that moment.

The Whipple house was an old farmhouse they'd tried to mod-
ernize by putting on red asphalt siding meant to look like brick.
Downstairs the rooms were big and drafty; upstairs they were small,
some of them unfinished and with bare floorboards, like Roger Whipple's room, which people would afterward say based on what the
police said was like an animal's pen, nothing in it but a bed shoved
into a corner and some furniture and boxes and things Mrs. Whipple
stored there.

Of the Whipples—there were seven in the family still living at
home—only Mrs. Whipple and her daughter Iris were home that
afternoon. They said they hadn't heard a sound except for kids playing in the back; they swore it.

Rhoda was bent on going home and leaving Rhea behind, but at
the end of the driveway something made her turn her bicycle wheel
back . . . so if you were watching you'd think she was just cruising
around for something to do, a red-haired girl with whitish skin and
freckles, skinny little body, pedaling fast, then slow, then coasting,
then fast again, turning and dipping and crisscrossing her path, talking
to herself as if she was angry. She hated Rhea! She was furious at
Rhea! But feeling sort of scared too and sickish in the pit of her
belly, knowing that she and Rhea shouldn't be in two places; something might happen to one of them or to both. Some things you
know.

So she pedaled back to the house. Laid her bike down in the dirt
next to Rhea's. The bikes were old hand-me-downs, the kickstands
were broken. But their daddy had put on new Goodyear tires for
them at the start of the summer, and he'd oiled them too.

You never would see just one of the twins' bicycles anywhere,
you always saw both of them laid down on the ground and facing in
the same direction with the pedals in about the same position.

Rhoda peered up at the second floor of the house, the shade
drawn over the window, the door still closed. She called out, Rhea?
Hey, Rhea? starting up the stairs, making a lot of noise so they'd
hear her, pulling on the railing as if to break it the way a boy would.
Still she was scared. But making noise like that and feeling so dis-

gusted and mad helped her get stronger, and there was Roger Whipple with the door open staring down at her flush-faced and sweaty as if he was scared too. He seemed to have forgotten her. He was wiping his hands on his overalls. He just stared, a lemony light coming up in his eyes.

Afterward he would say he didn't remember anything. Just didn't remember anything. The size of a grown man but round-shouldered so it was hard to judge how tall he was, or how old. His straw-colored hair falling in his eyes and his fingers twined together as if he was praying or trying with all the strength in him to keep his hands still. He didn't remember the twins in his room and couldn't explain the blood but he cried a lot, acted scared and guilty and sorry like a dog that's done bad, so they decided he shouldn't be made to stand trial; there was no point to it.

Afterward Mrs. Whipple kept to the house, never went out, not even to church or grocery shopping. She died of cancer just a few months before Roger died; she'd loved her boy, she always said; she said none of it was his fault in his heart, he wasn't the kind of boy to injure an animal; he loved kittens especially and was a good sweet obedient boy and religious too and Jesus was looking after him and whatever happened it must have been those girls teasing him; everybody knew what the Kunkel twins were like. Roger had had a lifetime of being teased and taunted by children, his heart broken by all the abuse, and something must have snapped that day, that was all.

The Whipples were the ones, though, who called the police. Mr. Whipple found the girls' bodies back in the icehouse hidden under some straw and canvas. Those two look-alike girls, side by side.

He found them around 9 P.M. that night. He knew, he said. Oh, he knew.

The way Roger was acting, and the fact that the Kunkel girls were missing: word had gotten around town. Roger taking a bath like that in the middle of the day and washing his hair too and not answering when anyone said his name, just sitting there staring at the floor. So they went up to his room and saw the blood. So they knew.

The hardest minute of his life, Mr. Whipple said, was in the icehouse lifting that canvas to see what was under it.

He took it hard too; he never recovered. He hadn't any choice but to think what a lot of people thought—it had been his fault. He was an old-time Methodist, he took all that seriously, but none of it helped him. Believed Jesus Christ was his personal savior and He never stopped loving Roger or turned His face from him, and if Roger did truly repent in his heart he would be saved and they would be reunited in Heaven, all the Whipples reunited. He believed, but none of it helped in his life.

The icehouse is still there but boarded up and derelict, the Whipples' ice business ended long ago. Strangers live in the house, and the yard is littered with rusting hulks of cars and pickup trucks. Some Whipples live scattered around the county but none in town. The old train depot is still there too.

After I'd been married some years I got involved with this man, I won't say his name, his name is not a name I say, but we would meet back there sometimes, back in that old lot that's all weeds and scrub trees. Wild as kids and on the edge of being drunk. I was crazy for this guy, I mean crazy like I could hardly think of anybody but him or anything but the two of us making love the way we did; with him deep inside me I wanted it never to stop. Just fuck and fuck and fuck, I'd whisper to him, and this went on for a long time, two or three years, then ended the way these things do and looking back on it I'm not able to recognize that woman, as if she was someone not even not-me but a crazy woman I would despise, making so much of such a thing, risking her marriage and her kids finding out and her life being ruined for such a thing, my God. The things people do.

It's like living out a story that has to go its own way.

Behind the icehouse in his car I'd think of Rhea and Rhoda and what happened that day upstairs in Roger Whipple's room. And the funeral parlor with the twins like dolls laid out and their eyes like dolls' eyes too that shut when you tilt them back. One night when I wasn't asleep but wasn't awake either I saw my parents standing in the doorway of my bedroom watching me and I knew their thoughts, how they were thinking of Rhea and Rhoda and of me their daughter wondering how they could keep me from harm, and there was no clear answer.

In his car in his arms I'd feel my mind drift, after we'd made love or at least after the first time. And I saw Rhoda Kunkel hesitating on the stairs a few steps down from Roger Whipple. I saw her white-faced and scared but deciding to keep going anyway, pushing by Roger Whipple to get inside the room, to find Rhea; she had to brush against him where he was standing as if he meant to block her but not having the nerve exactly to block her and he was smelling of his body and breathing hard but not in imitation of any dog now, not with his tongue flopping and lolling to make them laugh. Rhoda was asking where was Rhea? She couldn't see well at first in the dark little cubbyhole of a room because the sunshine had been so bright outside.

Roger Whipple said Rhea had gone home. His voice sounded scratchy as if it hadn't been used in some time. She'd gone home, he said, and Rhoda said right away that Rhea wouldn't go home without her and Roger Whipple came toward her saying, Yes she did, yes she *did*, as if he was getting angry she wouldn't believe him. Rhoda was calling, *Rhea, where are you?* Stumbling against something on the floor tangled with the bedclothes.

Behind her was this big boy saying again and again, Yes she did, yes she *did*, his voice rising, but it would never get loud enough so that anyone would hear and come save her.

I wasn't there, but some things you know.

THE BUCK

This is such a terrible story. It's a story I have told a dozen times, never knowing *why*.

Why I can't forget it, I mean. Why it's lodged so deep in me . . . like an arrow through the neck.

Like that arrow I never saw—fifteen-inch, steel-tipped, razor-sharp—that penetrated the deer's neck and killed him, though not immediately. How many hours, I wonder, till he bled to death, till his body turned cold and grew heavier—they say the weight of Death is always heavier than that of life—how many hours, terrible hours, I don't know.

I was not a witness. The sole witness did not survive.

Each time I tell this story of the wounded buck, the hunter who pursued him, and the elderly woman who rescued him, or tried to rescue him, I think that maybe *this* telling will make a difference. *This* time a secret meaning will be revealed, as if without my volition, and I will be released.

But each telling is a subtle repudiation of a previous telling. So each telling is a new telling. Each telling a forgetting.

That arrow lodged ever more firmly, cruelly. In living flesh.

I'd take comfort in saying all this happened years ago, in some remote part of the country. *Once upon a time*, I'd begin, but in fact it happened within the past year, and no more than eight miles from where I live, in a small town called Bethany, New Jersey.

Which is in Saugatuck County, in the northwestern corner of the state, bordering the Delaware River.

A region that's mainly rural: farmland, hills, some of the hills large enough to be called mountains. There aren't many roads in this part of New Jersey, and the big interstate highways just slice through, gouge through the countryside, north and south, east and west. Strangers in a rush to get somewhere else.

The incident happened on the Snyder farm. A lonely place, no neighbors close by.

The name "Snyder" was always known in Saugatuck County even though, when I was growing up, the Snyders had sold off most of their land. In the family's prime, in the 1930s, they'd owned three hundred twenty acres, most of it rich farmland; in the 1950s they'd begun to sell, piecemeal, as if grudgingly, maybe with the idea of one day buying their land back. But they never did; they died out instead. Three brothers, all unmarried; and Melanie Snyder, the last of the family. Eighty-two years old when she was found dead in a room of the old farmhouse, last January.

In deer-hunting season. The season that had always frightened and outraged her.

She'd been vigilant for years. She'd acquired a local reputation. Her six acres of land—all that remained of the property—was scrupulously posted against hunters ("with gun, bow and arrow, dog") and trespassers. Before hunting with firearms was banned in Saugatuck County, Melanie Snyder patrolled her property in hunting season, on foot, fearless about moving in the direction of gunfire. "You! What are you doing here?" she would call out to hunters. "Don't you know this land is posted?" She was a lanky woman with a strong-boned face, skin that looked permanently wind-burnt, close-cropped starkly white hair. Her eyes were unusually dark and prominent; everyone commented on Melanie Snyder's eyes; she wasn't a woman any man, no matter his age, felt comfortable confronting, especially out in the woods.

She sent trespassers home, threatened to call the sheriff if they didn't leave. She'd stride through the woods clapping her hands to frighten off deer, pheasants, small game, send them panicked to safety.

White-tailed deer, or, as older generations called them, Virginia

deer, were her favorites, "the most beautiful animals in creation."
She hated it that state conservationists argued in favor of controlled
hunting for the "good" of the deer themselves, to reduce their alarm-
ingly fertile numbers.

She hated the idea of hunting with bow and arrow—as if it made
any difference to a deer, how it died.

She hated the stealth and silence of the bow. With guns, you can
at least hear the enemy.

His name was Wayne Kunz, "Woody" Kunz, part owner of a
small auto parts store in Delaware Gap, New Jersey, known to his
circle of male friends as a good guy. A good sport. You might say,
a "character."

The way he dressed: his hunting gear, for instance.

A black simulated-leather jumpsuit, over it the regulation flu-
orescent-orange vest. A bright red cap, with earflaps. Boots to the
knee, like a Nazi storm trooper's; mirror sunglasses hiding his pale
lashless eyes. He had a large, round, singed-looking face, a small
damp mouth: this big-bellied, quick-grinning fellow, the kind who
keeps up a constant chatting murmur with himself, as if terrified of
silence, of being finally *alone*.

He hadn't been able to talk any of his friends into coming with
him, deer hunting with bow and arrow.

Even showing them his new Atlas bow, forty-eight inches, sleek
blond fiberglass "wood," showing them the quill of arrows, synthetic-
feathered, lightweight steel and steel-tipped and razor-sharp like no
Indian's arrows had ever been—he'd been disappointed, disgusted
with them, none of his friends wanting to come along, waking in the
predawn dark, driving out into Saugatuck County to kill a few deer.

Woody Kunz. Forty years old, five feet ten inches, two hundred
pounds. He'd been married, years ago, but the marriage hadn't
worked out, and there were no children.

Crashing clumsily through the underbrush, in pursuit of deer.

Not wanting to think he was lost—*was* he lost?

Talking to himself, cursing and begging himself—"C'mon,
Woody, for Christ's sake, Woody, move your fat *ass*"—half sobbing
as, another time, a herd of deer broke and scattered before he could
get into shooting range. Running and leaping through the woods,

taunting him with their uplifted white tails, erect snowy-white tails like targets so he couldn't help but fire off an arrow—to fly into space, disappear.

"Fuck it, Woody! Fuck you, asshole!"

Later. He's tired. Even with the sunglasses his eyes are seared from the bright winter sun reflecting on the snow. Knowing he deserves better.

Another time the deer are too quick and smart for him, must be they scented him downwind, breaking to run before he even saw them, only heard them, silent except for the sound of their crashing hooves. This time, he fires a shot knowing it won't strike any target, no warm living flesh. Must be he does it to make himself feel bad.

Playing the fool in the eyes of anybody watching and he can't help but think uneasily that somebody *is* watching—if only the unblinking eye of God.

And then: he sees the buck.

His buck, yes, suddenly. Oh, Jesus. His heart clenches, he *knows*.

He has surprised the beautiful dun-colored animal drinking from a fast-running stream; the stream is frozen except for a channel of black water at its center, the buck with its antlered head lowered. Woody Kunz stares, hardly able to believe his good luck, rapidly counting the points of the antlers—eight? ten?—as he fits an arrow into place with trembling fingers, lifts the bow, and sights along the arrow aiming for that point of the anatomy where neck and chest converge—it's a heart shot he hopes for—drawing back the arrow, feeling the power of the bow, releasing it; and seemingly in the same instant the buck leaps, the arrow has struck him in the neck, there's a shriek of animal terror and pain, and Woody Kunz shouts in ecstatic triumph.

But the buck isn't killed outright. To Woody's astonishment, and something like hurt, the buck turns and runs—flees.

Later he'd say he hadn't seen the NO TRESPASSING signs in the woods, he hadn't come by way of the road so he hadn't seen them there, the usual state-issued signs forbidding hunting, trapping, trespassing on private land, but Woody Kunz would claim he hadn't known it was private land exactly; he'd have to confess he might have been lost, tracking deer for hours moving more or less in a circle, not able to gauge where the center of the circle might be; and yes, he was excited, adrenaline rushing in his veins as he hadn't felt it in God knows how long, half a lifetime maybe, so he hadn't seen the signs posting the Snyder property or if he'd seen them they had not registered upon his consciousness or if they'd registered upon his consciousness he hadn't known what they were, so tattered and weatherworn.

That was Woody Kunz's defense, against a charge, if there was to be a charge, of unlawful trespassing and hunting on posted property.

Jesus is the most important person in all our lives!
Jesus abides in our hearts, no need to see Him!

These joyful pronóuncements, or are they commandments, Melanie Snyder sometimes hears, rising out of the silence of the old house. The wind in the eaves, a shrieking of crows in the orchard, and this disembodied voice, the voice of her long-dead fiancé—waking her suddenly from one of her reveries, so she doesn't remember where she is, what year this is, what has happened to her, to have aged her so.

She'd fallen in love with her brothers, one by one. Her tall strong indifferent brothers.

Much later, to everyone's surprise and certainly to her own, she'd fallen in love with a young Lutheran preacher, just her age.

Standing just her height. Smiling at her shyly, his wire-rimmed glasses winking as if shyly too. Shaking her gloved hand. Hello, Miss Snyder. Like a brother who would at last see *her*.

Twenty-eight years old! She'd been fated to be a spinster, of course. That plain, stubborn, sharp-tongued girl, eyes too large and stark and intelligent in her face to be "feminine," her body flat as a board.

In this place in which girls married as young as sixteen, began having their babies at seventeen, were valued and praised and loved for such qualities as they shared with brood mares and milking cows, you cultivated irony to save your soul—and your pride.

Except: she fell in love with the visiting preacher, introduced to him by family friends, the two "young people" urged together to speak stumblingly, clumsily to each other of—what? Decades later Melanie Snyder won't remember a syllable, but she remembers the young man's preaching voice, *Jesus! Jesus is our only salvation!* He'd gripped the edges of the pulpit of the Bethany church, God love shining in his face, white teeth bared like piano keys.

How it happened, how they became officially engaged—whether by their own decision or others'—they might not have been able to say. But it was time to marry, for both.

Plain, earnest, upright young people. Firm-believing Christians, of that there could be no doubt.

Did Melanie doubt? No, never!

She was prepared to be a Christian wife and to have her babies one by one. As God ordained.

There were passionate-seeming squeezes of her hand, there were chaste kisses, fluttery and insubstantial as a butterfly's wings. There were Sunday walks, in the afternoon. *Jesus is the most important person in my life, I feel Him close beside us—don't you, Melanie?*

The emptiness of the country lane, the silence of the sky, except for the crows' raucous jeering cries. Slow-spiraling hawks high overhead.

Oh, yes, certainly! Oh, yes.

Melanie Snyder's fiancé. The young just-graduated seminary student, with his hope to be a missionary. He was an energetic softball player, a pitcher of above-average ability; he led the Sunday school children on hikes, canoe trips. But he was most himself there in the pulpit of the Bethany church, elevated a few inches above the rapt congregation, where even his shy stammering rose to passion, a kind of sensual power. How strong the bones of his earnest, homely face, the fair-brown wings of hair brushed back neatly from his forehead! *Jesus, our redeemer. Jesus, our only salvation.* As if the God love shining in the young man's face were a beacon, a lighthouse beacon, flung out into the night, giving light yet unseeing, blind, in itself.

The engagement was never officially terminated. Always, there were sound reasons for postponing the wedding. Their families were disappointed but eager, on both sides, to comply. His letters came to her like clockwork, every two weeks, from North Carolina, where he was stationed as a chaplain in the U.S. Army. Dutiful letters, buoyant letters about his work, his "mission," his conviction that he was at last where God meant him to be.

Then the letters ceased. And they told Melanie he'd had an "accident" of some kind; there'd been a "misunderstanding" of some kind. He was discharged from his army post and reassigned to a Lutheran church in St. Louis, where he was to assist an older minister. But why? Melanie asked. Why, what has happened? Melanie demanded to know, but never was she told, never would a young woman be told such a thing, not for her ears, not for an ignorant virgin's ears; she'd wept and protested and mourned and lapsed finally into shame, not knowing what had happened to ruin her happiness but knowing it must constitute a rejection of her, a repudiation of the womanliness she'd tried so hard—ah, so shamefully hard!—to take on.

That feeling, that sense of unworthiness, she would retain for years. Studying her face in a mirror, plain, frank, unyielding, those eyes alit with irony, she realized she'd known all along—she was fated to be a spinster, never to be any man's wife.

And didn't that realization bring with it, in truth, relief?

Now, fifty years later, if those words *Jesus! Jesus abides in our hearts, no need to see Him!* ring out faintly in the silence of the old house, she turns aside, unhearing. For she's an old woman who has outlived such lies. Such subterfuge. She has taken revenge on Jesus Christ by ceasing to believe in Him—or in God, or in the Lutheran faith, or in such pieties as meekness, charity, love of one's enemies. Casting off her long-dead fiancé (who had not the courage even to write Melanie Snyder, finally, to release her from their engagement), she'd cast off his religion, as, drifting off from a friend, we lose the friends with whom he or she connected us, there being no deeper bond.

What is it?

She sees, in the lower pasture, almost out of the range of her vision, a movement of some kind: a swaying dun-colored shape, blurred by the frost on the aged glass. Standing in her kitchen, alert, aroused.

An animal of some kind? A large dog? A deer?

A wounded deer?

Melanie hurries to pull her sheepskin jacket from a peg; she's jamming her feet into boots, already angry, half knowing what she'll see.

Guns you could at least hear; now the slaughter is with bow and arrow. Grown men playing at Indians. Playing at killing.

The excuse is, the "excess" deer population in the county has to be kept down. White-tailed deer overbreeding, causing crop damage, auto accidents. As if men, the species of men who prowl the woods seeking innocent creatures to kill, need any excuse.

Melanie Snyder, who has known hunters all her life, including her own brothers, understands: to the hunter, killing an animal is just a substitute for killing another human being. Male, female. That's the forbidden fantasy.

She has never been frightened of accosting them, though, and she isn't now. Running outside into the gusty January air. A scowling wild-eyed old woman, sexless leathery face, white hair rising from her head in stiff tufts. She is wearing a soiled sheepskin jacket several sizes too large for her, a relic once belonging to one of her brothers; her boots are rubberized fishing boots, the castoffs of another, long-deceased brother.

Melanie is prepared for an ugly sight but this sight stuns her at first; she hears herself cry out, "Oh. Oh, God!"

A buck, full grown, beautiful, with handsome pointed antlers, is staggering in her direction, thrashing his head from side to side, desperate to dislodge an arrow that has penetrated his neck. His eyes roll in his head, his mouth is opening and closing spasmodically, blood flows bright and glistening from the wound; in fact it is two wounds, in the lower part of his neck near his left shoulder. Behind him, in the lower pasture, running clumsily after him, is the hunter, bow uplifted: a bizarre sight in black jumpsuit, bright orange vest, comical red hat. Like a robot or a spaceman, Melanie thinks, staring. She has never seen any hunter so costumed. Is this a man she should know? a face? a name? He's a hefty man with pale flushed skin, damp mouth, eyes hidden behind sunglasses with opaque mirrored lenses. His breath is steaming in the cold; he's clearly excited, agitated— dangerous. Fitting an arrow crookedly to his bow as if preparing, at this range, to shoot.

Melanie cries, "You! Get out of here!"

The hunter yells, "Lady, stand aside!"

"This land is posted! I'll call the sheriff!"

"Lady, you better gimme a clear shot!"

The buck is snorting, stamping his sharp-hooved feet in the snow. Deranged by terror and panic, he thrashes his antlered head from side to side, bleeding freely, bright-glistening blood underfoot, splattered onto Melanie Snyder's clothes as, instinctively, recklessly, she positions herself between the wounded animal and the hunter. She's pleading, angry. "Get off my land! Haven't you done enough evil? This poor creature! Let him alone!"

The hunter, panting, gaping at her, can't seem to believe what he sees: a white-haired woman in men's clothes, must be eighty years old, trying to shield a buck with an arrow through his neck. He advances to within a few yards of her, tries to circle around her. Saying incredulously, "That's my arrow, for Christ's sake, lady! That buck's a goner and he's *mine!*"

"Brute! Murderer! I'm telling you to get off my land or I'll call the sheriff and have you arrested!"

"Lady, that buck is goddamned dangerous—you better stand aside."

"*You* stand aside. Get off my property!"

"Lady, for Christ's sake—"

"You heard me: *get off my property!*"

So, for some minutes, there's an impasse.

Forever afterward Woody Kunz will remember, to his chagrin and shame: the beautiful white-tailed full-grown buck with the most amazing spread of antlers he'd ever seen—*his* buck, *his* kill, *his* arrow sticking through the animal's neck—the wounded buck snorting, thrashing his head, stamping the ground, blood everywhere, blood-tinged saliva hanging from his mouth in threads, and the crazy old woman shielding the buck with her body, refusing to surrender him to his rightful owner. And Woody Kunz is certain *he* is the rightful owner; he's shouting in the old woman's face, he's pleading with her, practically begging, finally; the fucking deer is *his*, he's earned it, he's been out tramping in the cold since seven this morning, God damn it if he's going to give up! Face blotched and hot, tears of rage and impotence stinging his eyes: oh, Jesus, he'd grab the old hag by the shoulders, lift her clear, and fire another arrow this time into the heart so there'd be no doubt—except, somehow, he doesn't do it, doesn't dare.

Instead, he backs off. Still with his bow upraised, his handsome brand-new Atlas bow from Sears, but the arrow droops useless in his fingers.

In a voice heavy with disgust, sarcasm, he says, "OK. OK, lady, you win."

The last glimpse Woody Kunz has of this spectacle, the old woman is trying clumsily to pull the arrow out of the buck's neck, and the buck is naturally putting up a struggle, swiping at her with his antlers, but weakly, sinking to his knees in the snow, then scrambling to his feet again; still the old woman persists; sure, she *is* crazy and deserves whatever happens to her, the front of her sheepskin jacket soaked in blood by now, blood even on her face, in her hair.

It isn't until late afternoon, hours later, that Woody Kunz returns home.

Having gotten lost in the countryside, wandered in circles in the woods, couldn't locate the road he'd parked his goddamned car on, muttering to himself, sick and furious and shamed, in a state of such agitation his head feels close to bursting, guts like a nest of tangled snakes. Never, *never*, is Woody Kunz going to live down this humiliation in his own eyes.

So he's decided not to tell anyone. Not even to fashion it into an anecdote to entertain his friends: Woody Kunz being cheated out of a twelve-point buck by an old lady? Shit, he'd rather die than have it known.

Sure, it crosses his mind he should maybe report the incident to the sheriff. Not to reiterate his claim of the deer—though the deer *is* his—but to report the old woman in case she's really in danger. Out there, seemingly alone, so old, in the middle of nowhere. A mortally wounded full-grown whitetail buck, crazed with pain and terror, like a visitation of God, in her care.

She's begging, desperate: "*Let* me help you, oh, please! Oh, please! Let me—"

Tugging at the terrible arrow, tugging forward, tugging back, her fingers slippery with blood. Woman and beast struggling, the one disdainful, even reckless, of her safety; the other dazed by trauma or loss of blood, not lashing out as ordinarily he would, to attack an enemy, with bared teeth, antlers, sharp hooves—

"Oh, please, you must not die, please—"

It's probable that Melanie Snyder has herself become deranged. All of the world having shrunk to the task at hand, to the forcible removal of this steel bar that has penetrated the buck's neck, fifteen-inch steel-glinting sharp-tipped arrow with white, synthetic quills—nothing matters but that *the arrow must be removed*.

The bulging eyes roll upward, there's bloody froth at the shuddering nostrils, she smells, tastes, the hot rank breath—then the antlers strike her in the chest, she's falling, crying out in surprise.

And the buck has pushed past her, fleeing on skidding hooves, on legs near buckling at the knees, so strangely—were she fully conscious she would realize, *so* strangely—into her father's house.

It won't be until three days later, at about this hour of the morning, that they'll discover her—or the body she has become. Melanie Snyder and the buck with the arrow through his neck.

But Melanie Snyder has no sense of what's coming, no cautionary fear. As if, this damp-gusty January morning, such a visitation, such urgency pressed upon her, has blotted out all anticipation of the future, let alone of danger.

In blind panic, voiding his bowels, the buck has run crashing into the old farmhouse, into the kitchen, through to the parlor; as Melanie Snyder sits dazed on the frozen ground beneath her rear stoop he turns, furious, charges into a corner of the room, collides with an upright piano, making a brief discordant startled music, an explosion of muted notes; turns again, crashing into a table laden with family photographs, a lamp of stippled milk glass with a fluted shade. A renewed rush of adrenaline empowers him; turning again, half rearing, hooves skidding on the thin loose-lying Oriental carpet faded to near transparency, he charges his reflection in a mirror as, out back, Melanie Snyder sits trying to summon her strength, trying to comprehend what has happened and what she must do.

She doesn't remember the buck having knocked her down, thus can't believe he *has* attacked her.

She thinks, Without me, he is doomed.

She hears one of her brothers speaking harshly, scolding: What is she doing there sitting on the ground?—*For the Lord's sake, Melanie!*—but she ignores him, testing her right ankle, the joint is livid with pain but not broken—she can shift her weight to her other foot—a high-pitched ringing in her head as of church bells, and where there should be terror there's determination, for Melanie Snyder is an independent woman, a woman far too proud to accept, let alone solicit, her neighbors' proffered aid since the death of the last of her brothers: she wills herself not to succumb to weakness now, in this hour of her trial.

Managing to get to her feet, moving with calculating slowness. As if her bones are made of glass.

Overhead, an opaque January sky, yet beautiful. Like slightly tarnished mother-of-pearl.

Except for the crows in their gathering place beyond the barns, and the hoarse *uh-uh-uh* of her breathing: silence.

She enters the house. By painful inches, yet eagerly. Leaning heavily against the door frame.

She sees the fresh blood trail, sees and smells the moist animal droppings, so shocking, there on the kitchen floor she keeps clean with a pointless yet self-satisfying fanaticism, the aged linoleum worn nearly colorless, yes, but Melanie has a house owner's pride, and pride is all. The buck in his frenzy to escape the very confines he has plunged into is turning, rearing, snorting, crashing in the other room. Melanie calls, "I'm here! I will help you!"—blindly too entering the parlor with its etiolated light, tasseled shades drawn to cover three quarters of the windows as, decades ago, Melanie Snyder's mother had so drawn them, to protect the furnishings against the sun. Surely she's a bizarre sight herself, drunk-swaying, staggering, her wrinkled face, hands glistening with blood, white hair in tufts as if she hasn't taken a brush to it in weeks, Melanie Snyder in the oversized sheepskin jacket she wears in town, driving a rusted Plymouth pickup truck with a useless muffler—everybody in Bethany knows Melanie Snyder though she doesn't know them, carelessly confuses sons with fathers, granddaughters with mothers, her own remote blood relations with total strangers—she's awkward in these rubberized boots many sizes too large for her shrunken feet, yet reaching out—unhesitantly, boldly—to the maddened buck who crouches in a corner facing her, his breath frothing in blood, in erratic shuddering waves, she is speaking softly, half begging, "I want to help you! Oh—" as the heavy head dips, the antlers rush at her— how astonishing the elegance of such male beauty, and the burden of it, God's design both playful and deadly shrewd, the strangeness of bone growing out of flesh, bone calcified and many-branched as a young apple tree—clumsily he charges this woman who is his enemy even as, with a look of startled concern, she opens her arms to him, the sharp antlers now striking her a second time in the chest and this time breaking her fragile collarbone as easily as one might break a chicken wishbone set to dry on a windowsill for days, and the momentum of his charge carries him helplessly forward, he falls, the arrow's quill brushing against Melanie Snyder's face; as he scrambles in a frenzy to upright himself his sharp hooves catch her in the chest, belly, pelvis; he has fallen heavily, as if from a great height, as if flung down upon her, breath in wheezing shudders and the blood froth bubbling around his mouth, and Melanie Snyder lies pinned beneath the animal body, legs gone, lower part of her body gone, a void of numbness, not even pain, distant from her as something seen through the wrong end of a telescope, rapidly retreating.

How did it happen, how strange; they were of the same height now, or nearly: Melanie Snyder and her tall strong indifferent brothers. Never married, none of them, d'you know why? No woman was ever quite good enough for the Snyder boys, and the girl, Melanie— well, one look at her and you know: a born spinster.

It's more than thirty years after they informed her, guardedly, without much sympathy—for perhaps sympathy would have invited tears, and they were not a family comfortable with tears—that her fiancé had been discharged from the army, that Melanie dares to ask, shyly, without her customary aggressiveness, what had really happened, what the mysterious "accident," or was it a "misunderstanding," had been. And her brother, her elder by six years, an aged slope-shouldered man with a deeply creased face, sighs and passes his hand over his chin and says, in a tone of mild but unmistakable contempt, "Don't ask."

She lies there beneath the dying animal, then beneath the lifeless stiffening body, face no more than four inches from the great head, the empty eyes—how many hours she's conscious, she can't gauge.

At first calling, into the silence, "Help—help me! Help—"

There *is* a telephone in the kitchen; rarely does it ring, and when it rings Melanie Snyder frequently ignores it, doesn't want people inquiring after her, well-intentioned neighbors, good Lutherans from the church she hasn't set foot in, except for funerals, in twenty-odd years.

The dying animal, beautiful even in dying, bleeding to death, soaking Melanie Snyder's clothes with his blood, and isn't she bleeding too, from wounds in her throat and face, her hands?

And he's dead, she feels the life pass from him—"Oh, no, oh, *no*," sobbing and pushing at the body, warm sticky blood by degrees cooling and congealing—the wood-fire stove in the kitchen has gone out and cold eases in from out-of-doors; in fact the kitchen door must be open, creaking and banging in the wind. A void rises from the loose-fitting floorboards as from the lower part of Melanie's body; she's sobbing as if her heart is broken, she's furious, trying to lift the heavy body from her, clawing at the body, raking her torn nails and bleeding fingers against the buck's thick winter coat, a coarse-haired furry coat, but the buck's body will not budge.

The weight of Death, so much more powerful than life.

Later. She wakes moaning and delirious, a din as of sleet pellets against the windows, and the cold has congealed the buck's blood and her own, the numbness has moved higher, obliterating much of what she has known as "body" these eighty-odd years; she understands that she is dying—consciousness like a fragile bubble, or a skein of bubbles—yet she is able still to wish to summon her old strength, the bitter joy of her stubborn strength, pushing at the heavy animal body, dead furry weight, eyes sightless as glass and the arrow, the terrible arrow, the obscene arrow: "Let me *go*. Let me *free*."

Fainting and waking. Drifting in and out of consciousness.

Hearing that faint ringing voice in the eaves, as always subtly chiding, in righteous reproach of Melanie Snyder, mixed with the wind and that profound agelessness of wind as if blowing to us from the farthest reaches of time as well as space—*Jesus! Jesus is our only salvation! Jesus abides in our hearts!*—but in pride she turns aside unhearing; never has she begged, nor will she beg now. Oh, never.

And does she regret her gesture, trying to save an innocent beast? She does not.

And would she consent, even now, to having made a mistake, acted improvidently? She would not.

When after nearly seventy-two hours Woody Kunz overcomes his manly embarrassment and notifies the Saugatuck County sheriff's office of the "incident" on the Snyder farm and they go out to investigate, they find eighty-two-year-old Melanie Snyder dead, pinned beneath the dead whitetail buck, in the parlor of the old farmhouse in which no one outside the Snyder family had stepped for many years. An astonishing sight: human and animal bodies virtually locked together in the rigor of death, their mingled blood so soaked into Melanie Snyder's clothes, so frozen, it is possible to separate them only by force.

YARROW

He was afraid to borrow the money from a bank.

It was a Saturday morning in early April, still winter, soft wet snow falling, clumps the size of blossoms.

A messy season, flu season, dirt-raddled snow drifted against the edges of things, mud thawing on the roads. A cavernous-clouded sky and blinding sunshine, and it was the longest drive he'd made in his truck in memory, three miles to his cousin Tyrone Clayton's house.

Tyrone saw it in his face. Asked him inside, asked him did he want an ale? Irene and the children were in town shopping.

The radio was turned up loud: Fats Domino singing "Blueberry Hill."

Mud on Jody's boots so he said he wouldn't come all the way into the house, he'd talk from the doorway. Didn't want to track up Irene's clean floor.

He could only stay a minute, he said. He had a favor to ask.

"Sure," Tyrone said. Laying his cigarette carefully in an ashtray.

"I need to borrow some money."

"How much?"

"Five hundred dollars."

Jody spoke in a low quick voice just loud enough for Tyrone to hear. Then exhaled as if he'd been holding his breath in for a long time.

Tyrone said, keeping his voice level and easy, "Guess I can manage that."

"I'll pay you back as soon as I can," Jody said. "By June at the latest."

"No hurry," Tyrone said.

Then they were silent. Breathing hard. Excited, deeply embarrassed. Tyrone knew that Jody needed more than $500—much more than $500—but the way things were right now he couldn't afford to lend him more. He just couldn't afford it, and even $500 was going to be hard. He knew that Jody knew all this but Jody had had to come to him anyway, knowing it, asking the favor, knowing that Tyrone would say yes but knowing that Tyrone could barely afford it either. Because Jody was desperate, and if Tyrone hadn't quite wanted to understand that until this minute he had to understand it now.

His cousin's young aggrieved handsome face inside a sallow face blurred and pocked by fatigue. Three days' growth of whiskers on his chin and he wouldn't meet Tyrone's eyes, he was that ashamed.

Tyrone said he could get to the bank Monday noon, would that be soon enough?

Jody said as if he hadn't been listening that he wanted to pay the going rate of interest on the loan. "Ask them at the bank, will you? And we'll work it out."

"Hell, no," Tyrone said, laughing, surprised. "I don't want any interest."

"Just find out," Jody said, an edge to his voice, "and we'll work it out."

Tyrone asked how was Brenda these days, he'd heard from Irene she was getting better? But his voice came out weak and faltering.

Jody said she *was* getting better, she rested a lot during the day, the stitches from the surgery had come out, but she still had a lot of pain and the doctor warned them about rushing things so she had to take it slow.

He did the grocery shopping, for instance. All the shopping. Not that he minded—he didn't, he was damned glad Brenda was alive—but it took time and he only had Saturdays really.

Then this afternoon if the snow didn't get worse he was hoping to put in a shift at the quarry, three or four hours. Shoveling, mainly, some cleanup.

He was speaking faster, with more feeling. A raw baffled voice new to him, and his eyes puffy and red-rimmed as if he'd been rubbing at them.

All this while Jody's truck was idling in the driveway, spewing out clouds of exhaust. He'd left the key in the ignition, which Tyrone thought was a strange thing to do, almost rude.

Snowflakes were falling thicker now, blown in delicate skeins by the wind. Twisting and turning and looping like narrowing your eyes to shift your vision out of focus so that it's your own nerve endings you see out there.

Wet air, colder than the temperature suggested. Flu season, and everybody was passing it around to everybody else.

Something more needed to be said before Jody left, but Tyrone couldn't think what it was.

He stood in the doorway watching Jody maneuver the truck out onto the road. It was a heavy-duty dump truck, Jody's own truck, a '49 Ford he'd have to be replacing soon. Tyrone was thinking they should have shaken hands or something, but it wasn't a gesture that came naturally or easily to them. He couldn't remember when he had last shaken hands with somebody as close to him as Jody, and this morning wasn't the time to start.

He watched Jody drive away. He hadn't gotten around to shaving yet that morning himself and he stood vague and dazed, rubbing his stubbled jaw, thinking how much it had cost Jody McIllvanney to ask for that $500, and how much it would cost him.

For the past year or more Jody's wife, Brenda, had been sick. Twenty-eight years old, thin, nervous, red-haired, pretty, she'd had four children now ranging in age from Dawn, who was thirteen years old and said to be troublesome, to the baby boy, who was only eighteen months. In between were two more boys, ten years and six years. Brenda had never quite recovered from the last pregnancy, came down with a bladder infection, had to have an operation just after Christmas—at a city hospital forty miles away, which meant people in Yarrow had to drive eighty miles round trip to see her.

Which meant, too, more medical bills the McIllvanneys couldn't afford.

The day before she was scheduled to enter the hospital, Brenda spoke with Irene Clayton on the phone and said she was frightened she was going to die.

"Don't talk that way," Irene said sharply.

Brenda was crying as if her heart was broken, and Irene was afraid she too would start to cry.

"I just don't think Jody could manage without me," Brenda was saying. "Him and the children—and all the bills we owe—I just don't think he could keep going."

"You know better than to talk that way," Irene said. "That's a terrible thing to say." She listened to Brenda crying and felt helpless and frightened herself. She said, "You hadn't better let Jody hear you going on like that."

The McIllvanneys lived in Brenda's parents' old farmhouse, which wasn't by choice but all they could afford. Some years ago Jody had started building his own house at the edge of town but he ran out of money shortly after the basement was finished—Jody was a trucker, self-employed; his work tended to be local, seasonal, not very reliable—and for more than a year the family lived in the basement, below ground. (The roof was tarpapered over and there were windows but still the big single room was damp, chilly, depressing; the children were always coming down with colds. Dawn called it a damn dumb place to live, no wonder the kids on the school bus laughed at them all. Living like rats in a hole!) After Brenda's mother died they moved into the old farmhouse, which was free and clear, no mortgage, except it had been built in the 1880s and was termite-ridden and needed repairs constantly. Rotting shingles, leaky roof, earthen cellar that flooded when it rained: you name it. Bad as the *Titanic*, Jody said. He wished the damn thing *would* sink.

When Brenda got pregnant for the fourth time Jody began working part-time at the limestone quarry in Yarrow Falls: hard filthy backbreaking work he hated, but it paid better than anything else he could find. Jody handled a shovel, he climbed ladders, he operated drills and tractors and wire saws; when it rained he stood in the pit, water to his knees, coughing up phlegm, his feet aching as if they were on fire. Just temporary work he hoped wouldn't kill him.

Worse yet, he told Tyrone, he might develop a taste for the quarry. Like most of the quarriers. The limestone, the open fresh air, the weird machines that were so noisy and dangerous—it was work not just anybody could do. You had to have a strong back and the guts for it, and anything like that, it tended to get under your skin if you weren't careful. It brought some pride with it after all.

The Clayton children, Janice and Bobby, were fond of their Uncle Jody, as they were taught to call him—Janice knew he was really a cousin of theirs, just as he was a cousin of their father's—except when he was in one of his bad moods. Then he wouldn't really look at them, he'd just mutter hello without smiling. He had a worse temper than their father, and he was a bigger man than their father: muscled arms and shoulders that looked as if they were pumped up and that the flesh would hurt, ropy veins, and skin stretched tight. But he could be funny, loud-laughing as a kid, with a broad side-slanting grin and a way of teasing that left you breathless and excited as if you'd been tickled with quick hard fingers. Their own father was lean and hard and soft-spoken, an inch or two shorter than his cousin. He worked at the Allis Chalmers plant in town and never had anything interesting to say about it—just that it was *work*, and it *paid*—while Jody had all sorts of tales, some believable and some not, about driving his truck. "Never a dull minute with Jody around!" Irene always said. Tyrone said that was true, but "You know how he exaggerates."

One summer when Janice was a small child her Uncle Jody came over to the house with a half-dozen guinea chicks in a cardboard box, a present for them, and Janice had loved the chicks, tiny enough to stand in the palm of her hand; they didn't weigh anything! No feathers like the adults, just fuzzy blond down, stubby wings, and legs disproportionately long for their bodies. They were fearless, unlike the adults that were so suspicious and nerved up all the time.

"They're pretty birds," Jody said. "I like seeing them around the place—you get kind of used to them."

The Claytons tried to raise the guinea fowl according to Jody's instructions but they died off one by one and in the end even Janice lost her enthusiasm for them. She'd given them special names—

Freckles, Peewee, Queenie, Bathsheba—but they disappointed her because all they wanted to do was eat.

They only liked her, she said, because she fed them.

After Jody borrowed the $500 from Tyrone he didn't drop by the house for a long time. And Tyrone didn't seek him out, feeling embarrassed and uncomfortable: he didn't want Jody to think he was waiting to be paid back or even that he was thinking about the money.

(Was he thinking about it? Only occasionally, when it hit him like a blow to the gut.)

Irene didn't hear from Brenda very often either, which was strange, she said, and sad, and she hoped the money wouldn't come between them because Brenda was so sweet and such a good friend and needed somebody to talk to what with Jody and Jody's moods—and that Dawn was a handful too, judging from what Janice said. (Dawn was a year older than Janice but in her class at school.) Irene said, "Why don't we invite them over here for a supper or something? We haven't done that in a long time." But Tyrone thought the McIllvanneys might misunderstand. "He'll think I'm worried about that money," Tyrone said.

It wasn't until midsummer that Jody made what he called the first payment on the loan, $175 he gave Tyrone in an envelope, and Tyrone was relieved, and embarrassed, and tried to tell him why not keep it for a while since probably he needed it—didn't he need it?—and there wasn't any hurry anyway. But Jody insisted. Jody said it was the least he could do.

Then word got back to Tyrone that Jody had borrowed money from a mutual friend of theirs at about the time he'd borrowed the $500 from Tyrone *and he had paid all of it back*: $350, and he'd paid it all back in a lump sum, and Tyrone was damned mad to hear about it. Irene tried to tell him it didn't mean anything, only that Jody knew Tyrone better, was closer to Tyrone, like a brother; also, if he'd only borrowed $350 from the other man it was easier to pay it all back and close out the debt. Sure, said Tyrone. That makes me the chump.

But he didn't mean it and when, a few days or a week later, Irene brought the subject up again, wondering when Jody was going to pay the rest of the money, he cut her off short, saying it was his

money, not hers, and it was between him and Jody and hadn't anything to do with her, did she understand that?

Janice didn't want to tell her mother, but when they went back
to school in the fall Dawn McIllvanney began to behave mean to
her. And Dawn could be really mean when she wanted to be.

She was a chunky thick-set girl, swarthy skin like her father's,
sly eyes, a habit of grinning so it went through you like a sliver of
glass; not a bit of friendliness in it. Called Janice "*Jan*-y" in a sliding
whine and shoved her on the school bus or when they were waiting
in the cafeteria line. "Oh, excuse me, *Jan*-y!" she'd say, making anyone who was listening laugh. Dawn was the center of a circle of four
or five girls who were rough and pushy and loud, belligerent as boys;
she got poor grades in school not because she was stupid—though
she might have been a little slow—but because she made a show of
not trying, not handing in homework, wising off in class and angering
her teachers. Janice thought it was unfair that Dawn McIllvanney
had such a pretty red-haired mother while she had a mother who
was like anybody's mother—plain and pleasant and boring. She'd
always thought, before the trouble started, that Brenda McIllvanney
would rather have had *her* for a daughter than Dawn.

Janice soon understood that Dawn hated her and she'd better
keep her distance from her, but it happened that in gym class she
couldn't and that was where Dawn got her revenge: threw a basketball
right into Janice's face one time, broke Janice's pink plastic glasses,
claimed afterward it was an accident: "*Jan*-y" got in her way. Another
time, when the girls were doing gymnastics, Dawn stuck her big
sneakered foot out in front of Janice as Janice—who was wiry and
quick, one of the best gymnasts in the class—did a series of cartwheels
the full length of the mat, and naturally Janice fell, fell sideways, fell
hard, seeing as she fell her cousin's face pinched with hatred, the
rat-glittering little eyes. Pain shot like a knife, like many knives,
through Janice's body, and for a long time she couldn't move—just
lay there sobbing, hearing Dawn McIllvanney's mock-incredulous
voice as the gym instructor reprimanded her. *Hey, I didn't do anything, what the hell are you saying? Look, it was her, she's the one, it
was her own damn fault, the little crybaby!*

Janice never told her mother about the incident. She tried not to think that Dawn, who was her cousin after all, had wanted to hurt her really—break her neck or her backbone, cripple her for life. She tried not to think that.

One warm autumn day Irene Clayton met Brenda McIllvanney in the A&P in town—Brenda, whom she hadn't seen in months— Brenda, who was thin, almost gaunt, but wearing a flowery print dress—red lipsticked lips and hard red nails and a steely look that went through Irene like a razor. And Irene just stood there staring as if the earth had opened at her feet.

In her parked car in the lot Irene leaned her forehead against the steering wheel and began to cry. She made baffled sobbing sounds that astonished and deeply embarrassed the children; Janice and Bobby had never seen their mother cry in such a public place, and for so little reason they could understand. She usually wept in a rage at them!

Bobby threw himself against the back seat, pressing his hands over his ears. Janice, in the passenger's seat, looked out the window and said, "Momma, you're making a fool of yourself," in the coldest voice possible.

Tyrone wasn't accustomed to thinking about such things, poking into his own motives or other people's. But he'd known, he said. As soon as he'd handed Jody the money, that was it.

Irene said she didn't believe it.

She knew Brenda, and she knew Jody, and she didn't believe it.

Jody had thanked him but he hadn't wanted to look at him, Tyrone said. Took the money 'cause he couldn't not take it but that was that.

"I don't believe it, *really*," Irene said, wiping at her eyes.

Tyrone said nothing, lighting up a cigarette, shaking out the match. His movements were jerky and angry these days, these many days. Often it looked as if he was quarreling with someone under his breath. Irene said, "I don't believe it, *really*."

Jody sold his truck, gave up trucking for good, worked full-time now at the limestone quarry, still in debt, and that old house of theirs looked worse than ever—chickens and guinea fowl picking in the grassless front yard amid tossed-out trash, Brenda's peony beds overgrown with weeds as if no woman lived in the house at all—but still, somehow, Jody managed to buy a '53 Chevrolet up in Yarrow Falls, and he and Brenda were going out places together again, roadhouses and taverns miles away where no one knew them. Sometimes they were alone and sometimes they were with another couple. Their old friends rarely saw them now.

Tyrone was always hearing from relatives that the McIllvanneys couldn't seem to climb out of their bad luck, though Jody was working ten, twelve hours a day at the quarry et cetera, poor Brenda had some kind of thyroid condition now and had to take medicine so expensive you couldn't believe it et cetera, and Tyrone listened ironically to all this and said, "OK, but what about me? *What about me?*" And there never seemed to be any answer to that.

If Tyrone ran into Jody in town it was sheerly by accident. And damned clumsy and embarrassing: Jody pretended he didn't see Tyrone, turned nonchalantly away, whistling, hands in his pockets: turned a corner and walked fast and disappeared.

Asshole. As if Tyrone didn't see *him.*

Tyrone complained freely of his cousin to anyone who would listen: old friends, mutual acquaintances, strangers. He was baffled and bitter and hurt and furious, wondering aloud when he'd get his money back. And would he get it *with interest* as Jody had promised.

When he'd been drinking a bit, Tyrone said that nobody had ever thought Jody McIllvanney would turn out the way he had, a man whose word wasn't worth shit—not much better than a common crook—a man who couldn't even support his wife and children. "Anybody that bad off, he might as well hang himself," Tyrone would say. "Stick a shotgun barrel into his mouth and pull the trigger."

He had to stop thinking about Jody all the time, Irene said. She was getting scared he'd make himself sick.

She'd lain awake too many nights herself thinking about the McIllvanneys—Brenda in particular—and she wasn't going to think about them any longer. "It isn't healthy," she said, pleaded. "Ty? It eats away at your heart."

But Tyrone ignored her; he was calculating (sitting at the kitchen table, a sheet of paper before him, pencil in hand, bottle of Molson's

Ale at his elbow) how much Jody was probably earning a week up at the Falls now that he'd been promoted from shoveler to drill runner. It made him sick to think that—subtracting union dues, Social Security, and the rest—Jody was probably making a few more dollars a week than he made at Allis Chalmers. And if Jody could get an extra shift time-and-a-half on Saturdays he'd be making a damn sight more.

When Tyrone stood he felt dizzy and panicky, as if the floor was tilting beneath his feet.

Most people in Yarrow were on Tyrone's side, but he sensed there were some on Jody's side and lately he'd begun to hear that Jody was saying things about *him*, bad-mouthing him so you'd almost think it was Tyrone Clayton who owed Jody McIllvanney money and not the other way around. Hadn't Jody helped him put asbestos siding on his house when he and Irene had first moved in? (Yes, but he, Tyrone, had helped Jody with that would-be house of his, helping to put in the concrete, lay the beams for the basement ceiling, tar-paper the goddamned roof in the middle of the summer.) Tyrone went out drinking to the places he'd always gone and there were the men he'd been seeing for years, men he'd gone to school with, but Jody wasn't there; there was a queer sort of authority in Jody's absence, as if, the more *he* said, the more his listeners were inclined to believe *Jody*. "I know things are still bad for Jody and Brenda," he'd say, speaking passionately, conscious of the significance of his words—which might be repeated after all to Jody—"and I don't even want the fucking money back, but I do want respect. I do want respect from that son of a bitch."

(Though in fact he did want the money back: every penny of it. And he tended to think Jody still owed him $500, the original sum, plus interest, no matter he'd insisted at the time of the loan that he didn't want "interest" from any blood relation.)

There were nights he came home drunk; other nights he was so agitated he couldn't sit still to eat his supper because he'd heard something at work that day reported back to him, and Irene tried to comfort him, Irene said he was frightening the children, Irene said in a pleading voice, Why not try to forget?—forgive? like in the Bible; wasn't that real wisdom?—and just not lend anybody any money ever again in his life. "What the hell was I supposed to do?" Tyrone would say, turning on her furiously. "Tell my own cousin I grew up with that I wouldn't help him out? Tell him to get out of that doorway there?" Irene backed off, saying, "Ty, I don't know what you were supposed to do, but it turned out a mistake, didn't it?" And Tyrone said, his face contorted with rage and his voice shaking, "It wasn't a mistake at the time, you stupid bitch. *It wasn't a mistake at the time.*"

One night that fall the telephone rang at 9 P.M. and Irene answered and it was Jody McIllvanney, whose voice she hadn't heard in a long time, drunk and belligerent and demanding to speak to Tyrone—who luckily wasn't home. So Jody told Irene to tell him he'd been hearing certain things that Tyrone was saying behind his back and he didn't like what he'd heard and if Tyrone had something to say to him why not come over to the house and tell it to his face, and if Tyrone was afraid to do that he'd better keep his mouth shut or *he'd* come over *there* and beat the shit out of Tyrone.

Jody was shouting, saying he'd pay back the goddamn money when he could, that was the best he could do; he hadn't asked to be born; that was the best he could do, goddamn it—and Irene, speechless, terrified, slammed down the receiver.

Afterward she said she'd never heard anyone anywhere sounding so crazy. Like he'd have killed her if he'd been able to get hold of her.

A chilly breezy November day but there was Jody McIllvanney in coveralls and a T-shirt, no jacket, bareheaded, striding along the sidewalk not looking where he was going: and Janice Clayton stared at him, shocked at how he'd changed—my God he was big now, what you'd call *fat!*—weighing maybe two hundred sixty pounds, barrel-chested, big jiggly stomach pressing against the fabric of his coveralls, his face bloated too and his skin lumpy. It was said that stone quarriers ate and drank like hogs, got enormous, and there was Jody the shape of a human hog, even his hair long and shaggy, greasy, like a high school kid or a Hell's Angel. Janice stood frozen on the sidewalk, her schoolbooks pressed against her chest, hoping praying her Uncle Jody wouldn't glance up and see her or if he did he wouldn't recognize her though her heart kicked and she thought, *I don't hate him like I'm supposed to.*

But he looked up. He saw her. Saw how she was shrinking out toward the curb to avoid him and so he let her go, just mumbled a greeting she couldn't hear, and the moment was past, she was safe, she pushed her glasses up her nose and half ran up the street to escape. She remembered how he used to call out "How's it going?" to her and Bobby instead of saying hello—winking to show that it was a joke (what did any adult man care about how things were going for children) but serious in a way too. And she'd never known how to answer, nor had Bobby. "OK," they'd say, embarrassed, blushing, flattered. "All right, I guess."

(Janice had no anticipation, not the mildest of premonitions, that that would be the last time she'd see her Uncle Jody, but long afterward the sight of him would remain vivid in her memory, powerful, reproachful, and the November day too of gusty winds and the smell of snow in the air, a texture like grit. Waiting for the bus she was dreamy and melancholy, watching how the town's southside mills gave off smoke that rose into the air like mist. Powdery, almost iridescent, those subtle shifting colors of the backs of pigeons— iridescent gray, blue, purple shading into black.

The guinea fowl had long since died off but Janice had snapshots of her favorites, their names carefully recorded.)

Shortly after the New Year, Tyrone was driving to town when he saw a man hitchhiking by the side of the road, and sure enough it was Jody McIllvanney: Jody in his sheepskin jacket, a wool cap pulled low over his forehead, thumb uplifted. His face looked closed in as a fist; he might have recognized Tyrone but gave no sign just as Tyrone, speeding past, gave no sign of recognizing him. It had all happened so swiftly Tyrone hadn't time to react. He wondered if Jody's new car had broken down and he laughed aloud harshly, thinking, Good. Serve him right. Serve them all right.

He watched his cousin's figure in the rearview mirror, diminishing with distance.

Then, for some reason he'd never be able to explain, he decided to turn his car around, drive back to Jody; maybe he'd slow down and shout something out the window or maybe—just maybe—he'd give the son of a bitch a ride if it looked like that might be a good idea. But as he approached Jody it was clear that Jody intended to stand his ground, didn't want any favors from him: you could see from his arrogant stance that he'd rather freeze his ass off than beg a ride from Tyrone; he'd lowered his arm and stood there in the road, legs apart, waiting. A big beefy glowering man you could tell wanted a fight even without knowing who he was.

Tyrone's heart swelled with fury and righteousness.

Tyrone hit the horn with the palm of his hand to scare the son of a bitch off the road.

He was laughing, shouting, *Thief! Liar! Lying betraying bastard!*

What did he do then but call Jody's bluff, aim the car straight at him, fifty miles an hour, and he'd lost control even before he hit a patch of cobbled ridged ice and began to skid—hardly had time before the impact to turn the wheel, pump desperately at the brakes—and he saw his cousin's look of absolute disbelief, not even fear or surprise, as the left fender slammed into him and the chassis plowed into his body and threw it aside and out of Tyrone's sight.

The steering wheel caught Tyrone in the chest. But he was all right. He was coughing, choking, but he was all right, gripping the wheel tight and pumping the brakes as the car leveled out of its wild swerve and came to a bumpy rest in a ditch. Scrub trees and tall grasses clawing at the windshield and Jesus, his nose was bleeding and he couldn't see anything in the rearview mirror but he knew Jody was dead: that sickening thud, that enormous impact like a man-sized boulder flung against the car, that's what it meant.

"Jesus."

Tyrone sat panting in his car, the motor racing, clouds of exhaust lifting behind; he was terrified, his bladder contracted, heart pumping like crazy, and it couldn't have happened, could it, that quickly?—hairline cracks on his windshield and his nose clogged with blood?—except he'd felt the body snapping beneath the car; it wasn't something you were likely to mistake as anything but death.

He didn't have to drive back another time. Didn't have to see the bright blood on the snow.

He pressed his forehead against the steering wheel. A terrible hammering in his chest he'd have to wait out.

"Damn you, fuck you, *Jody*. . . ."

Tyrone busied himself maneuvering his car out of the ditch, rocking the chassis, concentrating on the effort, which involved his entire physical being; he was panting, grunting, whispering *C'mon baby c'mon for Christ's sweet sake*; then he was free and clear and back on the road and no one knew.

He'd begun to shiver convulsively. Though he was sweating too inside his clothes. And his bladder pinched in terror as he hadn't felt it in a long, long time.

But he was all right, wasn't he? And the car was operating.

He drove on, slowly at first, then panic hit him in a fresh wave and he began to drive faster, thinking he was going in the wrong direction but he had to get somewhere—where?—had to get help.

Police, ambulance. He'd go home and telephone.

There's a man dead on the road. Hitchhiker and he'd stepped in front of the car and it was over in an instant.

Blood dripping from his nose onto his fucking jacket and those hairline cracks in the windshield, like cracks in his own skull. He was crying, couldn't stop.

He'd tell Irene to make the call. Wouldn't tell her who it was he'd hit. Then he'd drive back to Jody, *Hey, you know I didn't mean it why the hell didn't you get out of the way I was just kidding around, then the ice, why the hell didn't you get out of the way goddamn you you did it on purpose didn't you—*

But maybe it would be better if he stopped at the first house, a neighbor's house.

Police, or the ambulance? Or both? There was an emergency number he'd never memorized the way you were supposed to. . . .

His mind was shifting out of focus, going blank in patches, empty and white-glaring as the snowy fields.

Those fields you could lose yourself in at this time of year. Staring and dreaming, stubbled with grass and grain and tracked over with animal prints, but you couldn't see that at a distance—everything clean and clear, dazzling blinding white. At a distance.

It was a secret no one knew: Jody McIllvanney was dead.

Bleeding his life out in a ditch. In the snow.

He hadn't survived the impact of the car, Tyrone knew that. No chance of it, plowing into a human being like that full in the chest and the gut; he'd felt the bones being crushed, the backbone snapped—*felt* it.

He'd seen bodies crumpled, Jesus, he'd seen more than his fair share. Kids his own age, Americans, Japs, in uniform, near naked, bleeding, broken bones, eyes rolled up into their skulls. But mostly he'd been lucky enough to come upon them after death had come and gone and only the body was left.

No witnesses.

No one on the road this time of day.

He had to get help, but help was a long way off.

His foot pressing down hard on the accelerator, then letting up when the tires began to spin—it was dangerous driving in the winter along these roads, dangerous driving any time the roads were likely to be slippery—now approaching a single-lane bridge crashing over the bridge the floorboards bouncing and kicking and the car trembling. Oh, sweet Jesus, help me.

Explaining to someone, a patrolman on the highway, how it wasn't his fault. The hitchhiker standing flat-footed in the road, not dodging out of the way even when the car began to skid.

He'd lost control of the car. But then he'd regained it.

No witnesses.

How could he be held to blame?

If Jody had paid in installments, for instance $25, even $10 every month or so. Paring back on the debt just to show his good faith. His gratitude.

He couldn't be held responsible. He'd kill himself if they came to arrest him.

Except: no witnesses.

Except: his car was damaged.

The fender crushed, the bumper, part of the hood—that's how they would know. Blood splashed on the grill.

That's how they would find him.

That's how they would arrest him.

He and Jody used to go deer hunting farther north; you sling the carcass over the fender unless it's too big, then you tie it to the roof of the car. Twine tied tight as you can tie it.

He'd known without having to look.

Asshole. Bleeding his life out back in a ditch.

But who would know? If he kept going.

If he drove on past his house—just kept driving as if it wasn't any house he knew, any connection to him—drive and drive up into the northern part of the state until something happened to stop him. Until his gas gave out.

SUNDAYS IN SUMMER

Most of all you remember the condemned bridge over the creek: the rusted girders, the missing planks, how water rushed below rushing into your belly into your throat when you looked down. That sharp stink of oil and tar. Heat radiating from dead metal. The high arch of the bridge so ornate and useless, flakes of rust catching in your skin like tiny gnats. Come on, they called out, laughing. Why are you afraid? It's safe, it can't fall in. The bridge was blocked off by three squat wooden posts; there was a sign peppered with gunshot CLOSED TO TRAFFIC AND PEDESTRIANS. NO TRESPASSING UNDER PENALTY OF STATE LAW. None of the girls your age jumped or dived from the bridge to swim in the creek, mainly it was older boys, but sometimes, now, so many years later, in another life, you wake from a frightening dream and you realize you'd been diving again from the condemned bridge into the dark water below. The dream is ugly, exuberant. Look. Look. Look at me. Like your cousin Lyle, smiling, triumphant, wet hair plastered to his skull. The tavern on the creek was your parents' favorite tavern, everybody's favorite until the accident. So many Sundays the boys had jumped and dived from the old bridge and no one was hurt, no one was ever in trouble, until the bright hot muggy afternoon when your cousin Lyle climbed like a monkey up the slanted girders to the top of the bridge, twelve years old and he'd been drinking beer one of his older brothers gave him; he crawled on his hands and knees up the side of the bridge and from the topmost girder he jumped off into space waving and kicking, clowning as he dropped, but he hadn't remembered to jump from the center of the bridge where the creek was deep; he'd jumped close to shore where the water was shallow, debris from the bridge's construction had been dumped there long ago—cables, wires, chunks of concrete—and one of the cables tore him open, groin to torso. If you think about it you see yourself running from the bridge calling for help, running back over to the Victory Inn for help, you can feel your blood pump harder and your throat constrict, but in fact you weren't there at the time, you weren't at the bridge with the others, you were with your mother in the tavern, a chair pulled up next to hers, because you hadn't been feeling well, too much sun, too much excitement; you were lying with your head in your mother's lap dozing off to sleep, then waking, then dozing off to sleep again, waiting to go home. Momma was stroking your snarled hair, talking with her friends, laughing at their clever remarks, but you knew, didn't you, how she loved you best. That slow warm hand like words trying to be said on the back of your head, your neck.

Sundays. Those summers. You were too young to be left home alone; your parents took you with them when they went drinking. They'd start early, midafternoon. Monday began the week your father hated. He had to get up at six in the morning, drive fifteen miles to the city, sometimes he took his lunch in a paper bag and sometimes he bought it in a diner near the factory; forty years he was to work there—first the assembly line, then the machine shop—but he didn't know this at the time, couldn't have guessed. Otherwise even the long Sundays wouldn't have been enough. Starting out around four in the afternoon and when they brought you back home you'd be asleep in the back seat of the car, carried into the darkened house in your father's arms. *She's asleep. Don't wake her.* Carried so gently, you didn't ever want to wake. You'd be hearing the jukebox and seeing its rich glowing colors, you'd be hearing those shrill ribbons of laughter from people rowing boats in the dark in the creek splashing their oars; sometimes one of the men would get unsteadily to his feet, rocking the boat from side to side, the girl with him would scream with laughter begging him to stop. Often your parents argued about who should drive when it was time to go home. You've had too much to drink, your mother would say, and your father would deny it; he'd say *she'd* had too much to drink, and she'd deny it; she'd say he was drunk and he knew he was drunk and he shouldn't make jokes, why didn't he just give her the car keys and she'd drive; and he'd say he surely wasn't handing over his car keys to anyone, wife or not, so that was that. Your mother was upset but your father kept his voice light and bantering as he almost always did. And why should you care? You'd lie down at once in the back seat of the car and fall asleep; not even the bumping of the car's wheels across the cinder lot could disturb you.

Sometimes there'd been an argument between them earlier and your mother would lock herself and you in the car with the windows rolled up tight, she'd smoke her cigarettes, tell you to go to sleep and not to ask questions, then when your father came to the car she'd refuse to unlock it at first; he'd have to plead with her, rapping on the window, trying all the doors, saying he was sorry for whatever he'd said or done or had he gotten into a quarrel with another man, or in an actual fight? Late Sunday evenings were the dangerous time. The men in your parents' crowd weren't afraid of fighting. But your father would be repentant now. "Honey," he'd say, "sweetheart, I'm sorry, you know I'm sorry don't you," falling across the windshield hugging and kissing the glass, his hair in his face, pounding his fists on the roof of the car crazy in love, couldn't help himself. Until finally your mother would break down laughing and unlock the door and your father would swing in triumphant, clamping his forearm around her head and kissing her, and you knew now you could go to sleep, you knew nothing more was going to happen.

Your mother hated it when the men got into quarrels with one another, when they shoved or pushed or actually started hitting one another—her own father had been killed in a tavern fight when she'd been less than a year old. She'd never really known what had happened, nobody ever talked about it openly. Why did the men fight? They were drunk, they got into an argument. Yes, but why? They were drunk. Why did her father die? Hit in the head, punched hard, then kicked when he lay helpless on the ground; afterward it was said a blood vessel had burst in his brain and he couldn't have been saved even if he'd been rushed to a hospital. Why did he get beaten?

They were drunk. Was the other man arrested? Was he charged with murder? Why did it happen? They were drunk.

The Victory Inn was a country place, a large ramshackle wooden house with a wide veranda built high on the bank of the Cattaraugus Creek. Once it had been an actual inn; now it was just a tavern, a beer joint as your mother called it, one of your father's friends' hangouts. Behind it a grassy slope led down to the creek; there were picnic tables, giant whitewashed ornamental rocks, any number of weeping willow trees leaning over the bank. Your mother loved weeping willows, Why can't we have weeping willows at our place? she'd ask, and your father would say, You know they're weed trees— their roots get in everywhere and you have to dig them out after a few years. Yes, but they're so beautiful, your mother said.

There was a narrow dirt path, a fishermen's path, leading through grass and briars in the direction of the condemned bridge a half mile away, so overgrown it was like a secret path; adults rarely took it. Running panting, excited, with the other children you'd have to be quick and duck or branches would slap back into your face; you'd emerge at the other end bleeding from a dozen little scratches on your forearms and legs, tiny tears in your clothing from thorns, but it was nothing, you hardly noticed, who had time to care! It was always a shock to see the bridge, that bridge, built so oddly high above the water, old-fashioned, something unnerving about it—how, from beneath, the sky showed through the missing planks.

I don't want you climbing up on that bridge, your mother said. Stay away from that bridge, do you hear me? Are you listening? Your mother was so pretty people had been listening to her all her life, men at the Victory Inn turned to watch her, she behaved as if she didn't notice or maybe it was so your father wouldn't notice, his hot quick temper, the way his eyes, smiling, shifted suddenly in their sockets and had a look you didn't want to see. Don't play up on the bridge, honey, your mother said. Already there were faint white lines in her forehead from worrying; you'd made her laugh once half in anger, tracing a line with your finger, asking what was it, and she'd said, That's caused by you, by all the trouble you are! in a high surprised voice like someone on the radio. At the Victory Inn her breath always smelled of beer and cigarettes. But still there was a smell you knew better—warm, powdery, sweet. She wore sundresses with narrow straps, her hair all coppery curls tied up sometimes with a scarf. On her feet, Sundays, high-heeled white sandals that made a sharp clattering noise when she walked.

Do you promise? Momma asked.

Yes. I promise.

CLOSED TO TRAFFIC AND PEDESTRIANS. NO TRESPASSING UNDER PENALTY OF STATE LAW but Lyle and the other older boys tried to tear the sign down, managed actually to bend it a little; it was bolted too tightly to one of the wooden posts to wrench off.

After rain the creek was swollen and fast, mud-colored like coffee with too much cream in it, a pale sickish color. After rain the sun was always hotter, brighter, the air steamy, clouds of mosquitoes drifted in the scrubby bushes near shore. Sunshine like a fist striking you between the shoulder blades, but once you started to cross the bridge you weren't allowed to turn back—that was a rule you'd made up for yourself to punish yourself if you were afraid. One foot in front of the other, don't look down, grip the rail to keep your balance and don't look down, don't let the others' noise confuse you. Always you keep to one of the wide iron girders; never would you dare to walk on a mere plank suspended above nothing!—though, forty years later, you'll be dreaming about that, walking on a mere plank, feeling it start to give way beneath your weight. Don't look down at the water, keep to the girder, pay no attention to the boys stamping on the planks to make them rattle to frighten one another; they've broken a plank clean through and part of it falls into the creek; now they're tossing stones and clods of mud into the water, laughing, yelling, Bombs away! Bombs away, Tokyo! You don't want to look at the water rushing below but you can't stop yourself, that quick sensation in the pit of your stomach, sick, dizzy, excited, you don't know if you're terrified of it or if you like it, clutching the railing so hard tiny flecks of rust are all over your hand.

Lyle's father was your father's oldest brother, he'd punched Lyle once on the upper arm in your presence and hurt him so he cried, it was the only way of keeping a kid like that in line, your uncle said, but boys are boys, what can you do? A stocky suntanned boy with pale blue eyes like his father's and like your own father's—that look runs in the family, the men and boys, a certain set of the mouth, nose, dark brown hair looking almost black, straight as an Indian's. Lyle never cried now, though sometimes he made other children cry, including you, but he was good-natured at heart, that was what they said about all the men in your father's family: they're good-natured at heart, they don't mean any harm.

There was a time, you might have been nine years old, Lyle and his brother Rick teased you, pretending they were going to throw you off the bridge, but you didn't scream like the other girls would have screamed, you gripped the railing tight and wouldn't budge, your face closed up tight, God damn you, let me alone, damn you I'll kill you, let me alone, you whispered, and finally they gave up, Lyle couldn't pry your fingers loose. On the way back to the Inn he was worried you'd tell, he said, Hey, you know we didn't mean it, we were only fooling around, but you wouldn't look at him, you hated him so. You wondered what were the ways you could kill him without anybody knowing.

There's a snapshot of you aged five or six, dark-eyed, shy, half hiding behind your mother's skirt. Your mother bends over you, worried, taking no notice of the camera or of your impatient father holding the camera, it's her little girl she's concerned with and in another moment she'll kiss you, or slap you, or hug you, or pinch you hard, or lift you staggering in her arms. Only eighteen years old when she had her first baby, never really knew how to be a mother. How do you learn, who tells you? Her own mother was dead, her husband's mother was jealous of her, marrying her favorite son, spiriting him away. Why doesn't your mother like me? Momma sometimes asked, watching your father's face, and he'd look away embarrassed. She likes you well enough, honey, forget it, don't bother about her. He was the youngest of the four boys, always the favorite. Good-looking, energetic, spoiled. Now he was in the union at the plant he made decent wages, that was the important thing. One summer he and Lyle's father were going to buy a small fishing boat secondhand from a friend, *Heart's Desire* was the name of the boat, painted in shaky white letters on the prow, but nothing came of it. There's a snapshot of you and your mother and your father in the boat, though, Momma in a two-piece bathing suit, hair pinned up in back, curls on her forehead like Betty Grable, and your father is bare-chested, his chest swathed in dark hair, wide lopsided grin, one hand upraised, a blur.

Your father could lift you high above his head with one arm if you held yourself stiff and didn't wriggle. His shoulders and arms inside a white T-shirt bunched with muscle, cords standing out in his neck, a ropy vein in his forehead. That child raised over his head so still, passive, showing no sign of fear, she might even be asleep, dreaming. The snapshot shows your father with the larger of his harmonicas gripped in his teeth but you don't remember that. Your mother was calling out importantly, One—two—*three*, but she snapped the picture on the count of four. "Oh, damn, I think I ruined it," she said. "Can I try again?"

Sunday, summer, so hot the air rippled and creased in the direct sunlight, the current in the creek was slow, lazy, so your mother and your Aunt Bobbie went rowing, let you help row, both of them giggling, slightly drunk; your oar kept slipping, and after a few minutes your hands began to ache but you didn't want them to know. Momma said, Let me have that, please, you're not strong enough, you're going to hurt yourself, but you kept fumbling with it until your Aunt Bobbie laughed, blowing smoke out of her nostrils, and said, Hey, I'm bored with this—I'm thirsty too—let's go back. Up in the big noisy crowded room off the barroom you drank flat Cokes, syrupy Cokes that weren't as good as Cokes out of the bottle; you were lonely, pouting, eating potato chips and pretzels for something to do, lips greasy and salty, fingers greasy and salty reaching for more. Your mother or one of your relatives or a big-bellied man you didn't know but he was a friend of your father's from work would give you a nickel so you could play the jukebox: Frank Sinatra was always your mother's request, Bing Crosby, Dinah Shore, the others liked; one of the selections was "Ghost Riders in the Sky," you'd play it twenty times in a row if you could. What time is it, is it time to go home? No, it's early yet, be still, can't you go outside and play? Where are your cousins? Lay your head in my lap and stop wriggling, stop fussing, don't make your father angry, he's had enough of you for today. You weren't hungry for hamburgers charred on the outside and watery runny red on the inside, that was blood, you knew it was blood, you couldn't allow it to touch your tongue or you'd start to gag. Couldn't eat the french fries, sweet coleslaw in tiny fluted white paper cups. You were going to be sick anyway, suddenly—your mother's chair jerked back, your mother was leading you out into the entry to the women's rest room where she stood you at one of the sinks and ran the faucet fast and hard, holding you steady—but nothing happened. You were shivering, your teeth chattering, something so heavy and bloated in your stomach you wanted to vomit it up, but nothing happened. What time is it, I hate it here, I want to go home: but if you said anything your mother would only say, It's early yet.

She was standing close behind you, close and snug in case you should start vomiting after all. You could feel the swell of her belly, her breasts, her special heat you loved and the smell too of perfume and powder and cigarettes and that bitter beery breath you loved, but she was looking over your head at her reflection in the mirror, staring critically at herself. Primping her hair, licking her lips to make the red lipstick glisten with a sheen like a waxy red crayon.

Like a match set to dried grass so quick!—so terrible!—the way men start to fight each other. Suddenly you'd be hearing raised voices, the room would go quiet, the first blow and there'd be swearing, stumbling; if they were inside the tavern they'd fall against tables and chairs but the scuffle wouldn't last long; other men would pull them apart before anyone was hurt. Why are they fighting? you'd ask, but there wasn't any answer really. They're drunk, or He was asking for it, or You can't blame him, or It runs in the family, they're all like that. Except one time when your father got in an exchange with a man he'd gone to school with—to grade school, out in the country—because the man had said something insulting to your mother and the insult had to be repaid so they went out into the parking lot; people tried to stop them but they weren't going to be stopped; your mother was half sobbing, begging—Don't, oh, please don't for God's sake—pulling at your father's arm, trying to make him look at her: Can't we just go home?

Get her out of here, your father told your mother, meaning you. Get her the hell out of here, he said, meaning you, but you were too quick, you slapped at your mother's hands and ran away, ran outside to hide in the tall grass. Nobody was going to find you but nobody was looking for you, and after a few minutes you crawled forward, then went to hide behind a parked car to watch. There was a ring of men around the fighters but you could see through their legs; squatting, staring, keeping very still, you saw enough.

Where were you? your mother demanded to know, and you said you'd been hiding in the women's rest room, locked yourself in one of the stalls. She didn't ask again; she was wiping her face with a tissue, studying her reflection in her compact mirror. Not so pretty now, was she. Her lower lip looked swollen, bruised. Her eyes were red-rimmed and bloodshot. Your father hoisted you up on his shoulder and carried you bouncing out to the car. You could feel the terrible heat pulsing from him; he was still breathless, tense, telling your mother she shouldn't have worried, shouldn't have been carrying on like that in front of their friends as if she hadn't any faith in him. He was her husband, she had to have faith in him, didn't she? He couldn't let another man insult her, it was an insult against them both, deliberately intended, didn't she understand? Your father's shirt was torn and stained but it wasn't his blood, he said, it was the other man's blood. Driving fast along the Cattaraugus Creek Road, one elbow out the window, wind blowing in all the windows because he was so damned hot, out of breath, couldn't stop talking, loud and excited and happy, how he'd known to keep pushing forward to keep jabbing at the bastard's face with his left so's to confuse him, let him swing wild all he wanted and stay out of his way, then nail him when it was clear and he could land a clean blow. The secret is to put your full weight behind the punch, your father said, not just to swing from the shoulder.

Both your father's hands were bleeding, he'd had to wrap his right hand in some toilet paper, wound around the knuckles.

Your mother sat quiet, keeping to her side of the car. Your father said, "What were the two of you talking about anyway?" When your mother didn't answer he said in a lower voice, "I'm not blaming you or anything but you must have given him the wrong idea and what if I'd had to hurt him bad or kill him or something, all because of—" and still she didn't answer; now she was lighting a cigarette and your father knocked it out of her fingers. "Damn you," she said, "what do you think you're doing!" She'd begun to cry again. Your father said, "I'm not blaming you but I saw you. Looking up at him. I saw something."

"I wasn't. I wasn't looking at him."

"You were talking to him, weren't you? You must have been looking at him."

"Go to hell. You're crazy."

"I said I saw you."

"Then you're crazy," your mother said, her voice rising. "You're drunk! I hate you! I wish you were dead! Oh, Jesus, how could you do it!" turning on him, striking him on the head and shoulders with her fists but the blows were light, no strength to them; your father just swore in surprise and shoved her away and she quit.

For a while you lay unmoving, pretending to be asleep. You could hear their quickened breathing. Then your mother turned on the radio, the volume low; it was music, singing, bouncy and sweet, the Andrews Sisters, who were old favorites of hers.

Sunday. Late afternoon, summer. It's hours from night: the sun is fierce and bright melting into the sky turning everything white, blinding. You know you'll be punished but that won't happen for a long time, your mother won't know for a long time, you don't care if she does find out, why should you care, so much excitement, so much fun, there isn't anywhere else you want to be except on the bridge, at the railing, pitching stones to see how far you can throw, there isn't anywhere else for you. Your cousin Lyle and a redheaded fat-faced boy named Denny can throw the farthest and they're the most daring, keeping people in rowboats from rowing under the bridge. There are five or six of you here, noisy with laughter; beneath the bridge in the shadowy creek your reflection is mixed with the other reflections broken by stones then coming back together again, broken, reassembling, like jigsaw puzzle pieces; you wave one hand and there's a hand waving in the water, lean out far over the railing and there's a figure leaning out as if to mock you. When you pick up a heavy rock with a ribbed pebbly texture glinting like tiny chips of glass, the feel of it, the touch, pierces your skin and rushes up your arm, you throw it quickly to get it out of your hand.

LEILA LEE

Leila Lee knew within three weeks of her marriage to Lamar Pike that the marriage was probably a mistake. She knew, she knew. But it wasn't a mistake she had the spirit to undo: she was afraid of the man.

Also, he had more money than she'd guessed. As a bank clerk at the First National Bank of Chapelton, where Mr. Pike did much of his business, she'd known about some but not all of his finances. He was rich by local standards though his daddy, as he liked to say, had been dirt poor, and all the Pikes going back to one or another of his ancestors who'd been a well-to-do landowner in this part of the state but who had lost everything in the Revolution. (By which Mr. Pike meant the Revolution of 1776, so far as Leila Lee could make out. Her own ancestors, she thought, were probably living in caves at that time or swinging from trees—God knows. Fortunately Mr. Pike never troubled to ask her much about her background, let alone her ancestors.)

Though Leila Lee had been going out with Lamar Pike for only a few weeks before they were married—in a five-minute ceremony down at the county courthouse, only Mr. Pike's sullen twelve-year-old son a witness—she'd known him for months, in her capacity as bank clerk at the First National. He wasn't a tall man but he gave the impression of tallness. He gave the impression, even when he was standing still, of moving forward: stocky, compact, muscular, fattish, with a permanently flushed, ruddy skin and a perfectly bald head and steely gray-green eyes the color of ditch water. There was the look of a charging bull about him that frightened and excited Leila Lee when he started in her direction, which he nearly always did. (He was a man who liked attractive women. You could see it plainly in his face.) He was the owner of Pike Realty & Insurance but dressed like a farmer most of the time, in an old sheepskin jacket, soiled overalls, manure-splattered boots, work caps with HARDIN GRAINS or KAYO OIL stitched on their visors. Though he owned a new-model Lincoln Continental it was mainly his Bronco jeep he drove around town. In Chapelton he was something of a controversial figure, admired by some and cordially disliked by others, said to be a generous friend but a spiteful enemy, quoting the Bible when it suited him ("Iron sharpeneth iron" was one of his favored remarks) and smiling a fierce gap-toothed grin which could be as intimidating as another man's scowl. After they'd become acquainted Mr. Pike told Leila Lee, "I'm considered a cold son of a bitch by men who haven't found a way to cheat me. You may have heard some bad-mouthing about me?" And Leila Lee, who certainly had, opened her lovely eyes wider and said, "One thing I always hear about you, Mr. Pike, is that you're *generous*: always giving to charity and never saying no." This was the answer Mr. Pike wanted to hear, but he said with his quick ambiguous smile, "I don't never say no, honey. Try me."

Was he the kind of man who'd hit a woman? Leila Lee wondered. That was the main thing.

At that time Leila Lee was new to Chapelton and kept herself to herself as the saying went. Lived alone, dressed with a certain stylish flair, looked to be in her mid- or late twenties. (In truth she was thirty-four.) With her pretty rouged face and nerved-up manner and something in her warm brown eyes that spoke of hurt she naturally drew men to her, but until Mr. Pike came along her luck had been running worse than usual. She'd been married for the first time aged eighteen, for the second time aged twenty-three, which meant there were two ex-husbands out there for her to contemplate when she was in a weak mood. Also, there was a tragedy in her life, a medical secret it might be called, of which she didn't intend to speak to any prospective suitor.

By instinct Lamar Pike seemed to head for Leila Lee's wicket at the bank even before he caught sight of her. Close up, his face was

battered, wind- and sun-worn, a mass of thin lines that deepened
when he smiled. His skin was flushed, his nose slightly venous, something pushing and impatient in even his kindest, most courteous
remarks. And those gray-green eyes—Leila Lee seemed for a dizzying
instant to see herself by way of them and wasn't comfortable with
what she saw.

For some reason he never telephoned her, but when he spied
her at a wedding reception in a Chapelton hotel one Saturday afternoon in January he made straight for her, smiling his dazzling smile.
He came on to her like a well-practiced bull, edging out competition,
just slightly crowding her, putting her off balance and out of breath.
Within the space of an hour Leila Lee learned that Lamar Pike was
a widower, fifty-six years old, had just one child, a boy, and hoped
for more—though, as he said, squinching one eye at her as if in a
wink, he was in no hurry to remarry. "I don't want to make a mistake
this time around," he said ambiguously. Had he made a mistake,
Leila Lee wondered, the first time?

Leila Lee felt both intimidated and assured in Mr. Pike's presence.
He was the kind of man you had to keep stepping back from, while
he edged forward; he was the kind of man whose sexual interest—
it was almost a hunger, a greed—showed clearly in his face. He
wanted her, pure and simple, and there was safety in that. Leila Lee
understood that. In this situation it scarcely mattered what they were
saying: if Leila Lee spoke cleverly or couldn't think of the right words,
if she was quick-witted and funny and just a bit audacious or frankly,
physically, scared of him. Other men, who successfully resisted being
attracted to her in that way, were riskier, made her uneasy. She
understood they were assessing her as a person, not a pretty youngish
woman. She understood maybe that put her at a disadvantage.

Leila Lee couldn't see Mr. Pike that evening because she had
another engagement, but Monday afternoon when she left the bank
there he was in his hearse-black Lincoln Continental, waiting at the
curb, and did she want a ride home?—smiling at her so hard it hurt.
She felt an immediate stab of excitement but declined politely, saying
it was only a few blocks to her apartment building and she usually
just walked. Mr. Pike leaned over to open the heavy door. "Slide
in, honey," he said. So there was Leila Lee obeying. Mr. Pike helped
her settle herself in, his hand big and warm and strong, the biggest

hand, she thought, that had ever touched her. "No trouble to drive you home, Leila Lee," Mr. Pike said. "Unless you'd like to go for a ride along the river instead."

Leila Lee declined politely and told him her address: right off Main Street. Mr. Pike pulled out into traffic, using his horn. He opened the glove compartment and took out a silver flask, asked her did she want a drink, it was fine Kentucky bourbon and this was the time of day, just past 5 P.M., it went down best. Leila Lee declined, then said, "Well, I guess I wouldn't mind." The liquor burned her throat pleasantly and seemed within seconds to irradiate in her loins, a warm cozy glow Leila Lee halfway thought her companion could sense.

She noticed he'd gone past Main Street, seemed to be headed out of town. She said, "Where are we going, Mr. Pike?" and Mr. Pike said, "You'll know when we get there."

When he touched her, perspiration broke out on the small of her back and behind her knees. Oh, yes, Leila Lee thought.

Two months later Leila Lee was standing in Mr. Pike's kitchen preparing dinner as she did every night they didn't go out: slicing onions into one of her beautiful copper frying pans and blinking to keep her eyes clear and listening—it couldn't be called eavesdropping because she surely didn't want to do it—to Mr. Pike and his son, Lamar Jr., out in the breezeway.

Not that she could hear Lamar Jr.'s voice, only Mr. Pike's. What the boy had done now—or failed to do—Leila Lee hoped not to be told. He was hours late getting home from school, or he hadn't done his chores from the day before, or, if he'd done them, they had been done carelessly and would have to be done over. Much of the time the boy's misdeeds were less tangible: he didn't show proper respect for Mr. Pike or his new stepmother, didn't show a convincing Christian spirit when Mr. Pike led them in prayer at meals ("saying grace" was the primary concession Mr. Pike made to his Presbyterian heritage), didn't even *look* the way Mr. Pike believed he should—his neck appeared too thin for his head, his head too large for his shoulders, his shoulders, bladelike, curved inward as if he were intent upon making himself smaller. Lamar Jr. was twelve years old but nearly as tall as his father, who was five foot nine; he probably weighed eighty pounds less. One of the features Leila Lee liked in him was his brown-red hair, which was fine as baby's hair, though often disheveled and in need of shampooing. And he had a fine-boned, rather pretty face, the cheekbones delicately pronounced. His eyes were weak, however, and he wore glasses with thick lenses, which Mr. Pike seemed to take as a personal affront. ("That child didn't get bad eyes from *me*," he'd told Leila Lee on the very first occasion of their meeting, as if Lamar Jr., haughty, sullen, and absolutely silent, were not even present.) Nonetheless Leila Lee thought the boy's eyes were beautiful, thick-lashed as a girl's and with chiseled-looking brows, though eerily colorless—so faint a gray they seemed to vanish when Leila Lee looked at him head on.

She knew the boy hated her but tried not to feel it. She'd win him over in time, she thought. She had plenty of time.

Mr. Pike had moved from scolding Lamar Jr. to mocking him in his cold drawling voice, which meant he knew Leila Lee might be listening. He required an audience of more than just Lamar Jr. at such times. Though Leila Lee knew it really wasn't funny she sometimes couldn't keep from laughing at some of Mr. Pike's fantastical notions ("You look like a snake's gnawing your gut, boy"; "You look like there's a foot-long thorn wedged up your rear"), and even Lamar Jr. might laugh involuntarily, harsh mirthless laughter that took him by surprise. Most of the time, however, he provoked his father's wrath by failing to react at all, an expression on his face of an almost scholarly neutrality; he'd stand slouched, motionless, as if he were in the rain and simply waiting for it to stop. Once Leila Lee glanced through a doorway just at the moment Mr. Pike hauled off and slapped Lamar Jr. full in the face. The boy cried out in pain but didn't succumb to tears; backing away, cringing, he bared his teeth at his father, outlined in blood—a mocking little version of Mr. Pike's smile, it looked to Leila Lee. She had an instant's vertigo, seeing that.

When Leila Lee went out with Mr. Pike for their first formal evening he showed her several snapshots of his son, spreading them out on the table before her as if exhibiting evidence. "I love this boy more than anything in the world," he said with a curious air of baffled regret. "And he knows it—that's problem number one." Leila Lee examined the snapshots with unfeigned interest, thinking she'd never seen so *sad* a child. His face looked like the face of a child famine victim in a newspaper photograph. "He's smart for his age in some ways, in other ways not," Mr. Pike said. "I've had to discipline him." "That's too bad," Leila Lee said. "Yes, it is," Mr. Pike said, "but it has to be done." He looked up at Leila Lee as if appraising her. "He'll resent you," he said. Leila Lee sat very still. What was this man saying?

It seemed difficult for Mr. Pike to speak of his son by name. "My son" and "my boy" were more natural than "Lamar" since "Lamar" was Mr. Pike's own name. Leila Lee wasn't to know what to call him either; she'd have to settle for "Lamar" and call Mr. Pike something else. Mr. Pike was saying that after his wife's death something had seemed to curdle in his son—he'd been nine years old at the time—and he hadn't been the same since. He was sly and treacherous and duplicitous. You could see the mockery in his eyes; you could imagine the thoughts he was thinking, in his own head. His grades at school were all A's and B's but his teachers complained of him as a "disruptive" classroom presence; he "used profanity," "took the name of the Lord in vain." His sarcasm set a poor example for his classmates. He had no friends that Mr. Pike knew of and no interests except science fiction: reading it and even trying to write it, holed away up in his room. He wouldn't show what he'd written to anyone, especially not his father! "I could forgive that boy mouthing off at me," Mr. Pike said with a sigh, "but he doesn't do that, much. He just sits there thinking his own thoughts. Won't look at me or talk to me, unless I come down hard on him. Then he's likely to lie." Mr. Pike rubbed his eyes hard; for a moment he looked his age, or older. Leila Lee was moved to lay her hand atop his, she felt such a swerve of sympathy for him. "You look like a man who has endured a good deal," Leila Lee said with warmth. "A man of sensitivity who has suffered."

Mr. Pike thanked her. He appeared deeply moved. He told her again, as if it were a vow, that he loved his son more than anything else on earth and there could never be any woman he loved more: "The blood bond goes deepest." Leila Lee murmured an assent though she felt, in truth, a bit hurt. (Which was surely unreasonable? If Leila Lee had a child of her own she'd love it far more than she could ever love Mr. Pike or any other man. Wouldn't even *want* Mr. Pike or any other man, maybe.)

In all their times together Mr. Pike was moved to say very little about his late wife, Geraldine, except that she'd been a good woman, a good Christian woman who'd tried her best. Leila Lee asked how she died and Mr. Pike said, "Natural causes."

After they were married and Leila Lee came to live in Mr. Pike's splendid orange-brick house north of Chapelton, she realized she'd set her foot unknowingly in a battle zone. How it had to do with the first Mrs. Pike she didn't understand, and often thought it hadn't anything to do with that poor woman at all; it was just Lamar Sr. and Lamar Jr. in permanent opposition. There might be a truce and a cease-fire for a few days but it was never more than temporary and she'd given up hoping otherwise. Lamar Jr. ignored her if he couldn't avoid her, seeming to look right through her with his queer ghost-colored eyes. If he tried that with his father Mr. Pike would say sharply, "Look me in the face, boy, do you have something to hide?" Or he'd criticize the boy for his bad posture, or his sloppy clothes, or the way he'd done one or another of his household chores. (The current project, which promised to take a very long time, necessitated Lamar Jr.'s chopping the remains of an enormous oak tree into kindling-sized pieces of wood. The oak had died by degrees, and Mr. Pike had hired a tree service crew to fell it, but he had not directed them to cut the trunk and limbs into firewood, as they might have done easily with their chain saws; that task was Lamar Jr.'s. Swinging a man-sized ax would develop his arm and shoulder muscles, Mr. Pike said. *He* knew; he'd spent a boyhood doing just such work and saw now how precious it was. At any rate it would get Lamar Jr. out of his room and his nose out of his sickly books.)

Another area of trouble had to do with religion. Mr. Pike confided in Leila Lee that he didn't really "believe" as his parents had taught him—he'd been baptized in the Presbyterian faith—but he was convinced that the old ways were probably right. He made a point of keeping active in the local church by way of generous yearly contributions, and he considered himself, and was considered, a leading member of the local Christian community. (Mr. Pike also gave generously to the Chapelton volunteer firemen, and to the hospital fund, and to the county animal shelter services, and elsewhere. Charity donations were one of his hobbies.) Though he rarely attended ser-

vices at the Presbyterian church—even on the sabbath, he did business of a kind—he insisted that Lamar Jr. attend Sunday school classes
in the church basement and at Sunday dinner he quizzed him on
what he'd learned that day. Lamar Jr. was able to recite strings of
Bible verses with his eyes shut, head slightly swaying—"In the beginning was the Word, and the Word was with God, and the Word
was God"—in a high reedy flat voice, as if he wasn't listening to what
he said, had no need of listening. He had quick snappy answers to
all of Mr. Pike's questions, but Leila Lee guessed that the boy skipped
Sunday school as often as he could; by way of a remark made to her
by a neighbor in the A&P she had the idea he spent the time wandering in the cemetery behind the church. But no one was moved
to tell Mr. Pike. People felt sorry for Lamar Jr. as a boy who'd lost
his mother; they had an idea how hard it might be to be Lamar Sr.'s
only son.

Out in the breezeway Mr. Pike's voice rose suddenly. Leila Lee
stood tensed with a half-pared Spanish onion in one hand and a
bright-gleaming knife in another, waiting for the sharp sound of a
blow. "What I will not tolerate is *duplicity*," Mr. Pike was shouting.
"I will not tolerate *duplicity*. Do you understand?" Leila Lee held
her breath. There was a long terrible moment when something violent could have erupted but then, miraculously, the boy gave way,
murmured what sounded like an apology. "*Do* you understand?" Mr.
Pike repeated. And again the boy murmured words Leila Lee couldn't
quite hear but understood was an acquiescence.

It was at that moment, standing with her belly pressed against
the counter and the back of one hand pressed against her watering
eyes—standing there faint and sick with dread, as if she and not
Lamar Jr. had been in danger of being struck—that Leila Lee realized
for the first time, or allowed herself to think clearly for the first time,
that the marriage to Mr. Pike might have been—well, a mistake.

That night, undressing for bed, Mr. Pike declared to Leila Lee
that he could not, simply *would* not bear duplicity. "I could understand a son of mine rebelling with a fiery spirit, especially when he
was sixteen, seventeen years old—my own daddy could hardly handle
me—but this other, this—" Mr. Pike seemed to be addressing the
boy by way of Leila Lee, as he frequently did at such times. His voice
was loud and hurt and baffled, and Leila Lee was thinking, not mean-

ing to be cruel, that he looked his age. His chest muscles were sagging into fat and the flesh around his middle *was* nothing but fat. "This doubleness, *duplicity: I won't tolerate it.*" Leila Lee had noticed since coming to live with Mr. Pike that he used the word "duplicity" often to characterize his son; he seemed to be fascinated by the word itself. He pronounced it with an especial venom, as if it were a foreign word, something he'd had to reach out for, to describe the wickedness in his own home. "I do believe the boy lies now for the pure pleasure of meanness in lying. And for mocking his father. 'Except ye become as little children, ye shall not enter the Kingdom of Heaven'—huh!"

Leila Lee said hesitantly, "You're sure you aren't too hard on him, hon?" Mr. Pike stared at her. "Hard on him? I been feeling I'm too lenient." Leila Lee said, "Well, he was crying today." Mr. Pike said, "He was not crying today. Out in the breezeway?" Leila Lee said, "He was crying in his room." Mr. Pike said, "How do you know what he was doing in his room?" Leila Lee said, "I heard him." Mr. Pike was advancing upon her in his stocking feet. His face looked raw and reddened and his eyes were drained of color. "Did he go bellyaching to you?" he asked quietly. Leila Lee said, backing away, "No, hon. He never does that." Mr. Pike said, "He did, didn't he?" Leila Lee half screamed, "*No.*" She was biting her lip, trembling. The look in Mr. Pike's face was not a loving one at the moment. "If I ever hear that that boy is going bellyaching to you, or to anyone—" Mr. Pike said. His voice quavered with an unfocused rage. He flexed his fingers; he was breathing as deeply and erratically as he sometimes breathed at night, when his breath seemed to catch deep in his throat and there was a click, a moist choking sound, and the deep rhythms of his snoring were interrupted. "If I ever hear *you're* covering up for *him*—"

Mr. Pike was looking at Leila Lee as if he'd never seen her before. He'd gotten into the habit of shoving her sometimes, even hitting her now and then, not hard, but, yes, *hitting*, as a way of emphasizing his words. The blows didn't hurt, or in any case didn't really hurt; Leila Lee understood that it was simply the way Mr. Pike was, using his hands to make himself understood. Now he poked her in the chest with a forefinger as he spoke. He shoved her backward in little staggering steps until she felt the edge of the bed against the backs of her knees. He was trying hard not to lose control, Leila Lee could

see that, and something in her face—some look of appeal or terror—
helped to calm him down. She could always count on that: Lamar
Pike was a gentleman almost by instinct.

His face creased as if he were about to cry. He said, "If I didn't
love that boy so much. . . ."

In all fairness to Lamar Pike, Leila Lee had to acknowledge that
he was the most affectionate man she'd ever known. Lusty and loving
and doing what he would with his hands and his mouth and the rest
of him: that was just his way. If he pushed her around sometimes,
at other times he stroked and caressed and petted her as if he couldn't
get enough of her, coming into the kitchen behind her, for instance,
and sliding his arms around her and burying his face in her neck,
calling her honey, sweetheart, darling, his beautiful beautiful baby,
his Leila Lee who made all things new. Sometimes he couldn't seem
to help kissing her, nuzzling her ear, running his big hands across
her breasts even when Lamar Jr. might be in view—so that Leila Lee,
laughing, would say, "Hon, *please*." She knew it was expected of her.
A man of Mr. Pike's temperament would be deeply offended by a
woman with appetites like his own.

Of course they were still in their honeymoon phase, Leila Lee
thought. She could count on some of this abating before long.

Mr. Pike was affectionate too, in his rough jocular way, with
Lamar Jr., laying a heavy hand on one of the boy's thin shoulders or
rubbing his knuckles just a bit too hard across the boy's head. It was
well-intentioned, fatherly, loving, and Leila Lee saw and appreciated
how the boy held himself stiff and polite and didn't shrink away as
he surely wanted to do. She could envision a time not long past when
Mr. Pike had held his small son on his lap, rode him on his shoulders,
carried him high and proud in his arms. She wondered if poor Lamar
Jr. could remember that time.

Mr. Pike liked to touch people, that was it. He showed he was
there, that way, and that *they* were there. It was as simple as that.

And he liked to touch animals, particularly his fancy pedigree
cattle. The creatures were such big hefty brutes—cows and steers
both—that they scarcely knew they were being petted and admired.
You'd need a sledgehammer or an ax to fell one of these babies, Mr.
Pike liked to boast. Leila Lee sometimes watched from the living

room window as he inspected them in the front pasture: stroking their enormous heads, slapping their sides and haunches, talking animatedly to them. Leila Lee wondered what he said to the cattle, that stocky but quick-stepping figure in a worn sheepskin jacket, bald head gleaming with pride and pleasure in the midst of his herd. Black Angus are an expensive hobby, Mr. Pike admitted, but a man must have some beauty around him.

Seeing how he loved the cattle—those ugly smelly things!—Leila Lee was moved to think that she loved him after all. He had a kindly heart. He never did hurt by actual intention.

Fifty-six, and shortly fifty-seven years old, and Mr. Pike was hoping for a baby, that Leila Lee knew. She knew.

Thus far, however, he shied away from speaking directly of it; he was that kind of old-fashioned man. Leila Lee wondered nervously how long his patience, or his old-fashionedness, would last.

She dreaded the day he would ask her certain questions or, worse yet, haul her off to a doctor and ask *him* certain questions. She could always say it was all a surprise to her, but that might be difficult to believe and Mr. Pike would see she'd been duplicitous too. She wondered what would happen then.

She smiled at him and he didn't see. She spoke his name as his father never did: "Lamar." And he didn't hear.

Like tossing a ball at a playmate and the playmate won't catch it, turns coolly aside. You little bastard, Leila Lee thought one day, I'll make you like me. I'll make you *love* me.

When he came home from school there she was, waiting. She wore a pretty yellow angora sweater and pleated slacks and her hair was combed and she wanted to know how his day had gone. And Lamar Jr. stared at her and asked, "Why?"

Leila Lee, thrown off balance, could only stammer, "Why *what?* What do you mean?"

The boy's silvery eyes shifted and seemed to become transparent. "Why do you want to know about crap like that?" he said, edging toward the stairs.

Another time, when Leila Lee set out fresh-baked oatmeal cookies for Lamar Jr. and poured him a glass of milk, he said, "Thank

you, ma'am," in his polite flat voice and carried the snack upstairs
to his room. Leila Lee was left alone in the kitchen staring after him.
She'd begun to cry without knowing it.

But she persisted. She wasn't going to give up. Weeks and then
months of stratagems: asking Lamar Jr. head-on questions he couldn't
avoid answering, looking him full in the face so that he couldn't avoid
looking at her, making him *see* who she was. When Mr. Pike disci-
plined him most harshly, and not always fairly, Leila Lee sought him
out afterward to console him with a few carefully chosen ambiguous
words that, if ever repeated to Mr. Pike, would not have caused
offense. "You shouldn't provoke your father, Lamar," she said, wetting her lips. "You know how he loves you, and how it hurts him to
punish you. And it hurts me to be a witness to it." "Yes, ma'am,"
the boy said, keeping his face neutral, his voice clear of irony. At
such times he held himself still as a wild creature and Leila Lee wanted
to fold him in her arms. Or did she want to slap his arrogant face,
as Mr. Pike did? She reached out to touch his shoulder, his head,
his fine soft hair. Naturally he stiffened against her but he didn't
lunge away.

Other times she tried humor—the boy, for all his sulking, did
have a sharp sense of humor. And she tried shocking him: standing
right in his path with her hands on her hips and saying frankly that
she was here, in his father's house, and she wasn't going to go away.
Wasn't he a smart enough boy to accept that and make the best of
it? It wasn't until the end of the summer that she tried something
even bolder and more risky: saying in a gentle but emphatic voice
that if she *did* go away, his mother wouldn't come back. "I hope you
don't have some strange notion in your head that it's me against her.
Do you?"

Lamar Jr.'s eyes snapped open at this remark. He said sullenly,
"I know that. I'm not a moron."

Leila Lee looked into the matter of the first Mrs. Pike, this Geraldine of whom Mr. Pike so rarely, and then so reluctantly, spoke.
Snapshots showed a plump-faced but pretty woman with permed hair
and a look of being startled by the camera. Her clothes and personal
effects had been parceled out to her kin after her death and there
was little in the house to remind anyone of her. The wife of one of
Mr. Pike's business associates happened to mention to Leila Lee one

evening when the four of them were together that "Geraldine was just no match for Lamar, poor thing—couldn't keep up with him," but Leila Lee had the impression that the woman was pitying more than sympathetic. She learned too how Geraldine had died: cirrhosis of the liver.

Another wife of another business associate confided in Leila Lee that the Pikes had had trouble of some mysterious kind with Lamar Jr. long before Mrs. Pike died. Maybe he was *born* with some sort of trouble, Leila Lee was told.

By the time school started in the fall—Lamar Jr. was in eighth grade now; he'd be thirteen in another month—Leila Lee had succeeded in befriending him to a degree. It pleased her that he'd have his after-school snack downstairs in the kitchen with her, not locked away in his room. Once Mr. Pike came home in the early evening, the household atmosphere was usually too highly charged for Leila Lee to talk to Lamar Jr., so she had to take advantage when she could. (The supper table was a field of tension you entered at your own risk; it put Leila Lee in mind of one of those insect-zapping mechanisms people installed by their outdoor swimming pools.)

Leila Lee inquired as to Lamar Jr.'s eighth-grade teachers, and it was chilling, how the boy ticked them off one by one: Mr. Humphreys the math teacher was a "fool," Miss Stoner the English teacher was a "hypocrite," Mrs. O'Mara the music teacher was "a decent sort." The principal of the school was a "mere politician." Leila Lee laughed in astonishment at Lamar Jr.'s superior tone. "Sounds like you don't get along any better at school than you do at home," Leila Lee said.

Lamar Jr. shrugged his shoulders. He said indifferently, "*My* kingdom is not of this hick town."

It was a remark that floored Leila Lee; she'd never heard anything like it in her life, apart, maybe, from television and movies where amazing remarks just rolled off people's tongues as if they were natural. And it was blasphemy, wasn't it, if there still was such a thing?

Leila Lee had gotten the idea of reading some science fiction herself, or trying to. It was risky because Lamar Jr. might think she was spying on him, but she'd gone so far as to check out books from

the public library that Lamar Jr. had checked out. She had some luck
with some of the books but no luck at all with the others: you needed
to twist your mind into all sorts of strange contortions to read this
sort of thing, she thought, and she maybe couldn't do it. Or maybe
hadn't the right kind of mind.

It turned out that Lamar Jr. did condescend to answer her questions, though he would never initiate any conversation of his own
on the subject. Leila Lee appreciated it that he hadn't mocked her
for her ignorance or turned aside in one of his cold trembling rages
when his fingers flexed like his daddy's and you had to hold your
breath and hope nothing would happen. She hoped to appeal to the
boy's better side: told him with a breathy little laugh that the books
he liked were so strange, she halfway feared, reading just a few pages,
she'd lose her sanity! "Most days it's enough for me to cope with
the real world," she said, "let alone all these others."

Lamar Jr. said haughtily, "Which world is 'real'?"

It crossed Leila Lee's mind then that maybe there really was
something wrong with the boy, some derangement too elusive to be
named. And you couldn't blame the poor deceased mother for it.

It was an eye-stopping house to which Lamar Pike had brought
his bride, a half mile north of Chapelton and atop a lovely scenic
hill. Though a sign at the end of the drive said PIKE FARM—
REGISTERED BLACK ANGUS, the house was far from a farmhouse of
any conventional sort. It was in fact a split-level ranch with a number
of showy picture windows and a good deal of white ornamental
wrought iron. A fancy orange brick that was almost *too* vivid, Leila
Lee thought, and something seemed to be wrong with the foundation,
which showed here and there through the evergreen shrubs like an
exposed gum in a mouth, but of course she loved it; the first time
she'd seen it her eyes had misted over with surprise and pleasure.
Mr. Pike said, watching her face, "Do you like it, honey? I designed
it myself."

One of the unusual features about the orange-brick house was
its antique front door. It was an authentic Presbyterian, or Christian,
door dating from 1786, Mr. Pike said with pride, made of heavy oak,
carved to form a cross at the top with an opened Bible suggested in
the lower half. Leila Lee's initial thought was that the battered old

door jarred with the style of the house but in time she was to stop minding it, or even seeing it. Mr. Pike was particularly proud of the door because it had belonged to one Jepheth Pike, who had settled this part of the country when it was all wilderness and Chapelton wasn't anything but a ferry landing. A long long time ago, Mr. Pike said reverently, "And here we are now!" Leila Lee allowed herself to be hugged, hard; to be kissed and nuzzled and fondled, though they were standing outside in a blowy winter cold. There was something sad about the antique door no one ever used except company, but Mr. Pike's mood was anything but sad. That day, he'd hurried her inside and upstairs to his bedroom. They didn't have much time, he said, before Lamar Jr. was due home from school.

That spring Leila Lee put in pansies and petunias and bright Oriental poppies in the long bed fronting the house but many of the flowers died out in a few weeks, the earth was so pocked with pebbles, broken slate, chunks of concrete. Mr. Pike approved of her working in the flower beds, as the first Mrs. Pike had done; he conceded that the place needed a woman's touch in small things. But his main interest in the farm was his cattle, of course. He had three cows, five steers, and two yearling heifers in his herd. You wouldn't have thought so few cattle would add up to so much work but Mr. Pike seemed to relish the work, when he had time for it. Most days Lamar Jr. did the routine tasks. (If the boy hated his daddy's pet cattle as much as Leila Lee guessed he did, he had enough sense to keep quiet about it.) One morning Leila Lee chanced to note Lamar Jr. crossing the barnyard weighed down by heavy buckets in both hands and how, even so—not thinking to set the buckets down—he paused to watch his father in the pasture in the midst of the herd. It seemed to Leila Lee an eerie thing: that she and Lamar Jr. were thinking the exact same thought at the exact same moment. If Mr. Pike lavished half as much attention and good feeling on his son as on those ugly smelly beasts, there wouldn't be half so much trouble in the household.

(Or was that all wrong? Leila Lee wondered. That boy's mind wasn't the kind an ordinary person could read.)

Leila Lee's private feelings about religion were ambiguous. It would not have been inaccurate to say that she didn't know what she believed or even, precisely, what she'd been told—as a child (baptized in the Methodist faith) and as a young adult (converted to Roman Catholicism at the insistence of her first husband). When life went well she didn't think about God, but when life snarled she found herself thinking about God a good deal, as if trying to bargain with, or outguess, Him. It was a losing proposition! Leila Lee supposed, trying to see the humor in it. He had all the cards on His side.

Leila Lee's parents, who had been Methodists in a casual way, were dead now and fading rapidly into oblivion. Leila Lee had feuded with them for years so it was hard to believe they would be united again in another world, or would want to be. Her ex-husbands, who were still alive (so far as she knew), had the feel about them, when she thought of them, of being dead. And good riddance. It had been her first husband who'd infected her with a filthy disease aged nineteen that turned into an inflammation of her ovaries and . . . the rest of it.

She had her doubts about God though she wasn't too proud, these days, to pray to Him in her thoughts—just quick fleeting thoughts having to do with Lamar Jr. (She was worried Mr. Pike would seriously hurt the boy some day soon. Did she imagine it or was his temper getting worse?) She had her doubts even more about Jesus Christ, but she remembered from her somewhat confused days as a Roman Catholic how she'd been fascinated by certain things in their hometown cathedral: the elaborate altar, the votive candles in their little red glasses, the statues of Jesus Christ with His heart raw and exposed and of the Virgin Mary grieving over Christ as He lay dying, or dead, with His head in her lap, the folds of their voluminous robes commingled. The mother's sorrow at outliving her son. . . . Leila Lee could summon tears even now, thinking of that statue. She'd gone through a phase when it was the Virgin Mary she prayed to exclusively, and not any of the men.

It was difficult too for Leila Lee to gauge her husband's views on religion. He led her and Lamar Jr. in brief prayers of thanksgiving before meals, and he quizzed Lamar Jr. on his Sunday school lessons when he remembered to, and he did give sizable contributions to the church. But he seemed not to believe in God as such, or in any case not in God's world. It was a dog-eat-dog world, he often said, with an air of satisfaction. You had to keep going or your competitors would devour your rear.

He was always quoting from the Bible but Leila Lee didn't know how to react. His tone was both lugubrious and ironic—sometimes funny. After news came of the death of an old business rival he rubbed his hands energetically and said with his big smile, "You see? 'They that live by the sword shall perish by the sword.'" Another time, watching television, a newsreel came on of famine victims in one or another African country and Mr. Pike said, sighing, "'The poor ye *always* have with you,'" and switched to another channel.

Why didn't he bring some of his friends home with him after school, Leila Lee suggested to Lamar Jr., though she knew, or suspected, that the poor child had no friends. "Yes, ma'am," he said, fixing her with a polite bored look. "I will do that."

He did his homework, and he did his daily chores, and he had his science fiction interests, and he watched a few select television programs a week. Sometimes he tramped in the woods and fields for hours but he insisted upon going alone: wouldn't let Leila Lee accompany him, though she promised to walk fast and not hold him back. When a neighbor's dog trotted after him he sent the dog back home because, as he said, the dog would interfere with his thoughts!

One day, with Mr. Pike's permission, Leila Lee took Lamar Jr. on a trip to a natural science museum in another city. The two of them, alone together for hours, got along fairly well by Leila Lee's estimate though not wonderfully well as she had hoped. The science museum was a dull, quiet, serious place that seemed truly to intrigue Lamar Jr., and Leila Lee did the best she could to follow along behind him. Anything that was "educational" had its appeal for Leila Lee's stepson no matter how boring: fossil exhibits, extinct bird exhibits, dusty tableaux of prehistoric animals and slack-jawed Neanderthal cavemen (and women, Leila Lee noted with surprise; somehow she'd never thought of actual women living back then). There was, in a darkened room, a model of the solar system in which miniature planets and their satellites orbited at mysteriously varying speeds around a sphere that resembled a swollen orange. Leila Lee would have been shaken to realize how small Earth was, and how insignificant, if she hadn't been so glassy-eyed with boredom by then. Also, you could see that the planets hadn't been dusted in some time and the "sun" hadn't the slightest suggestion about it of heat.

Another time, in November, Leila Lee took Lamar Jr. to visit the Surratt Patriot's Mansion some twenty-five miles upriver. The excursion was a few days after, and meant in partial recompense for, a particularly unhappy session between Mr. Pike and Lamar Jr., during which time Mr. Pike had been forced to discipline the boy by swatting him about the head and shoulders with a folded newspaper. Exactly what Lamar Jr. had done to merit this punishment Leila Lee didn't know because it was none of her business and she had no inclination to ask Mr. Pike to explain. Discipline was his domain.

From the outside the Surratt Mansion, which dated from 1760, looked disappointingly like an ordinary log-and-mortar house— hardly a mansion even by the standards of the eighteenth century. Inside, it seemed even smaller, consisting of two floors, no more than six or seven rooms, a precariously steep stairway. But the antiquated furnishings and the funny wavy-glass windows—the very look of the place—were fascinating, Leila Lee thought. To think that men and women lived so long ago, in such a place, in the very midst of the wilderness and susceptible to attack by Indians, wild beasts, and one another! She wondered if they were people like herself, if the women were women like herself. She wondered what it could have been like, for a woman to give birth in such circumstances.

Lamar Jr. had been quiet, you might even say sullen, for most of the morning. But once inside the mansion he asked the guide a number of sharp suspicious questions that caused everyone in their little group of twelve or so visitors to look at him. Leila Lee didn't know whether to be proud of the boy (for naturally he'd be thought to be *her* flesh-and-blood son) or embarrassed. Lamar Jr. did have a way about him that was—well, abrasive, smart-alecky, as Mr. Pike said; his voice could take on a sneering high-pitched tone that grated the nerves. One of his questions touched Leila Lee's heart—"How did so many people live crowded together in a house this size?"— asked in genuine perplexity. The guide, a fat, friendly woman, said with a smile that that was how people lived, in those days. "Maybe they didn't know they were crowded together," she said.

Lamar Jr. took the reply as a rebuff, it seemed. He clammed up tight for the rest of the downstairs.

Upstairs were three bedrooms, one of them a long open drafty room the guide referred to as the children's room, though it was also the place, the very spot, where the patriot Surratt (a young man of twenty-four) had been killed by Hessian soldiers. He'd been pursued into the house and up the stairs and in full view of his mother and young sisters he was shot at close range in the chest—"with a gun very like the musket on the staircase wall behind you," the guide said with a dramatic rise in her voice. (Everyone turned, startled, to look.) Next the guide stooped fatly to point out bloodstains in the pine floor and everyone crowded around to examine them, each in turn. Lamar Jr. adjusted his glasses and said skeptically, "That could be any kind of stain." The guide ignored him as best she could. One of the women in the group said quickly, "Goodness, that must have been a tragic day for this house!" The guide said, "Yes, it was."

On the way home Leila Lee took Lamar Jr. for lunch at a garish roadside place called Bobby's she'd been brought to a few times before meeting Mr. Pike. It was out of the ordinary for Lamar Jr. to be treated to a restaurant lunch, but the boy seemed unimpressed, even bored, by the setting. He drummed his fingers on the tabletop and hummed under his breath as Leila Lee tried to make conversation. He studied the menu, closed it, slapped it down, then took it up again and studied it again and closed it again and slapped it down. Leila Lee was facing him for the first time that day, and she couldn't help but see that the boy, aged thirteen, was looking *old*. His skin had drained to a pale sickly hue and his ghost eyes were more transparent than ever. Mr. Pike is killing him, Leila Lee thought in a panic.

But it was a thought you couldn't do anything constructive with, so Leila Lee shoved it aside and took a sip of her peach daiquiri. (One of the attractions of Bobby's, she'd have had to admit, was their peach daiquiris. They also served banana, pineapple, orange, lime, and another kind of daiquiri she couldn't recall, though she'd had them all at various times.) She reached over boldly to lay her hand atop Lamar Jr.'s and said, "Wasn't that Surratt Mansion *interesting!* So much history in such a little space! I'd love to go back another time, wouldn't you?" Lamar Jr. stared at her hand as if it were some sort of dead thing touching him, but he made no movement to push it away. He was a polite boy, at heart. Leila Lee took another swallow of her daiquiri and said, in a confidential voice, "You know, Lamar, your daddy loves you above anything on earth. He does, that's a fact. He told me point-blank he loves you more than he loves *me*, or ever could. He told me that before we were married, to give me fair warning, I believe. What do you think of that?"

At that moment their waitress arrived to take food orders. She was a pudgy bright-smiling youngish woman in spike-heeled shoes, a tight-fitting jersey blouse, and scarlet satin shorts with *Bobby's* monogrammed on the cuffs—Leila Lee had forgotten how the waitresses dressed here, or she maybe wouldn't have brought Lamar Jr. for lunch. But the boy seemed scarcely to notice the smiling young woman, let alone her costume. He gave his order in a flat, bored voice and shoved the menu aside. Leila Lee flushed with embarrassment; she disliked any kind of unnecessary rudeness, especially in public. And she always took the part of waitresses, knowing what they were up against.

When they were alone she said to Lamar Jr., "It's wrong of you to take out bad feelings on innocent people. You're a smart boy and you should know that."

Lamar Jr. stifled a yawn. He said, "Who should I take them out on, guilty people?"

"The trouble with you is, you're too damned smart."

"Maybe I'm not smart enough."

"That's a way of looking at it," Leila Lee said angrily. She paused, thinking hard. She said, "I shouldn't bring up such a subject—your daddy would disapprove—but you know, Lamar, he *is* a businessman. It's what finances our household. It's what puts food on your plate. He never talks about such things to you or to me, but I happen to know that a businessman has got to take out his meanness in some way close by that can't fight back, like other businessmen can fight back. Does that ring true? You got to understand your daddy in his own world."

Lamar Jr. showed some quickening of interest at this but his response was an ironic drawl. "How's a businessman sure there's anything that can't fight back?"

"It's the way things are. The way the world is set up," Leila Lee said. She had found a tiny fly in her drink and was trying to fish it out with the corner of a paper napkin. "And in fact—I shouldn't be telling you this!—your daddy had a specially worrisome week last week. Some other man beat him out to a big purchase where there's going to be a mall built in a few years."

Leila Lee ordered a second peach daiquiri but was too polite to say anything about the tiny fly. When their food arrived—a hamburger plate for Lamar Jr., a salad plate for Leila Lee—Lamar Jr. ate with little appetite at first, as he commonly did at home, then with more and more appetite as Leila Lee watched. So skinny! She'd love to fatten him up! She said gently, "You know, Lamar, your daddy *does* love you above anything on earth. That's the important thing. That's what I hope you'll remember from today."

Lamar Jr. didn't so much as glance up from his hamburger. He said, "Next time he lays a hand on me I'm going to kill him."

It happened on the first day of December, a Monday, a schoolday, and it happened so swiftly and, in a terrible way, so naturally, Leila Lee was always to understand that it couldn't have *not* happened. And what she herself had to do with it, what blame or what fault or what complicity, she would not have wanted to say.

Lamar Jr. was out behind the house chopping wood and Mr. Pike arrived home in the early dusk and so far as Leila Lee could determine he simply took up again an unresolved quarrel of the previous day— or was it the previous week?—and when he advanced on Lamar Jr., the boy feinted at him with the ax, and that infuriated Mr. Pike so he lost control and lunged after him, and Lamar Jr. danced out of the way.

Some of this Leila Lee had the misfortune of seeing, since she was in the kitchen speaking on the telephone when Mr. Pike's jeep pulled up around back, but she couldn't hear a word of what they shouted at each other. She heard them shouting, but that was all. She saw Mr. Pike advancing upon Lamar Jr. and she saw Mr. Pike's arm reared back to strike a blow and she saw the first swing of the ax, which looked to her (she'd remember this: she'd swear to this) like an accident of a kind, that strange kind of accident that happens while you watch it happen and it's your own action that is causing it but at the same time it *isn't*—just something that happens.

In recounting the episode Leila Lee would speed things up but of course it required more time than this to occur. Ten minutes? Fifteen? She'd tensed a little as she frequently did when she heard Mr. Pike coming home—the jeep made a louder, bouncier sort of noise coming up the driveway than the Lincoln—and then Mr. Pike was out there with Lamar Jr. and his breath was steaming and they appeared to be discussing something earnestly and Lamar Jr. was cringing back like a dog when it's scolded, and then Leila Lee began to hear loud voices (or was it just Mr. Pike's voice?) and still it was a few minutes before what happened happened so she had time to think what *she* should do: hurry to the back door and call out to Mr. Pike that he was wanted on the telephone, or maybe she was feeling faint, or maybe some madman had just dialed their number and was at that very instant whispering foul things to her over the phone— or if she'd had the slightest bit of courage she wouldn't just call to her husband from the doorway but run right out into the December chill and shout, "You! Stop! Don't lay a hand on that boy! You hateful hateful man!"

But Leila Lee was a coward, or at any rate couldn't move from where she stood. Just stood there paralyzed, half knowing what was going to happen as if it were a television movie she'd seen a long time ago and was only now recalling as she saw it a second time.

She got off the telephone: how she did it gracefully, and without arousing any alarm, she'd never remember afterward.

Even then she took time enough to get her heavy cable-knit sweater hanging from a peg near the door. And going outside it was like she was swimming upstream, throwing herself against the current. She did at last begin to scream but it was involuntary now, seeing Lamar Jr. with the ax in both his hands, swinging it in a wide terrible arc at Mr. Pike, who was staggering backward—for the first time, Leila Lee had time to think even at this instant, in his life. She screamed, "Lamar! No!" but no force on earth could have interrupted the ax's wide swinging arc.

Mr. Pike had tried to shield himself with both his arms but the ax struck them down. And then, swung again in a second arc, the ax struck him broadside on his head and blood seemed to burst from him like something from a burst balloon, and he fell heavily to the ground and Leila Lee knew he must be dead but she kept crying, pleading, "Lamar! Don't! Oh, don't—*please!*"

All this while Lamar Jr. uttered no words, not even in anger, but Leila Lee was to recall that sobbing noises came from him in spasms, involuntary as her own screams. And there suddenly was Mr. Pike fallen: Leila Lee's husband of ten months and fourteen days lying dead, his poor skull smashed, in the graveled driveway of his own homestead. And there was crazed Lamar Jr., standing over him with his legs spread, bringing the ax down another time, and another. . . . And then catching sight of Leila Lee where she stood not ten feet away, he stared at her baffled and eager as if she were a vision of some kind just arisen out of the earth before him. He was breathing hard, his eyes showed round and intent behind his crooked glasses, and Leila Lee stood swaying with her eyes shut and a voice that must have been her own said clearly, inside her head: I will be next.

Long afterward Leila Lee would wonder what force had driven her out there when her deepest instinct should have been to run into another part of the house and bolt the door and get on the telephone and dial the emergency number: ambulance, police, fire company, what would it matter? And why, seeing Mr. Pike broken and dead, all that blood around him, and worse, splashed in the gravel, she'd stood her ground for as long as she had. Why she had stared at her stepson so—not calmly, exactly, more with a look of sorrow and resignation. "Oh, what have you done!" she whispered.

And Lamar Jr., splattered in his father's blood, stood staring at her with the ax at rest against his bent knee. As if he'd been using that man-sized instrument all his life and knew the most efficient leverage for it, right hand closed about the end of the handle, left hand gripping it close by the head.

Leila Lee tried not to look at the body at his feet but at Lamar Jr. She knew it was important not to look away from his eyes. She said, wetting her lips, "I'll say I did it."

The things that transpired after this, Leila Lee wasn't to remember clearly. She knew that if she let herself break down and begin crying in earnest, that wild wailing hopeless crying that springs out of your chest unbidden, she'd never be able to stop or know how to deal with Lamar Jr. (Who appeared to be in a state of shock: allowing her to lead him by the hand into the house but saying not a word, just moving like a person in a dream putting one foot in front of the other.)

The first thing she did was make him remove his bloodstained clothes and get into the shower. Didn't watch him undress, of course, but stood on the other side of the bathroom door giving instructions. "Wash clean," she said several times. "Scrub yourself. Be sure to shampoo your hair; it's surely in your hair." She laid out for him a fresh pair of trousers and a long-sleeved white shirt—a white shirt seemed appropriate under the circumstances.

She changed her clothes too, for some reason she couldn't have named. Took off her flannel slacks and put on a woolen skirt and a blue cardigan sweater Mr. Pike had bought her. Fluffed out her hair with the brush, dabbed on fresh lipstick, eyed herself in the mirror, and saw that she looked so near to the way she always looked it might almost be that nothing had happened out back, or that it hadn't happened yet.

Lamar Jr. wasn't in his room when she went to get him and for a moment she tasted panic. What if he'd gone back outside to get the ax? He'd dropped the ax in the gravel and given it a little kick as if to get it out of sight, but of course it was in plain sight.

She found the boy sitting hunched in the dark on the top step of the three steps leading down to the darkened family room. She said, a little out of breath, "Lamar, are you all right? You're all right, aren't you?" He made some vague sound that might have been words. Just sitting there hugging his knees, staring ahead. Leila Lee touched his hair, which was damp and neatly combed, and he didn't flinch or stiffen against her. She said, "Are you hungry? You must be hungry. It's past suppertime; you must be hungry."

She said, "We could go out for hamburgers at Howard Johnson's. You're all dressed and so am I."

She said, "I just don't know if I'm up to making any meal in that kitchen tonight."

Lamar Jr.'s eyes, fixed on her now, seemed to be coming slowly into focus. He stirred, got slowly to his feet, then just stood there.

Leila Lee could see that he was trembling deep inside his body where no one could comfort him.

"You've got to eat, Lamar," she said, meaning to be practical. "You've got to keep up your strength for—"

She fell silent. *For all that lies ahead*, she'd meant to say. But what would it be that lay ahead? Beyond the next hour, or this evening, or tomorrow morning?

Leila Lee tried to order her thoughts, which were breaking and scattering in all directions, like bees scared out of a hive. Of the two of them it fell to her to be in charge and she had to think what to do or there'd be worse trouble than there was. She intended to tell them—the police, the authorities—that she'd done it, not her step-son, but her mind was beginning to flinch away from what "it" was, exactly. And if they guessed she was lying, what would she do then?

"I wonder if we should move him," she said suddenly. "Into the house, maybe. The basement? Just to get him out of the—where he is."

Lamar Jr. said faintly, "I don't know."

It was the first thing he'd said in some time, and Leila Lee was a little disappointed in it. The boy was watching her with a forehead creased as an old man's and a look of calm childlike trust.

"Or maybe . . . we could wrap him in a canvas and carry him in the jeep. . . . Down to the river, maybe. Is the river frozen over yet?" Leila Lee asked. She spoke energetically, in odd rhythmic surges. It wasn't her normal way of speaking but it seemed right. "That way no one would know. We'd tell people he just disappeared. Or we'd tell them he went on a trip, make up some place for him to go to. I believe he was due to fly to Houston next week. We could say he went a few days early."

For some reason her heart gave a lurch and she knew she'd have to ease away from that subject. It was all too complicated for them to consider right now. She would have to tell herself the story over and over carefully in her head and she would have to get Lamar Jr. to memorize his part but it was too complicated at the moment. She felt light-headed and excited and exhausted all at once, that state of mind where you don't dare trust your judgment and should make no crucial decisions.

She asked Lamar Jr. again if he was hungry and he wiped his nose with the edge of his hand before replying. The lenses of his glasses were smudged with fingerprints; Leila Lee couldn't see his eyes but she knew they were there, fixed trustingly upon her. "I guess so," he said.

"Well, that's a good sign," Leila Lee said with a cheerfulness she didn't altogether feel.

She seemed to have changed her mind about going out to eat. It was beginning to snow and the wind sounded mean and there were perfectly good leftovers in the refrigerator—fried chicken, mashed potatoes, the remains of a macaroni-and-cheese casserole—Mr. Pike's favorite foods and Lamar Jr. liked them well enough too. She loaded things on a tray and carried them into the family room where Lamar Jr. was sitting quietly, his hair neatly combed and his fresh white shirt giving him a Sunday morning kind of look.

The family room was walnut-paneled with a mammoth fieldstone fireplace and low-slung "modernistic" furniture, as Mr. Pike called it. Leila Lee considered it the most attractive room in the house and always regretted they never seemed to use it as a family. Its advantage tonight was that its windows faced out the front of the house, not out the rear. And the largest of their several television sets was here.

Leila Lee switched on the television to keep them company. As the bright-colored images shifted into focus she felt relaxed and almost safe for the first time in—however long it had been. She'd stopped keeping track of the time since she'd heard Mr. Pike's jeep careen up the drive.

They watched with varying degrees of attention a documentary called "The World of Trees: Acacia to Yew." Next came a network news program, so Leila Lee switched channels to a newlyweds' quiz show; she didn't want her nerves jangled any worse than they'd been. They ate slowly and distractedly as they watched and when Lamar Jr. seemed to be finished Leila Lee took the plates away and brought him a napkin for his greasy mouth and hands. He hadn't eaten much but it was more than she'd expected. She asked did he want ice cream, there was a quart of raspberry ripple in the freezer, but he shook his head no. Leila Lee was moved to recall how, a long time ago, he'd say "No, thank you, ma'am" in his cold flat nasty voice and she had hated him or hated the idea of him, and her needing to court him. But that was all over now.

Mr. Pike was nudging Leila Lee awake and saying, "Where are you, hon? Why don't you come to bed?" his tone not pushy but sad-sounding and pleading. Leila Lee opened her eyes wide as she customarily did when she was caught off guard or feeling guilty but she couldn't see Mr. Pike, who was crouched right over her. Yet there were his eyes!—she *could* make out his eyes!—that greeny-gray color she'd be seeing the rest of her life in reflections off windows or water puddles, or in the sky at certain times of morning when the light isn't sunlight but something else. She drew breath to speak and explain herself, she meant to assure Mr. Pike she'd be there immediately, but somehow it happened not just that Mr. Pike was gone but that, for a long terrible moment, everything was gone. Leila Lee's eyes were opened wide seeing nothing.

Then she was awake, and there was the television still on, some late-night movie she halfway thought she'd seen before. Her mouth was so parched it ached, and her eyes were caked with sleep as if she'd been sleeping for many hours instead of—how many had it been? The clock on the mantel said 12:25. Lamar Jr. was at the other end of the sofa sobbing quietly to himself, that kind of sobbing you know has been going on a long time, and Leila Lee stared at him not knowing why they were where they were, or why the boy was crying like that, choking back worse sobs, and then suddenly she knew: she remembered. In a rush of sick terror she said, "Oh, Lamar! Oh, Lamar, *honey*—"

Leila Lee saw that the boy seemed to be caving in on himself. His skeleton seemed to be collapsing. She reached out for him with no mind that doing so might make things worse, the two of them crying and choking, and nothing decided about what came next. Limp and unresisting he slid like sand into her arms. Lay with his head in her lap like a small child. She smoothed his hair, she stroked his heated face, she tried to unclench his fingers that were trembling with tension. She saw that his nails were edged with dried blood and that it would take some work to get them clean.

Still, she closed her eyes in a kind of weary gratitude and rested her head atop his. His hair was clean, at least: baby-fine and soft and smelling of nothing but cleanness. This is peace, Leila Lee was thinking. Even the murmurous noise of the television movie was far away. This is love, this is the end of things.

In this posture they remained for a very long time.

THE SWIMMERS

There are stories that go unaccountably wrong and become impermeable to the imagination. They lodge in the memory like an old wound never entirely healed. This story of my father's younger brother, Clyde Farrell, my uncle, and a woman named Joan Lunt with whom he fell in love, years ago, in 1959, is one of those stories.

Some of it I was a part of, aged thirteen. But much of it I have to imagine.

It must have been a pale, wintry, unflattering light he first saw her in, swimming laps in the early morning in the local YM-YWCA pool, but that initial sight of Joan Lunt—not her face, which was obscured from him, but the movement of her strong, supple, creamy-pale body through the water and the sureness of her strokes—never faded from Clyde Farrell's mind.

He'd been told of her, in fact he'd come to the pool that morning partly to observe her, but still you didn't expect to see such serious swimming, 7:45 A.M. of a weekday, in the antiquated white-tiled Y pool, light slanting down from the wired glass skylight overhead, a sharp medicinal smell of chlorine and disinfectant pinching your nostrils. There were a few other swimmers in the pool, ordinary swimmers, one of them an acquaintance of Clyde's who waved at him, called out his name, when Clyde appeared in his swim trunks on the deck, climbed up onto the diving board, then paused to watch

223

Joan Lunt swimming toward the far end of the pool . . . just stood watching her, not rudely but with a frank childlike interest, smiling with the spontaneous pleasure of seeing another person doing something well, with so little waste motion. Joan Lunt in her yellow bathing suit with the crossed straps in back and her white rubber cap that gleamed and sparked in the miniature waves: an attractive woman in her mid-thirties, though she looked younger, with an air of total absorption in the task at hand, swimming to the limit of her capacity, maintaining a pace and a rhythm Clyde Farrell would have been challenged to maintain himself, and Clyde was a good swimmer, known locally as a very good swimmer, a winner, years before, when he was in his teens, of county and state competitions. Joan Lunt wasn't aware of him standing on the diving board watching her, or so it appeared. Just swimming, counting laps. How many she'd done already, he couldn't imagine. He saw that she knew to cup the water when she stroked back, not to let it thread through her fingers like most people do; she knew as if by instinct how to take advantage of the element she was in, propelling herself forward like an otter or a seal, power in her shoulder muscles and upper arms and the steady flutter kick of her legs, feet flashing white through the chemical-turquoise glitter of the water. When Joan Lunt reached the end of the pool she ducked immediately down into the water in a well-practiced maneuver, turned, used the tiled side to push off from, in a single graceful motion that took her a considerable distance, and Clyde Farrell's heart contracted when, emerging from the water, head and shoulders and flashing arms, the woman didn't miss a beat, just continued as if she hadn't been confronted with any limit or impediment, any boundary. It was just water, and her in it, water that might go on forever, and her in it, swimming, sealed off and invulnerable.

Clyde Farrell dived into the pool and swam vigorously, keeping to his own lane, energetic and single-minded too, and when, after some minutes, he glanced around for the woman in the yellow bathing suit, the woman I'd told him of meeting, Joan Lunt, he saw to his disappointment she was gone.

His vanity was wounded. He thought, She never once looked at me.

———

My father and my Uncle Clyde were farm boys who left the farm as soon as they were of age: joined the U.S. Navy out of high school, went away, came back, and lived and worked in town, my father in a small sign shop and Clyde in a succession of jobs. He drove a truck for a gravel company; he was a foreman in a local tool factory; he managed a sporting goods store; he owned property at Wolf's Head Lake, twenty miles to the north, and spoke with vague enthusiasm of developing it some day. He wasn't a practical man, and he never saved money. He liked to gamble at cards and horses. In the navy he'd learned to box and for a while after being discharged he considered a professional career as a welterweight, but that meant signing contracts, traveling around the country, taking orders from other men. Not Clyde Farrell's temperament.

He was a good-looking man, not tall, about five feet nine, compact and quick on his feet, a natural athlete, with well-defined shoulder and arm muscles, strong sinewy legs. His hair was the color of damp sand, his eyes a warm liquid brown, all iris. There was a gap between his two front teeth that gave him a childlike look and was misleading.

No one ever expected Clyde Farrell to get married, or even to fall seriously in love. That capacity in him seemed missing, somehow: a small but self-proclaimed absence, like the gap between his teeth.

But Clyde was powerfully attracted to women, and after watching Joan Lunt swim that morning he drifted by later in the day to Kress's, Yewville's largest department store, where he knew she'd recently started work. Kress's was a store of some distinction: the merchandise was of high quality, the counters made of solid burnished oak; the overhead lighting was muted and flattering to women customers. Behind the counter displaying gloves and leather handbags, Joan Lunt struck the eye as an ordinarily pretty woman, composed, intelligent, feminine, brunette, with a brunette's waxy-pale skin, carefully made up, even glamorous, but not a woman Clyde Farrell would have noticed much. He was thirty-two years old, in many ways much younger. This woman was too mature for him, wasn't she—probably married or divorced, very likely with children. Clyde thought, In her clothes she's just another one of them.

So Clyde walked out of Kress's, a store he didn't like anyway, and wasn't going to think about Joan Lunt, but one morning a few days later there he was, unaccountably, back at the YM-YWCA, 7:30

A.M. of a weekday in March 1959, and there too was Joan Lunt in
her satiny-yellow bathing suit and gleaming white cap. Swimming
laps, arm over strong slender arm, stroke following stroke, oblivious
of Clyde Farrell and of her surroundings so Clyde was forced to see
how her presence in the old, tacky, harshly chlorinated pool made
of the place something extraordinary that lifted his heart.

That morning Clyde swam in the pool, but only for about ten
minutes, then left and hastily showered and dressed and was waiting
for Joan Lunt out in the lobby. Clyde wasn't a shy man, but he could
give that impression when it suited him. When Joan Lunt appeared
he stepped forward, and smiled, and introduced himself, saying,
"Miss Lunt? I guess you know my niece Sylvie? She told me about
meeting you." Joan Lunt hesitated, then shook hands with Clyde and
said, in that way of hers that suggested she was giving information
meant to be clear and unequivocal, "My first name is Joan." She
didn't smile but seemed prepared to smile.

Close up, Joan Lunt was a good-looking woman with shrewd dark
eyes, straight dark eyebrows, an expertly reddened mouth. There
was an inch-long white scar at the left corner of her mouth like a
sliver of glass. Her thick shoulder-length dark brown hair was carefully waved, but the ends were damp; though her face was pale it
appeared heated, invigorated by exercise.

Joan Lunt and Clyde Farrell were nearly of a height, and comfortable together.

Leaving the YM-YWCA, descending the old granite steps to Main
Street that were worn smooth in the centers, nearly hollow with
decades of feet, Clyde said to Joan, "You're a beautiful swimmer—
I couldn't help admiring you, in there," and Joan Lunt laughed and
said, "And so are you—I was admiring you too," and Clyde said,
surprised, "Really? You saw me?" and Joan Lunt said, "Both times."

It was Friday. They arranged to meet for drinks that afternoon,
and spent the next two days together.

In Yewville, no one knew who Joan Lunt was except as she
presented herself: a woman in her mid-thirties, solitary, very private,
seemingly unattached, with no relatives or friends in the area. No
one knew where exactly she'd come from, or why; why here of all
places, Yewville, New York, a small city of less than thirty thousand

people, built on the banks of the Eden River, in the southwestern
foothills of the Chautauqua Mountains. She had arrived in early
February, in a dented rust-red 1956 Chevrolet with New York State
license plates, the rear of the car piled with suitcases, cartons, clothes.
She spent two nights in Yewville's single good hotel, the Mohawk,
then moved into a tiny furnished apartment on Chambers Street.
She spent several days interviewing for jobs downtown, all jobs you
might call jobs for women specifically, and was hired at Kress's and
started work promptly on the first Monday morning following her
arrival. If it was sheerly good luck, the job at Kress's, the most
prestigious store in town, Joan Lunt seemed to take it in stride, the
way a person would who felt she deserved as much. Or better.

The other saleswomen at Kress's, other tenants in the Chambers
Street building, men who approached her—no one could get to know
her. It was impossible to get beyond the woman's quick, just slightly
edgy smile, her resolute cheeriness, her purposefully vague manner.
Asked where she was from she would say, "Nowhere you'd know."
Asked was she married, did she have a family, she would say, "Oh,
I'm an independent woman, I'm well over eighteen." She'd laugh to
suggest that this was a joke, of a kind—the thin scar beside her
mouth white with anger.

It was observed that her fingers were entirely ringless.

But the nails were perfectly manicured, polished an enamel-hard
red.

It was observed that, for a solitary woman, Joan Lunt had curious
habits.

For instance, swimming. Very few women swam in the YM-
YWCA pool in those days. Sometimes Joan Lunt swam in the early
morning, and sometimes, Saturdays, in the late morning; she swam
only once in the afternoon, after work, but the pool was disagreeably
crowded, and too many people approached her. A well-intentioned
woman asked, "Who taught you to swim like that?" and Joan Lunt
said quietly, "I taught myself." She didn't smile, and the conversation
was not continued.

It was observed that, for a woman in her presumed circumstances,
Joan Lunt was remarkably arrogant.

It seemed curious too that she went to the Methodist church
Sunday mornings, sitting in a pew at the very rear, holding an opened

hymnbook in her hand but not singing with the congregation, and that she slipped away afterward without speaking to anyone. Each time, she left a neatly folded dollar bill in the collection basket.

She wasn't explicitly unfriendly, but she wasn't friendly. At church, the minister and his wife tried to speak with her, tried to make her feel welcome, *did* make her feel welcome, but nothing came of it; she'd hurry off in her car, disappear. People began to murmur there was something strange about that woman, something not right, yes, maybe even something wrong; for instance, wasn't she behaving suspiciously? Like a runaway wife, for instance? A bad mother? A sinner fleeing Christ?

Another of Joan Lunt's curious habits was to drink, alone, in the early evening, in the Yewville Bar & Grill or the White Owl Tavern or the restaurant-bar adjoining the Greyhound bus station. If possible, she sat in a booth at the very rear of these taverns, where she could observe the front entrances without being seen herself. For an hour or more she'd drink bourbon and water, slowly, very slowly, with an elaborate slowness, her face perfectly composed but her eyes alert. In the Yewville Bar & Grill there was an enormous sectioned mirror stretching the length of the taproom and in this mirror, muted by arabesques of frosted glass, Joan Lunt was reflected as beautiful and mysterious. Now and then men approached her to ask was she alone? did she want company? how's about another drink? but she responded coolly to them and never invited anyone to join her. Had my Uncle Clyde approached her in such a fashion she would very likely have been cool to him too, but my Uncle Clyde wasn't the kind of man to set himself up for any sort of public rejection.

One evening in March, before Joan Lunt met up with Clyde Farrell, patrons at the bar of the Yewville Bar & Grill, one of them my father, reported with amusement hearing an exchange between Joan Lunt and a local farmer who, mildly drunk, offered to sit with her and buy her a drink, which ended with Joan Lunt saying, in a loud, sharp voice, "You don't want trouble, mister. Believe me, you don't."

Rumors spread, delicious and censorious, that Joan Lunt was a man-hater. That she carried a razor in her purse. Or an ice pick. Or a lady's-sized revolver.

It was at the YM-YWCA pool that I became acquainted with Joan Lunt, on Saturday mornings. She saw that I was alone, that I was a good swimmer, might have mistaken me for younger than I was and befriended me, casually and cheerfully, the way an adult woman might befriend a young girl to whom she isn't related. Her remarks were often exclamations, called across the slapping little waves of the turquoise-tinted water, *"Isn't* it heavenly!"—meaning the pool, the prospect of swimming, the icy rain pelting the skylight overhead while we, in our bathing suits, were snug and safe below.

Another time, in the changing room, she said almost rapturously, "There's nothing like swimming is there? Your mind just *dissolves."*

She asked my name, and when I told her she stared at me and said, "Sylvie. I had a close friend once named Sylvie, a long time ago. I loved that name, and I loved *her."*

I was embarrassed but pleased. It astonished me that an adult woman, a woman my mother's age, might be so certain of her feelings and so direct in expressing them to a stranger. I fantasized that Joan Lunt came from a part of the world where people knew what they thought and announced their thoughts importantly to others. This struck me with the force of a radically new idea.

I watched Joan Lunt covertly and I didn't even envy her in the pool, she was so far beyond me; her face that seemed to me strong and rare and beautiful, and her body that was a fully developed woman's body—prominent breasts, shapely hips, long firm legs—all beyond me. I saw how the swiftness and skill with which Joan Lunt swam made other swimmers, especially the adults, appear slow by contrast: clumsy, ill-coordinated, without style.

One day Joan Lunt was waiting for me in the lobby, hair damp at the ends, face carefully made up, her lipstick seemingly brighter than usual. "Sylvie!" she said, smiling. "Let's walk out together."

So we walked outside into the snow-glaring windy sunshine, and she said, "Are you going in this direction? Good, let's walk together." She addressed me as if I were much younger than I was, and her manner was nervous, quick, alert. As we walked up Main Street she asked questions of me of a kind she'd never asked before, about my family, about my "interests," about school, not listening to the answers and offering no information about herself. At the corner of Chambers and Main she asked eagerly would I like to come back to her apartment to visit for a few minutes, and though out of shyness I wanted to say No, thank you, I said yes instead because it was clear that Joan Lunt was frightened about something, and I didn't want to leave her.

Her apartment building was shabby and weatherworn, as modest a place as even the poorest of my relatives lived in, but it had about it a sort of makeshift glamour, up the street from the White Owl Tavern and the Shamrock Diner, where motorcyclists hung out, close by the railroad yards on the river. I felt excited and pleased to enter the building and to climb with Joan Lunt—who was chatting briskly all the while—to the fourth floor. On each floor Joan would pause, breathless, glancing around, listening, and I wanted to ask if someone might be following her? waiting for her? but of course I didn't say a thing. When she unlocked the door to her apartment, stepped inside, and whispered, "Come in, Sylvie!" I seemed to understand that no one else had been invited in there before.

The apartment was really just one room with a tiny kitchen alcove, a tiny bathroom, a doorless closet, and a curtainless window with stained, injured-looking venetian blinds. Joan Lunt said with an apologetic little laugh, "Those blinds—I tried to wash them but the dirt turned to a sort of paste." I was standing at the window peering down into a weedy back yard of tilting clotheslines and windblown trash, curious to see what the view was from Joan Lunt's window, and she came over and drew the blinds, saying, "The sunshine is too bright, it hurts my eyes."

She hung up our coats and asked if I would like some coffee? Fresh-squeezed orange juice? "It's my half-day off from Kress's," she said. "I don't have to be there until one." It was shortly after eleven o'clock.

We sat at a worn dinette table, and Joan Lunt chatted animatedly and plied me with questions as I drank orange juice in a tall glass, and she drank black coffee, and an alarm clock on the windowsill ticked the minutes briskly by. Few rooms in which I've lived even for considerable periods of time are as vividly imprinted in my memory as that room of Joan Lunt's, with its spare, battered-looking furniture (including a sofa bed and a chest of drawers), its wanly wallpapered walls bare of any hangings, even a mirror, and its badly faded shag rug laid upon painted floorboards. There was a mixture of smells: talcum powder, perfume, cooking odors, insect spray, general mustiness. Two opened suitcases were on the floor beside the sofa bed, apparently unpacked, containing underwear, toiletries, neatly folded sweaters and blouses, several pairs of shoes. A single dress hung in the closet, and a shiny black raincoat, and our two coats Joan had hung on wire hangers. I stared at the suitcases, thinking, How strange; she'd been living here for weeks but hadn't had time yet to unpack.

So this was where the mysterious Joan Lunt lived, the woman of whom people in Yewville spoke with such suspicion and disapproval! She was far more interesting to me, and in a way more real, than I was to myself; shortly, the story of the lovers Clyde Farrell and Joan Lunt, as I imagined it, would be infinitely more interesting, and infinitely more real, than any story with Sylvie Farrell at its core. (I was a fiercely introspective child, in some ways perhaps a strange child, and the solace of my life would be to grow not away from but ever more deeply and fruitfully *into* my strangeness, the way a child with an idiosyncratic, homely face often grows into that face and emerges, in adulthood, as "striking," "distinctive," sometimes even "beautiful.") It turned out that Joan liked poetry, and so we talked about poetry, and about love, and Joan asked me in that searching way of hers if I was "happy in my life," if I was "loved and prized" by my family, and I said, "Yes, I guess so," though these were not issues I had ever considered before and would not have known to consider if she hadn't asked. For some reason my eyes filled with tears. Joan said, "The crucial thing, Sylvie, is to have precious memories." She spoke almost vehemently, laying her hand on mine. "That's even more important than Jesus Christ in your heart, do you know why? Because Jesus Christ can fade out of your heart, but precious memories never do."

We talked like that. Like I'd never talked with anyone before.

I was nervy enough to ask Joan how she'd gotten the little scar beside her mouth, and she touched it quickly and said, "In a way I'm not proud of, Sylvie." I sat staring, stupid. The scar wasn't disfiguring in my eyes but enhancing. "A man hit me once," Joan said. "Don't ever let a man hit you, Sylvie." Weakly I said, "No, I won't."

No man in our family had ever struck any woman that I knew of, but it happened sometimes in families we knew. I recalled how a ninth-grade girl had come to school that winter with a blackened eye, and she'd seemed proud of it, in a way, and everyone had stared—and the boys just drifted to her, staring. Like they couldn't wait to get their hands on her themselves. And she knew precisely what they were thinking.

I told Joan Lunt that I wished I lived in a place like hers, by myself, and she said, laughing, "No, you don't, Sylvie, you're too young." I asked where she was from and she shrugged—"Oh, nowhere"—and I persisted: "But is it north of here, or south? Is it the country? Or a city?" and she said, running her fingers nervously through her hair, fingering the damp ends, "My only home is *here, now*, in this room, and, sweetie, that's more than enough for me to think about."

It was time to leave. The danger had passed, or Joan had passed out of thinking there was danger.

She walked with me to the stairs, smiling, cheerful, and squeezed my hand when we said goodbye. She called down after me, "See you next Saturday at the pool, maybe," but it would be weeks before I saw Joan Lunt again. She was to meet my Uncle Clyde the following week, and her life in Yewville that seemed to me so orderly and lonely and wonderful would be altered forever.

Clyde had a bachelor's place (that was how the women in our family spoke of it) to which he brought his women friends. It was a row house made of brick and cheap stucco, on the west side of town, near the old now-defunct tanning factories on the river. With the money he made working for a small Yewville construction company, and his occasional gambling wins, Clyde could have afforded to live in a better place, but he hadn't much mind for his surroundings and spent most of his spare time out. He brought Joan Lunt home with him because, for all the slapdash clutter of his house, it was more private than her apartment on Chambers Street, and they wanted privacy badly.

The first time they were alone together Clyde laid his hands on Joan's shoulders and kissed her, and she held herself steady, rising to the kiss, putting pressure against the mouth of this man who was virtually a stranger to her so that it was like an exchange, a handshake, between equals. Then, stepping back from the kiss, they both laughed; they were breathless, like people caught short, taken by surprise. Joan Lunt said faintly, "I—I do things sometimes without meaning them," and Clyde said, "Good. So do I."

Through the spring they were often seen together in Yewville; and when, weekends, they weren't seen, it was supposed they were at Clyde's cabin at Wolf's Head Lake (where he was teaching Joan Lunt to fish) or at the Schoharie Downs racetrack (where Clyde gambled on the Standardbreds). They were an attractive, eye-catching couple. They were frequent patrons of local bars and restaurants, and they turned up regularly at parties given by friends of Clyde's and at all-night poker parties in the upstairs rear of the Iroquois Hotel. Joan Lunt didn't play cards but she took an interest in Clyde's playing, and, as Clyde told my father admiringly, she never criticized a move of his, never chided or teased or second-guessed him. "But the woman has me figured out completely," Clyde said. "Almost from the first, when she saw the way I was winning and the way I kept on, she said, 'Clyde, you're the kind of gambler who won't quit because, when he's losing, he has to get back to winning, and, when he's winning, he has to give his friends a chance to catch up.' "

In May, Clyde brought Joan to a Sunday gathering at our house, a large noisy affair, and we saw how when Clyde and Joan were separated, in different rooms, they'd drift back together until they were touching, literally touching, without seeming to know what they did, still less that they were being observed. So that was what love was! Always a quickness of a kind was passing between them, a glance, a hand squeeze, a light pinch, a caress, Clyde's lazy fingers on the nape of Joan's neck beneath her hair, Joan's arm slipped around Clyde's waist, fingers hooked through his belt loop. . . . I wasn't jealous but I watched them covertly. My heart yearned for them, though I didn't know what I wanted of them, or for them.

At thirteen I was more of a child still than an adolescent girl: thin, long-limbed, eyes too large and naked-seeming for my face, and an imagination that rarely flew off into unknown territory but turned, and turned, and turned upon what was close at hand and known, but not altogether known. Imagination, says Aristotle, begins in desire: but what *is* desire? I could not, nor did I want to, possess my Uncle Clyde and Joan Lunt. I wasn't jealous of them, I loved

them both. I wanted them to *be*. For this too was a radically new
idea to me, that a man and a woman might be nearly strangers to
each other, yet lovers; lovers, yet nearly strangers; and the love
passing between them, charged like electricity, might be visible, without their knowing. Could they know how I dreamt of them!

After Clyde and Joan left our house, my mother complained
irritably that she couldn't get to know Joan Lunt. "She's sweet-
seeming and friendly enough, but you know her mind isn't there for
you," my mother said. "She's just plain *not-there*."

My father said, "As long as the woman's there for Clyde."

He didn't like anyone speaking critically of his younger brother
apart from himself.

But sometimes in fact Joan Lunt wasn't there for Clyde: he
wouldn't speak of it, but she'd disappear in her car for a day or two
or three, without explaining very satisfactorily where she'd gone or
why. Clyde could see by her manner that wherever Joan had gone
had perhaps not been a choice of hers, and that her disappearances,
or flights, left her tired and depressed, but still he was annoyed; he
felt betrayed. Clyde Farrell wasn't the kind of man to disguise his
feelings. Once on a Friday afternoon in June before a weekend they'd
planned at Wolf's Head Lake, Clyde returned to the construction
office at 5:30 P.M. to be handed a message hastily telephoned in by
Joan Lunt an hour before: *Can't make it this weekend. Sorry. Love,
Joan.* Clyde believed himself humiliated in front of others, vowed
he'd never forgive Joan Lunt; that very night, drunk and mean-spirited, he took up again with a former girlfriend . . . and so it went.

But in time they made up, as naturally they would, and Clyde
said, "I'm thinking maybe we should get married, to stop this sort
of thing," and Joan, surprised, said, "Oh, that isn't necessary, darling—I mean, for you to offer that."

Clyde believed, as others did, that Joan Lunt was having difficulties with a former man friend or husband, but Joan refused to
speak of it, just acknowledged that, yes, there was a man, yes, of
course he was an *ex*, but she resented so much as speaking of him;
she refused to allow him reentry into her life. Clyde asked, "What's
his name?" and Joan shook her head, mutely: just no; no, she would
not say, would not utter that name. Clyde asked, "Is he threatening

you? Now? Has he ever shown up in Yewville?" and Joan, as agitated
as he'd ever seen her, said, "He does what he does, and I do what
I do. And I don't talk about it."

But later that summer, at Wolf's Head Lake, in Clyde's bed in
Clyde's hand-hewn log cabin on the bluff above the lake, overlooking
wooded land that was Clyde Farrell's property for a mile in either
direction, Joan Lunt wept bitterly, weakened in the aftermath of
love, and said, "If I tell you, Clyde, it will make you feel too bound
to me. It will seem to be begging a favor of a kind, and I'm not
begging."

Clyde said, "I know you're not."

"I don't beg favors from anyone."

"I know you don't."

"I went through a long spell in my life when I did beg favors,
because I believed that was how women made their way, and I was
hurt because of it, but not more hurt than I deserved. I'm older now.
I know better. The meek don't inherit the earth, and they surely
don't deserve to."

Clyde laughed sadly and said, "Nobody's likely to mistake you
for meek, Joan honey."

*Making love they were like two swimmers deep in each other, plunging
hard. Wherever they were when they made love, it wasn't the place they
found themselves in when they returned, and whatever the time, it wasn't
the same time.*

The trouble came in September. A cousin of mine, another niece
of Clyde's, was married, and the wedding party was held in the
Nautauga Inn, on Lake Nautauga, about ten miles east of Yewville.
Clyde knew the inn's owner, and it happened that he and Joan Lunt,
handsomely dressed, were in the large public cocktail lounge adjacent
to the banquet room reserved for our party, talking with the owner-
bartender, when Clyde saw an expression on Joan's face of a kind
he'd never seen on her face before—fear, and more than fear, a
sudden sick terror—and he turned to see a stranger approaching
them, not slowly, exactly, but with a restrained sort of haste: a man
of about forty, unshaven, in a blue seersucker sports jacket now

badly rumpled, tieless, a muscled but soft-looking man with a blunt, rough, ruined-handsome face, complexion like an emery board, and this man's eyes were too bleached a color for his skin, unless there was a strange light rising in them. And this same light rose in Clyde Farrell's eyes in that instant.

Joan Lunt was whispering, "Oh, no—*no*," pulling at Clyde's arm to turn him away, but naturally Clyde Farrell wasn't going to step away from a confrontation, and the stranger, who would turn out to be named Robert Waxman, Rob Waxman, Joan Lunt's former husband, divorced from her fifteen months before, co-owner of a failing meat supplying company in Kingston, advanced upon Clyde and Joan, smiling as if he knew them both, saying loudly, in a slurred but vibrating voice, "Hello, hello, hello!" and when Joan tried to escape Waxman leapt after her, cursing, and Clyde naturally intervened, and suddenly the two men were scuffling, and voices were raised, and before anyone could separate them there was the astonishing sight of Waxman with his gravelly face and hot eyes crouched holding a pistol in his hand, striking Clyde clumsily about the head and shoulders with the butt, and crying, enraged, "Didn't ask to be born! God damn you! I didn't ask to be born!" and, "I'm no different from you! Any of you! *You!* In my heart!" There were screams as Waxman fired the pistol point-blank at Clyde, a popping sound like a firecracker, and Waxman stepped back to get a better aim, he'd hit his man in the fleshy part of a shoulder, and Clyde Farrell, desperate, infuriated, scrambled forward in his wedding party finery, baboon-style, not on his hands and knees but on his hands and feet, bent double, face contorted, teeth bared, and managed to throw himself on Waxman, who outweighed him by perhaps forty pounds, and the men fell heavily to the floor, and there was Clyde Farrell straddling his man, striking him blow after blow in the face, even with his weakened left hand, until Waxman's nose was broken and his nostrils streamed blood, and his mouth too was broken and bloody, and someone risked being struck by Clyde's wild fists and pulled him away.

And there on the floor of the breezy screened-in barroom of the Nautauga Inn lay a man, unconscious, breathing erratically, bleeding from his face, whom no one except Joan Lunt knew was Joan Lunt's former husband; and there, panting, hot-eyed, stood Clyde Farrell over him, bleeding too, from a shoulder wound he was to claim he'd never felt.

Said Joan Lunt repeatedly, "Clyde, I'm sorry. I'm so sorry."

Said Joan Lunt, carefully, "I just don't know if I can keep on seeing you. Or keep on living here in Yewville."

And my Uncle Clyde was trying hard, trying very hard, to understand.

"You don't love me, then?" he asked several times.

He was baffled, he wasn't angry. It was the following week and by this time he wasn't angry, nor was he proud of what he'd done, though everyone was speaking of it and would speak of it, in awe, for years. He wasn't proud because in fact he couldn't remember clearly what he'd done, what sort of lightning-swift action he'd performed, no conscious decision had been made that he could recall. Just the light dancing up in a stranger's eyes, and its immediate reflection in his own.

Now Joan Lunt was saying this strange unexpected thing, this thing he couldn't comprehend. Wiping her eyes, and, yes, her voice was shaky, but he recognized the steely stubbornness in it, the resolute will. She said, "I do love you. I've told you. But I can't live like that any longer."

"You're still in love with *him*."

"Of course I'm not in love with him. But I can't live like that any longer."

"Like what? What I did? I'm not *like* that."

"I'm thirty-six years old. I can't take it any longer."

"Joan, I was only protecting you."

"Men fighting each other, men trying to kill each other—I can't take it any longer."

"I was only protecting you. He might have killed you."

"I know. I know you were protecting me. I know you'd do it again if you had to."

Clyde said, suddenly furious, "You're damned right I would."

Waxman was out on bail and returned to Kingston. Like Clyde Farrell he'd been treated in the emergency room at Yewville General Hospital; then he'd been taken to the county sheriff's headquarters and booked on charges of assault with a deadly weapon and reckless endangerment of life. In time, Waxman would be sentenced to a year's probation: with no prior record except for traffic violations, he was to impress the judge with his air of sincere remorse and repentance. Clyde Farrell, after giving testimony and hearing the sentencing, would never see the man again.

Joan Lunt was saying, "I know I should thank you, Clyde. But I can't."

Clyde splashed more bourbon into Joan's glass and into his own. They were sitting at Joan's dinette table beside a window whose grimy and cracked venetian blinds were tightly closed. Clyde smiled and said, "Never mind thanking me, honey, just let's forget it."

Joan said softly, "Yes, but I can't forget it."

"It's just something you're saying. Telling yourself. Maybe you'd better stop."

"I want to thank you, Clyde, and I can't. You risked your life for me. I know that. And I can't thank you."

So they discussed it, like this. For hours. For much of a night. Sharing a bottle of bourbon Clyde had brought over. And eventually they made love, in Joan Lunt's narrow sofa bed that smelled of talcum powder, perfume, and the ingrained dust of years, and their love-making was tentative and cautious but as sweet as ever, and driving back to his place early in the morning, at dawn, Clyde thought surely things were changed, yes, he was convinced that things were changed; hadn't he Joan's promise that she would think it all over, not make any decision, they'd see each other that evening and talk it over then? She'd kissed his lips in goodbye, and walked him to the stairs, and watched him descend to the street.

But Clyde never saw Joan Lunt again.

That evening she was gone, moved out of the apartment, like that, no warning, not even a telephone call, and she'd left only a brief letter behind with *Clyde Farrell* written on the envelope. Which Clyde never showed to anyone and probably, in fact, ripped up immediately.

It was believed that Clyde spent some time, days, then weeks, into the early winter of that year, looking for Joan Lunt; but no one, not even my father, knew exactly what he did, where he drove, whom he questioned, the depth of his desperation or his yearning or his rage, for Clyde wasn't of course the kind of man to speak of such things.

Joan Lunt's young friend Sylvie never saw her again either, or heard of her. And this hurt me too, more than I might have anticipated.

And over the years, once I left Yewville to go to college in another state, then to begin my own adult life, I saw less and less of my Uncle Clyde. He never married: for a few years he continued the life he'd been leading before meeting Joan Lunt, a typical bachelor life, of its place and time; then he began to spend more and more time at Wolf's Head Lake, developing his property, building small wood-frame summer cottages and renting them out to vacationers and acting as caretaker for them, an increasingly solitary life no one would have predicted for Clyde Farrell.

He stopped gambling too, abruptly. His luck had turned, he said.

I saw my Uncle Clyde only at family occasions, primarily weddings and funerals. The last time we spoke together in a way that might be called forthright was in 1971, at my grandmother's funeral. I looked up and saw through a haze of tears a man of youthful middle age moving in my general direction: Clyde, who seemed shorter than I recalled, not stocky but compact, with a look of furious compression, in a dark suit that fitted him tightly about the shoulders. His hair had turned not silver but an eerie metallic-blond, with faint tarnished streaks, and it was combed down flat and damp on his head, a look here too of furious constraint. Clyde's face was familiar to me as my own, yet altered: the skin had a grainy texture, roughened from years of outdoor living, like dried earth, and the creases and dents in it resembled animal tracks; his eyes were narrow, damp, restless; the eyelids looked swollen. He was walking with a slight limp he tried, in his vanity, to disguise; I learned later that he'd had knee surgery. And the gunshot wound to his left shoulder he'd insisted at the time had not given him much, or any, pain gave him pain now, an arthritic sort of pain, agonizing in cold weather. I stared at my uncle, thinking, *Oh, why? Why?* I didn't know if I was seeing the man Joan Lunt had fled from or the man her flight had made.

But Clyde sighted me and hurried over to embrace me, his favorite niece still. If he associated me with Joan Lunt—and I had the idea he did—he'd forgiven me long ago.

Death gives to life—to the survivors' shared life, that is—an insubstantial quality. It's like an image of absolute clarity reflected in water, then disturbed, shattered into ripples, revealed as mere surface. Its clarity, even its beauty, can resume, but you can't any longer trust in its reality.

So my Uncle Clyde and I regarded each other, stricken in that instant with grief. But, being a man, *he* didn't cry.

We drifted off to one side, away from the other mourners, and I saw it was all right between us, it was all right to ask, so I asked had he ever heard from Joan Lunt, after that day? Had he ever heard *of* her? He said, "I never go where I'm not welcome, honey," as if this were the answer to my question. Then added, seeing my look of distress, "I stopped thinking of her years ago. We don't need each other the way we think we do when we're younger."

I couldn't bear to look at my uncle. *Oh, why? Why?* Somehow I must have believed all along that there was a story, a story unknown to me, that had worked itself out without my knowing, like a stream tunneling its way underground. I would not have minded not knowing this story could I only know that it *was.*

Clyde said, roughly, "*You* didn't hear from her, did you? The two of you were so close."

He wants me to lie, I thought. But I said only, sadly, "No, I never heard from her. And we weren't close."

Said Clyde, "Sure you were."

The last I saw of Clyde that day, it was after dark and he and my father were having a disagreement just outside the back door of our house. My father insisted that Clyde, who'd been drinking, wasn't in condition to drive his pickup truck back to the lake; and Clyde was insisting he was; and my father said maybe yes, Clyde, and maybe no, but he didn't want to take a chance: why didn't *he* drive Clyde home; and Clyde pointed out truculently that, if my father drove him home, how in hell would he get back here except by taking Clyde's only means of transportation? So the brothers discussed their predicament, as dark came on.

GETTING TO KNOW
ALL ABOUT YOU

In 1962, in Rome, New York, we lived in our last house together as a family, my parents Darrell and Trix and my brother Wesley and me. In December of that year, when we split up—my mother to the state psychiatric hospital at Cattaraugus, my father to wherever, elusive man, he went—Wesley was seventeen and I was fifteen, "coming up fast on the outside lane," as Trix used to say. Trix often joked about me in some obscurely threatening (but comical) relationship to her, not because I resembled her—I was tall and rangy and freckled and homely, taking after Darrell's side of the family and not hers—but because I was her only daughter and in theory the baby of the household. Like a kitten we'd owned once that, small enough to fit in the palm of a child's hand, nonetheless growled deep in his throat when teased, I seemed to disconcert my mother simply by growing: as if I were betraying a contract of a kind between Trix and me. Sometimes, in one of her moods, she would contemplate me for so long I'd have to ask uneasily, "What are you looking at?" and, quick and glib, not missing a beat, she'd say, "That's what I was wondering too."

Trix's favored mode of discourse with my brother and me was the riddle, the rejoinder, the question-turned-on-its-head; she would have made, we joked, a great writer of those little fortunes extracted from Chinese fortune cookies. (When the four of us ate in Chinese restaurants—and we were always eating in Chinese restaurants—Trix was the one to make a fuss over the fortunes, insisting we read them aloud; or she'd read them aloud for us, smiling and nodding sagely, as if, however bland or innocuous or frankly nonsensical the fortunes were, they nonetheless yielded their secret meanings to her. The most cryptic, or the funniest, like ONE MOUTH, TWO EARS, USE ACCORDING, she brought home and taped to the refrigerator door.) Once, hurt by something Trix had said, I told Darrell that Trix just didn't take us seriously; and Darrell said, "Oh, no, honey, you've got it backwards: Trix takes you and your brother too seriously. That's the problem."

Had there been a problem? I hadn't known until that moment.

Those years, we were always moving; one "rental unit" to another, one city to another. Wesley and I were accustomed to transferring to new schools in the middle of a term, leaving behind newly made friends with the ease with which the family left behind, in each rental, things we'd outgrown or broken or no longer wanted, in the expectation that the next tenants might make some use of them. Both Darrell and Trix worked, but the nature of their work was often mysterious to Wesley and me, involving as it did abrupt starts and stops, deals that fell through, disappointments, betrayals. They were trained dancers, wonderful dancers: Trix had, if she was in one of her strong phases, a beautiful throaty alto voice—it resembled Nina Simone's—but most of the jobs they were forced to accept were not very glamorous, in fact frankly degrading; Darrell's most lucrative work was short-haul (i.e., nonunion) trucking, and Trix's was cocktail waitressing. (Sometimes the tips Trix brought home were so lavish, involving ten- and even twenty-dollar bills, she dared not show them to Darrell but only to Wesley and me, smiling mysteriously and winking, a cautionary finger to her lips.) Both clerked in stores, tried stints of door-to-door selling; Darrell hired himself out as an organist for special occasions, and Trix sang at weddings, though the pay in such instances wasn't much to brag about and the "exposure" negligible. We moved frequently because one or the other of them or both felt the urge; because a town's resources were exhausted; because Darrell had quit his job or was fired, or Trix had quit hers or was fired, or they'd run into "trouble" with the bank. There was also a "drinking problem"—my parents spoke of it, when they spoke of it, as a single problem, as if, like the rusted yet still rather classy-looking 1955 Cadillac that Darrell had bought third- or fourth-hand for a song, it was shared by them both and a vexation to both. (Though Darrell's drinking went back for years, and Trix's was relatively recent. "Since peeking over into the abyss," she joked. By which she meant turning thirty.)

As near as Wesley and I could determine, Darrell was Trix's primary reason for drinking, and Trix was Darrell's primary reason for drinking; and each liked to drink with the other, even while discussing "the problem." By the time Wesley was a senior in high school and I was a sophomore, it wasn't unusual for our parents to sit at the kitchen table or on the back (outside) stairs, drinking and smoking and talking for hours, out of the range of our hearing (unless we eavesdropped), drinking wine or beer or, if they could afford it, their favorite whiskey, Jack Daniels. In the morning, before leaving for school, Wesley and I would throw together breakfast, invariably cold cereal sweetened with teaspoonfuls of sugar, while Darrell and Trix slept in, the door to their bedroom conspicuously closed if not frankly locked (I tried the door a few times, not actually to open it—I would not have dared—but just experimentally, to see), and we'd discover the empty bottles set neatly inside the heavy-duty A&P shopping bag Trix used as a wastebasket beneath the kitchen sink, covered in ashes and cigarette butts, and, on the table and windowsill, the melted-down remains of the candles Trix liked to burn in the dark, those squat colored candles that give off a sharp odor of incense as they burn. The apartment so smelled of this incense, Wesley worried that he might carry the odor to school with him in his clothes, or in his hair, and that his classmates might ridicule him behind his back.

I felt a pang of resentment, that my brother cared about anything so petty and so futile as high school popularity. "They probably do," I said, meanly. "They probably ridicule us both. But Trix's incense is the least of it."

"Trix" was a derivation of Trish, our mother's girlhood name, or cognomen, as she called it; Trish was itself a derivation of Patricia. Trix disliked her original name because she thought it prissy and old-fashioned, but she didn't much like "Trix" either. When she and Darrell had had hopes of a career of some kind in show business her stage name was Roxanne, which seemed best to suit her; she was a small, slender, willful woman, with enormous eyes and small-boned delicate features and pale, almost platinum-blond hair, worn in straight-cut bangs to her eyebrows to disguise, as she said, her "rather low and undistinguished" forehead. A friend of mine once observed that Trix was a strange name; and that it was strange too, wasn't it, for my brother and me to call our parents by their first names? I explained, as Darrell and Trix had schooled us to explain, "Our family doesn't set much store by local customs, actually," and the girl looked at me in astonishment. I didn't tell her that if I'd called Trix "Mom," let alone "Mommy," she would have been infuriated. As it was, Trix liked to joke that she was "clearly too young to be the mother of such *hulking* offspring."

Before they were married, or in any case before they became parents, Darrell and Trix had hoped to be professional dancers— ballroom dancers, as they called it—which evoked, in Wesley's and my imagination, a vision of long-gowned beautiful women and men in tuxedos, a scene out of *Gone With the Wind* or one of the Fred Astaire–Ginger Rogers movies we watched on the late show. They had taken lessons from a "dancing master" in Buffalo, New York; there were piles of snapshots of the two of them from that time, "The Marvelous McIntyres" as they'd hoped to be called: Darrell startlingly young and handsome, with exaggerated sideburns and sleek oiled pompadoured hair, Trix (Roxanne?) as beautiful as any Hollywood starlet, blond hair in a shoulder-length pageboy perfect as a wig, and features dramatically emphasized—eyebrows darkened, eyes outlined in mascara, smile wide and earnest cutting into her dimpled cheeks. She was something of Doris Day, Dorothy Collins, Grace Kelly. (Yet even then, Darrell said, rather proudly, she could "turn into a hellcat at the drop of a hat.") "It says something, doesn't it, about the politics of this family," Wesley one day observed, when the two of us, alone together, bored, were paging another time through Trix's brimming album. "The disproportion of snapshots *before* and *after*." I said, "Before and after what?" "Before our births and after our births, stupid," Wesley said. "Haven't you ever noticed?"

It was obvious, yet I had not noticed. There must have been three times as many snapshots of Darrell and Trix, singly or together, as there were of them with us. I said, weakly, "Well, Trix's camera is broken." Wesley laughed. He said, "Of course, you and I aren't so *photogenic* as they are." He flipped through the pages, whistling thinly through his teeth. "Did you know there's a word, *xenogenic?* I discovered it the other day in the dictionary; it means 'offspring markedly different from parents.' " "So what does that mean?" I asked. "It means 'offspring markedly different from parents.' " "Yes, but what does that *mean?*" There were times when I hated Wesley intensely, though Wesley was my only friend.

He regarded me pityingly through his glasses. He was a tall weedy boy with a head too large for his narrow shoulders, bony elbows and wrists, "ferret-faced," as Trix affectionately called him; his facial skin so without color, like mine, that a half-dozen oversized freckles seemed to float in it, like seeds in watery milk. But his eyes were brightly watchful, and I feared his sharp tongue. It was generally granted in the household that Wesley was the smarter of the two of us, the brainier, though often, because of his asthma, his heart palpitations, and his tight-wired nerves, he had to suffer the humiliation of bringing home report cards less impressive than mine.

He said, "That I was right to believe what I've believed all along, that there isn't much genetic connection between us: between us, I mean, and them. We're just these sort of *things* they had, probably by accident, and wouldn't mind dumping, if they could get away with it."

"That isn't true," I said. "You shouldn't say things like that."

"You think Darrell and Trix wouldn't give us up, trade all this in"—he made a careless gesture meant to indicate the apartment we were currently renting (low water-stained ceilings, well-worn sticky linoleum in all the rooms, a fourth-floor walk-up in an aging brick tenement a few blocks from the less than thriving downtown of Schenectady, New York)—"if they could retrieve the way they were in the snapshots and have a real career? If they could be stars, be *famous*, be *rich?*"

I didn't want to answer; there was no answer. To say yes would provoke Wesley into derisive laughter, to say no would be a betrayal of Darrell and Trix. I said, in the quietest meanest voice, "You're just saying what you'd do in their place."

How hard our parents had tried to break into show business, whether they'd even auditioned for anything, Wesley and I couldn't determine; it was better not to ask. If Trix was in one of her cheery clownish moods she'd turn a question upside-down and toss it back into our faces; if she was in a depressed mood she'd say, "Oh, it was just a fairy tale, one of your father's pipe dreams." I had a vision of the past disappearing like a cloud of pipe smoke, though my father did not smoke pipes: only cigarettes.

Camels were his brand, Winstons Trix's. But naturally they smoked each other's, when they were caught short.

From Schenectady we moved to Utica, where Darrell worked for a while as a security guard at a Mayflower Movers warehouse and where, though she wanted badly to work—"anything to get out of this damned apartment"—Trix had difficulty finding a job that suited her. She was a waitress in a hotel restaurant but the tips were poor; she was a saleswoman (ladies' lingerie) in a downtown department store but the pay was too low; she was, for a mere week, a secretary-receptionist for a tool manufacturing company whose owner decided suddenly to file for bankruptcy. She wound up, as, she said, she knew she would—"it must be a law of physics with me, like gravitation"— as a cocktail waitress at the Golden Slipper, the best-known or perhaps the most notorious supper club in the city, in which, required to wear leather miniskirts, tight low-cut satin blouses, black net stockings, and spike-heeled shoes, she made a good deal of money from tips and got into the habit of drinking on the job. The patrons, she said, were to blame; they insisted. "A man doesn't like to drink alone," she said. "It's like, you know, making love alone. It lacks class."

It was at the Golden Slipper that Trix acquired a boyfriend named Roy Blume, a former policeman, "retired" from the force after a crackdown of some kind and dealing now in real estate. He drove a white 1959 Cadillac Seville which was often parked outside our apartment house when Wesley and I came home from school. "Look," I'd say, "he's here again," and Wesley would shrug his shoulders in a show of indifference. If Darrell didn't seem to care, why should *he* care? Upstairs, in the kitchen, Trix and Roy Blume were likely to be frying up hamburgers and onions or defrosting a frozen pizza in the oven, drinks in hand. When we appeared Trix would cry out gaily, "Don't tell me you kids come home for lunch now!"

and Wesley would say, "It's after four o'clock, Trix; it's a little late for lunch." Roy Blume, grinning, his big face flushed with pleasure, said, "It's never too late for lunch if you're goddamned hungry!" And he and Trix laughed as if he'd said something funny. I laughed too; it seemed the easiest way.

Wesley would stare at us all in disgust. He never stayed: picked up his schoolbooks and ran back down the stairs. I'd call after him to wait for me and he'd shout back, "You—you stay here! I don't want you tagging after me." There was a branch library a few blocks away where he could do his homework until it closed at nine o'clock. By then, Roy Blume would be gone; Trix would usually be gone too, on duty at the Golden Slipper. I'd be in the apartment alone, the radio turned up high, humming to myself, my stomach stuffed with the salty greasy delicious food Trix and Roy Blume had prepared. I'm happiest like this, I'd think. Catching sight of my pale grave freckled face in a mirror, my eyes still damp from so much laughter.

Roy Blume was married, with a family: one of his daughters was in Wesley's high school class. Trix didn't seem to care; she wasn't in love with him, just enjoyed his company, she said: "All I want is to know I'm alive for God's sake; is that too much to ask?" I worried sometimes that Trix would run off with Roy Blume and leave us alone with Darrell. (Whom we rarely saw, these days. He worked nights at the warehouse and slept into the afternoon.) I asked Wesley what did he think would happen and Wesley said he didn't know and didn't want to know. "But something has to happen, doesn't it?" I asked. Wesley said indifferently, "Ask *them*."

Those rare evenings Darrell happened to be home he was likely to be in a volatile mood. Like Trix he had a quick, hot temper; unlike Trix he sometimes shoved, slapped, punched. He'd begun to put on weight around the middle; his face was still lean, angular, with a fair, thin skin; his hair, receding in patches, was still a darkish brick-red, tight springy curls that were often damp with perspiration. When I saw Darrell outside the house on the street or downtown, by accident, I'd stare at him in surprise that *that man* could be my father; he looked too energetic, too special, to be contained in a family, in any set of rooms. I thought, He won't be with us for long.

And he did want to move out of Utica; he thought the city's

atmosphere "actively conducive to ill health." But where to go next? And where, if we went through the trouble of moving, would turn out better, in the long run, than here? "You can't take that attitude," Trix said nervously. "If you take that attitude, you're dead." "No," Darrell said, smiling. "*You're* dead."

They must have quarreled about Roy Blume, but I tried not to hear. Sitting up late at night, in the kitchen, in the dark, Trix's candles lit and giving off their harsh rich fragrance, talking earnestly, sometimes laughing, raising their voices. Wesley and I had separate bedrooms, of course, but I could sense him through the wall, awake as I was, eyes wide open like mine, hearing, even when not quite hearing, our parents' murmuring voices in the night. Is that what love is? I wondered. Is that what you do, married, a man and a woman: talking together, hour after hour, and drinking?

From Utica we moved to Rome: "A distinction," Trix said dryly, "without a difference." She had come to dislike the Golden Slipper but at least it was a job, and Darrell was having trouble keeping a job, what with his hot temper, and his pride, and his drinking, and his sense, for which none of us could blame him, of being undervalued by the world. "Forty-three years old and nothing to show for it," he said. Trix piped up, "You hear that, guys? He doesn't give a damn for *us*." "I'm not counting people outside my individual self," Darrell said in an aggrieved voice. "You must know what I mean, surely. My individual *soul*." "You have two soles, sweetie," Trix said, nudging him, pointing to his feet. "Two soles, one mouth, use according." And we all laughed.

Wesley had it analyzed, the way Wesley had most things analyzed: if Darrell tried to be serious, Trix clowned; if Trix tried to be serious, Darrell clowned. That way one of them was always covering for the other.

Roy Blume showed up at the apartment a final time, with an enormous order of Chinese take-out food, including Peking duck, Darrell's favorite, and we all ate together, including Darrell, who had quit his job at the warehouse a few days before. Everyone got along, there was a good deal of joking and laughing, and at one point Trix even sang, though this was after Wesley and I had gone to bed at midnight. Early on there'd been a little tension, when Trix complained teasingly about Darrell, as she often complained, that he blamed her for everything: "If a tree fell over on our roof this very instant he'd blame me. If lightning struck us all dead he'd blame me. Just the way his eyes fix on me I can see he blames me." Darrell laughed pleasantly and said, "I guess somebody's got a guilty conscience." Trix said nothing, and Roy Blume, handing around fortune cookies, said nothing. Darrell added slyly, "Or a guilty ass." But no one heard him, we were all busily breaking apart our fortune cookies and seeing what our fortunes were. Trix said gaily, "OK, guys, who wants to go first? Roy? Judith? Wesley? Darrell? *Me?*"

Wesley was my only friend, but he was also my only enemy. He was the only person in my life who, while he didn't want me to do badly or come to harm, didn't want me to do *too* well or be *too* happy. His liking for me was calibrated in terms of himself primarily: whether I made him look good or bad by comparison. Most of the time, I made him look good.

If we happened to pass each other in a school corridor, Wesley might look through me or he might, for no clear reason, call out loudly, "Hey, kid sister, how's it going?"—as if we were the kind of people who addressed each other like that. Wesley acted out of character so often, and so convincingly, you wouldn't have known (I suppose this was the point) what his character was. A girl from one of my classes with whom I happened to be walking once said wistfully, when Wesley called out his cheery greeting in the corridor, she wished *she* had a big brother. "It must make life easier, somehow."

"Oh, yes. It does," I said enthusiastically. And wondered if, saying it, I had made it true.

Though Wesley was shy and nervous and sharply critical of both his reedy nasal voice and his skinny body, he made it a point always to speak up in class, never to sit passively. His strategy, he explained, which should be mine too, was to establish himself within a few days of transferring to a new school as quick, smart, bright, articulate: "You have to make your impression right away, and it has to be a strong one.

"Otherwise," he added, "you're lost."

He was extremely intelligent—too smart for his own good, as Trix observed—but school examinations, even tests and small impromptu quizzes, filled him with dread. Since junior high school, the only way Wesley could get the high grades he wanted and deserved, was to study beforehand for hours: to write out laborious answers to hypothetical questions and to memorize the answers. When the test papers were passed out he'd quickly scan the questions, and those initial five or six seconds determined his fate. If he'd guessed right about the questions he had a chance to score as high as 100; if not, he was lucky to pass. "It's all so damned humiliating," he said, "but what can I do?" Trix said coolly, "You could hang yourself." Wesley laughed, shocked, but said without missing a beat, "And after *that?*"

I thought he took himself too seriously; what did it matter, really: tests, grades, report cards . . . all of it? In my worst moods, depressions that lasted, like overcast skies in this part of New York State, for days, I couldn't see what difference it made if you succeeded in school or failed, if you were "smart" or "stupid." The two smartest people of my acquaintance, including all the teachers I'd ever had, were Darrell and Trix: and what had smart got them?

For the first time in my memory, after one of our moves, there were boxes and cartons left unpacked: things Trix couldn't get around to dealing with. She had to look for a new job, and Darrell needed the car (he'd gotten a job selling shoes at a discount store in a mall), and the bus schedule was a problem, and the kitchen of the new rental needed cleaning, scrubbing, scouring, and she didn't feel well, not like her "old self"; an hour or two out of bed and she was exhausted as if she hadn't slept for days. She'd lie on the sofa, with a drink, the glass resting on her abdomen, sometimes just club soda with ice, but she needed, it seemed, the good feeling of a glass between her fingers, the solace of liquid and slow-melting ice; she'd lie and watch daytime television and if I came to join her she'd ask me if I didn't think—"Please tell me the unvarnished truth, now"— that she could act as well as the soap opera actresses and was as good-looking as they were, or almost. "Yet they have their careers and I have nothing," Trix said, puzzled. "Well, I shouldn't say I have *nothing*, I have my *life*." She smiled at me and her cheeks dimpled. "I have you and I have Darrell and Wesley. Promise you won't leave me, Judith?" Trix's serious moods made me uneasy, so I tried to make a joke, saying, "Where would *I* go?" In my bleached jeans, shapeless shirt, my hair a mess and my skin pallid as curdled milk, the possibility of my leaving home did seem preposterous.

Trix got a job eventually, selling catalog orders for a discount clothing company that operated out of Hoboken, New Jersey. For this she needed the car, and Darrell considered buying another car, but there wasn't enough money for payments, let alone a down payment and insurance and the rest. Darrell solved the problem by quitting his job—or getting fired; it wasn't exactly clear which, and there surely wasn't much point in making it clearer. He said, "A man can't look himself in the eye, jamming ladies' smelly feet in shoes all day long." Trix said, "A man hadn't better cuddle up to his honey, jamming ladies' smelly feet in shoes all day long." And they kissed and cuddled like young lovers, and tickled each other, and made plans, or talked about making plans, for the future. The catch phrase for the future was *what we try next*.

In this new house, Wesley was more methodical about spying on Darrell and Trix—"It scares me not to know what they're up to"— because, though small, it was an actual house, with an upstairs and downstairs, in which eavesdropping wasn't always so easy. Darrell had leased the property for a year, on his own, without consulting Trix, and Trix hated it immediately, sniffing the air: it was in a semi-rural "residential" neighborhood of unpaved dead-end streets that trailed off into fields, and one of these streets, close by, trailed off into the city dump. Darrell had not noticed the dump, he admitted. He guessed that the real estate agent, showing him the property, had been careful to take another route.

Trix said, "I think you did this on purpose."

Darrell said, "Why would I do it on purpose? Do you think I'm crazy?"

Trix said, "I think you're bent on punishment."

"On punishing who, myself?"

"If I'm you, and we're all you," Trix said wildly, making a gesture that included Wesley and me, "then that's who. And you know it, you fucker. *You can't deceive me.*"

Our first night in the house, we were kept awake by noise in the neighborhood: motorcycles, mainly. Two or possibly even three of our new neighbors not only drove motorcycles but appeared to be trading in them, repairing and selling. Trix observed dryly, "I suppose we'll end up buying a motorcycle too. If you can't lick 'em, join 'em."

Darrell said, as if the thought had come to him too, but not as a joke, "I wouldn't actually mind, in fact. But I'd want the real thing, a Harley-Davidson, not some prissy little Jap import."

Trix said, "Motorcycles are suicide."

"So? You only live once, love."

"You only *die* once."

After this move Darrell and Trix began to quarrel more frequently and more seriously. Trix quit her job ringing doorbells—"You feel like a hooker peddling the wrong product"—and got another as a cocktail waitress, at an extravagant roadhouse restaurant called the Mauna Loa; Darrell was driving a truck again, for a local cement company. He'd had several near-offers for managerial positions but they failed to come through at the last minute—Darrell didn't have a high school diploma, for one thing. And he wasn't confident he could trust former employers to write him helpful letters of recommendation.

Again, Trix had a boyfriend, or boyfriends. It was dangerous for her to leave the Mauna Loa alone (she worked until 2 A.M.), so someone usually drove her, and Darrell, home by that hour, waited up for her . . . sitting out on the front porch, in good weather, and drinking, and waiting. Sometimes when Trix came home they would prepare a late meal together, laughing and banging around in the kitchen; sometimes they fought. Upstairs in our beds Wesley and I cowered, not wanting to hear the things our parents screamed at each other, oblivious of the neighbors. In the morning, cleaning up after them, Wesley might ask, as if clinically, "Do you think people deserve to live, Judith, who make messes like this? Do you think there is any moral justification for them?" We were getting more fussy, both of us, about keeping things clean; the old house was infested with mice, cockroaches, termites, and, in season, ants . . . a certain species of large nimble black ant that seemed one day to be everywhere, underfoot and overhead. I said, "Maybe things will get better, once we're settled." Wesley said, "We *are* settled." I said, "When Darrell gets a better job." "But Darrell isn't going to get a 'better' job," Wesley said meanly, "because no one is stupid enough to give him one." "You don't know everything, Wesley. You can't predict the future." "I know Darrell is a drunk. A souse. A lush." "He's trying to cut back on his drinking, he says." "*He* says." "And so does she." "*She* says." But our bickering was halfhearted; we lacked the proper style. We'd turned into caretakers of our parents like a middle-aged spinster sister and bachelor brother who have been together all their lives and know nothing else.

That summer, Darrell began to get into trouble with the police. There had been problems now and then, in other cities, often with overdrawn bank accounts and "bad" checks, but this was another kind of trouble.

The first arrest was for fighting, in a tavern; the second, more serious, arrest was for selling merchandise (three portable televisions) that turned out to have been stolen . . . though not, luckily, by Darrell McIntyre. Darrell had to post $1,500 bail (which Trix borrowed from the owner of the Mauna Loa), and though in the end charges were dropped he had to pay his attorney $350, which he couldn't afford. He raged about the unfairness, the injustice: "Under the fucking U.S. legal code a man has to defend himself even if he's innocent! Especially if he's innocent! And no matter how it turns out he winds up paying the equivalent of a fine!" For weeks he talked of virtually nothing else.

After this, as if Darrell had crossed an invisible line and the crossing was irremediable, police came to our house fairly frequently with questions to ask of Darrell: not so much in suspicion of him as with the expectation that he might help them with other cases. Burglaries, bad checks, armed robbery, even the stranglings of young women in the area that had begun eighteen months before . . . there would be a loud knock at the door, and Trix would give a little scream, "Oh, Christ, *no*, not again, it's the police *again!*" Darrell always insisted he knew nothing, absolutely nothing; he had no friends in the city, no connections, so please would they leave him alone? He didn't care about himself, he said, but he was worried for his family. "What's it look like if a patrol car is parked in our driveway half the time?" he asked. "I don't want the house firebombed."

Darrell was infuriated by the police but knew he must speak civilly to them. They had, after all, so much power, and he had none. And the more he groveled before them, the more he pleaded, the angrier he would be when they left. Trix, frightened, cautioned us to stay out of his way. "Don't, you know," she whispered, a finger to her lips, "*provoke*."

After these visits from the police Trix tried to comfort Darrell: babied him, sat up with him and talked, and drank. I could hear their low murmurous voices coming up the heating duct, pure sound, without discernible words. Wesley felt obliged to eavesdrop on them at such times, sitting on the darkened stairs in his pajamas. Next day he'd tell me, in a voice heavy with sarcasm, that Trix did actually talk baby talk to Darrell and that he loved it, unless he lost his temper suddenly and told her to shut up. "They've been reminiscing about the 'dancing master' lately," Wesley said. "Wondering if he's still alive. And what went wrong with their careers." "Are they talking about moving again?" I asked. "I don't think so, they don't talk much about the future," Wesley said. "Or about us. Just themselves. *What went wrong*." "Maybe you shouldn't spy on them," I said. "Darrell won't like it, if he catches you." "I don't do it for fun," Wesley said angrily. "I feel *sorry* for them, I want to *help* them, I don't know for Christ's sake what to *do*." His eyes were bright with tears; his hands shook. He said, in the next breath, "I've got to get out."

One night in October, after Trix had been sent home early from the restaurant in a taxi—there'd been a disagreement of some kind with one of her customers—Wesley and I eavesdropped together, sitting on the stairs. Darrell said at one point, "That does it, you're never going back," and Trix said, "Honey, I'd go crazy at home, nothing to do but *think*," and Darrell said, "Don't tell *me*. I am your husband, and I say enough is enough." Trix dissolved into giggles, and for some reason Darrell laughed too, and in a while the familiar smell of incense wafted up the stairs, and we heard the ice cube tray from the refrigerator being emptied into its container. They were talking more quietly now so Wesley and I slipped farther down the stairs, until we were nearly at the bottom. Darrell was saying, "The curious thing is, love, nothing actually did go wrong with us. We are the same person we always were . . . the same people, I mean . . . the same two people. Outside and in."

Trix began singing, " 'Getting to know you . . . ' " and Darrell joined in, laughing, suddenly, and then they were on their feet, dancing. Not caring, suddenly, how much noise they made, if they woke us, if we were emboldened to spy on them. It was clear they were enjoying themselves. Wesley and I watched, abashed. Even drunk they were still good dancers, executing, as if by instinct, difficult exotic steps. Darrell was in his undershorts, and shirtless; Trix had stripped off her silky muumuu and danced in her black lace brassiere and half-slip, in her stocking feet. I thought, We'll be punished seeing them like this. It's wrong, seeing them like this. But it was hard to break away.

Wesley intended to go to college: "away" to college, as he pointedly said. There was no money, of course, and no promise of money, but he worked after school and Saturdays, at an A&P, and saved as much as he could. He wanted to go to a private university like Cornell, Rochester, or Syracuse, and not one of the branches of the state university; for this he would need a tuition scholarship, at least, and all the financial aid he could get. He wanted to study biochemistry, maybe medicine . . . if he could afford medical school.

On her good days Trix fantasized "Wesley McIntyre, M.D.," and talked excitedly, if fuzzily, of his future. On her bad days, which had become, by this time, most days, she accused him of planning to abandon her, of "grinding his heel" in her and Darrell's faces. Wesley said, pained, "Mother, don't be absurd." Trix shot back, "What is 'Mother' if not absurd? 'Mother' is such a definition." And she crinkled her face as if she meant to cry but couldn't remember how.

Wesley said to me, "She isn't going to let me go. I know it."

Once things begin to go bad in a family they go bad quickly, like fruit that's ripening one hour and rotting the next. Even as it happens it's impossible to believe that it *is* happening, that it won't somehow reverse itself and take you back to where you were.

All that year Darrell had become increasingly bitter and irritable. His weight shot up to over two hundred pounds and Trix no longer dared tease him by poking him in the gut or trying, with a pretense of comic failure, to close her arms around his waist. He swore at her and at us, pushed us around, gave us open-handed cuffs to the face, back, buttocks. When he drank his face lost its contours and resiliency; his skin became the color and texture of bread dough. My handsome father! Darrell whom I adored! He took a special dislike to Wesley, who slunk out of the room when Darrell entered and who couldn't keep his food down, some nights, after one of our contentious meals. At the same time Wesley was capable of defying Darrell, flaring up suddenly and wildly; the boys' gym coach at the high school had taught the boys the basic principles of boxing, and here was skinny bespectacled Wesley, one hundred fifteen pounds, striking out at Darrell with his fists, his head ducked, chin to his shoulder, knees bent. Darrell wheezed with laughter, forgetting to be angry. He cried, "Willie the Wisp! Our own Willie the Wisp! Trix, come here! Bring the camera! Our own Willie the Wisp!" as Wesley danced around him, jabbing frantically with his left fist, trying to set up leverage for a right cross. He dared to hit Darrell's forearms, even his exposed face, but his blows seemed to make no difference: Darrell just laughed.

Trix ran into the room not with her camera—which was, in any case, still broken—but with the ice cube tray, which she emptied, as efficiently as she could, over both their heads.

One night a few weeks before Christmas, Wesley and I were wakened by noises out front: a car motor, doors slamming, men shouting, the sound of fighting—and the car drove off. Darrell hauled Trix into the house and in the kitchen proceeded to beat her up; there was a sound of breaking glass, Trix's breathless screams, Darrell's cry of "Bitch"—a word he never used. Wesley said, "I'm going to call the police. He's drunk, he's killing her. Listen!" We cowered together on the stairs. Again Wesley said, "I'm going to call the police," but he didn't move, and I didn't move, and finally the noises subsided. We could hear them in the kitchen, crying. Both of them, crying. And in the morning Trix had a bruised face, a blackening eye, her makeup heavy, and her lips very red. She said, without looking at me, "If either of you tell on us I'll personally strangle you. Got it?"

But later that month, December 29 to be exact, it happened again, a loud argument downstairs that wakened me from my sleep: Trix's desperate childlike screams and Darrell's shouts and the sound of things being thrown around. It was three in the morning, and Trix had just come home from the Mauna Loa. This fight was prolonged and terrible and within a half hour the police arrived, and as soon as they entered the house Darrell went berserk.

And that was it: and irrevocably. As we didn't quite grasp at the time.

Darrell was booked on several charges, the most serious being felonious assault and resisting arrest; the police had beaten him badly, overpowered him, dragged him out to the squad car in handcuffs. Trix was taken semiconscious to the emergency room of the closest hospital, and hospitalized, and eventually kept for psychiatric observation; given so extreme a state, alternately depressed and violent, threatening to kill herself (and, I learned afterward, her daughter Judith), the attending physician had no choice but to commit her to the psychiatric ward for fourteen days' observation . . . then for thirty days . . . and at last she was formally committed to the State Hospital for the Insane at Cattaraugus.

It was not believable. But it was happening.

"We're being punished now, it's starting now," I told Wesley. "The things we said, how we watched them, spied on them . . . it's starting now and it won't ever end."

Wesley said, "For God's sake don't talk like that. They'll be all right. You know Darrell. You know Trix. It's probably some crazy joke of hers, getting back at us, making us worry."

I'd begun to cry, and then I was laughing. I thought of how, the first time we'd seen Trix in the intensive care ward of the hospital, we hardly recognized her. *Is that Trix? That isn't Trix.* Darrell had beaten her so savagely her face was no longer a face but something else, raw flesh, swollen, bruised, misshapen. *That can't be Trix. Not our Trix.* Her skull had been fractured in a fall and several of her ribs were broken. IV tubes were feeding her, keeping her alive. I'd said, as if a stranger's voice were speaking through me, dull and numbed, "Oh, hey, look, he didn't mean *this*. I hope the police understand; he didn't mean *this*."

Weeks later when we visited her at the state hospital, Trix seemed scarcely to recognize us or to care that we'd come. She was further changed: her face mottled and wizened, as if it had been soaked in water; her body limp, listless, frail, with a look of being uninhabited. Two of her front teeth were missing. Her white-blond hair was mostly white and cropped brutally short. For several painful minutes she refused to look at us; she stared into a corner of the ward or shut her eyes tight, rocking back and forth and humming to herself. Then she said, with a sudden bitter violence, "What are you staring at, you two . . . two little *fuckers*."

We tried to talk to her, tried to explain. If it was the police she was angry about, we hadn't called the police and we didn't know who had.

(I had not called, I'd been too terrified. And Wesley swore *he* hadn't.)

"Whoever did call the police," Wesley said, "—it must have been a neighbor—it's a good idea they did, isn't it? They saved your life, didn't they?"

Trix snorted in derision and turned away. That was it, that was going to be it for the day: she turned to a wall, hugged herself hard, began to hum. No melody I could recognize, just sound, angry and buzzing. I could see that my mother had found a place where no one knew her, no one remembered her as she had been or expected anything of her. And that place suited her. So why were we, whoever we were, here? All we did was agitate the air.

But our mother was severely depressed, we were informed. She suffered from "delusions," "hallucinations," "compulsive thoughts." If she were to be taken off drugs she was likely to become violent: digging at herself with her nails, raking her face, her arms, raving, demanding to be released, threatening the staff physician, the attendants, the other inmates, whom she accused of spying on her and mimicking her behind her back. She spoke of getting out of the hospital and finding her husband and strangling *him*. And her children too . . . if she could find them.

Years of excessive drinking had permanently damaged her health: her liver and her heart. And, though X rays had not indicated any blood clotting, the skull fracture might have permanently affected her brain.

We tried to explain that Mother—shrewdly, we now called Trix "Mother"—often said things she didn't mean. She was emotional at times but basically she was an intelligent, reasonable woman; she was a very intelligent woman. "That is her problem, in fact," Wesley said daringly. "She and my father both . . . have never been able to use their intelligence." "And why is that, do you think?" the doctor asked. His question was sincere enough, but neither Wesley nor I could think of an answer.

Darrell too was gone. Both his children had betrayed him, he said, and that "canceled out all debts." He owed us no favors any more than we owed him.

A few days after being released from jail he forfeited his bail bond and disappeared, taking the Cadillac and a few clothes, both his own and Trix's. When we came home from school that day we found a scrawled note on the kitchen table: *Lousy little traitors, stew in your own juice.*

So far as we knew he never came back to Rome, nor did he try to visit Trix at Cattaraugus. He telephoned the hospital often, they said, and demanded to speak to her, but was refused, and hung up without leaving his telephone number. He called us too, at the high school, saying it was a "family emergency" but declining to identify himself. He asked solely about Trix, not about us: Was there any change in her? What sorts of things did she say about him? Did she forgive him? Did she still love him? When was she going to be discharged? He couldn't talk long, he said, he knew our conversations were being monitored by the police; he knew they were after him, had him on their wanted list, were determined to throw him into jail. "You crushed our life flat, like an empty beer can, you two," he'd say, his voice slurred, gravelly, "so I hope you're happy now. You two." If we protested he interrupted and repeated what he said: "*You two.*" He never asked after us: how we were; where, even, we were living. He must have known we could take care of ourselves and didn't after all require any parents.

The run-down house at the city limits had reverted to other tenants. Wesley and I were no longer living together. He was the lucky one: boarding with his chemistry teacher until the fall, when he'd start college at the University of Rochester. (Wesley must have done well on his college entrance examinations, for which he'd studied obsessively, even during the frantic uprooted days when our family was first broken up. When the letter from Rochester came with its good, impossibly good, news, my brother wept as I'd never seen him weep, not even that night our parents were taken away.)

Because there was no one to take me in—Darrell and Trix had always been boastful of having "severed all ties" with their families— I was remanded to a county welfare shelter for adolescents: runaways, delinquents, sociopaths, and psychotics; girls in every state of pregnancy; children whose parents had kicked them out or whose parents, like ours, had simply disappeared. Wesley felt sorry for me, or guilty about me, but in truth I didn't much mind my new surroundings; like Trix, I paid very little attention to them. I'd found a place where no one knew me.

The spring and summer of 1963, Wesley and I took the Greyhound bus up to Cattaraugus to visit Trix on alternate Saturdays, three and a half hours going and three and a half hours returning, that numbing exhausting interminable trip, with its numerous local stops, of which it is better for me not to speak. Wesley worked at calculus problems or studied the books that were to be his textbooks at Rochester; I read novels from the public library or sat, dazed, too depressed to read, staring out the bus window. What frightened us about Trix was her peacefulness in her new life. She'd become an inmate, an invalid, *that* was her talent: a frail, listless, aging woman, with a voice that always sounded unused when she finally spoke; her skin, that had been so lovely, now marred, mottled, creased. Her eyes seemed smaller too, dulled by drugs and inertia . . . and peace. I dreamt of those eyes, vacuous as suns, reflecting the glare of the fluorescent lighting and nothing else.

She doesn't want to get well, she isn't even *trying*, Wesley said; God damn her, God damn them both. I said, Why should she want to get well? Trix has been there, she knows.

We no longer talked, ever, about the night Darrell had beaten Trix, the night the police came. Though once, returning from Cattaraugus, the week before Wesley was scheduled to leave for Rochester, I said suddenly, "You called the police, didn't you?" And Wesley said calmly, as if he'd been waiting for this—this accusation that was nothing more than a statement of fact—"I thought you'd called them."

My heart contracted in hatred of him. Liar, I thought. Oh, liar.

But I said, "Look, it doesn't matter. Someone had to call them. He was killing her, he was out of his mind. He had to be stopped." I paused, hearing my brother's hoarse asthmatic breath; I felt his agitation, his hatred of me. I said, "Someone had to stop him."

"Funny," Wesley said, looking me directly in the eye, "I've always thought it was you."

After that we saw each other at ever-increasing intervals for the next five or six years. There was never an actual day, still less an hour, when we said goodbye—not even at Trix's funeral. She died in the hospital of a stroke only fifty-one years old, in 1972. We'd long since stopped hearing from Darrell, of course, and by that time we were living hundreds of miles apart, so it has been easy to let go.

I'm thinking, though, that I will get in touch with Wesley when I figure out the answer to that doctor's question. One day, I seem to know, I will. And then I'll call Wesley right away, or write him a letter, if I have his address. One day.

CAPITAL PUNISHMENT

It will be over Evander Jones that the trouble begins between Hope Brunty and her father, but even if Hope guesses this, at the time she doesn't care. At the time, she is fifteen years old and a sophomore in high school.

Hope's parents have been divorced for six years. She hasn't seen her mother in nearly five years; Mr. Brunty was "awarded custody" of her.

Hope's mother's name is Harriet but it is a name never spoken at home. Hope never hears her father speak it. She knows that her mother has remarried, that she has moved away to California. She has three small children: twin boys and another daughter. Is this girl Hope's half-sister? She has no interest in her, keeps forgetting her name. She has no idea how old the child is. The woman she remembers as her mother is thin, nervous, pretty, with pale heated skin, plucked eyebrows, a red lipsticked mouth, hennaed hair. She smells perfumy, but also of cigarettes; her breath smells sometimes of sweet red wine. When she cries Hope runs away to hide. When she and Mr. Brunty speak in quick raised voices to each other she runs away to hide. Why is the slick flirty image of Chiquita the Banana mixed up with Hope's mother in Hope's mind? She is two or three years old, staring from the picture of the red-mouthed smiling woman with the high-piled black hair to her mother, who stands above her—her mother who is saying something to her she can't understand. One of the women is tiny and flat, only a drawing. The other is "real."

Hope's mother lives with her new family in Redwood City, California, which is thousands of miles away. Too far to visit if she is ever invited. Hope dreams sometimes of a city that is a redwood forest, tall straight trees stretching out in all directions and the shade so dark it is always night. In this city, no houses or inhabitants are visible.

Since Mrs. Brunty moved away from the one-story asphalt-sided shingle-roofed house on Lewiston Street where Hope and her father live, Hope has grown into a big healthy strapping girl, as the relatives say. How she's grown! they are always saying, looking to Mr. Brunty as if he were to be congratulated, or blamed. Mr. Brunty is a big man himself, accustomed to being the biggest man wherever he goes. People naturally make way for him, the way smaller dogs defer to larger. Hope has seen him edge into the front of a line, push out of a doorway ahead of others; she has been with him numberless times in the car when he bullies his way forward and others drop back intimidated. She does not know whether Mr. Brunty is aware of these habits or whether they are unconscious, "just his way." She overhears the relatives tell Mr. Brunty that Hope takes after *him* and she feels a thrill of pride nonetheless.

Once Hope overheard Mr. Brunty telling a friend of his, a man, that all the things women pretend to like in you—a sense of humor, for instance, teasing and kidding around, standing up for your own rights and not letting over people run over you, that sort of thing— they'll twist around one day when they want to, until they're the exact same things they hate in you. Say your hair is brown, Mr. Brunty said. Say your eyes are blue. Say you tell certain jokes they always laughed at only now they can't stand. Most of all it's you being the man you are and not some other man they'll twist around when it suits them, when they're ready.

His heart had been broken, he said, but it could only be broken once. The women he knew now he could take them or leave them and he hoped they understood that.

"I hope they feel the same way about me," he said.

Evander Jones, the death row prisoner who went insane while awaiting execution, is related in some mysterious way to one of

Hope's classmates at Locktown High School: a boy named Delano Holland who had been elected vice-president of their class in eighth grade. He was the first Negro elected to any class office in the history of the school district, which was part of the excitement of electing him. Hope Brunty helped in his campaign and has considered herself a friend of his ever since.

The rumor is that Evander Jones is Delano's half-brother even though he's so much older than Delano: thirty-seven, it said in the paper. Nobody wants to ask Delano about Jones and in the past week or two Delano hasn't been coming to school regularly but once, when he does, Hope Brunty approaches him in the cafeteria line in that way of hers that's shy but pushy too and she asks how he is, how things are going, she says she hasn't seen him around much she hopes they are still friends, and Delano goes stiff, smiling his twitchy smile and looking over her head. Since eighth grade he has grown into a lanky curve-shouldered boy who speaks to whites in monosyllables or doesn't speak at all.

Hope loses her courage and doesn't ask whatever it was she'd wanted to ask. She *is* pushy, but there are limits.

She has grown into the kind of girl who doesn't have boyfriends but who does have boy pals, boy buddies. Sometimes they get rowdy joking around in the halls, shouting with laughter; Hope is a big-boned girl who isn't afraid to punch back when she's rabbit-punched, but it's all just teasing, it's all just fun. The boys seem willing to forgive her for being an A student and Hope knows that being rowdy among them is better than nothing at all.

But Delano Holland doesn't like her any more. The other black boys don't like her any more. And the black girls: she'd never had any friends among them anyway. She'd tried, but she never had a one.

Mr. Nicholson, their tenth grade civics teacher, brings up the subject of Evander Jones in his class, invites discussion: should a person who has been sentenced to death be executed if he has been declared by doctors *non compos mentis*? (Mr. Nicholson writes *non compos mentis* on the blackboard.) When the debate club argues the question, the "moral, ethical, and/or legal" issues involved, Hope Brunty, though only a sophomore, stands out among the debaters opposing execution—she is so passionate, so serious, remarkably mature for a girl her age except for her habit of now and then interrupting others, saying hurtful sarcastic things.

Still, Hope's side wins. Which thrills her so much that for a brief while she almost thinks that things in the real adult world have been altered.

"Now, Daddy, please pay *attention*," Hope says excitedly. She has hurried him into the living room to see the six o'clock news, which features, tonight, four nights before the scheduled electrocution, an interview with the doomed man up at the Mecklenburg Prison. "You sure are damned bossy these days," Mr. Brunty says. Hope says, "Daddy, don't *talk*."

There is Jones in his dull gray prison uniform smiling and blinking and craning his neck, fixing his wide-open stare at the television camera. His eyes are disconcertingly big—pop eyes. He is a much smaller man than Hope expects, with a very dark skin that looks oiled. His hair is trimmed short, a tight little cap of wool going unevenly gray.

He is flanked by two white men, one of them a regular newscaster, the other a lawyer from the State Bureau of Public Advocacy. As they introduce him Jones squirms and twitches and continues to stare at the camera as if he's unaware of what is being said about him, or uninterested. It is immediately obvious, Hope thinks, frightened, that the man is "not right."

Mr. Brunty too seems shaken. He says they shouldn't show such things on television: a poor bastard off his rocker like that.

Hope pokes him in the arm. "Daddy, *hush*."

Evander Jones is a war veteran, was awarded a Purple Heart, honorably discharged at the end of the war. Nine years ago he was convicted of first-degree murder in a drugstore holdup and sentenced to die in the electric chair, but his case was reopened and the date of execution postponed several times and finally it was discovered that the man had gone insane on death row and did not understand that he was going to die. He seemed not to know where he was or why he was there.

Jones is not faking! His is an authentic case. He has been examined by officials and psychiatrists many times since the situation came to light, and not even those in the employ of the state are willing to testify that he is sane. He suffers from acute paranoid schizophrenia: auditory hallucinations, obsessive thoughts, fixed delusions. Nine years of incarceration on death row are responsible, the lawyer says. In a truly humane society capital punishment would be abolished; it is a barbaric custom—an eye for an eye, a tooth for a tooth. (Indeed, the fact that Evander Jones has gone insane came to light only after another inmate on death row was discovered hanging in his cell a few weeks ago. The man's method was said to be "ingenious" but authorities would not give details.)

At first Jones sits smiling and mute as the white men in their suits and ties discuss him. It is revealed that the governor will make an announcement about his case sometime before 11 P.M. on Friday, the time of his scheduled execution. It is mentioned that public opinion is "sharply divided": most of the telephone calls and telegrams the governor has received are in favor of his execution being postponed (or the sentence commuted altogether), but some are in favor of no interference. Jones, asked how he feels, sits mute for a long awkward moment as if he has not heard the question or has not understood it. "What is your feeling about your situation, Mr. Jones?" the newscaster asks in his earnest, compassionate voice, and Jones begins to squirm with what appears to be pleasure. His pop eyes widen, his purplish-black skin exudes moisture. His voice leaps from him like a small frenzied animal, and at first neither Hope nor Mr. Brunty can understand a word.

He has had, Jones says excitedly, "a Visitation from the Lord." He has seen "the Way, the Truth, and the Light." How long ago he doesn't know—it could have been yesterday, it could have been the hour of his birth. An angel appeared to him. Jesus Christ appeared to him. He is ready, he says, for "the Rapture." He is ready for "the Trumpet Call."

The lawyer tries to interrupt Jones to ask him about the circumstances of his trial—an all-white jury, a white judge, his common-law wife's testimony discredited—but Jones keeps on talking, more and more rapidly. Mr. Brunty says it isn't right for them to listen to this—the man is obviously crazy as a loon and he's going to turn the television off—but Hope gives a little scream and holds him back. "Daddy, what do you mean? Daddy, don't you *dare!*"

Jones is saying that he listens every instant for the Trumpet Call. There is a Rapture that is hard to bear but it must be borne. He is hopeful to be embraced in the Bosom of the Lord. "Praise the Lord! Praise the Lord! The Lord giveth and the Lord taketh away! Blessed be the name of the Lord!" he cries. "I am ready. I am hopeful. Goin' to meet the Lord. The Rapture is hard to bear but the Rapture is upon us. Oh, yes, Lord. Oh, yes, Lord. I bein' the first to go pavin' the Way for the rest of them sinners, oh, yes, Lord!" A warm light seems to break from his face and ray outward—but the interview is over. Jones is rudely interrupted in mid-syllable.

The news anchorwoman concludes by saying that the controversy has attracted national and international attention. Is Evander Jones's imminent execution a miscarriage of justice, as some argue, or a grim necessity, as others insist? Viewers are invited to call WWCT-TV immediately following the show or write postcards voicing their opinions. But they must hurry!

Bright and sassy, a commercial for new Buicks comes on the screen and Hope and Mr. Brunty sit there staring at it. Hope's face is streaked with tears; she waits—she is waiting—for her father to glance at her, to notice. But he doesn't. He heaves himself from his chair with no comment and goes out into the kitchen. Opening the refrigerator, Hope hears, getting another beer.

Hope tests certain words, phrases. She is consciously improving her vocabulary in what might be called an exalted direction but she experiments with other words too, murmuring them under her breath, gauging their weight. She thinks of Mr. Brunty, whom she loves, as a "big lug." A "big dumb lug." A "big dumb ox."

She will leave him soon though he doesn't know it. She will leave Locktown altogether—a place of "mediocre sensibility" (as her civics teacher, Mr. Nicholson, has said), "to all intents and purposes soulless."

Hope sees that Mr. Brunty's eyes, though they are a pale washed-out blue, resemble Evander Jones's eyes: protuberant, heavy-lidded. The man is fattish and graying and his nose is getting red-veined but he's still considered a handsome man. Women are attracted to him, that's for sure. (Hope has never cared in the slightest what her father does with his string of girlfriends so long as he doesn't do it anywhere near her and doesn't talk about it. She's satisfied not even knowing any names.) Both Mr. Brunty and Hope have big broad faces and squarish jaws and noses that are disproportionately small—snubbed—as if they'd been pushed in as a prank, like clay noses. Genetic determinism, Hope thinks. They'd studied all that grim stuff in biology class.

Once when Mr. and Mrs. Brunty were quarreling in the kitchen very late at night Hope appeared in her pajamas in the doorway and saw that they weren't people she knew, exactly: there was this shiny-faced woman in a nightgown slapping at this big joking-angry man and the woman wasn't covered the way she was supposed to be—the top of her nightgown had been yanked down over one shoulder; one of her breasts was exposed—and the man, when he turned to see Hope, when his wild eyes fastened on her—she saw a thin trickle of blood running down from his nose and splashing onto the bronze-fuzzy hairs that covered his chest. Hope began to scream.

A long time ago.

In secret they are making their plans: telephoning one another and speaking in lowered voices or in whispers; none of their parents is to know. Who initially made the suggestion about cutting classes, taking the Greyhound bus to the capital, joining what newspapers have called the "coalition" of diverse groups protesting Evander Jones's execution—whose sense of justice sparked the adventure, the trespass into adult territory—no one will want to say afterward. It wasn't Hope Brunty, the only sophomore in the group, but as soon as Hope learned of their plans she insisted upon being included.

Originally there are quite a few students from Locktown involved: twelve members of the debating team, among them four girls. By Wednesday evening two or three have backed out; by Thursday morning all but six have backed out. Hope Brunty is the youngest, and the only girl.

The first Miles Brunty knows of his daughter Hope's involvement in the demonstration for Evander Jones is when the call comes for him from the juvenile detention facility where Hope is being held.

Five to twelve of a Thursday morning and he's told to take a telephone call up front and his heart stops for a moment, then starts in
again with a deadly little kick. You aren't called out of the machine
shop to be told good news; that's the kind that can wait.

It takes Mr. Brunty several minutes to understand what he hears.
He must make an effort to comprehend the fact that Hope isn't in
Locktown as he'd assumed, she isn't in school as he'd assumed, she
is one hundred fifteen miles away at the state capital in a juvenile
detention facility. She was brought in with a number of other minors
after an unauthorized gathering on the steps of the capitol building
got out of hand and she is being held pending release in his custody.
The word "minor" strikes Mr. Brunty's ear oddly—he isn't accustomed to hearing his daughter so designated.

"Is she all right? Is my daughter all right?" he asks excitedly. And
the police matron, who knows what he means by "all right," assures
him that, yes, she is.

Maybe a bit shaken. Like many of the younger demonstrators.

Mr. Brunty, who is very agitated, is carefully told that none of
the minors involved has been formally arrested; none will be charged
with any crime or misdemeanor. But should he wish to engage legal
counsel he has the opportunity now to do so.

And when he comes to get his daughter he should bring identification for both himself and her and Hope's birth certificate. Does
he understand? The police matron speaks slowly and patiently, re-
peating her information several times. She is accustomed to dealing
with parents in various states of shock and incomprehension.

Afterward it will come out that Hope and five other students
from Locktown High School took a bus to the state capital that
morning, instead of going to school, so that they could participate
in a demonstration in support of Evander Jones (in support of the
postponement of his execution, that is) planned by a number of
liberal and pacifist organizations in the state. In all, approximately
one hundred fifty people turned out, among them a sprinkling of
high school students; unfortunately a number of angry and in some
cases violent demonstrators turned out against *them*—which the or-
ganizers seemed not to have foreseen.

"She isn't hurt? You're sure?" Mr. Brunty asks. And the police

matron assures him she is not. And puts Hope, who is crying, on
the line.

It takes him an hour and forty-five minutes to get to the detention
facility—which looks, and smells, more like a clinic than a jail—and
once he's there they make him wait. The place is busy, crowded,
understaffed; other parents have come to get their children; there is
a constant milling in the lobby and in the lounge where Mr. Brunty
paces, telling himself repeatedly that the main thing is his little girl
is all right.

That's the main thing, the rest will come later.

He finds himself thinking past Hope to Hope's mother. How,
one night a long time ago, after he and Harriet had made love, one
of their not-great times, he'd said something he maybe shouldn't
have said, and after a moment Harriet said, "Then you won't mind
me leaving you, will you . . . you won't mind it a lot, will you," and
he knew the woman wasn't joking. And she wasn't asking it as a
question either.

He's called into a windowless room; he's asked questions, told
to fill out forms, sweating inside his clothes (he'd gone home to
change into a suit, clean white shirt, tie) like a guilty man. Several
times he tells the juvenile officers that he'd had no idea what Hope
was up to, no idea at all! Misunderstanding him, they assure him he
isn't to blame.

He and Hope are brought together in another windowless room,
walls painted a pale sickly green and fluorescent lighting that throws
queer dented shadows downward on their faces, and here is Hope
stumbling into his arms sobbing as he hasn't heard her sob in years:
Daddy, thank God you're here, oh, Daddy, I'm so sorry, I'm so
scared, I'm so *scared*. What strikes him is how tall she's grown, how
solid and ample and heated her flesh. He embraces her, deeply
moved, embarrassed, not really knowing what to do. He looks over
her head at the juvenile officers as if hoping for support or solace.
He has never seen Hope quite so agitated in any public place, before
witnesses.

He calls her sweetheart, comforts her, tells her not to cry, she's
coming home now. It's all over now, he says. Or whatever he says:
it's as if another man, another father, were standing in his place,

clumsy and flush-faced in his suit and tie, saying words not his but appropriate to the occasion.

It's a long drive, Mr. Brunty thinks, back home. He hopes they get there.

Of course Mr. Brunty is aware of the fact that Hope isn't like other girls her age. His sisters and aunts are always taking him aside to ask, Shouldn't Hope lose a little weight? Does Hope have any boyfriends? Why is Hope so unfriendly? (Meaning, Why does Hope think she's so superior to us?) Mr. Brunty tells them he's damned grateful his daughter is as different from her mother as night and day. Or he tells them it isn't any of their business, which it isn't.

These teenaged girls Mr. Brunty sees downtown or in the neighborhood, strolling along the sidewalk as if they owned it, breathless and giggling and quick to notice if they're being watched: he *is* grateful his own daughter bears so little resemblance to them. The other day he'd happened to be watching this girl no older than Hope with her hair peroxided and falling down her back and her face all gummed up like a grown woman's, wearing tight jeans and a skimpy red halter top and this was in a Rexall's where she was leaning against a counter, arms straight out, chewing gum, studying things for sale on the counter but at the same time pushing in with her arms against her breasts to make the cleavage more noticeable, and she wasn't unaware of Mr. Brunty close by, not by a long shot. Hot little bitch, Mr. Brunty thought. Did they know what they were inviting, watching a man old enough to be their father slantwise like that? Damp pink tongue wetting her lower lip as if, sure, she *was* just contemplating the top of the counter.

Most summers Hope wears jeans too but they're loose-fitting, and her shirts and pullovers are likely to be loose too; she wears soiled white sneakers that make her feet look enormous, and sometimes an old sweat-stained visored cap backwards on her head, as if for a joke—the way Mr. Brunty wears his. You wouldn't know, seeing her loping along the street or sprawled in the living room reading one of her library books, that she was an honor student at the high school; would hardly be able to tell if she was a boy or a girl.

And she's increasingly critical of him: nagging him about his table manners, his taste in television programs, his lack of a "political conscience." Since the Evander Jones publicity hit the newspapers and TV she'd picked at him, saying some people (like him?) are born morally "apathetic," and the way the word "apathetic" rolled off her tongue allowed Mr. Brunty to know she was using it to mock him. Not just that she was saying *he* was apathetic but she chose to use a word no one had ever used in Mr. Brunty's presence, that he knew of. A word she probably thought he didn't understand, being a seventh-grade dropout from a country school and not a hot-shit honor student like herself.

They were in the kitchen just before supper. Mr. Brunty stopped what he'd been doing and looked at her, and after an uneasy moment she glanced around and saw him. And her eyes pinched a little and he could see that she knew: she knew how close she was to trouble. Her mouth opened just slightly and the peeved-looking expression on her face faded and though Mr. Brunty had not taken a step in her direction she stumbled back, clumsy, banging her hip against the edge of a counter.

Mr. Brunty said quietly, "You want to say all that again? Explain what it is you been saying? Spell it all out for me? Do you?" and Hope, to give her credit, laughed a little and shook her head no, no, no, no, she didn't.

On the interstate he questions her but doesn't push her, doesn't want to get her crying again. That scared him—the way she'd broken down and pushed herself, big as she is, into his arms. As one of the officers told him, young people are naturally idealistic and what his daughter did, what most of the demonstrators did, was generous and civic-spirited—a little imprudent, as it turned out, but they couldn't have known that beforehand.

"I understand that," Mr. Brunty said curtly. Though he was thinking, What about her deceiving *me*?

So he asks Hope a few questions, mainly why she got involved with something that had so little to do with her. And how could she and her friends have thought that the governor would be influenced by *them*? That isn't the way politicians operate, Mr. Brunty says.

Hope says quietly that there were a lot of people involved, not just kids. He'd see on the television news. "And it isn't over yet," she adds.

"What isn't over yet?"

"The governor still has to make his decision."

There is a queer dazed sleepwalker's look to Hope that Mr. Brunty doesn't like. She is sitting unnaturally straight beside him (she usually slouches in the car) as if she's afraid to relax. He can feel the tension in her body.

Hope fumbles for a tissue in her purse and blows her nose noisily. She seems to be breathing hard, almost panting; she runs her fingers repeatedly through her snarled hair. It's like her, Mr. Brunty thinks, not to have a comb. The only fifteen-year-old girl in the state without a comb.

Suddenly he asks, "You're sure nobody laid a hand on you? No cop or—"

"No."

"You were all piled into a police van, weren't you?"

"It was all right."

"Were you handcuffed?"

"*No*, Daddy."

"And you're sure nobody at school put you up to this? This Mr. Nicholson you're always talking about?"

"Yes, Daddy. I'm sure."

"You're sure?"

"Daddy, *please*." She laughs in a harsh melancholy way—no mirth, just a hissing expulsion of air.

Mr. Brunty lets it go for the time being. He's thinking all along that this is the girl who deceived him. Not lying exactly because he hadn't asked her point-blank that morning was she going to go to school that day or did she have other plans? So it wasn't exactly lying but could he ever believe her again?

He's thinking it has been years since he has laid a hand on his daughter and he can't start in again now. Not now. One blow and she'd try to defend herself, she'd fight back, and God knows what would happen then, if she provoked him. So he can't start.

Though it's too early for supper they stop at a restaurant on the interstate; Mr. Brunty missed lunch and is ravenously hungry.

Hope says wanly that she hasn't much appetite. The way human beings behaved that day, pushing and jostling one another, so much anger and so much hatred, all that that says about human nature—she doubts she'll ever have much appetite for food ever again.

"You'll eat," says Mr. Brunty. "If you know what's good for you."

The restaurant is surprisingly crowded for this hour of the afternoon but they are waited on quickly and their food is brought to them with startling swiftness, on gray lightweight plastic plates. Thin slices of fatty roast beef, scoops of lukewarm mashed potatoes, canned peas and tiny diced carrots. Two small bowls of applesauce. During the course of the meal Mr. Brunty thickly butters five or six pieces of white bread and wipes his plate as he eats: an old habit Hope has criticized in the past but now she keeps very still. Mr. Brunty says of the food, "It isn't bad, is it? Not as bad as it looks." Meaning to be friendly he adds, "This will save you cooking supper, at least."

Hope sighs and picks at her food as if to please him. Very likely she was fed at the detention facility, and Mr. Brunty had noticed a wall of vending machines in one of the corridors. Candy bars, potato chips, peanuts. When Hope feels sorry for herself she stuffs herself with things like that, hidden away in her room with the door shut against him.

He sees that she went off that morning, all that distance, in ordinary school clothes: plaid blouse, cotton skirt, white ribbed cotton socks. In her over-the-shoulder bag is a wallet containing $2.35 and the return Greyhound ticket, a small note pad, and a ballpoint pen. (Hope had intended to write up the demonstration for the school newspaper.) Her blouse is sweat-stained under the arms and her skirt is, as usual, badly rumpled, as if she has been sleeping in it. There is a strange flush to her face like sunburn.

Mr. Brunty feels sorry for Hope, picking at her food like that. He is about to ask if she wants to order something else from the menu when her eyes suddenly snap up at him. "I will never forget this day," she says. "This is a day of ignominy."

"A day of what?"

"Shame and disgrace."

Mr. Brunty stares at her. He says, "Yes, it is. It certainly is. I buy that—it certainly is."

"I suppose you're happy with the way things turned out."

"Happy? Driving across the state to bail you out? Are you serious?" Mr. Brunty laughs angrily. "When we get home—"

Hope's mouth is trembling. Her eyes brim again with tears and Mr. Brunty is panicked she will start crying again, here in the restaurant. Those half-dozen times Harriet lost control—went into hysterics, laughing, crying, gasping for breath, clawing at her own face with her nails—had scared him shitless.

Mr. Brunty changes the subject, asks Hope if she would like to order something else from the menu: a tuna fish sandwich, maybe. He will eat what's left of her roast beef and order another beer.

Hope says politely, "No, thank you."

"You sure?"

"*Yes*, Daddy."

"You don't need to be sarcastic."

"I wasn't being sarcastic."

"Everything you say is sarcastic."

"Then what can I do about it?" Hope gives a sudden scream, bringing both fists down hard on the tabletop. "If everything I say is sarcastic what can I say that isn't?"

Mr. Brunty is appalled; other customers have turned to look at them. "Take it easy, for Christ's sake," he says.

They sit trembling, not looking at each other. After a moment Mr. Brunty says cautiously, "You're all right now, you're safe now, and you know it."

"What do I know? I don't know anything!" she says. Then, in a quieter voice, "I feel sick, Daddy. I'm going to the rest room." But she doesn't budge from her side of the booth, remains sitting with her elbows on the table, fists pressed against her face. Big sad homely girl, *his* girl. Mr. Brunty feels a pang of helpless love for her, and dislike.

He finishes his food and most of Hope's. Orders another beer. And asks, as if casually, why Hope and her classmates got involved with Evander Jones in the first place: she never did explain. Some poor black bastard none of them had ever heard of a few days ago.

Hope sighs and shrugs.

Mr. Brunty says, eyeing her with derision, "Did you kids think he'd give a damn about you? You think he even *knows* about *you*? He doesn't."

Hope rubs her hands briskly over her eyes. "That isn't the point, Daddy," she says.

"Why isn't it the point? What point? People like that don't care for us, so why should we care for them? You tell me; you got all the answers."

"If you have to ask a question like that, Daddy, you can't understand any answer I can give you."

"What's that supposed to mean?" Mr. Brunty asks belligerently. "I'm just asking, in plain English. A man like that—a Negro or whoever, a complete stranger—in prison because he shot and killed another man—"

"Maybe he *didn't*, maybe he was *innocent*," Hope interrupts. "He didn't get a fair trial."

"You think he cares about *you?* Even knows about *you?* He'd slit your throat if he could."

"Daddy, that isn't the *point*," Hope says weakly. "You just don't get the *point*."

"I'm sitting here waiting for you to tell me," Mr. Brunty says, trying to keeping his voice low. "Aren't I listening? So tell me."

"Tell you what?"

"Why I should care about somebody who doesn't care about me. Tell me."

"Because—"

"Yes?"

"Because—it's why we're here."

"Here? Where?"

"Here on earth."

"*Where?*"

"Oh, Daddy, never mind," Hope says. "I don't know."

Mr. Brunty leans forward, staring at his daughter. He is thinking she's somebody he doesn't know and wouldn't be talking with, sitting in this booth with, if it weren't for the accident of—their connection. If it weren't for a chain of things he can't quite remember now except to know that they happened and that, when they began happening, it was without his full knowledge or consent.

You could say that in a way they hadn't anything to do with him.

"Why we're here, right here, right now—that's the question," Mr.

Brunty says loudly. "I mean right here in this booth in this god-damned joint in the middle of nowhere."

When Hope doesn't reply he says, as if he can't resist prodding her, pushing, "This poor asshole Jones! You might as well kiss him goodbye, you and your friends. He's good as dead this minute. Want to bet? He's good as dead this minute."

Hope looks up at him, her eyes pinching. "That isn't so," she says. "You're just saying that."

"Good as dead," Mr. Brunty repeats, lighting up a cigarette.

"The governor—"

"The governor! Come off it! If he lets one of these guys live he'll have to let them all live. Open the prisons and turn them all out."

Hope fixes him with a look of loathing. She says, "I don't believe anything you say. I don't even listen to anything you say! You're such a hypocrite—telling people my mother left us when you know you made her leave."

"I what?"

"You *made* her leave."

"You don't know what the hell you're talking about."

"You forced her out and then you told everybody she left *you*. You said she left *us*. That's what hypocrisy is!"

"I never forced anybody to leave," Mr. Brunty says angrily. He is aware of a couple in the adjoining booth listening to their conversation, which only makes him all the angrier. "What the hell do you know about it? You were only a little girl at the time."

Hope has shifted into her old self: mocking, derisive, tough as nails. Mr. Brunty could reach out and slap her smug face.

"Hypocrite," she says. "You know what you are."

"I never made anybody leave me! Your mother—"

Hope stretches her mouth and sings, "I never made anybody leave . . . me" to the tune of "You'll Never Know How Much I Love You."

"Yeah," says Mr. Brunty. "You don't know *shit*."

Hope giggles and falls silent. Just in time, her father is thinking.

She snatches up her purse and announces she's going to the women's room.

———

Mr. Brunty finishes his beer and lights up another cigarette and goes to pay the cashier. Hope is taking her time about coming back; by now it's early evening and the restaurant is getting crowded. Many families with young children. Squalling babies. Mr. Brunty is thinking that one third of a man's life is a hell of a long time to be on death row, but that's how things work out: an eye for an eye, a tooth for a tooth.

The women's rest room has double doors that are continually swinging in and out. Each time a figure appears Mr. Brunty thinks it's his daughter, and each time it's a stranger. Where is she? Keeping him waiting on purpose? She wouldn't have gone directly to the car, he's sure, but where the hell is she? Five minutes, ten minutes: Mr. Brunty tosses his cigarette onto the dirty tile floor and grinds it out with the heel of his foot, though there's an ashtray a few feet away.

The woman cashier, Mr. Brunty's age, perky and heavily made up and not bad-looking except for the pinkish synthetic wig she's wearing, calls over, "You look like you're waiting for somebody!" as if it were a witty remark.

Mr. Brunty says coldly, "That's right," and gives the bitch a look that shuts her up fast.

Fifteen minutes. He begins to understand that something is wrong. Half-consciously he has drawn closer to the doors as if, at a slant, he might see inside, might catch a glimpse of Hope. Women going in and coming out begin to eye him suspiciously. When the next woman comes out—a hefty girl carrying a baby—Mr. Brunty stops her apologetically to ask if she has seen a girl who resembles Hope. He refers to Hope as "my daughter, fifteen years old, sort of big for her age," and tries to remember what she is wearing.

The girl is sympathetic but says she doesn't know if she noticed anyone like that inside; would Mr. Brunty like her to go back and check? "No, that's all right, sorry to bother you," Mr. Brunty says. A moment later he could kick himself.

He is thinking such weird thoughts like things scuttling in the dirt when you overturn a rock: what if Hope has hanged herself in one of the toilet stalls? (That would be just like her.) She might also have slashed her wrists in a place he couldn't enter and that would be just like her too. . . . Hadn't he read that women are more likely to slash their wrists than to hang themselves? Or take an overdose of pills.

He has been waiting for Hope so long that women leaving the rest room are all women he has seen going in. And no Hope! In desperation he stops a friendly-looking woman of about his age and asks her did she happen to see a girl resembling Hope, but the woman seems not to have heard his question or not to wish to answer it. In a vehement voice she tells him that there is a pack of women inside— some mothers changing their babies' diapers too—and it isn't a very pleasant place. "You wouldn't get that in the men's room," she says with an air of reproach. Mr. Brunty sees that the woman is slightly off—that look in the eye, that eager smile—and he tries to edge away. "You have to wait a long time in there to use the toilet," the woman says. "You know why?" "Why?" Mr. Brunty asks reluctantly. "Because some of the toilets don't work," the woman says. "They don't flush. It's a disgrace—it's disgusting." "Yes," Mr. Brunty says, edging away.

Two teenaged girls leave the rest room, laughing loudly together, both smoking cigarettes. Mr. Brunty wonders if, on the sly, Hope smokes cigarettes like so many teenagers. He decides he will forgive her if he learns that she does.

The cashier in the pink wig is watching him. Mr. Brunty regrets having snubbed her because now he might enlist her help.

Then it occurs to him that Hope has climbed out a rear window to escape from him—what could be simpler, more obvious—as he'd seen a tricky woman do in a TV movie the other night. This beautiful model desperate to escape some nut who'd threatened to kill her and in a restaurant in New Orleans the woman pushed open a window and forced herself—this took time; this was tense and dramatic— through an excruciatingly small narrow space. "Sweet fucking Jesus," Mr. Brunty says, wiping his hands on his trousers. He wonders if he is losing his mind.

He leaves the restaurant to see if Hope is hitchhiking on the highway; that would be the way her mind worked. But no one is there. Trucks roar past, semidetached rigs, thunderous vehicles, strangers' cars—nothing.

He goes to his car and unlocks the door, his hands shaking. His heart is beating hard and his senses are keenly but pointlessly alert, as if he is about to fight another man. No one inside the car but of course he knew that; the doors were all locked.

Then he hears someone speak, drawling, and of course it's Hope, sauntering toward him from a grove of picnic tables close by. Her hair is flying in the wind, still snarled, but her face looks washed, scrubbed. She regards her daddy with an expression of wide-eyed innocence.

"Where were you?" Mr. Brunty says angrily. He's embarrassed that he must look so worried.

Hope opens her eyes still wider. "Where were *you?*" she says. "I've been waiting out here for ages."

"I was waiting for you inside," Mr. Brunty says. He feels clumsy, exposed. His heart is still beating uncomfortably hard and he looks at his daughter with a peculiar eagerness, as if he is waiting for her to say something further, to explain herself, or him.

But she doesn't, of course. She is playing dumb. She repeats that she was waiting for him out here, and as she settles into the passenger's seat she stretches and yawns and adds with a small mock-smile, "Didn't think you'd lost me, did you?"

Years later when Hope Brunty is living in New York City her father, from whom she has been amicably estranged for a very long time, sends her a clipping from the Locktown newspaper. For a moment Hope has no idea what it is, what it can possibly have to do with her.

A woman named Evita Swann—a black woman, judging from her photograph—was arrested by Locktown police on charges of passing bad checks and while under questioning suddenly volunteered the information that, twenty-nine years before, she had lied to police; she'd lied on the witness stand in a murder trial. She had sworn that her common-law husband Evander Jones—one of the last prisoners in the state to be executed before the repeal of capital punishment—had been with her on the night of the murder, but in fact he had not been with her. Where he'd been, she never knew. "He never told me and I never asked," she said. The article is headed WOMAN CONFESSES PERJURY AFTER 29 YEARS.

Hope reads the clipping several times, feeling a rush of hurt, indignation. Isn't it like her father to send her something like this—torn from the newspaper, with no accompanying note!—when they correspond so rarely.

Isn't it like him, not to forget.

She has not thought of Evander Jones in many years and does not want to think of him—of that incident—now. She crumples the clipping and throws it away. She tells herself it's amusing, really: an old man, Miles Brunty, with nothing better to do with his time.

By degrees—by default, it sometimes seems—Hope has become one of the adults of the world though she has never married, has had no child. She finds herself, in young middle age, waiting with apprehension for news of her relatives' deaths though she is not close to her relatives; she waits with a particular dread for news of her father's death, knowing that, when he dies, she will grieve terribly for him; her life will be wrenched in two. Yet, mysteriously, she seems powerless to forestall the guilt while he is alive.

She loves Mr. Brunty yet cannot get along with him, just as he loves her (she believes) and cannot get along with her.

Hope left home, left him, when she was seventeen years old and had yet to complete her senior year at the high school. She boarded with a family who lived near the school and worked part-time at a dairy to support herself; she'd wanted, stubbornly, even defiantly, to support herself that final year in Locktown.

A few months after Hope moved out, Mr. Brunty remarried—a woman he'd been seeing off and on for years, a solid, likable person, in fact—and Hope felt no animosity toward her, only a cheery forced uneasiness: some disappointment perhaps that the woman wasn't glamorous.

Why leave home? Did you and your father quarrel? So Hope was asked repeatedly and she evaded answering because she didn't really know why she'd left home. Because it was time: she was quite mature for her age. Because Mr. Brunty had not tried to stop her. "Do what you want to do," he'd said ironically. "It's what you're going to do anyway."

And then of course Hope had gone away to the state university

and after that to a distinguished eastern university and she never
went back to Locktown to live, rarely went back to visit. Her life is
busy, crowded, stimulating, rewarding; she has many friends and she
believes passionately in her work and she isn't lonely, though living
alone. Though it sometimes surprises her to be referred to as a
"success." She thinks of her life as constant striving, constant pressure—is this what "success" is?

Mr. Brunty, she has heard, is proud of her, in her absence.

Mr. Brunty, she has heard, *does* love her—though he never writes
and their telephone conversations are strained and Hope feels more
comfortable with his wife, whom she scarcely knows.

In recent years she has come to think of him often, far oftener
than he might guess. He is a riddle to her; or, rather, *she* is a riddle
to herself, in relationship to him: a knot she can't untie. This evening,
alone, Hope will prepare a solitary meal, will read a book while she
eats, or try to read, thinking all the while about Mr. Brunty—who'd
ripped that news item out of the paper to send to her—wondering
what thoughts had gone through his mind, what feelings of vindic-
tiveness, satisfaction, irony. Or had he wanted her simply to know—
to know how one strand of one story turned out, after so many
years. All stories come to an end eventually but do we know their
endings?

She recalls with shame that sly mean-spirited trick of hers, that
inexplicable child's trick she'd played on her father that day: slipping
out of the women's room in the restaurant, hurrying outside to hide
around the corner of the building, heart beating hard in excitement.
Why had she done it? Had it been deliberate? Or had it just happened, one of those numberless things that take place between
people who live together for a long time, who are bound together by ties of blood, feeling, fate? Hope recalls laughing to
herself; Hope recalls the sheer childish impulsiveness of what
she'd done. Hiding from Daddy, and would he know where to find
her and would he worry, would he be frightened, when he couldn't
find her?

Capital punishment, she'd thought. Now you know.

Of course it was a senseless thing to have done on that day of
all days. Seeing the fatigue and worry in her father's face, the deep-
ening lines, the pale eyes so like her own. And that look of help-

lessness as he'd turned to her, car keys in hand. He hadn't caught on that it was a prank. That she'd meant it to wound.

"Did you think you'd lost me?" Hope dared to ask. Brazening it out, stretching and yawning. And the way he'd looked at her, blinking, squinting as if to get her into focus, told her no, probably not, he hadn't caught on and never would.

HOSTAGE

By the age of fourteen Bruno Sokolov had the heft and swagger of a near-grown man. His wide shoulders, sturdy neck, dark oily hair wetted and combed sleekly back from his forehead like a rooster's crest, above all his large head and the shrewd squint of his pebble-colored eyes gave him an air unnervingly adult, as if, in junior high school, in the company of children, he was in disguise, yet carelessly in disguise. He wore his older brothers' and even his father's cast-off clothing, rakish combinations that suited him, pin-striped shirts, sweater vests, suspenders, bulky tweed coats and corduroy trousers, cheap leather belts with enormous buckles, even, frequently, for there were always deaths in those big immigrant families, mourning bands around his upper arm that gave him a look both sinister and holy, to which none of our teachers could object. He was smart; he was tough, the natural leader of a neighborhood gang of boys; he carried a switchblade knife, or was believed to do so. He had a strangely scarred forehead—in one version of the story he'd overturned a pan of boiling water on himself as a small child, in another version his mother in a fit of emotion had overturned it on him. He spoke English with a strong accent, musical yet mocking, as if these sounds were his own invention, these queer eliding vowels and diphthongs, and he had remarkable self-confidence for a boy with his background, the son of Polish-Russian immigrants—out of bravado he ran for, and actually won, our ninth-grade presidency, in a fluke of an election that pitted our teachers' choice, a "good" boy, against a boy whom most of the teachers mistrusted or feared. Even when Bruno Sokolov spoke intelligently in class there was an overtone of subtle mockery, if not contempt, in his voice. His grades were erratic and he was often absent from school—"family reasons" the usual excuse—and he was famous for intimidating or harassing or actually beating up certain of his classmates. His play at football and basketball was that of a steer loosed happily among heifers, and when, as our class president, a black snap-on bow tie around his neck, he addressed the rowdy assemblage from the stage with the aplomb and drawling ease of a radio broadcaster or a politician, shrewd eyes glittering with a sense of his own power, we felt— aroused, laughing at his jokes, a shiver of certitude rippling among even the dullest of us like a nervous reflex through a school of fish— that we were in the presence of someone distinctive, someone of whom, however we might dislike him, we might be proud.

I didn't know him. I didn't belong to his world. Though my family lived only a block or so from his family in a neighborhood of row houses built in the 1890s and hardly renovated since that time, my grandparents had emigrated from Budapest in the early 1900s and Bruno's parents had come from Lublin, a Polish city near the Russian border, in the early 1930s, and that made a considerable difference. And I was younger than Bruno, younger than most of my classmates—I had been skipped a grade in elementary school, a source of obscure pride and shame to me—so that if he happened to glance toward me, if his squinty amused stare drifted in my direction, there was nothing, it seemed, on which it might snag. I was small, I was brainy, I was invisible. For my part I observed Bruno Sokolov scrupulously, in classes, in the school corridors, making his way down the stairs, pushing ahead in the cafeteria line, actions he seemed to perform without thinking, as if the very size of his body had to be accommodated, his needs and impulses immediately discharged. Even to be teased by Bruno Sokolov was an honor of a kind but it was not an honor casually granted, for the Sokolovs, poor as they were, crowded into their shabby row house with its rear yard lifting to a railway embankment, nonetheless took themselves seriously: they were displaced tradesmen, not Polish peasants.

The immigrants' world retained its taxonomical distinctions of class, money, power, "breeding." In America, you were hungry to move up but you had no intention of helping others, outside the family, to move up with you.

The places where imagination takes root. . . . There was an oversized winter coat Bruno Sokolov wore in bad weather, cossack-style, navy blue, with upturned collar, deep pockets, and frayed sleeves, the mere sight of which made me feel confused, light-headed, panicked. There was the back of Bruno's big head, observed slantwise from me in English class, the springy oily dark hair often separating in quills, falling about his ears, and every few weeks a fresh haircut, done at home, crude and brutal, shaved at the neck. There was the sound of his suddenly uplifted voice, ringing and abrasive, often drawling in mockery, the give-and-take, foulmouthed, of young adolescent boys, and my immediate sense of alarm when I heard it, but also my envy: a sharp stabbing envy that cut me like a knife, for of course Bruno Sokolov never spoke my name, even in derision. He gave no sign of knowing it.

The infatuation was hardly love, not even affection, for I often fantasized Bruno Sokolov dying, a violent cinematic death, and took a vengeful pleasure in it; but there was about my feeling for him that sense, common to love, of futility and wild optimism conjoined, a quickening of the pulse even at the very instant that the quickening, the hope, is checked: *No. Don't.*

Midway in the school year when we were in ninth grade Bruno's father died a strange and much talked-of death and I waited for weeks to tell Bruno how sorry I was that it had happened, approaching him one day, in the corridor outside our homeroom, with an aggressive sort of shyness, and Bruno stared down at me with a look of blank surprise as if a voice had sounded out of the very air beside him, a voice wrongly intimate and knowing. He was taller than I by more than a head, his height exaggerated by the springy thickness of his hair and the breadth of his shoulders. The shiny-smooth skin of his scar, disappearing under his hair, was serrated and would have been rough to the touch. His eyes were heavy-lidded from lack of sleep or grief and he stared at me for what seemed a long time before saying, with a shrug of his shoulders, "Yeah. Me too." And that was all.

My heart was beating rapidly, wildly. But that was all.

Even by the standards of our neighborhood Mr. Sokolov had

died an unusual death. He was a large fleshy man with deep-set suspicious eyes and bushy but receding hair that gave him a perpetually affronted look; he dressed formally, in dark tight-fitting suits with old-fashioned wide lapels, starched white shirts, dark neckties. He and two brothers owned a small neighborhood grocery with a meat counter, a real butcher's shop as my mother spoke of it, and Mr. Sokolov so dominated the store, took such edgy excitable antagonistic pride in it, that many customers, including my mother, were offended by his manner. In Bruno's father Bruno's coarse sly charm was mere coarseness; he was in the habit of issuing commands, in Polish, to his brothers, in front of customers; the neighborhood belief was that he wasn't quite "right in the head"—and certainly the dislocations of language made for constant misunderstandings, and constant misunderstandings made for what is called, clinically, paranoia, that sense that the world's very tilt is in our disfavor and that nothing, however accidental-seeming, is accidental. Mr. Sokolov's short temper led him into arguments and even into feuds with neighbors, customers, city authorities, local police; he was tyrannical with his family—three sons, two daughters, a wife who spoke virtually no English—he was driven to fits of rage when his store was vandalized and burglarized and police failed to arrest the criminals, or even to give the Sokolovs the satisfaction that they were trying to find them. (All this was "Mafia-related." It was an open secret that the small neighborhood tradesmen were being extorted or were engaged in some elaborate process of attempting to resist extortion.) Mr. Sokolov died, in fact, defending his store: he was hiding at the rear when someone broke in, and he attacked the intruder with a meat cleaver but was himself shot in the leg, and when the man ran limping and bleeding out into the alley Mr. Sokolov pursued him with the cleaver, limping and bleeding too and shouting wildly in Polish . . . and somehow Mr. Sokolov and the other man both disappeared. A trail of their commingled blood drops led to an intersection close by, then stopped. Police theorized that a van had been parked there and that Mr. Sokolov was taken away in it; he was missing for several days, the object of a much-publicized local search; then his body, or rather parts of his body, began to be discovered: floating in the canal, carelessly buried at the city dump, tossed into the weedy vacant lot behind St. John the Evangelist Church, to which the Sokolovs be-

longed. The murderer or murderers were never found and twenty
years later, long after Bruno Sokolov himself had died, in Korea,
one of his cousins ran for mayor and narrowly missed winning, on
the strength of a passionate campaign against "organized crime" in
the city.

On Saturday mornings in all but the worst winter weather I took
two city buses downtown to the public library, where, in a windowless
ground-floor room set aside for "young adult" readers, I searched
the shelves for books, especially novels, the search invested with a
queer heart-stopping urgency as if the next book I chose, encased
in its yellowing plastic cover, YA in tall black letters on its spine,
might in some way change my life. I was of an age when any change
at all seemed promising; I hadn't yet the temperament to conceive
of change as fearful. I didn't doubt that *the* book, *the* revelation,
awaited me, no matter that the books I actually did read were usually
disappointing, too simplistically written and imagined, made up of
characters too unswervingly good or bad to be believable. It was the
search itself that excited me: the look and the feel of the books on
their bracketed metal shelves, the smell of the room, a close, warm,
stale mixture of floor wax, furniture polish, paper paste, the faint
chemical scent of the middle-aged librarian's inky-black dyed hair.
Sometimes the very approach to the library—my first glimpse of its
Greek Revival portico and columns, its fanning stone steps—aroused
me to a sickish apprehension, as if I understood beforehand that
whatever I hoped to find there I would not find or, by the act of
finding it, making it my own, I would thereby lose it. The library
was further invested with romance since every second or third Saturday I caught sight of Bruno Sokolov there too . . . and one day
when I was sitting on the front steps, waiting for the bus, Bruno
stooped over me unannounced to ask, in his oddly breezy, brotherly
manner, what I'd checked out and to show me what he had: adult
science fiction by Heinlein, Bradbury, Asimov. Did he have a card
for upstairs, for adult books? I asked, surprised, and Bruno said,
"Sure." Another time he showed me a book with a dark lurid cover,
a ghoulish face with red-gleaming eyes, Bram Stoker's *Dracula*—he
hadn't checked it out of the library but had simply taken it from a
shelf and slipped it inside his coat. Not stealing exactly, Bruno said,

because he'd bring it back, probably. "The kind of stuff I like, it's things that make you think, y'know, the weirder the better," he said, smiling and showing big damp yellowed teeth. "Stuff that scares you into thinking, y'know what I mean?" His eyes were heavy-lidded, his lips rather thick, the lower lip in particular; the curious scar high on his forehead gleamed with reflected light. I saw with surprise his thick stubby battered-looking fingers clutching the book, dirt-edged nails, the knuckles nicked and raw, as if he hurt himself casually without knowing what he did, or caring. Or maybe his hands were roughened from work at the grocery. Or from fighting.

"Yes," I said, looking up at him. "I know what you mean."

I watched him walk away, my eyes pinching, following his tall figure in its forward-plunging impatient stride until he was out of sight. *Thief*, I thought. *I could turn you in.* It was only the second or third time we'd spoken together and it would be the final time. And I guessed he didn't know my name. Or even know that he didn't know.

It wasn't long afterward, on another Saturday morning, in late winter, in the library, downstairs, alone, emerging from the women's lavatory—that place of ancient toilets with chain-activated flushes, black-and-white-checked tile encrusted with decades of dirt, incongruously ornate plaster moldings—I heard someone say in a low insinuating voice, "Little girl? Eh? Little girl? Where're you going?" and was crudely awakened from my brooding trance, the usual spellbound state in which I walked about when I was alone in those days, dreaming not so much of Bruno Sokolov or one or another boy I knew as of the mysterious stab of emotions they aroused, the angry teasing hope they seemed to embody. I'd just pushed through the heavy frosted-glass swinging door and saw, there, a few feet away, in the cavernous poorly lit corridor—this was in an alcove, not far from the young adult reading room—one of the hellish sights of my life: a man approaching me, smiling at me, intimate, derisive, accusatory. I had vaguely recalled this man following me down the stairs but I must have told myself, if I'd told myself anything, that he was simply headed for the men's lavatory. "Little girl—c'mon *here*," he said, less patiently. Did he know me? Was I expected to know him? I had seen him around the library and on the street outside, dressed shabbily yet flamboyantly in layers of mismatched clothing, overcoat, sweaters, shirt, filthy woolen scarf wound around his neck, unbuckled overshoes flapping on his feet; he was one of a number of oldish odd-looking and -behaving men who haunted the library, in cold weather especially, spending much of the day in the reference room, where they made a show of reading, or actually did read, the daily newspapers, turning the pages harshly, as if the world's events filled them with contempt. Sometimes they dozed, or muttered to themselves, or drank from pint bottles hidden in much-wrinkled paper bags, or forgot where they were, the precariousness of their welcome, and addressed someone who didn't know them and who quickly edged away. If they caused much disruption one of the librarians, usually a stocky woman with pearl-framed glasses (whom I myself feared for her air of cold authority), ushered them outside and shut the door behind them. Upon rare occasions police were called but I had never actually seen a policeman arrive.

But here, now, today, for no reason I could guess or would ever be explained to me, one of these men had followed me downstairs to the women's lavatory, speaking excitedly, scolding me, now walking straight at me as if he meant to run me down. He grabbed hold of my arm and wrestled me back against the wall, and the things I was carrying—my little beige leather army surplus purse, an armload of library books—went flying. I saw his coarse-veined face above me, and his white-rimmed rheumy mad eyes, felt his whiskers like wire brush against my skin, and must have screamed, though I don't remember screaming, and he panted, and cursed, and spoke to me with great urgency, now dragging me to the doorway of the men's lavatory, where, I suddenly knew, he would assault me, keep me hostage, kill me—there was no hope for me now. Had I not read of such horrors hinted in the newspaper or heard of them, whispered, never fully articulated . . . ?

Yet I might have escaped my assailant, had I squirmed, ducked under his arm, twisted free. He outweighed me by more than one hundred pounds but I might have escaped him and run upstairs screaming for help except that I could not move; all the strength had drained from me. It was as if the mere touch of an adult, an adult's terrible authority, had paralyzed me.

But we were making noise, and the noises echoed in the high-ceilinged space. And then the frosted-glass window of the door to the lavatory shattered and fell in pieces around us. By now the librarian from the young adult room had emerged, and another woman was poking her head around a corner staring at us incredulously, and someone cried out for the madman to leave me alone, and the madman shouted back in a rage, and how many minutes passed in this way, or was it merely seconds, while I crouched unable to move yet trembling violently in a crook of a stranger's arm, breathing in the odors, the stench really, of his desperate being, a sharp smell of alcohol and dirt-stiffened clothing, and I might have thought of praying, I might have thought of God, but all thoughts were struck from my brain, like shadows in a room blasted by light, and even the thought that I would be held hostage and mutilated and murdered and shamed before all the world had not the power to make me fight as I might have and should have fought.

A number of people had gathered but were shy of approaching us. The librarian with the pearl-framed glasses was trying to reason with my assailant, who, gripping me hard, with a kind of joy, kept saying, "No! No! No, you don't—stay away!" His arm was crooked around my head, his elbow pinioning my neck; I half crouched in an awkward position, the side of my face against his coat, the rough material of his coat, and my hair bunched up fallen into my face; I did not think I was crying, for I had not the space or the breath for crying, yet my face was wet with tears, my nose ran shamefully as a baby's—and all the while we swayed and lurched and staggered together, as in a comical dance, which, having begun, we could not end, for there was no way of ending, no way of escaping the corner we had backed into. Several times the word *police* was uttered and several times the madman threatened to "kill the little girl" if any police should so much as appear. Shouts and cries burst about us like birds' shrieks echoing in the passageway and then dipping abruptly to silence. My assailant had pulled me into the lavatory, the outer area of sinks and tall narrow mirrors and naked light bulbs, identical to the women's lavatory, it seemed, yet a forbidden space, and I was able to think clearly, for the first time since the madman had grabbed me, *He will have to kill me now to prove he can do it.*

And then the door was pushed open and Bruno Sokolov appeared, crouched, unhesitating, moving swiftly—he had shoved his way past the witnesses in the corridor, paying no attention to them,

drawn by the excitement, the upset, the prospect of a fight, not
knowing who I was until he saw me and perhaps not even knowing
then, for there wasn't time to think; in describing what happened I
am trying to put into words quicksilver actions that took place within
seconds or split seconds: Bruno, fierce and direct as on the basketball
court when he deliberately ran down another player, pulling the
madman off me, yanking him away, the two of them screaming at
each other, cursing, like men who know each other well, and there
was Bruno of a height with my assailant fending off the man's frenzied
windmill blows, the two of them now struggling by the sinks, Bruno
punching, stabbing, kicking, a blade flashing in his right hand and
blood splashing on the floor, thick sinewy worms of red splashing
on the tiled floor. . . . Bruno had taken out his switchblade knife
and was gesturing with it, cautiously at first, then more recklessly—
"Let the girl go! Let the girl *go!*"—as the man backed off and Bruno
blindly advanced, now striking the knife at him, slashing him, so the
man fell clumsily to his knees shrieking in pain, a sort of hysterical
terror, trying to shield his face with his arms. And there was Bruno
in a pea-green army surplus jacket, bareheaded, frightened and dangerous, crouched above him, his face so doughy-pale and contorted
I would scarcely have recognized it, his voice high-pitched, chanting,
"Let the girl *go*, let the girl *go*," as, not seeming to know what he
did, caught up in the rhythm of an impersonal action, he brought
the knife against the man again and again. . . . But I ran out of the
lavatory and into the corridor, where a woman caught me in her
arms and half carried me in haste down the hall to a cubicle of an
office and shut the door and locked it, and a call was placed to the
emergency room of the closest hospital—the word *assault* was uttered, *assault against a young girl*—and I saw it was the librarian with
the pearl-framed glasses, now agitated, as solicitous of me as a
mother.

So I knew I would be safe.

My assailant was a man of fifty-eight, an ex-mental patient now
living on a disability pension from the U.S. Navy in a downtown
hotel for transients. He did not die from Bruno Sokolov's attack but
he was in critical condition for some weeks, semiconscious, and when
conscious rarely coherent, unable to explain why he had assaulted

me or even to recall that he had done so. Nor did he remember the junior high school boy who'd stabbed him with a wicked eight-inch switchblade knife, wounding him in the chest, belly, groin, arms, and face. His memories, such as they were, were concentrated upon a childhood spent in a rural settlement in western Pennsylvania half a century ago.

Following this much-publicized incident things were never the same again for Bruno Sokolov. As a minor who had, in a sense, behaved heroically, he was not formally charged with any crime (possession of a deadly weapon, for instance, or "aggravated assault"), and naturally witnesses testified in his behalf: he had rushed into the lavatory and thrown himself on the madman in order to save me, and then he had fought him, nearly killing him, in self-defense. (So I testified too. So I told everyone. Though I always knew that in the strictest sense it wasn't true.) But a juvenile-court judge placed him on six months' probation, during which time he was obliged to seek psychiatric therapy and to register as an outpatient at a state psychiatric facility, and the shame of that connection so qualified the glamour of Bruno's heroism and what, literally, he had nearly done—*killed a man! an adult man! stabbed him to death with a switchblade!*—that in school he became increasingly withdrawn and sullen; his grades sharply declined, and he had to resign his class office. There were intervals when he simply stayed away from school; the psychiatric therapy was extended for an indefinite period.

There were problems in the Sokolov family as well, arising from, exacerbated by, Bruno's notoriety—it was said he ran away from home, tried to enlist in the army but was rejected, so he returned to work in the grocery store after school and Saturdays—and it seemed now incredible that this hulking moody expressionless boy might ever have run for, let alone won, one of our class offices; clearly, he wasn't the type. Nor did he play on any of the sports teams any longer; he seemed hardly a schoolboy now, yet not a man either, bored, ironic, and truculent, out of scale in our classrooms and in our corridors, slamming his locker door shut as if he meant to break it, and should a textbook fall from his hand he'd be likely to give it a kick, but not out of clowning high spirits and not inviting you to laugh, sharing a joke, because there was no joke, only Bruno

Sokolov's dangerous eyes shifting like water under wind, and then he'd be gone, no backward glance, hardly more than a tight ticlike grimace to acknowledge the tie, the bond, the secret between us, unspoken, that we were kin almost as blood relatives are kin who have virtually nothing to do with each other publicly and do not in a sense "know" each other at all, a phenomenon common with school-children though perhaps not limited to them. *It's because of me*, I would think, staring after him, *what he is now—my fault*. Though at more sober moments I understood that what Bruno Sokolov had done had nothing to do with me, or no more to do with me than it had with the ex-mental patient he had nearly killed.

By sixteen Bruno Sokolov had quit school, by seventeen he had joined the army, by eighteen he'd been shipped overseas to die within a few months at the battle of Taegu, Korea: Private First Class Bruno J. Sokolov, his photograph, tough-jawed, squinty-eyed, hopeful, in the evening paper. And the other night I dreamt of him, a boy thirty-four years dead, remembering in the dream what I'd forgotten for years, that none of his friends had ever called him Bruno but always Sokolov or Sokki—"Sockie"—a harsh sibilant magical sound I had yearned to have the right to say, shouting it in the street as others did, and he would have turned, and he would have seen me, and he would have raised his hand in recognition. As if that might have made a difference.

CRAPS

Just when I thought he'd drifted off to sleep, his head heavy and warm on my shoulder, Hughie says, What's that story you were going to tell me about Vegas? And I tell him quickly, There's lots of stories about Vegas.

Late Sunday morning I'm lying on top of the bed half dressed with Hughie, my ex-husband, sort of cradled in my arms—he'd dropped by earlier just wanting to talk, he said, in one of his moods where he needs consolation and some signs of affection—and lying together like this, just lying still and drowsy, is an old habit of ours but it's Hughie who always requires it, these days. We fit together like a hand and a glove—Hughie's head on my right shoulder and my arm under his neck (where, sometimes, it goes to sleep, gets so numb I can't feel it there), his right arm cradling my breasts from beneath, and his right foot tucked between mine. There are these old habits you slip into no matter how you actually feel about each other, or anything else. Or where your mind drifts, late Sunday morning.

I was seventeen when I met Hughie, who is twenty-two years older than me. I was twenty-seven when I asked him please to leave. The divorce came through in about eighteen months but we're still friends; you could say we are like brother and sister if it was qualified to mean not always getting along with each other but always there; in a small town like this where's there to go? After the divorce, last year, we have actually gotten along better. Hughie is always changing jobs and changing woman friends and stopping drinking (and starting again) and none of what he does is my problem now, though naturally, being the way I am, I take an interest. But I don't let it hurt me, now.

He's away for months and doesn't call and I'm busy with my own life; then suddenly he'll drop by, lonely, depressed, three days' beard and bloodshot eyes and I won't lend him money if that's what he wants (sometimes I think he's just testing me, anyway) but I'll make him supper, or sometimes he has brought something special to eat, or a bottle of wine, sometimes even flowers. Flowers! I can't help laughing when he holds them out to me like a guilty little boy. He was always ready to spend our money on things we didn't need and I saw through that long ago but here's the same Hughie; they don't change. All other things change but they don't change, men like him.

So what's this story about Vegas? Hughie says. I'm waiting.

It isn't any story, I tell him. What's Lynn been telling you behind my back?

Some guy you met at craps. Some millionaire Texan.

I didn't meet him at craps and he wasn't any millionaire Texan and why don't you stay quiet, if you're going to stay here at all. You said you just wanted to nap.

So Hughie draws this long deep breath and burrows his face in my neck and lies very still. You've been to Vegas yourself, I say, you know what it's like. Hughie doesn't answer but I can tell he's waiting for me to go on. Of course it was a real surprise to *me*, I say, walking into the casino with Lynn and already at 9 A.M. there's so many people gambling, at these machines that look like video games. Almost the first people I saw, I swear they looked like your parents: this elderly couple playing the slots side by side, and she's winning some, a few quarters, and he doesn't care to be interrupted, just keeps on playing, leaning real close to the machine like he can't see too well, dropping in a quarter and pulling the lever, dropping in a quarter and pulling the lever, over and over the way they do, and it *is* fascinating, sort of, you can see how people get hooked. Lynn and I spent the morning on the machines and won some, lost some, the way you do. We saw some people Lynn said were probably retired to Vegas just for the slots and some of them, their right hands were actually deformed, like with arthritis, shaped like claws, pulling the lever a thousand times a day. But you could see they were happy, doing what they want to do.

There's lots of Vegas stories we heard just in the brief time we were there, and new ones every day. A man drives across the desert with two suitcases in the car, one empty and one filled with five-hundred-dollar bills; he's got five hundred thousand dollars and places a bet on some heavyweight boxer that the odds are six to one against—and he wins! And they fill the second suitcase for him with thousand-dollar bills and he drives off again and nobody even knows his name. That's a true story, supposed to have happened just a few weeks before. Then there are these millionaire, I mean billionaire, Arab sheiks that fly in for the poker games, these special poker games at some club not open to the general public where there's no limit on bets. I saw some of them, I think, just caught a glimpse. Up at the Sands some man died at blackjack, he'd been at the table for a long time they said and had a coronary for no special reason—I mean, not because he'd won a lot of money, or lost. We were in Vegas at the time but not in that casino, thank God! One thing that did occur, in the Rainbow Casino, it's sort of disgusting, a woman lost control of her bladder, playing the slots and not wanting to take time off, I suppose; people all started walking away fast, as Lynn and I did. Can you imagine! And she wasn't all that old either, around fifty, but a drinker—they must be the worst kind, hooked in with the slots on top of drinking.

Lynn's crazy about the slots but she said we should set ourselves a limit, make it seventy-five apiece, and see how far that would go, which is the only sensible way to approach gambling, and I wasn't playing ten minutes before I won a hundred and sixty dollars, which was one third of a jackpot for that machine. I was excited as a kid, jumping up and down; if it'd been me alone I would have quit right there and gone off and celebrated with a drink and something rich and fancy like a chocolate eclair, but Lynn just laughed and kissed me and said to calm down. Wait till you win a real jackpot, she said. That'll be time to celebrate, then.

I forgot to mention all the conventions being held in the big hotels, and people drinking too much and acting like kids: the National Association of Morticians was one of them, the Fred Astaire Dance Association was another, a bunch of hypnotists, veterinari-

ans—you name it! A lot of them fattish bald guys wearing badges
with a look like they're running loose, no wives to crimp their style.
I mean *a lot*.

I did see one sight that scared me, a little: that night, late, we
were walking with these guys we'd met through Caesar's Palace—
you know what that place is like, my God!—and there's this nice-
looking woman about my age playing the slots, all alone evidently,
with her cigarettes and her drink and one of those waxy paper buckets
half filled with coins, and all of a sudden she hits the jackpot and
it's one of the big jackpots, one thousand silver dollars, and the
machine lights up, you know, the way they do, and plays some hon-
keytonk music, and people come over to watch, especially tourists
who've never seen a big jackpot, and all she does is light up a cigarette, her hands are shaking and she doesn't even look at the coins
spilling out, she's half turned away from the machine, her face so
sad you'd think she was about to cry, and all the while the silver
coins are tumbling out and filling the trough and spilling onto the
floor and on and on and on! I mean, it keeps *on*, one thousand coins!
It's just such a happy sight, the machine lighting up, and the silly
music like cartoon music, but she isn't taking the least bit of happiness
from it—just tired-looking and so sad it was painful to look at her.
This man I was with, Sonny, he said, She's waiting for the jackpot
to finish so she can keep on playing. That's all she wants, to keep
on playing. A jackpot like that gets in the way.

And that turned out to be the case. At least with that woman—
we stood off a ways and watched.

OK, Hughie says. Now tell me about Sonny.

What I was needing, I thought, was a new life. Not a new *life*,
that sounds sort of extreme, but some new outlook on *this* life. Some
new surprise, a set of new feelings. I want a baby but that's not it;
I been wanting a baby for a long time. (Which was one of the reasons
Hughie and I broke up. He has kids from his first marriage and
definitely doesn't want any more.) That might be part of it but that's
not it. Some nights, after work, thinking how there's nobody prominent in my affections any longer and nobody I even know of I'd
like to be prominent, not in this town at least, where everybody
knows everybody else's business and some of them, the men, have

the idea I'm still married to Hughie or belong to him at least—some nights I'd start in crying for no reason I could name. Or, not even crying, just my throat closing up, that feeling of some old hurt returning.

So Lynn, my crazy friend Lynn, she comes over and shows me this charter-airline stuff, these brochures about Vegas, how cheap it is to fly there and how the hotels, some of them, aren't really that expensive, considering where you are—the big-name stars playing out there, the quality entertainment. Lynn has been to Vegas a half-dozen times and always enjoyed herself, and she told me if I was feeling bad this was the time to go—mid-January and the holiday season dead and gone and anybody's spirits just naturally need picking up. It didn't matter whether you were sad or not, Lynn said, this time of year would do it.

So I said no, then I heard myself say yes—you know how Lynn is with me. She just winds me around her little finger.

Hughie stirs and says, Oh, yes? And who wants to be wound?

I give him a pinch and tell him be quiet. Does he want to hear this or doesn't he?

Go on, he says. I'm waiting for Sonny, the millionaire Texan.

Anyway, as you know, it was my first time in Vegas. The first time flying over the Rockies like that, and the Grand Canyon—my God, that's beautiful; the whole time in the air was beautiful, sort of like a dream—Lynn hates window seats so I was sitting next to the window and we're flying at thirty thousand feet or whatever the pilot said, over these mountains, these snowy peaks, then over clouds like snow crust—miles and miles of it, I mean *hundreds* of miles of it—and I guess I got sort of hypnotized looking out. It's a funny feeling you have, flying over a big stretch of cloud, like a field piled with snow, but there are people living below it not able to guess how big the field is and how there's other people flying above it. How they're down there hidden and you're up above, flying over.

Hughie is lying heavy against me with his chin sort of sharp on my shoulder. He's breathing hard and steady so I think he might be dropping off to sleep. But he says, a little too loud in my ear to suit me, OK, OK, I'm waiting for the high roller. So I tell *him* OK: this guy, Sonny Drexel as he introduced himself, from Oklahoma City, a rancher he said he was, him and his buddy were watching Lynn

and me at blackjack, where we hadn't any luck—all those damn games
go fast, the serious ones; you put your chip down and Christ it's gone
before you know what happened. (Which is why some people prefer
the slots—you go at your own speed and never lose much.) So these
two, Sonny and Brady, said they'd stake us just to keep us in the
game, and we all played for a while and got along pretty well, though
Lynn and I never did get any luck, me especially. The strange thing
is, Sonny said I was luck for him, wearing my turquoise dress, you
know that one, and a black velvet ribbon in my hair, that makes me
look ten years younger than I am—that's what caught his eye, he
told me afterward, the ribbon, reminded him of his little girl. That
is, when she was actually little. I guess she's all grown up, now, and
then some.

How old was he? Hughie asks.

He *looked* like middle forties, maybe fifty, but I calculated later
on he was around sixty—

Sixty!

—but didn't act it at all, good-looking in this cowboy style you
see out in Vegas, a suede hat with silver studs, and snakeskin boots,
designer jeans, jeweled bracelet on one wrist and wristwatch on the
other, even some rings—the rings all had special meanings. Like one
was a birthstone, one used to belong to his great-grandfather, that
sort of thing. Lynn says the serious gamblers are all superstitious,
they don't do anything by chance. What Sonny reminded me of was
one of these cigarette billboard ads, an older man I mean, with pale
hair you can't tell is blond or silver, and longish sideburns, and a
creased, kindly, slightly puzzled face as if he'd been looking too long
into the sun. His voice was higher-pitched than you'd expect. Brady
was younger, heavier, with a coarser skin. What the connection was
between them I never did learn.

The two of them were taking a break from craps; I got the idea
they'd done pretty well judging from the good mood they were in,
especially Sonny, buying drinks for Lynn and me and some Japanese
tourists we got to talking with at the bar in the Tropicana, then this
expensive supper they bought us at the Barbary Coast where we saw
some of the floor show, a kind of Ice Capades with singing and
rainbow lights and acrobatics—it was beautiful to see, and Lynn and
I loved it, but Sonny got restless so we had to leave. Brady was

ragging him about not being able to stay away from the craps table for more than an hour or two like he needs his oxygen replenished, and Sonny laughs but you can tell he's annoyed. That kind of a man, you can get intimate with him to a degree and think you know him, but the least hint of familiarity he draws back and chills you out. I picked up on that right away.

Another thing Brady ragged him about was going to the john all the time and washing his hands. He's afraid of germs, Brady said, and Sonny said, You'd be too if you could see them with the naked eye, and we all laughed and Brady said, Can *you* see them with the naked eye? and Sonny laughed too but said in this serious voice, Sometimes. And I don't like it.

And I did notice, the short period of time I was in the man's company, he must have excused himself a dozen times to go to the lavatory. Only when he was shooting craps he didn't, of course—it was like he was another person then. When he was hot, I mean. Really rolling high and nothing could have stopped him.

So we went back to the Dunes and Sonny and Brady got into a game and Sonny was shooting and almost right away got hot. Won eighteen hundred dollars in less time than it takes me to say it! He had me stand on his left-hand side, told me not to move an inch if I could help it. At first he didn't want me to bet, thinking that might go against his own luck, but after a while, when he kept winning and so many other people were betting on the game, he said it might be all right so I started placing little bets on what they called the pass line—the easiest bet. And naturally I won too, though it didn't seem real or right, betting with chips he'd given me and following what he did.

Craps isn't my favorite game, it's so fast and nervous and wild, and so complicated, Christ—like some game that was invented to keep ordinary minds at a distance. All Lynn and I did was bet on the pass line and later on the come line—we wouldn't have wanted to bet no pass and go against Sonny—but these other gamblers got involved, and of course Brady was doing all kinds of things, special bets we couldn't follow. And the smart thing about Sonny was, he knew when to quit for a while—with this big pile of chips he'd built up in half an hour—and let somebody else shoot, so he could bet or not bet, depending. He told me what to do and I did it and most

of the time I won, but if I lost he told me to stop for a while till my
luck returned; he said you can feel your luck in you like a pressure
in the chest and head but not a cruel pressure, a feeling that's high-
wired and happy, and you can feel it drain away, sudden, he said, as
water draining out of a sink. A gambler moves by instinct, he said,
like a man dousing for water.

I had a granddaddy who could douse for water, I said.

We'll talk about it some other time, he said.

So after Brady shot for a while and did OK, Sonny took over
again and you could tell something would happen: this feeling all
around the table, like the air's charged up. Of course we'd all been
drinking this while, I don't know how long, Lynn and me excited
and giggling like high school girls, arms around each other's waist,
saying, This is something different, isn't it! This is something different
from the old home routine! And Sonny started his roll and I placed
bets on the pass line, which is the only bet I ever felt easy with, that
I understood: before the shooter rolls the dice, you place your bet,
and if he rolls seven or eleven you and him both win and he keeps
the dice to roll again. If he hits two, three, or ten the bet is lost but
he keeps his point and goes on rolling until either he makes his point
and you both win or he shoots seven and the bet is lost. I *think* that's
how the game goes.

That's how it goes, Hughie says. He's wider awake than I thought
he would be, which is flattering. Except it's two, three, or twelve on
that first roll.

And anyway I won my bets. But like I say it didn't seem real, or
exactly right.

Around 4:30 A.M. Sonny quit for the night. He'd been playing
in all about fifteen hours, he estimated, in the past twenty-four and
needed some rest. As far as I could calculate—they didn't like to
talk about these things, like it was in bad taste—he'd won about
twenty-five thousand just the time I was with him.

Called me his good luck talisman, said he'd always want me by
his side. All the time he was shooting he hadn't touched me, but
now he put his arm around me so tight it was hard to walk and sort
of leaned on me, calling me pretty girl, pretty Irene, Irene-y, I'll see
you in my dreams. He was drunk I guess but not so you'd really
notice. Had a way of talking that was a combination of a high-class

gentleman and a country boy—a sort of twangy accent, warm and rich like Johnny Cash.

He *was* sweet. Next day down in the promenade—we were staying in the big Hilton, there's all these boutiques and special stores there—he bought me a Japanese kimono, the most beautiful thing, turquoise with a brocade design like a sunburst, gold, red, green: just so beautiful. And some black silk pants to go with the kimono, and some gold lamé sandals with spike heels. And some gold teardrop earrings, and a bottle of perfume. And—

Uh-huh, says Hughie, his leg muscles twitching the way they do when he's asleep but he isn't asleep now, I get the drift of it.

It wasn't *that*, I tell Hughie, I liked him for himself. He was a fine, sweet, generous, thoughtful man. And a gentleman.

Hughie keeps quiet, not wanting to pick a fight and get kicked out of here on his ass as he's in danger of being. My heart's beating hard just at that one thing he said, his sly innuendo that I don't have to swallow any more than I swallowed any of his shit and he knows it—he's the boy who knows it no matter what he goes around town telling his buddies.

He was a gentleman, I say. There aren't many of that kind around.

Hughie doesn't say a word but I know he's fully awake and listening.

I *will* say, though, when we first got to his room—a real nice room in the Hilton Tower, nothing like what Lynn and I were sharing at our motel—I started in feeling very strange and wanted to just say good night and leave. Before, you know, it was too late and Sonny got the wrong idea. I'm just standing there, afraid if I sit down I'll fall asleep—I was more exhausted all of a sudden than I've ever been in my life—and my eyes weren't focusing right, everything sort of swimmy and blurry. I was drunk but that wasn't the only thing. There's this man I don't even know whistling to himself and taking off his shirt and his chest is covered in what looks like actual fur: gray-grizzled, silvery, matted. And his nipples dark as a woman's. And fat loose around his waist though his ribs were showing. And some sort of scar, or burn, on his back that looked just terrible. It's like him and me were married and had been married a long time, he's tossing his things around, whistling loud and happy, has me help him with his boots—these snakeskin boots like nothing you've ever seen, Lynn says something like that would go for five hundred dollars if not a thousand. You don't even see them in any store around here.

So I'm feeling very, very strange, this sickish feeling in my stomach, and Sonny's in the bathroom running the water loud and still whistling. He's happier now than down in the casino, like it was all held in, down there, and now it's coming out—just how happy he is, and how powerful it is, that kind of happiness!—like it would be too much for an ordinary person.

Sonny comes out of the bathroom drying his hands on a towel and when he sees me it's like he's almost forgotten I was there: this big smile comes over his face that looks as if it could stretch his face out of shape. Kisses me, and stands back staring at me, tells me how much I mean to him, how pretty I am, will I be his pretty pretty girl forever, and he takes the velvet bow out of my hair and kisses it solemn and serious and I'm thinking to myself, God, am *I* doing this? This is *me?* In a hotel room with some guy who, nice as he is, I don't know, just met? And I'm laughing too, giggling and scared, 'cause it's so easy, you could see doing this every night, I don't mean for the money or even for the man but just—the fact of how easy it is, once it starts.

Hughie stirs. Irene, he says, and it's the first time I have heard him call me Irene in a long time, this is a hard story to hear.

I told you, be quiet. Or don't you want to hear it?

I *want* to hear it, Hughie says, but I guess I want some parts of it to go by fast.

There's nothing to go by fast, I say, since all that happens is I sort of pass out on one of the beds and Sonny loosens my clothes and takes off my shoes and that's all—he sleeps in his own bed like a gentleman. And that's all.

Then the next morning I wake up pretty late, around eleven, and already he's in the shower, he orders us breakfast from room service which neither one of us can stomach, except for the Bloody Marys, and we go downstairs and pick out those nice things—which were a surprise to me, I swear, completely unexpected. Where Brady and Lynn are, I don't know, and I didn't like to make any inquiries.

Later on we drove over to Vegas World in this special car of Sonny's, Italian, hand-built, he said, like a custom-made suit, some sort of Ferrari with a long name, bright red like lipstick and capable

Sonny said of doing 175 miles an hour under the right road conditions. How'd I like to go for a drive in the desert maybe the next day? Sonny asked. Out to Death Valley maybe. I told him I'd like that a lot, but I seemed to know we'd never get there, that something was due to happen; it was like a movie where things are going so well you know they can't last. Also, it was only a few blocks to Vegas World but the sunlight hurt our eyes, even with dark sunglasses. What the actual desert would be like I didn't want to think.

(It's kind of a startling thing, leaving the inside world and going to the outside, that you've sort of forgotten is still there. This ordinary sunshine and ordinary sidewalks and traffic lights and things, and people in it that didn't seem to have anything to do with all that was happening in the casinos. It made me feel sort of sickish, I told Sonny, and he said yes but you get used to it.)

At Vegas World it's sort of like a circus for adults but Sonny wasn't interested in any of it, just headed straight for the casino. And what a crowd packed in! Not just every slot machine taken, but people waiting for some to open up. Sonny staked me to some blackjack again, but I didn't do too well, then for a few turns at roulette, ditto; he didn't play because as he said you get to know which game is yours and which isn't.

Also, he said, the games were too simple. Didn't command his fullest concentration.

So it was back at craps, and he had me stand close beside him, on his left, wearing my new outfit, including the shoes, and the black velvet ribbon in my hair. And again Sonny got on a roll, couldn't seem to make a mistake; he doubled his bet, and won, and doubled, and won, and there was this feeling of—it's hard to explain—a kind of excitement at the table, happiness so strong it's scary. That it could go through you like electricity, and kill you, bend your skull out of shape. Some of it's because other people get caught up in the betting, strangers that a few minutes ago didn't know one another but suddenly they're all united, close as old friends or something deeper, sisters and brothers—the exact same blood.

So he did real well again but never allowed himself to show what he was feeling. I could never be like that, I guess; I could never be a real gambler! All my feelings show on my face.

So we went back to the Hilton, this is maybe 6 P.M. that day, and Sonny's in a state like I don't believe I have ever seen any person in, giving off heat like a radiator, I swear I could almost feel the waves of it, and I was pretty high too, and we're kissing a little, sort of fooling around, but more like kids, or puppies, than, you know— like he's too worked up for anything to actually happen. His skin is burning like fever, but without sweat. And his eyes, this tawny cat color, the eyeball and the iris or whatever it's called sort of run together, like a man with jaundice, and I notice he's breathing hard, and loud, but don't make much of it. Whatever we're doing he stops all of a sudden and goes into the bathroom to wash his hands—I mean, I guess that's what he was doing—then he comes back and looks at me and says, Get dressed, honey, let's go back to the casino. And I can't believe it.

So we go back out again, this time down to the Sands, and in the car he's talking a mile a minute, to me you'd naturally think but really to himself. I listened hard but I can't remember much of it now. He did want me to marry him, that's for sure—come back with him to Oklahoma City to this new house he planned to build. He didn't ask me anything about myself, such as did I have any children, let alone did I want any children, so I sat there nodding and agreeing but thinking he probably wasn't serious, really. What he said, he meant, but only while he was saying it.

Then at the Sands his luck turned on him after about an hour, I don't know why. I mean—I don't know why he didn't know it was going to turn, the way he'd said he always did. Right in the middle of one of these red-hot rolls—what you would think was a red-hot roll—when he'd made, I calculated, about twenty-two thousand in not much more time than it's taking me to say so, he rolled the wrong numbers and lost the bet; and that was the beginning of the end. The two or three guys that'd been betting don't come won really big, and Sonny just stood there like he couldn't believe he was seeing what he was seeing. And the terrible thing is, the girl just raked in the chips like nothing had gone wrong, or even changed. Not the slightest understanding in her face of what had happened.

Now, *I* seemed to know that poor man should quit right then but he didn't pay the least heed to me, and when I put my hand on his arm he pushed away like I was something nasty. Don't touch! he said.

And this feeling came over me like the floor was tilting, and I thought, I know the truth of why we're here on earth, human beings here on earth: it's to love one another if we can, but if we can't—if we try, but can't—we're here to show kindness and gentleness and mercy and respect to one another, and to protect one another. I don't know how I knew but I *knew*.

But would he pay any attention to me? He wouldn't. Saying he wanted to marry me one minute and telling me to go to hell, calling me cunt, the next. For all the good I meant to do him.

So his luck ran out, and I don't know how much he lost, but people made big money betting against him, and in the end nobody wanted to look at him. I should mention he was wearing the suede cowboy hat and the same black silk shirt with one of these little string neckties he'd been wearing the day before, and the fancy boots. And a leather belt with a big silver buckle. And hot as he was he wasn't sweating much. (*I* was the one that was sweating now!)

I recall one final sight: the girl in her costume with *Sands* stitched in gold on the back, black jumpsuit and tight belt and black spike heels, hair blonder and puffier than mine, she took this little Plexiglas rake of hers and just raked Sonny's chips away, and took a crumpled-up five-hundred-dollar bill from him the same way except that she pushed it down a little slot in the table like a mail slot. And it just disappeared.

So finally Sonny turned away, his face like paper that's been burnt through but hasn't burst into actual flames yet. Finish up your drink, Blondie, he says to me, smiling. I'm hurt to think the man has forgotten my name.

We went back to the Hilton and he made some calls, then went out, saying he'd be gone awhile. I watched some television and washed my hair and finished this champagne we'd got the night before, and it got late but I was too worked up to sleep. I had the drapes open looking over at Vegas World—that's the tallest building, all colored lights like fireworks. But everywhere on the Strip there's lights: the Sahara, the Oasis, the Golden Nugget, Caesar's Palace, all the rest. Off in the distance the mountains you can't see and I never did get to see except from the air and going to and from the airport in the cab.

Around 4 A.M. when I was actually asleep a little, with all the
lights on, Sonny came back to the room. He had that look so drunk
it might be said to be sober. He sat on the edge of the bed and
kneaded his chest with both hands like it hurt him inside. In this
calm voice he said, I have led the wrong life. I have done wrong
things. At the very time of doing them I knew they were wrong, but
I did them nonetheless. I did them *nonetheless*—this word drawn out
slow, in a whisper.

He started to cry so it was painful to watch. Begging me not to
leave him now his luck had run temporarily out.

I was crying too. I told him I'd stay with him as long as he wanted.

He said, I'm not from where I said. I'm from a different place.
Not even Oklahoma. I've been a bad husband and father. There's
people back home loved me and gave me their trust, and I let them
down. I let them down a lot of times. Right now they don't even
know where I am.

I was sort of cradling his head, stooping over him. I said, Don't
think about that now, Sonny, and he shot back, Don't think about
it *now?* When the fuck *am* I supposed to think about it, then?

But right away he changed his tone back. Said, Dolly, I'm a dead
man.

What? I asked.

I'm dying, I'm a dying man, he said. I'm next thing to dead.

Are you serious? Should I call a—

You can't leave me just yet, he said, gripping my arm hard. You
know I'm crazy about you; I'd love you if I could.

That didn't make any sense so I said, You can love me, why can't
you love me? And he says right away, in this voice like we've been
quarreling, Dolly, if I *could*, I *would*.

He grabs me around the hips so hard it hurts and pulls me down
onto the bed. Then he's on me pawing and grunting and making this
terrible hoarse sobbing noise, and I'm there not helping him much
but just waiting for it to get over. I think, He can't do it, he's too
drunk, or too sick, or too old, and that's more or less the way it was,
I guess, but I wasn't paying close attention, shutting my eyes tight
and seeing all kinds of things that had nothing to do with him or
what was going on. I could see the wheat field out behind here, the

way the wind makes it look like waves. And the Grand Canyon, when the pilot turned the plane for us, explained some things to us, those natural rock formations, what a canyon actually is.

And other things too. Lying there with my eyes shut like they are now, my mind taking me far away from where I was.

Afterward I couldn't wake him. It was almost noon and he was lying on his back with his mouth open and saliva on the pillow and I seemed to know he wasn't just sleeping or even blacked out but something more serious. I tried to wake him, slapped his face and got a washcloth soaked in cold water, and that didn't help; oh, Christ, I'm thinking, the man is in a coma, he's going to die. The loud wheezing breath in a rhythm not like a normal breath: he's going to die. No matter what I do, shaking him, shouting in his ear, *I can't wake him up*.

I remembered something I'd read about brain death, a coma caused by too much alcohol and pills—did I mention Sonny'd been taking some kind of pills, just popping them now and then, not too many, and I didn't know if they were for his health, or what, like my daddy has to take heart pills every day of his life and glycerine if he gets pains in his chest—but I didn't want to ask Sonny; I figured it was too personal a question.

I got so scared, I guess I panicked. Thinking if he's going to die I will be involved. I would be a witness, and maybe arrested. Called to testify. Or charged with murder like that woman, that actress, who gave John Belushi a shot of heroin and he died. And she was tried and found guilty of murder!

So I got dressed and left. I left the kimono behind, and the jewelry, and even the perfume, and the shoes—it was the only decent thing to do. I wasn't thinking too clearly but I thought he could sell them back, maybe, to the stores. Or pawn them. I found some hundred-dollar bills loose in my purse and left them too, on the bedside table where he couldn't miss them.

So I went downstairs to the lobby, and in the lobby I called the house physician and told him Sonny's room number and hung up quick before he could ask any questions. I went back to our motel and nobody was there, thank God, and I took a long bath and tried to keep myself from thinking. I fell asleep in the bath and sometime that afternoon Lynn helped me out and dried me and seeing my face she just said, Don't tell me, so I didn't tell her. I never did tell her much of it.

Before we left Vegas I called Sonny's room but the phone just rang and rang. I asked at the desk was Sonny Drexel still registered and the girl said there wasn't any Sonny Drexel listed and had not been, and I said, That can't be right, and the girl repeated what she'd said, and I asked who was registered in 2023 up in the tower and she said, in the snottiest voice possible, The Hilton does not give out such information.

And that was the end of that. Like that—it was the end of that.

Hughie? You listening?

But Hughie's asleep by now. Warm moist breath against my neck like a baby's. Pressing heavy against me, foot twitching between mine, like always. He's here, then he's gone.

DEATH VALLEY

The colors of winter here were dun, a bleached brown, layers of rich cobalt blue. The light fell vertical, sharp as a knife. And there was the wind.

He observed as she shaded her eyes, which were not strong eyes, against the glare. "That looks like water," she said brightly. "Or ice."

"Those are salt flats."

"What?"

"Salt. Salt flats."

"It *looks* like ice."

Her tone was lightly combative. As if sexual banter were her primary mode of discourse.

She said, "I was always wondering about the name. Since I was a little girl."

"The name?"

"Death Valley. It's something you hear about, or see in the movies. The old movies. You know: 'Death Valley.' You sort of wonder."

It was then he realized how young she was. Twenty years younger than he, by a generous estimate. At that age you can still reasonably think death is romance.

It was their second day. He had rented a car, a classy-looking metallic-gray BMW, and driven her out into the desert. She'd never seen the desert, she said; she'd never seen Death Valley. There was an air of mild reproach in her voice, as if he, or others like him, had cheated her of a vision that was her due.

In the big casino, where they'd met, there were no clocks on the walls because the principle of time did not apply. Nor did the principle of day and night apply. Like the interior of a great head, he thought. And even in the desert where the winter light fell sharp and straight and blinding it didn't seem like day, exactly, but like something else.

She was saying, persisting, hair blowing prettily across her face, "Are you sure that isn't water, *really?* It looks so much like water."

"Taste it and see."

In the casino at Caesar's, at the craps table he always played at Caesar's, he'd said, smiling, "Pray for me, sweetheart," turning to her as if he'd known absolutely she would be there, or someone very like her. Not a hooker but a small-town girl, a secretary or a beauty salon worker, here in Vegas for a three-day weekend with a girlfriend from the office or the beauty salon, come to play the slots and to test her luck. With her hair cascading in shiny synthetic-looking curls halfway down her back, and her eyes like an owl's with makeup, and glossed lips, wasn't she there to bring him good luck? Her or someone like her.

At craps the play is fast and nerved up and choppy like a wind-whipped sea whose waves crash in one direction, then in another, and then in another. Pray for me honey, he'd said, and twenty minutes later walked away with $14,683, not the very most he'd ever won in Vegas but the most he'd won in a long time. The girl, whose name was Linda, pressed her hand against her heart, saying it was going like crazy from all the excitement; how could people *do* such things, take such risks? He kissed her solemnly on the cheek and thanked her. His lips were cold.

She hadn't prayed for him, she said. She'd had her fingers crossed but she hadn't prayed because God is God no matter who you are or think you are; God is a wrathful God you best did not provoke.

She rolled her almost-pretty owl's eyes as if she knew, as if she'd had a personal run-in with God.

"It's just your special luck," she said, drawing her fingers slow across his sleeve.

"You think I'm a lucky man?" he said happily.

"I *know* you're a lucky man: I just saw."

He kissed her on the lips, smelling her sweet sharp perfume, and through it he saw the bargain-rate motel room she and her girlfriend were renting for the weekend, the beaverboard walls, the stained venetian blinds pulled against the sun, the window air conditioner with its amiable guttural rumble. The girlfriend had a date for the night but Linda was alone. The kind of girl, baby fat in her cheeks, a little pinch of it under her chin, who wouldn't be alone for long and surely knew it.

But she surprised him, the quickness with which she framed his face in her hands, a dozen bracelets jingling, and kissed him, lightly, on the lips, like a woman in a movie when the music comes up.

"Well," he said, smiling his wide white happy smile, his sort of surprised smile, "I guess I *am* a lucky man."

Linda was the kind of girl too, in bright blurry makeup and highlighted ashy hair, chunky legs shaved so smooth they gave off a kind of sheen, like pewter, who has carried with her in secret since the age of sixteen a razor blade sharp as on the day of its purchase, never once used. It is likely to be wrapped in several turns of Kleenex placed carefully against the bottom of her leather shoulder bag. No one knows it is there, and often she too forgets.

An older woman, a friend, advised her to carry the razor blade with her at all times, if not on her actual person (which would be tricky) then within reach. The logic is, If you never have to use it you're in luck, right? If you have to use it and you have it, you're in luck, right? So how can you lose?

So sometimes without knowing what she does her fingers seek out the blade, the shape of the blade, neatly wrapped in its several turns of Kleenex, pressed, there, flat against the bottom of her bag. He guessed it was probably like that.

It was their second day, the first day after their first night; driving out from Vegas into the desert she'd laid her head sleepily against his shoulder, as if she had a right. Perfectly manicured pink-lacquered nails on his thigh, digging lightly into his sharp-pressed chino pants.

He told her with the air of one imparting a secret that he drove out into the desert as often as he could, not just to get away from Vegas but to be alone. To listen, he said, to the wind.

"Is it always so windy?" she asked.

"And I like the quiet."

"The *quiet?* But it goes on," she said, her reedy childlike voice beginning to falter, "such a long way."

He'd stopped the car, thinking this was a good place. Back a lane leading off the tourists' loop road, where no one was likely to come. Just this side of Furnace Creek one turn beyond a turnoff for a deserted mine where he'd brought another girl a few months back. There was a dreamy illusion they were the only visitors in this part of Death Valley today, but maybe it wasn't an illusion.

She'd said back in the room she was crazy about him, but now she was holding herself just a little off; he sensed it and liked it, that edge between them, not just the loneliness of the place but the sun did it, the starkness, the sudden wonder why you are here and why with this person, some stranger you hardly know and whose actual name you could not swear to.

"Is that tumbleweed?" she was asking. "I always wondered what tumbleweed was."

"It's something like tumbleweed," he said, "some kind of vegetation that dries out, tumbles in the wind, scatters its seeds that way. It's a weed."

"Everything's a weed, isn't it, in a place like this?"

He laughed; she had him there. "Everything's a weed," he conceded.

She had a way of surprising him now and then. He liked her; he really did. "You have named the secret of the universe," he said, smiling. *"Everything's a weed."*

He was laughing, and then suddenly he was coughing. She asked was he all right and he said yes, then started in laughing again, or maybe it was coughing. In a kind of paroxysm, like sex. But not always shared, like sex. Not always something you want to see, in others. Like sex.

"Lie down, honey, let's try it here."

He spoke half seriously but teasing too so that she could take it that way if she wanted. Behind the purple-tinted glasses her eyes widened in alarm. She said, "Here? I'd rather go back to Vegas."

He laughed and wiped his mouth with a tissue. He was excited but couldn't keep from yawning; his eyes flooded with tears. "I thought you were a big growed-up girl," he said, winking. He saw that his watch had stopped almost exactly at twelve noon.

She decided he was teasing, maybe he was teasing; she laughed and walked off a little, saying it was a shame she'd left her camera behind, wouldn't you know it, Death Valley and she'd left her camera behind. You could see she was trying. Squinting at these mountains that were not Kodacolor mountains with dazzling snowy peaks but just rock formations lifting out of the earth, weirdly striated.

The striations of the brain, out there. Terrible to see if you saw them.

Vegetation that looked like it was actually mineral.

Rocks, crumbled earth. Dun-colored bleached-looking dead-looking earth.

And the dunes, and the sand in ripples like washboards. And the wind.

She said, licking her lips, uneasy because he'd been silent for so long, hands in his chino pockets, not following her with his eyes as she strolled about, in her tank-top jersey blouse with the spaghetti straps to show she wasn't wearing a bra and the black-and-white striped miniskirt that fitted her hips snug and sweet, as if to set her off the way, say, a model is set off against a dull dun-colored background. "I suppose many people have died out here—pioneers, I mean—crossing the desert? In the old days?"

"I wouldn't doubt it," he said.

"The Donner party—the people who had to eat one another's flesh in order to survive—didn't they cross Death Valley?"

"I don't believe so."

"I thought that was their name. I saw a television show about them once."

"That was the name but I don't think the Donners crossed Death Valley. I think it was Idaho. Somewhere in Idaho."

"It was just heartbreaking, the television show. Once you got to know them, the men and women and the little kids, your heart just went out to them. My God! Turning cannibal!" She spoke vehemently, gesturing with both hands. The wind blew thinly through her hair. "Our ancestors endured so much, it's a miracle we came into being at all."

She looked at him; he was smiling. She shaded her eyes against him and said, "OK, what's up? Did I say something stupid, or what?"

"You said something wonderful."

"Yeah? What?"

" 'It's a miracle we came into being at all.' "

"Yeah?"

"Yeah."

"Just something, you know, nice. I don't like to talk about it, actually."

"But is it strong, is it sweet, is it a little painful, what *is* it? I'm just curious. What women feel."

"I don't like to talk about it actually."

"Why not?"

"I—"

"You said you were married, once. When—when was it?—you were nineteen."

"What's that got to do with it?"

"You're not a kid."

"No. I guess I'm not a kid." She cut her eyes at him, meaning to shift the subject. "You'd maybe prefer a kid?"

"As I said, I'm just curious. How long the sensation lasts, for instance, afterward. Minutes? Hours?"

"Oh, I don't know, you know," she said, shy again, not looking at him, a blush starting up from her neck. "A long time sometimes, hours sometimes. I guess it depends."

"On what?"

"How strong it was in the beginning."

"If you love the guy a lot—or don't, much—does that affect the orgasm too?"

"I guess so."

"But don't you *know*?"

She stood mute and resisting, her face, beneath the heavy pancake makeup, decidedly pink. "I guess I don't. I guess it's something that just . . . happens."

"The orgasm, you mean. Can't you say the word?"

She stood smiling, staring at their feet. Sandals with just enough heel to make it unwise for her to have worn them, out here. And if she'd have to run, and kick the shoes off, the sand would be like liquid fire against her feet.

Her purse too, the shoulder bag, left behind in the car. She'd never get to it in time.

"Say it," he said, bending a little to look in her face. Teasing. "Can't you say it? Orgasm."

She laughed nervously, and shook her head, and said, "It makes me feel funny. I don't like it, you looking at me so close."

"Why does it embarrass you?"

"I don't know. I'm not embarrassed."

"A big girl like you."

"I'm not embarrassed, I don't *like* it."

"You look embarrassed. But very sweet too."

"Well."

"You know you're a great-looking girl, don't you? Where did you say you were from? Oh, yes: you and your girlfriend, from Nebraska."

Her face crinkled in childish dislike.

He said, quickly, with an air of apology, "No, I mean Columbus, Ohio. You and two girlfriends from Columbus, Ohio." He was teasing, poking her with a forefinger. In the plump resilient flesh just below her breasts. "The big weekend in Vegas. Right? First time in Vegas, right? And last night you won a hundred and twenty dollars at the slots, you were telling me. Two separate jackpots."

There was a silence. She said, quietly, "I think I'd sort of like to go back now, to Las Vegas. This place is kind of weird."

"I thought you wanted to see the countryside. The 'natural rock formations.' "

"It makes me feel . . . sort of strange, here. Like it's a dream or something."

"A dream of yours or a dream of the landscape?"

She peered at him, suspicious. "What's that mean?"

"What?"

"What you just asked me?"

"*You* were saying it, honey, not me. That it's like a dream here. Where anything can happen."

She laughed again, not exactly frightened yet but on the edge of it. He was thinking how her mouth was her cunt actually, the fat lips glossed up the way they were. The night before he'd taken a wad of toilet paper and was a little rough playing daddy, scolding her to keep it light—he was careful to keep it light—wiping the lipstick off, the apricot makeup, layers of pancake makeup and grainy powder that had caked over her young skin. Without the makeup her skin was doughy and a little coarse but he preferred it to the other. If there was anything he loathed it was female makeup smeared on him, the madman look of lipstick around his mouth, enlarging his mouth.

He kissed her, and whispered some things in her ear, and she slapped at him and said they'd better go back to the car, at least. And he kissed her again, forcing her mouth open, how wet it was, but not really warm, and how he felt, in that instant, the power flow down from his torso into his belly and loins, the first time he'd felt it that day. Last night, he must have felt it too but couldn't remember, he'd been too drunk.

He was thinking, those years he'd worked out every day, lifting weights, keeping himself in condition, he'd had that feeling a lot: you walk in someplace where no one knows you but they glance up in acknowledgment of you, in approval or even admiration, and that does it: sets you up for the rest of the day.

She didn't like him roughhousing; she said, little-girl hurt, "You got the wrong idea about me, mister," and he said, smiling, "You've got an ass, don't you? You've got a cunt. You *are* a cunt. So where's the 'wrong idea'?" But now he'd gone a little too far too fast and she was hurt and beginning to be frightened. Seeing her face he was repentant at once, saying he was sorry, damned sorry. Wouldn't hurt her for the world.

She went ahead of him to the car, swaying a little in the sandals like a drunken woman. He caught up to her, kissed her, apologized another time. He yawned; moisture flooded his eyes. In the car they drank from the bottle he'd brought along, good strong smooth delicious Jim Beam, my pal Jim Beam, don't go anywhere without him. He talked about getting married, it was time for him to settle down,

Jesus, it was past the time, he had a hunch he should consolidate his luck and he should do it right now. She lay with her head against his shoulder, just a little uneasy against his shoulder, and he asked if she'd ever heard of the poet Rilke, the great German poet Rilke, and she said she'd maybe heard of the name but couldn't swear to it. Guardedly she said she didn't read much poetry now; used to read it, had to memorize it, back in high school. He was feeling good so he recited what he could remember of one of the *Duino Elegies*, the words pushing through in their startling order which he had not known he still knew, but of course there were only snatches, shreds. "*And that is how I have cherished you—deep inside / the mirror, where you put yourself, far away / from all the world. Why have you come like this / and so denied yourself. . . .*"

His voice trailed off, he sensed her embarrassment, they sat for a while without speaking. Except for the wind it was absolutely silent, but you stopped hearing the wind after a while.

She said, clearing her throat, "It's funny: in the shade it's sort of chilly, but in the sun, out there, it's so hot."

In that instant he hated her. He was very happy. He said, "It's winter, sweetheart. After all."

She was preparing to cry but holding back, thinking was he the kind of man who feels sorry when you cry or was he the kind of man who gets really angry. So he warned her, "I'm getting just a little impatient, honey," and that quieted her fast. He got her into the back of the BMW, and they kissed awhile, he called her honey and sweetheart and said how crazy he was about her, his good luck talisman dropped from the sky. She was still stiff, scared, but he unzipped his trousers anyway, closed his fingers around the nape of her neck; she began to say, "No, hey, no, I don't want to, not here," whimpering like a child, and he said, "Here's as good as anywhere, cunt," so that quieted her, and she did it, she went through with it, in the back seat of the rented car awkward as kids playing in some cramped secret place. And he drifted off thinking of how wild it would be, how no one could stop it from happening; this is the one who's going to lean over quick to get her purse from the front seat and take out the razor blade and unwrap it while his eyes are shut and his face all slack and dreamy like the bones had melted . . . and then she'll bring the blade's edge against his neck, where the big blue artery is throbbing. And there's an immediate explosion of blood and his eyes are open now and he's screaming, he's clutching at his throat with his fingers as if to close the wound, just with his fingers, and she scrambles out of the car, running stumbling in the sand, screaming, How do you like it? How do you like it? Filthy shit-eating bastard, how do you like it?—running until she's out of the range of his cries. Until the cries subside.

Then she waits, her heart pounding hard, so scared she's begun to leak in her panties. But at the same time there's a part of her brain reasoning, I'm safe here, what can he do to me here? He can't do anything now.

And she's thinking too, Anything I did to him, it's been done before by somebody to somebody, not once but many times.

She thinks, shivering, There is that consolation.

When she returns to the BMW, she sees his body on the ground a few yards from the car where he fell, must have tried to crawl a little, though there is nowhere his crawling could have taken him. She sees he isn't breathing, must be dead; and so much blood in the sand, soaked up in the sand, and in the back seat of the car, horrible to see. She tries not to look but has to get the car keys from his pocket, his trousers around his ankles, unzipped, and his jockey shorts open, everything looking so tender and exposed like veins on the outside of the body, and soaked too with blood. The wild thought comes to her, How will they take photographs of him for the papers, lying the way he is, how will they manage to show it on the television news?

Sweet, sweet Linda. God, how sweet.

Back in Vegas, he dropped her off at her motel, said he'd call her around nine, and she said, "Oh, sure, I'm gonna hang around here all night in this shithole and wait for you to call, that's great, thanks a lot, mister," and he said, "If I say I'm going to call I'm going to call, why are you so angry? Nine P.M. sharp, or a little after," and she got out of the car, moving stiffly, as if her joints ached; then she leaned in the window, face puffy and mouth bruised-looking. "Fuck you, mister," she said, "in no uncertain terms."

He sat in the car, the engine idling, and watched her walk away and had to give her credit: she didn't once glance back. Holding herself with dignity in that wrinkled miniskirt that barely covered her thighs, walking as steady as she could manage in the tacky fake-leather sandals, as if it mattered, and she mattered, which actually scared him a little—that evidence of the difference between them when he hadn't believed there could be, much.

WHITE TRASH

Poor skinny thing you're thinking but it's how models are skinny, with style—pelvic bones sticking out and tight little buttocks, tiny breasts and cunt, hair bleached a perfect bone-white, all these frizzy wild curls. Funky clothes I got on sale where the high school girls shop, pink V-necked sweater spangled with tiny silver stars, slithery black rayon skirt, black mesh stockings, and these spike-heeled shoes I love with the ankle straps, open toes: sexy, giggly, Melanie's looking good again and feeling good to match.

You'd guess maybe twenty-three, twenty-four years old? Could be I'm pushing thirty. Or had that birthday not knowing it 'cause I was elsewhere.

Mayweather Smith the jazz pianist looks at me close, lifting his lip from his big white wet teeth in a kind of smile goes through me like a razor, says, Why you hangin' around like this? Lookin' for trouble? And I come back quick and snappy 'cause it's one of Melanie's good nights, saying, You want to give me trouble?

Which makes the man laugh. Snorting kind of laugh and he's a big man leaning close shifting in his chair so his fancy wide leather belt gives a creak like something on a horse.

Mayweather Smith takes a big swallow of the whiskey and water I bought him and says, Don't want to give nobody trouble, specially not a pretty little girl like you. Don't want to get it neither. I too old for that kind of shit. Too busy too. You understand?

Sure I understand, I say.

Picks up his beret that he wears at the piano and don't exactly look at me, saying he better get back saying he'd be happy to play any piece I request, so I tell him, Play "Cry Me a River" and he walks away without a word but the first number is my number and I'm thinking, Mmmmm, Melanie, you're the luckiest woman alive.

Been gone from home for maybe one week. I'm not counting the days. Staying at this cinderblock motel on South Main Street where it's closed-up looking after 6 P.M. except for a barbecue place and some liquor stores and the Lucky Deuce where Mayweather Smith is playing jazz piano THUR. FRI. SAT. NITES as they advertise. Just luck I dropped in there, which is why it's "Lucky Deuce" maybe. Two nights in a row listening to Mayweather Smith play his special kind of jazz and I'm crazy about him just don't want the piano to stop just could sit there at my own little table close by listening and eating him up with my eyes. No matter Mayweather Smith is col- lapsed-looking and there's these pouches around his eyes and a mean sour bad-tasting look 'cause it's clear he was a damned handsome man once and not that long ago. (First time I seen him I sat there staring so hard watching his hands, his fingers on the keyboard, didn't even know I was falling in love, didn't give a shit for that kind of connection right then, 'cause I was blown away thinking Jesus that man is *black* like *black* only got invented not just the outermost part of the skin that you can see but going deep inside. Blood and bones and marrow—*black*. Deep as you want to dig—*black*. That special kind of black skin that's got a purplish sheen to it like oily patches on the surface of the water.)

The man has got his dignity. Knows how good he is even if he's casting pearls before swine down here on lower Main. In this burnt- out city that looks, certain neighborhoods, like the end of the world.

The first night he acted mostly like I wasn't there (too many other men paying attention to me: the only white woman in the place, and alone), only thanked me for the drink I bought him, nodded at me, not smiling, raised his beret just a touch, and went right on playing piano. Big hands stretching on the keyboard so it almost looks easy. And Melanie sits there blinking back tears feeling the music so strong

knowing this is the one. All them white men and two actual husbands
and this is the one, getting back to the black boyfriend I had when
I was fifteen years old. God, it's been a long time hasn't it? I'm ready.

He was shaving off three days' beard sick-looking in the mirror
'cause he'd missed work those three days and was worried would
they take him back. Wouldn't make no telephone call—that's how
he is. Walking past where the bathroom door was open I caught his
eye in the mirror that nasty look he gave me and I started screaming
at him, yelling at him standing there in his undershirt and shorts
judging me making a judgment on me and here I wasn't back home
a week, that morning. I wasn't off the pills one day. Started screaming
and must have slapped him 'cause the razor sank into his cheek, made
a bloody slash, and I kept hitting him saying, I hate you! I hate you!
Why didn't you die instead! not knowing what all I said but knowing
it was right.

Other times the bastard slapped me hard right back, but this time
he just stood there looking at me. Dripping blood down his chin,
chest, onto the floor. Just looking at me like he saw something in
my face I didn't know about.

Spent all day at the mall seeing movies and walking through the
stores. Came back and the fucker was gone (left the TV on) so I
packed up some things and walked right out not caring who saw. He
tried to scare me lots of times saying he'd kill me if I walked out on
him (like I walked out on this other guy we both knew), but he ain't
going to kill nobody: got to find me first.

There was a baby so small and shriveled it could fit in Melanie's
two hands. Too small to draw breath so it died. I told them I wasn't
a junkie, think I'm crazy? Tried some things over the years for
personal reasons but not while I was pregnant. "White trash" I know
they been calling me on the street, but I wasn't ever a junkie and
surely not this past year. I can sue for malpractice I told them at the
clinic, got excited saying I'd burn the place down so they called a
guard, they got guards on duty there twenty-four hours a day which
I should have remembered. Saying it was my fault my "condition"
to blame for the baby never drawing breath like he did (or they said:
how do I know they're telling the truth?), then they put me in

restraint which wasn't necessary and stuck me full of needles making
my head bad. So I had this mixed-up dream that the baby wasn't
born yet but the labor had started and wasn't ever going to stop.
Melanie being punished by the Lord God of Wrath for something
she never done. Or if she done it, it was all a long time ago running
with some other crowd.

Explaining all this to Mayweather Smith. A man capable of jazz
piano like that—you know he's going to understand. Specially a black
man 'cause they know how it is with women, they're the ones really
know. Not these shithead white men that always let you down.

Both my husbands were white, which is why I know. Back in
high school I had a black boyfriend, Jimmy Fox was his name, he
was a lot older than me which was one of the reasons we broke up
but I don't know why we broke up really, that never made a whole
lot of sense to me. I was too damned smart in those days thinking
I'd be a beauty queen or some damn thing, or a model. Wanted to
be a singer too with a rock band but none of it came to nothing.

If that baby was black he'd be alive right now. That I'd swear to.

The smart-ass intern at the clinic asking me questions then asking
my husband, and him standing there shamefaced staring at the floor
like he didn't know English. He needed a shave that day too but was
wearing that silky blue shirt of his half open to his belly button and
the off-white sport coat in some fabric you think's going to shine in
the dark—a pimp's outfit from Louis the Hatter's—and *he* thinks *he's*
superior to blacks. (He's from Tennessee just like me. White trash
just like me if it comes down to it.) Melanie be quiet, he's saying.
Melanie shut your mouth, he's saying. That fucker standing there'd
betray Jesus Christ Himself if he had the chance.

So I been spending some time with friends but know enough to
be cautious about wearing out my welcome. Also I like to move on:
get restless staying in one place. Riding the city bus for the hell of
it—can't afford taxis—down Mohegan to South Main, South Main
to Griffith, Griffith to Bonaventure, back up to Brush. You get into
conversations on the bus with people you never saw before and will
never see again, older women especially, they're kind-hearted, they
know how the world is, once they get past not liking me 'cause of
my hair and the way I dress, the eye shadow, et cetera. Once I start
in telling them about that poor sad tiny baby that never had a chance,

weighing three pounds maybe. As if that was my fault along with
everything else!

Look at my arms if you think I'm a junkie! I told them. Pulling
up my sweater sleeves to show Mayweather Smith too and his big
eyes bulging. Any fucking needle marks you see were done by the
city. Not authorized by me.

You sure had you some bad times, Mayweather Smith says, staring. Pretty little thing like you.

Skinny I look but it's with style. And my legs ain't skinny either,
not for a woman my size. (I been size four since ninth grade. Standing
five foot one in the highest high heels like the ones I'm wearing right
now.)

Pretty little thing like you, says Mayweather Smith. Could lift
you in one arm without no trouble, couldn't I?

Took the bastard long enough to come to Melanie's table is what
I'm thinking but mmmmmmm that smell of hair lotion or pomade
or what you call it, that special smell mixed in with something to-
bacco-y, sort of dry. He's a good-looking man yet. Big broad face
like something carved and deep-set eyes oh, Christ, you could look
in forever like listening to him at the piano forever never wanting
it to end. I'd like to lick his face with my tongue—those oily little
beads you almost can't see, globules of sweat. Run my tongue along
his skinny little mustache, push it in his mouth right with everybody
watching like they never saw a white woman before, independent
like me.

What's your last name, Melanie, he's asking, ain't you got no last
name? I got too many last names, I tell him. This makes him pause
then shake his head, laughing like I said something real witty. Angling
to know am I married and where's my husband but I turn a little
cool and signal for the waiter to bring us two more drinks—it's getting
on toward closing time: 2 A.M. is the hour.

He don't know what to make of Melanie and that's just fine.
Trying to jive me at first with nigger talk like he'd just come up
from Georgia, then lapsing back to his regular talk. The way blacks
do whites sometimes and you can't blame them I suppose but that
particular game makes me madder than hell like they blame you for
being white and them black. I let him talk, though. Feeling a nice

buzz behind my ears and between the legs too from that nice mellow sound I been hearing. You a jazz fan? he asks, leaning close helping himself to one of my cigarettes, and I tell him, Sort of, yeah I guess I am, but I never heard nothing like tonight. He says, Never? lifting his lip from his teeth in that mean tight smile and I know to say, Never in person anyway. I'm a little shaky he's going to walk away and that's that but I can't let him know it. They can smell fear on you sometimes like a dog.

Got him a sly peekaboo tongue fat and wet as a cow's tongue. And that wet little click in his throat like he's trying not to laugh.

Too many white women crowding him when he was young, maybe. Makes a man spoiled.

There's some loud drunk voices and almost a fight and two guys are pulled off each other. Almost dropped my drink it scared me so—happens so fast and so loud. Mayweather Smith makes a face of disdain, turning a shoulder on the commotion like he's embarrassed of it, with me here. Just some local assholes, he says. We better get goin'.

All this time Melanie's hand is laying on his arm and he just lets it lay, don't shift it off and don't take hold either. Melanie's digging her red-painted nails in, light and playful like a cat does kneading your arm 'cause it reminds them of their lost momma cat they can't hope to remember any other way.

Mayweather Smith's car is a Cadillac Eldorado a few years old and there's rust on the fenders, but what I can see looks good. That's a comfort sure enough. White finish and red leather interior, powder-gray fancy cushioned seats, still some of that nice smell of an expensive car. My favorite kind of car I'm telling him and he helps me walk in this damned gravel helps me climb inside otherwise I'd have trouble. Sweet brown sugar I been waiting for all my life.

Inside the car's so cold! Hits me like a punch in the face. Teeth chattering and I can't stop shivering so it's like a fit, a convulsion and I've seen what a convulsion can do, but Mayweather Smith's holding me saying, OK, honey, OK, you'll get warm in a minute. Turning on the heater full blast. I lost more weight than I knew so the damp winter cold goes through my bones, scares me like it could

kill me. Like one of them bag ladies they found the other morning
in a doorway close by City Hall froze clean through. And no last
name.

Goin' to warm you up fast, honey, says Mayweather Smith, getting excited taking hold of me so I couldn't breathe too well at first.
Had to fight to get breath, then I was sobbing and laughing choking
and it was over. He says, Did I hurt you, little honey? sounding
concerned but maybe also teasing a little, that Deep South nigger
accent. Sweating like a pig so it's near rolling off his face.

No you did not, I tell him.

We're driving somewhere and it's raining, half rain and half sleet,
the windshield wipers going and the wheels sliding a little on the
pavement. Mayweather Smith passes me the bottle—Four Roses it
says on the label—helps me hold it to take a drink but even so some
of it dribbles down my chin onto my nice suede coat. Ain't you
somethin' he says. Melanie what's-her-name. You goin' to be nice
to my friends like you been nice to me?

Somewhere else we're stopping again by some viaduct. Not a
neighborhood I know. The thing that scares me is I might be going
to get sick and oh, Christ, if that happens! puking in the front seat
of Mayweather Smith's Cadillac and I'll kill myself if I do, jump off
the fucking bridge. Oh, Christ, please don't let it happen and in a
few minutes I'm OK. The heat's on steady now and the shivering is
stopped but I better not have any more to drink, I'm explaining to
Mayweather Smith. He's gripping my buttocks so they'll bruise but
I'm not going to cry: they don't like tears. Somebody told me once
(my momma?) and that's surely so. Black or white or whatever, they
don't like it.

(Almost I'm forgetting who this is: big black man with a face like
a mask carved out of something hard and oiled, panting and grunting
and near-snorting. Pop eyes. Wide black nostrils like a horse. Oh,
God, Melanie's blown away like she wanted: shit-faced drunk and
happy like she hasn't been in a long long time.)

Then it's sometime later and I'm trying to tell him about my baby.
He's saying over and over Un-huh—lifting the bottle to drink—un-
huh honey that sure is sad. Wish to hell I knew you then, I say. Wish
the baby was black and it'd had a chance to live. You think it'd had

a chance somehow? I ask Mayweather Smith and he says he don't know.

I get started crying which is what I don't want: mascara running down my face and it's already smeared and caked no doubt looking like hell. Wish I'd known you a long time back, I'm telling him almost like we been arguing the point, 'cause it's hard when you don't love anybody and there's nothing to keep you on earth. Yeah honey, Mayweather Smith says, sighing, wheezing like the start of the blues, that sure is so.

My baby was going to be called Dwight, I tell him, after my deceased daddy.

That so? says Mayweather Smith.

He drove us all up from Blount County, Tennessee, when I was nine years old, I say. I never had no wish to go back like my momma did—she *did* go back. Died there too which was her wish.

I'm trying to say more words but something like a dream washes over me and I lose the way. Hoped to tell this man about my husband who ain't worth shit and the clinic and the doctor that never was any doctor only an "intern" younger'n me and how when my baby died they wouldn't let me have him, wouldn't let me try to nurse him, just saying he was dead, he ain't living, and I went a little crazy demanding him 'cause I had milk for him but they wouldn't hand him over. And Mayweather Smith looks at me and says, Honey, that sure is sad.

I don't want money from them, like if I sued them or something, I say. I just want justice.

That's right much to want, Mayweather Smith says.

Then he starts in sort of slow and rambling telling me a story of his own that I miss the actual beginning of. How his brother Carlyle who was his baby brother was killed by police, white police in Cleveland in March 1958, and no justice ever done.

He says, Carlyle just walkin' in the neighborhood with his friends and the police car comes by and stops and they call for the boys to halt and naturally the boys take off running like hell but Carlyle is the slowest and they catch him. Aged seventeen and they killed him like a dog. You ever heard of the police choke hold, honey? he says, taking hold of me. What they do to people resistin' arrest? I don't know what he's saying but I tell him yes. Like this, honey, he says, closing his hands around my neck. There's this big artery you press in, see, to slow down the blood, see? Closing his hands around my neck so I'm scared, getting scared I won't be able to breathe. Hey, honey, you got to hold still, he says, otherwise you could get hurt. See? It's to slow down the blood goin' to the brain, pressin' on this special artery: ten seconds or so and you're out cold, fifteen seconds or so and you're dead. Ain't that somethin'? he says. That wet little click in his throat. Jiving me with his nigger accent. Weird thing about it, honey, it's the white man's technique ain't meant to hurt, they say. Kills you dead but ain't meant to hurt.

I'm trying to breathe twisting around trying to get loose of him scared as hell he's going to strangle me not knowing what he's doing. I know he don't mean to hurt. I know it but I can't help it. He's so drunk I don't want to rile him up more but I got to pry his fingers loose. Whispering, Hey don't, honey, Mayweather honey, maybe you better let me go, but he don't appear to be listening, he's kissing me up and down my opened front using his tongue that's wet and floppy saying things I can't hear. Pretty little white cunt, he's saying, pretty little platinum-blond white honey-cunt, he's saying, so I know to lay real still, not riling him up more, and it gets over with finally and it's OK. He lets me go and it's OK.

Gettin' late, he says, wiping his face with his handkerchief. We better move on.

I'm laying real still dozing off in this tub in this water gone lukewarm thinking, Oh, shit, I'd turn on the hot water but the faucet's too far to reach. Or maybe the hot water's all run out? Eyelids are puffy and I don't need to see Melanie stretched out in this tub to her full length. It's the Holland Hotel on Brush Street behind the old sports arena maybe a mile from the Lucky Deuce where Mayweather Smith is booked for the rest of the month. He's on the telephone in the next room. Or is that somebody else's voice. Now he's leaning in the doorway here poking his head in smiling that wet wide smile and his eyes yellowish white threaded with blood like he's been staring too long at something hard to see. My eyelids are heavy but I ain't surprised to see him there, or anybody. Saying, You coming in or going out? Or just standing in that fucking doorway letting the cold air in?

III

TWINS

1

They were identical twins, born within seconds of each other: Lee and Lester.

Lee was my father, now deceased, and Lester was, or is, my uncle, whom I'm not sure I have ever seen. I know I never met him face to face. If he's still alive he would be sixty-six years old now, but I doubt that he's living since my father, his twin, is dead.

When I was a boy all the family stories were about my Uncle Lester, or Les as he was usually called, and none were about my father because Uncle Les had run off years before and nobody knew where he was. He'd been only twenty-four when he disappeared. He got in trouble so he handled it the only way he knew—drove off in the 1939 Nash he and my father owned together and didn't call home for three weeks. After that it was months. Then years. His brother Lee was the only person he contacted but he never said much about what he was doing, when he was coming home; he'd make vague promises to come back (if he wasn't in any danger of being arrested?) but nothing came of it. He wasn't lying exactly, Father said. You had to understand Les to know what he meant. You had to know what his words actually meant when he said them.

Of the twin boys it was Les who'd been the sly one, people said. Sweet-faced but tricky. Playing pranks as a boy—some of the pranks not so funny. He'd always wanted to be a radio comedian like Jack

Benny or a movie actor like Cary Grant, John Wayne, Clark Gable, somebody up there on the screen bigger than life you had to admire. But he'd been an athlete too, in high school—both brothers were excellent athletes, big husky boys who played quarterback on the football team. They were the crowd's favorites: Lee and Les Waller. Les and Lee. Who was who? Did it matter? The Waller twins: you could only tell them apart by the numbers on their football jerseys. Their photographs had been published in the local newspapers many times, back then in 1937–1940. A long time ago.

Then they graduated from high school, then they went into the U.S. Navy, then when they came home, discharged from service, things didn't go so smoothly for them, Les in particular. I was never told much about those years. Nobody seemed to remember. The stories were mainly about Uncle Les after he'd driven away, after his life seemed to come into focus as a mystery. "When do you think we'll hear from Les again?" It was always asked of my father. "How long has it been, now?" Father would shrug his shoulders as if his clothes didn't fit him comfortably; he'd mumble something in reply or say nothing at all—he was the kind of man who could say nothing, just nothing, when people stood there waiting for him to speak. He'd just stand there silent. And you couldn't guess what he was thinking: did he miss Les badly, did he hate Les for all the attention he was still getting, did he maybe have secret news of Les nobody else could be told? Father never offered one word more than was required, though it was said that, at his store downtown, he could talk expansively and humorously, like any good salesman.

But Les had been the "friendly" twin, the "popular" twin, and people remembered him that way. They spoke of Les as if he'd been better-looking than my father, when the two had looked exactly alike, judging from snapshots! And he'd had a quicker temper too, which was how he'd gotten into trouble.

The children in our family—by which I mean my two older sisters and our half-dozen cousins—grew up hearing so much about Uncle Les it almost seemed he hadn't disappeared at all. Les this, Les that, d'you remember the time when, what do you think Les would make of, wasn't he something!—the football game that had won the trophy for East High, the Halloween party he'd dressed up as a woman complete with wig and makeup and black net stockings and spike-heeled shoes, the feud he'd had with Lee for a solid week when he behaved as if Lee wasn't there: just looked right through him. And poor Lee hadn't known how to take it; he'd been angry sometimes, other times so sad-looking you'd think his heart had broken. There were tales of Les's exploits in the navy too, as if he'd been alone, without Lee. It was as if the brothers had started out equal—in fact (as Grandmother had carefully noted in the twins' baby book) the infant to be baptized Lee had actually been born first, ten seconds ahead of his brother—then as time passed Les just naturally overtook Lee and seemed to force him into the background. He had more friends than Lee because he had Lee's friends as well as his own; he took any girlfriend away from Lee he wanted—except for Mother. Years after he'd left home any visitor to one of our family gatherings, not knowing the circumstances, would have assumed that Les was close by, not hundreds (or thousands) of miles away; he'd have assumed that Les was as immediate a presence as Lee. "When is Les coming back?" Lee was always asked. As if Lee himself, standing there, somehow didn't count.

Once when I was very young a telephone call came for my father from Uncle Les, long distance. Somewhere in Florida. In those days a long distance call was done by way of operators and was much more of a production than it is now. Father hurried into his and Mother's bedroom to take the call, closing the door behind him, and my mother kept my sisters and me away, saying, "It's Les! It's your Uncle Les after all this time!"—her voice excited but sounding frightened too. When the others reminisced about Uncle Les, Mother often sat silent—she was jealous of the attention he got, maybe, but also didn't seem to approve of him: there was something tricky, something untrustworthy, about Les; he was the opposite of Lee, no matter that they looked alike. When people used to ask her how it felt, being married to a man who had a twin somewhere in the world, she'd cut them off short, saying, "It doesn't feel any different from being married to a man with a brother—it's the same thing exactly." It might have been that, deciding to marry Lee, she had to turn her heart against Les forever.

An hour passed, and still the bedroom door was closed against us, though the telephone conversation seemed to have ended. Finally my mother got up her courage to knock on the door. "Lee? Honey?

Are you still on the phone? Is something wrong?" At first my father
wouldn't answer, then he shouted at her through the door, a furious,
despairing sound; he told her to get away, just get away and leave
him alone, take the kids away too. His voice was like no voice I'd
ever heard before. We went downstairs, all of us frightened. Father
too had a temper that erupted now and then. "Is Daddy crying?" I
asked. I was frightened but I wanted to laugh. My mother gave me
a little slap, not to hurt, just to shut me up. "It's his business what
he's doing," Mother said. "And don't you ask him about this later
on."

Uncle Les had disappeared ten years before I was born and I
wondered would I ever see him. There were always rumors that he
was coming home soon: for Christmas, for Grandfather's funeral, for
his joint birthday with Father (which was June 11, a day my father
seemed to dread). Somebody must have sighted a man who resembled Les (or Lee) and word quickly spread and Father would be asked
at the store or on the street, Was it true Les was on the way home,
and was he *really* coming this time? And Father would say, embarrassed or irritated or trying to make a joke of it, "I'd be the last to
know!" (Though that surely was a lie.) At rare and never predictable
intervals Les sent postcards home just to let people know (as he said)
he was still alive. The cards came from Key West, Florida; from
Anchorage, Alaska; from New York City; from Mexico City; from
the state of Washington. Once he sent a postcard from San Francisco
showing Alcatraz Prison and his message was only *They'll never take
me alive!* Most of his messages were scrawled and difficult to decipher,
not about anything much, work he'd been doing or hoped to do,
weather, jokes of one kind or another, things you'd have a hard time
remembering an hour later. Only one card really stood out, a Kodacolor picture of the Rocky Mountains west of Pueblo, Colorado,
looking like fake painted scenery with the message *I have slept in
places I can't name. I am sad thinking of home & all you there & I promise
I'll be back soon.* His telephone calls were to my father exclusively,
always person-to-person, charges reversed, a sore point with my
mother. (Who had a fixed idea that Father was sending Les money,
in secret. Which Father furiously denied. His brother, he said, had

too much pride to *beg*. If she knew Les she'd known damned well he would never *beg*.)

So Les was gone, and stayed away, and years passed: ten years, fifteen years, twenty. My grandparents died still waiting for him, each thinking Les would show up for their final illnesses, and always you found yourself thinking yes he could—he might—arrive at the hospital at the very last hour. Or he'd show up at the funeral service. Or at the cemetery. Hadn't he always wanted to be an actor in the movies, and wasn't this the sort of thing that happened in the movies, the prodigal son come home? Except he never did come home. Always he was expected, and never once did he come.

It wasn't until I was much older, away at college, that it occurred to me—the most obvious yet somehow unthinkable thought—that Uncle Les had a life of his own, perhaps a wife and children, *that had nothing to do with us*. No one in the family ever conceded such a possibility. All he did, or could be imagined doing, was in reference to the family he'd left behind, and by extension the circle of friends, acquaintances, high school classmates he'd known. Eagerly, for years, we scanned newspaper photographs, checked out *Life, Time, Collier's*, always with the vague expectation that Uncle Les would one day be revealed and that in his revelation he'd be speaking to us, citing us. *Where I come from. My family. My twin brother. My life.*

Not meaning to be rude, people were always asking Father if there was any kind of psychic connection between him and Les: "ESP" they called it, or "mental telepathy." Did Father know where Les was at this very moment? If he was shown a map of the United States (for instance) and closed his eyes, could he maybe touch with his finger the place Les was? Did he dream about him? Did he have hunches about him? They wanted to believe in the romance of twins but Father would have none of it. His reply was always the same: No, he hadn't any psychic connection with Les any more than he had a psychic connection with anybody, and no, he didn't know where the hell his brother was because where his brother was was his brother's business, wasn't it. And what was it to them? Though I was rarely present when Father was asked such questions I can imagine his voice at such times—slowly gathering momentum as if he was holding back great anger. He was in fact an angry man, a disappointed man, though he showed little emotion; he was contemptuous of men who showed their emotions. In his presence, however, you caught clearly the drift of his thoughts without his having to express them. If he wanted the subject of a conversation changed it was quickly changed. "No, I don't have any 'psychic connection' with anyone," he said, giving the words a twist to show what he thought of them. "Don't have it and don't want it."

The reason my Uncle Les ran away as he had, taking the 1939 Nash he only owned half of and breaking, as everybody said, his mother's heart, was: he'd almost killed a man in a fight and if he hadn't escaped the police would surely have arrested him on charges of assault and battery.

So Uncle Les had been a wanted man at the time of his disappearance!

This was a part of the story that came out only by degrees. Piecing it together was like piecing together a jigsaw puzzle you'd never seen whole. It can be done, but it takes time.

And while it was all right for us to ask questions of a certain kind, it was a mistake to ask other questions. Like the time I asked Father, in front of a roomful of relatives, "Would Uncle Les have been sentenced to the electric chair if that man died?" I was maybe nine, ten years old at the time and didn't know any better. I thought that having an uncle who had died in the electric chair would be an exciting thing.

After Father and Uncle Les were discharged from the navy and came back home to live, it seemed one or the other of them—but particularly Les—was always getting into a fight. Father was going out with Mother, whom he'd marry in another year, but Les was going out with any number of women, and it was over one of these women he got into the most serious fight of his life and came near to killing a man. If Father hadn't intervened, he would have killed him. Mother said this all the time, interjected it when she could: "If it hadn't been for Lee . . ." and her voice would trail off into a reproachful silence. And not even Father could contradict her.

A man named Cadwaller had insulted a girl Les was seeing at the time, or maybe Les himself, saying something he shouldn't have said, and Les naturally had to fight him. And (the men were fighting at work, at the Olcott gypsum plant) Les happened to pick up a hammer and began hitting Cadwaller on the head. He hadn't known what he was doing, my father said, just went wild and reached for the hammer 'cause Cadwaller had been fighting dirty, using his knee, and so forth, and when you're fighting like that you don't think clearly, you just want to get it over with—stop the other man from killing you. It's a natural instinct, Father said.

If it hadn't been for Father, everybody said, Cadwaller would probably have been killed. That was no exaggeration. Les had fractured his skull with the first hammer blow and was set to deliver a second. But Father pulled Les off the man and wrenched the hammer out of his hand and the fight was over. Cadwaller was unconscious, bleeding like a stuck pig, had to be taken to the hospital in an ambulance, by the time he was discharged from the hospital three weeks later Les was long gone and nobody (except maybe Lee) knew where he was. It was a sign of Cadwaller's meanness that he tried to say both twins had attacked him, Lee and Les together. They did everything together, those two, didn't they? And how could you tell them apart?

Mother used to wonder aloud whether Les had ever thanked Father. She was certain he had not. But she couldn't ask Father, that was risking a fight. She resented it that Father's family and relatives—a whole wide circle of relatives—continued to speak of Les as if he'd been a hero of some kind, and not a hotheaded fool who'd almost committed murder. She resented it that Father didn't get credit for really being the hero.

"It's no wonder your father is a bitter man," Mother said in a low angry voice my sisters and I wondered were we meant really to hear.

The family snapshot album was filled to overflowing with snapshots of the twins—as infants, as little boys, as growing boys, as high school boys in their football uniforms, as young men in their navy uniforms—usually standing side by side like Siamese twins, arms around each other's waist or shoulders. They were likely to be wearing identical clothing. Each the "mirror image" of the other. Lee and Les. Les and Lee. Even when they were pictured with girlfriends the twins stood side by side with their girls on the outside, leaning in. And the girls tended to look alike too, or tried to look alike—dark red lipstick, penciled-in eyebrows, hair curled under in pageboy style. You couldn't tell Les from Lee, Lee from Les. Most of the grownup pictures didn't have any identification at all.

In family pictures, when the boys were younger, one of the twins always seemed to be staring off to the side, a subtle little smirk on his face, while the other looked at the camera head on, smiling like a good boy. "Which one is you?" I'd ask Father. Father never did much more than glance at the snapshot. "That one," he'd say, tapping one of the figures with his thumb. "How can you tell yourself from Uncle Les, though?" I asked. "Can you remember where you were standing?" But Father wasn't interested in talking about it. When others looked through the family albums he left the room. Lee, Les. Les, Lee. I was fascinated by their high school yearbooks, their identical photographs and nearly identical captions. Later, when I went to their high school, I was fascinated by photographs of the varsity football team on which the boys had played, preserved there in the big glass display case in the school's foyer. In the second row in their football uniforms—shoulders grotesquely padded, helmets in hand—were Les and Lee, Lee and Les, my father and my uncle. But which was which? You could see, looking carefully at them, that it didn't matter what the caption said. They were the same boy, doubled.

"But how can you tell yourself from Uncle Les?" I asked Father so many times he finally told me never to ask the question again. I'd wanted badly a twin of my own, especially as I got older. For then I'd never be alone even when I was alone. Would I? If I couldn't tell myself apart from my twin, nobody else could either.

The old snapshots fascinated me. They still would, but I don't allow myself to look at them any longer. There's a limit to how many times you can think a certain thought, how many times you can let it overcome you. The thought doesn't wear out or break; you are the one who wears out. Or breaks. You have to make a choice, and I made my choice even before Father's death.

But still! Still, the snapshots fascinated me. If I close my eyes now I can see them again. But in no particular order. In a jumble like a dream going on and on and on but circling back upon itself. Lee and Les as teenaged boys, Lee and Les in their smart navy uniforms, Lee and Les as infants a few months old, lying close together in their crib. The images have meaning that no amount of staring and studying can exhaust but there's a danger in giving in to them, isn't there? You can sense, I think, the danger I am in. And if you draw back just slightly—if you make the sudden unpremeditated judgment *He's the one who's crazy*—I would not blame you. I don't believe it is true in any literal sense but I would not blame you.

I had to stop looking at the twins' pictures because something about them reached out to me to drain my strength if I kept on too long. A sick feeling would wash over me like the sensation you get when you stand up too quickly and the blood drains out of your head. Mother scolded me for spending so much time looking at the old snapshots. "You know your uncle is never going to come home," she'd say, as if it was only Uncle Les I was looking at.

Maybe I thought that having a twin, being a twin, holds you in the world a little more steadily than I am held in the world at this moment. Maybe I still think so, but what's to be done?

2

When I got to be eleven, twelve, thirteen years old, Father began to hear from Uncle Les more frequently. Suddenly it was every few months, always a late-night telephone call. From Galveston, Texas, where Les was working for an oil drilling company and making good money; from Anchorage, Alaska, where he was salmon fishing and could make six thousand dollars in a single season; from Monterey, California, where he was in a carnival or circus of some kind—no, he belonged to a troupe of "performing artists" who traveled around the United States giving shows with carnivals or circuses or fairs. All Uncle Les's news was optimistic and boastful but it tended too to be vague; Father had learned never to question him directly.

Mother hated the calls because for days afterward Father would be affected. He wouldn't, she said, be himself; it was as if another man, a stranger, had come to take his place. And as Father got older it seemed to get worse. He'd be sullen or very talkative, or cheerful and whistling and joking or depressed, or just quiet—terribly quiet. He was thinking about Les all the time but he wouldn't talk about him and that was the strange unnerving thing. Once Mother said angrily, "Nobody else is real to you but that goddamned Les, isn't that it?"

Father was slow to be provoked into fighting, maybe because of his own bad temper. He said she didn't know the first thing about the situation, so why didn't she keep still.

But Mother couldn't stop. "He's evil, really, in his heart. Isn't he? And you know it! And you can't do a damned thing about it, can you!"

Father stared at her but said nothing. In middle age he'd grown heavy, not fat but just heavy, solid, as if his flesh were hardening on his bones. Now that his hair was receding his very skull seemed to be larger: the bones of his forehead, the ridge over his eyes, were particularly defined. Lines crisscrossed his face in unexpected ways. For a man of his size he carried himself well, a bit self-consciously. He'd even become rather vain about his appearance in recent years; he owned Waller's Hardware on Main Street and was one of the town's "leading merchants." (This wasn't true. But it got said.) He seemed to have settled into his life without being happy with it: you got the impression he couldn't take it too seriously. What was important was happening someplace else.

Now Mother was saying, "He's evil, he's sick, isn't he! And you must know it! And you're crazy to put up with him—those telephone calls, person-to-person, *collect*—all these years!"

Father backed away. His mouth twitched, he was closing his hands into fists, you could see he wanted to hit Mother, he wanted to hurt her, but he wasn't going to.

"All these years!" Mother cried after him, as he walked out of the room. "God damn you both!"

By the age of thirteen I was beginning at last to resemble my father. Before, I'd taken more after my mother; now the balance was shifting toward my father: my sandy hair darkening, my face getting fuller, harder. I could see how that bony ridge over my eyes would get more prominent and I liked the idea. I regarded myself in the mirror with satisfaction. Thinking, It's Uncle Les I look like too.

That was the summer the strange thing happened that cut our lives in two. At the end of August, Father drove a carload of us to the state fair two hundred miles away because he'd got the idea from an advertisement he'd seen that his brother Les would be appearing there, with a troupe called the Monterey Ensemble. Mother thought it was a terrible idea; she seemed frightened of it. At first she didn't want to come along but then she said, yes, she'd better. She was worried about how Father would react when he didn't find Les but she worried too about what might happen if he *did* find him.

The state fair was gigantic, and the Monterey Ensemble was only one of numberless small attractions. We had a difficult time locating the shabby tent in which their performance was held, and as soon as we settled in our seats I knew we shouldn't have come. The atmosphere in the tent was rowdy—the audience was slow to settle down—it seemed the show was for children primarily, yet in some respects it seemed too sophisticated, or in any case too ironic, for children. Perhaps the performers were angry at their audience; the bleachers were only two thirds full. They strutted about in a peculiar swaggering manner, brash as adolescents. The youngest was about twenty years old and the oldest at least my father's age.

The first performers were jugglers, and they were very good, a man and a woman in bright spangled costumes who tossed Indian clubs and other odd-shaped items into the air with an extraordinary carelessness. My father was keyed up as I had never seen him, but absolutely still, watching the performers intently though it was immediately clear that the man wasn't his brother. He'd brought along a pint of bourbon in a paper bag and was sipping from it now and then.

Accompanying the performers was a clown musician playing drums, cymbals, horns, and other noisy instruments. He was bald and fat, with a bright lipsticked smile that never changed. I stared at him, dreading to think it might be Uncle Les but clearly it was not; that man looked nothing like Father. I could see that Father was watching him too, anxiously, but he never turned into Uncle Les.

Father stared at the jugglers with such concentration he forgot
to applaud at the end of the act.

Next were acrobats, then a mime with a seemingly elastic spine
and long rubbery arms and legs, then a trio of clowns who made the
audience roar with laughter, they were such crude buffoons, knocking
one another down into the sawdust, kicking one another's rears.
Shortly the entire troupe had introduced themselves. Was that all?
None of the men resembled my father closely enough to have been
his twin.

Unless it one of the clowns. Or the mime, made up grotesquely
in white face, high arched eyebrows painted above his own eyebrows,
small scarlet cupid's-bow mouth. Mother leaned over to Father and
said, "He isn't here!" with an air of vast relief but Father said nothing.
He sipped from the pint bottle; he studied the performers. He was
staring, staring. His eyes darted from place to place and tiny beads
of perspiration stood out on his forehead. It was as if he knew Les
was here but didn't know which person he was.

Of all the performers the clowns predictably drew the most laughter and applause. The mime drew the least, not because he wasn't
good—he was very good—but because his routines went so swiftly,
were so complex, it was difficult for the younger spectators to follow
them. And there was that air about him of swagger and irony, a
suggestion of mockery. He might have been anywhere between thirty
and fifty years old. He wore black tights that emphasized his near-
emaciated body—his ribs poked through the fabric—and an absurd
curly black wig; his makeup was dead white, his eyes luridly outlined.
How antic he was, even when his audience sat silent and baffled,
how graceful his movements. As we stared at him it came to seem
that he might resemble my father after all though he was probably
years younger, and he was certainly smaller. If it was Uncle Les the
flesh had melted away from his face, leaving it narrow and bony,
especially at the forehead. The man had a pinched, foxy look beneath
his makeup that was disquieting to see.

After a few minutes Father whispered, "That's him."

The mime was climbing a flight of stairs, knocking on a door,
opening the door to let himself in, kissing himself on the mouth, all
very swiftly and it almost seemed naturally; it was remarkable how
convincing his gestures were. He had an animated conversation,

tossed himself downstairs, picked himself up from the sawdust floor, strode away in dignity. The audience was slow in responding so he stood with his hands on his hips in an arrogant posture, staring out at us. He did a somersault, bounced to his feet, stood again with his hands on his hips, head flung back, staring. Father broke into loud applause as if he meant to prod the audience into clapping. He got to his feet, raising his hands high so that the mime could see him. "Bravo!" he called out.

Mother pulled him back down, greatly embarrassed. He was drunk, she said. And that wasn't Les.

"Yes, that's him," Father said stubbornly. "Which of the others can he be?"

"That man doesn't look anything like you," Mother said. "He's years younger."

Father was on his feet again, applauding.

The mime bowed in his direction. Miming delight, gratitude, as if nothing pleased him more than Father's enthusiasm.

Mother tried to pull him down again but Father brushed her hands away. He was swaying drunk on his feet. In a stage whisper, cupping his hands to his mouth, he said, "Hello, Les!" His gravelly whisper carried through the tent. "Hello, Les—it's Lee. You can't fool me—it's Lee. Les? Hey? It's Lee! See who I am?"

The mime was staring at him blankly, showing no sign of recognition.

"Hey, Les—it's Lee! Your brother Lee! You can't fool me, Les!" Father said.

The mime's lips drew back from his teeth in a parody of a smile. A parody of recognition. He mimicked delight, rolling his eyes at the audience; he signaled for Father to join him in the ring. It *was* Uncle Les, wasn't it? Greatly changed and hideously made up, but wasn't it him? Father certainly thought so. He didn't hesitate a moment; he obeyed the mime's summons and stepped forward, staring, shambling, dazed as a man in a dream.

The mime lured him forward. And he obeyed. We all stared transfixed with misery: how could this be happening? Father drunk on his feet, a big man, graceless, stumbling, drawn forward to make a fool of himself before an audience of silly children. A savage blush mottled his neck and face; he'd sweated through his summer shirt.

The mime mocked a friendly greeting, reaching out to shake hands with Father and then, as Father responded, drawing quickly back. He mocked Father's embarrassment and confusion. As in a mirror he aped Father's gestures. The audience exploded into laughter. As Father stood flat-footed in the spotlights, smiling fatuously, the mime danced about him, rousing the audience to ever greater fits of laughter. He was quick as an eel, manic, sinister, funnier than any of the clowns; he lifted his wig as if it was a hat (beneath, his hair was gray-brown like Father's, cut brutally short), and so mesmerizing was the gesture you could see how close Father came to mimicking it.

A second time the mime tricked Father into reaching out to shake hands. He ducked under Father's arm, danced away behind him. It was the most humiliating sight I have ever witnessed. Father was surely aware of the audience of rowdy children laughing at him, he must have been aware of the mime, or of Les, mocking him, yet he couldn't seem to break away. He stood there dazed and clumsy, blinking into the lights. He spoke to the mime, who mocked his speech, he smiled at the mime, who mocked his smile as in a funhouse mirror. Adroitly the mime danced behind him to give him a quick kick in the seat of the pants—not hard, but hard enough to jolt him. Why didn't he fight back, I wondered, why didn't he kick the mime in return? It would have seemed natural, there in the spotlights. In the squalid little sawdust ring, with everybody laughing.

The comedy must have lasted no more than five minutes, though it seemed much longer. Then the mime relented, as if knowing he'd gone too far. Or maybe he suddenly felt sorry for his victim. He backed off, bowing low, and released Father from his spell. And one of the clowns escorted Father back to his seat.

And Father sat down heavily beside me, panting, soaked in sweat. I couldn't bear to look at him.

Afterward Mother said, "How could you!" and Father said, "It *was* Les," but he sounded merely stubborn. He sounded miserable and ashamed. When he'd gone to speak with the mime after the performance the mime had disappeared and nobody in the Monterey Ensemble admitted to knowing where he was. Father waited around for an hour but the mime never reappeared. The members of the Ensemble must have thought Father was a real character, imagining the mime might be his brother. His twin brother! It was true they looked a bit alike but weren't they different ages and wasn't the mime from Oregon, wasn't his name Miles Starr? Nobody had ever heard him called Les. Father said that "Miles Starr" was obviously a stage name.

But if Les didn't want to see him, Father said philosophically, if, after all these years, his brother truly didn't want to see him—he would respect his brother's wishes. He wasn't the kind of man to force himself on anybody else. He had too much pride.

3

Father died of a heart attack some years later, aged fifty-six. Up to the day of his death he never mentioned the mime—never alluded to the Monterey Ensemble or the round trip of nearly five hundred miles he'd taken us on that day. He rarely spoke of his brother Les. It was as if the subject had worn him out, exhausted him.

If Uncle Les telephoned or sent him a card I was never told; when I talked to Mother, I never asked. I'd left home, moved hundreds of miles away, lost touch for months at a time. I could go for a very long time without thinking about my Uncle Les.

My life as a child began to seem like something seen through the wrong end of a telescope. It was all there if you cared to look hard enough. But why look? It will only bring pain.

A few months before Father died, as he and Mother were getting undressed for bed one night, he said suddenly, short of breath, "My brother is dying." Mother asked him how did he know and he said he just knew. And in the morning he said flatly, "My brother is dead. It's all over." Mother told him not to be silly, he was just imagining it, it was just something he'd dreamed. He didn't bother quarreling with her. But after that, she said, he wasn't the same man. Just sunk in on himself, old and tired, not speaking to her for hours at a time as if he'd forgotten she was there. He stayed down at the hardware store after closing hours—doing what? Waiting out his life. Going through the motions. And she was damned bitter about it.

I asked Mother what Father's voice had sounded like, that night. Just an ordinary voice, she said. What kind of a look did he have on

his face? I asked. She hesitated and said, Just an ordinary look. I
don't believe that, I said. Believe what you want, she said. Then she
relented; she said he'd looked excited, scared, his eyes dilated, his
skin pale and clammy. He was like a man dreaming with his eyes
open and he'd frightened her. "Do you think it was true," I asked,
"about Uncle Les dying? Do you think he's dead too?" "I hope so,"
Mother said savagely. "I've spent most of my life hating that man."

Now that Father is dead I seem to see him sometimes, or is it
Uncle Les, especially when I'm away from home. In airports, in
passing cars, in stores, in crowds—when I'm not prepared. In mirrors
new to me. Public rest rooms, for instance, where the light is poor
and your face swims up toward you like something you can't know
and can't guess until you see it. I am married, I have children, I have
my work, I am rarely alone and yet always lonely, and I'm wondering:
Is this common? Will it get worse? Is it something you can die of?

THE CRYING BABY

Precisely when the sound was first heard in our household I cannot say, for of course it was not recorded, unless my family without my knowledge or consent has recorded these matters for their own or for medical purposes, but I believe it must have been last autumn, probably mid- or late October, when the furnace usually begins to heat the house, so that the familiar sounds of our furnace masked the baby's weaker cries or were confused with them. And when, frightened, I paused in my kitchen work, or hurriedly shut off the vacuum cleaner, or ran stumbling to find my husband, or one of the children (though the five of them are fully grown and no longer live under their parents' roof, the two youngest, my girls, frequently return home to visit; they have come early to the knowledge that the world is a lonely place, not likely to be redeemed by the charity of our hearts), to ask if they too heard the sound, or had they indeed heard any strange startling sound, it was natural that each in turn had the power to convince me that there was no sound other than that of the old furnace with its heaving sighs, its faint whistles and rattles and subterranean quarrels; and if, stubborn woman as I am under duress or doubt, I persisted, begging them to listen—*Don't you hear it? It sounds like a baby crying*—in turn in all innocence they assured me there was no sound resembling the one I was in terror of hearing. And as the days passed, and the weeks, and the baby's crying returned at odd and never predictable hours of the day and night, now weak and nearly inaudible, now unmis-

---

349

takable, now plaintive, now enraged, in their impatience they chided me out of hearing the very fibrillations of the air I heard, or laughed me out of their possibility, or dismissed the very premise—that there was or even could be a sound new and haunting and foreign to all our ears of a true distinction emanating from the walls or the floorboards, or pushing through the ducts, vents, and water pipes, as profound in its own element as strands of hair whorled in the wrong direction, or a tremor of wavy glass in an otherwise clear pane, or italic print. They chided me for "hearing things," singly and in a chorus, and when my sons came home for their fond Sunday dinners they too took up the cry as if to beat me into a shamefaced submission: Mother, you must be hearing things!

So I'd date its origin in October of last year, nearly eleven months ago. When our furnace first came on. Which does not explain of course why the mysterious sound (whether mechanical or human) continued to be heard occasionally when the furnace was not in operation; why it *is* heard over and beyond the distracting noises of the furnace; why, in that stark silence when the thermostat shuts off the furnace and our ears are assailed by a sudden absence of sound, the sound is likely to continue independent of all other sounds—the sound of the crying baby, I mean.

In the beginning, yes, I was so shaky in my own judgment, and so fearful of madness, I tried to enlist others to hear what I heard and to substantiate my claims. Father of course, my daughters and my sons, for by instinct we are led to trust what's nearest or what, in any case, blind touch guides us toward, but also, to my deeper shame, persons outside the family who thereafter carried tales of me about the county like infected individuals spewing contagion at every orifice: friends who dropped by to visit and chat, neighbors I may have summoned of my own volition, a cosmetics saleswoman who rang the doorbell, the monkeyish little man employed by the gas company who came one snowy day to repair my stove. And there were others. I would not want to think how many others. Casting off my pride to ask as if I were hearing the crying baby for the first time, "Do you hear *that?*" or, cocking my head, guessing how the lenses of my glasses caught the light with a stern maternal reprimand, "What on earth *is* that? It sounds like a crying baby."

Most times they simply frowned, hearing nothing: polite, puzzled, even regretful; though once or twice as if in compliance to my motherly will they seemed, yes, to hear . . . to hear something. But did they hear what I heard, did the very hairs on the napes of their necks stir as mine did? I could not believe it.

And then, that winter day, it was the man who came to repair the stove who cocked his head as I did and screwed up his face with the effort of concentration, even as the eerie forlorn breathless heart-rending wail could scarcely fail to be heard, rising, as it seemingly did, from the very floor at our feet. "Yes, ma'am, I think I *do*. I think I do hear something. It follows me around, like, some kind of a sound," he said, giving his repair kit an exasperated shake, "but I don't know what it *is*, ma'am, I never tried to put a name to it."

This unexpected reply so shocked and stymied me and seemed in a way to have put me in my place, I stood staring down at the little man—he shorter than I by two or three inches, and lighter by thirty pounds—and could think of no proper retort; even as, like water disappearing down a drain, a finite quantity of water down an infinite length of drain, the baby's crying began to subside and a coarse sort of kitchen silence intervened. At last, fumbling, muddleheaded, I managed to stammer, "But the sound I mean is *here*, in my house; it is a sound to be heard only *here*," following the repair man to the door as if in appeal, and out onto the porch steps. "I've thought, sometimes, it sounds almost like—a baby's crying." But the wizened little man merely nodded, repair kit snug under his arm and cloth cap snug on his head, and said, as if the words were a small prayer with which he had learned to comfort himself, "*I* never tried to put a name to it."

I should not attempt to deny that, in the beginning, the mysterious sound filled me with a terrible uneasiness, intensifying at times to animal panic, for as the mother of the household, though my childbearing years are long past, I know myself responsible for all life herein, or all human life, and instinct urges me to offer help, yes even to offer suck, to any motherless or apparently abandoned or maltreated infant within my reach. Yet how, given the phantom elusiveness of the crying, was an infant within my reach?

The sound seemed to come from the walls much of the time, but if I approached and pressed an ear against the plasterboard it often happened that the sound teasingly retreated, or transformed itself into the rumble of mere plumbing. A telephone's sudden ringing might swallow up the crying and bear it away to nothingness. And there was the interference, on quieter days in particular, of heart and pulse beat, the shadowy roaring of the inner ear or the brain's labyrinthine passageways, into which it is a fearsome thing to inquire. Sometimes the sound seemed to be localized in the kitchen, sometimes in another room, upstairs or down, or in the basement, or in the attic, or in the garage adjoining the house; sometimes it began when I switched on the television set and vanished immediately when I switched off the television set; and similarly with faucets, the vacuum cleaner, the washing machine. For a day or so my husband convinced me that it was the wind in the chimney, and on another day he convinced me that it was the wind in the television antenna, and later the wind in the telephone wires outside the house, but further investigation proved, to my distress and to his impatience, that, plausible as these explanations were and, since plausible, seductive, they were simply not true. And indeed as it developed, as I quietly acquiesced to the arguments of my family and relatives, of course the sound might have been traced to a neighbor's crying baby, or to a neighbor's television set or radio turned up unforgivably high, or to a sick, injured, penned-up, or crazed animal in the neighborhood, or to birds, or to sirens, or to train whistles, or to diesel trucks, or to jet planes, or to sonic booms, or even to a malfunctioning of my own hearing, such sources *might* have explained away the baby's crying; yet upon thorough investigation, to the annoyance of all, did not: for one by one they were considered.

My hearing, for instance. Of course Father hauled me downtown to the ear doctor, who tested me with electrical beeps and whirs and poked a tiny flashlight into my brain and for good measure, to boost his fee no doubt, ejaculated a syringe of warm throbbing water into both my ears to dislodge the wax, or a pretext of wax. But the unassailable fact was that my hearing was normal for a woman of my age (I am fifty-two years old) and general health. Weeks later, when I persisted in hearing what was there to be heard and scarcely to be denied, Father hauled me a greater distance to a clinic where enormous humming machines scanned the interior of my skull but failed to detect a brain lesion, or a tumor, or any evidence of a stroke however minute. Anticipating the diagnosis of "schizophrenic"—for this perennial cliché pops effortlessly to even professional lips—I insisted upon the fact, for indeed it was a demonstrable truth, that the mysterious sound could be heard only in our house and only at certain wayward and unpredictable times; never did it sound in my head: "Of course I can tell the difference."

And with the passing of time I learned gradually to dissemble out of prudery and caution, assuring my family that, no, I no longer heard the baby's crying, or, if seemingly I heard it, I attributed it to something else and deftly turned my attention elsewhere, to the impedimenta of my cooking, for instance, or my housewifery, as infinite in its systems as any galaxy of household pipes or electrical wiring bearing away effluvia or easing along through conductors what is called, simply, "power"—for how otherwise were our lives together to be borne?

Frowning worriedly at me my daughters would sometimes ask, was I certain or was I telling them and Father only what I believed they wanted to hear? if indeed they *did* want it, for all human motives are ambiguous, and I would reply curtly, with a derisive little laugh, yes I was certain, yes of course—"For why should I lie?"—even as, perhaps, at that very moment, even as I regarded the young women with a face of wounded innocence, the thin forlorn wail of unspeakable heartbreak penetrated the wall at my back, or the ceiling above my head, or the floorboards upon which, so seemingly stolid and with dominion, my slippered feet rested. For by this time my judgment had shifted; my gravity's center had shifted; there was no algorithm to be shared with the "flesh of my flesh, blood of my blood" from whom I knew myself permanently estranged.

And there was a spell of weeks when, resistant to my apparent fate, I quickly inserted plugs of soft pink warmly malleable wax into my ears when I began to hear the baby's crying, that kept all household sounds at bay but picked up, on some principle of physics far beyond my ken, rhythmic buzzings and hummings and vibrations as of the ether itself, that void of sheer number. And in truth, so armed, or armored, I could not hear the baby's crying and went about my round of household tasks and sipped my afternoon coffee in the delirium of a willed and unnatural silence . . . until at last, unable to bear it any longer, with the helpless violence of the pelvic muscles springing to orgasm, I tore the obscene little clots of wax out of my ears and confronted what it was: the baby's continued crying or, more profound yet, the nullification of that sound I had tried in my vanity to deny.

Why some are chosen to bear witness while others pass their days in deaf contentedness is, too, beyond my ken, but if I know myself chosen why then I acknowledge my chosenness and will try to be equal to the task.

Noting the variables of the baby's crying while scrubbing the lino-leum-laid floors, polishing the furniture, which gleams from the most recent polishing, vacuuming the carpets worn thin and frayed and decent from countless vacuumings, scouring the sinks and the tubs and the toilets, removing, with a practiced sweep and twirl of the mop, the gauzy stalactites of cobweb in the corners of the ceiling, washing walls, windows, mirrors in which there floats a face no longer young but fired with the energies of youth, a stubborn grip to the jaws, heavy brows and bone at the brow, bone at the wide bridge of the nose, the steely unflinching light in the eyes, all the while *noting the variables*: for instance, the high thin wirelike wails that might well be confused, by cruder ears, with mere wind, or winds; and the thicker cries, or murmurings; and a hoarse sound as of gasping for air; and sounds of sheer tremulous emotion—whether fury, hurt, terror, even joy—with the power to stab any mother, perhaps any woman, starkly in the womb, in the pit of the womb—ah! have pity! the mere hearing of it!—as if the umbilical cord that binds us all one and another to each has yet to be cut.

The crying is most distinct on days when I am alone in the house, and when the sky is overcast, like a low ceiling; when my family is not only absent but not likely to return for hours; when the telephone or doorbell has not rung for hours; though my capacity for hearing it, my desire alternating with my dread, has no relationship to the sound that I can determine . . . like God's grace conferred upon the heads of the blessed, answering to no human summons, never to any demand. As the baby's crying begins, dissonant, terrifying, of a beauty too austere to be named, my cheeks too bell outward with unvoiced screams and my eyes release a harsh salt mist. Why do you haunt me? Are you the infant of my house, of the earth beneath the house? *Am* I your mother? *Is* this your womb, carried now limp and useless as a deflated balloon squeezed inside an aging woman's puffed belly?

And why?

And how long?

But the baby's crying merely continues, spinning and coiling about my dazed head. And if, in mute appeal, I raise my hand, the sound intensifies, unless indeed it abruptly diminishes, as the sound of a weak-tubed radio intensifies and diminishes when you pass your hand over it. For there is, and can be, no reply: no signal from *that* side to *this*.

Nonetheless! in the space of a brisk no-nonsense housekeeping of the kind I have been doing, and handily, for thirty-odd years, I pass from anticipation to fear to resignation to impatience to panic to a faint-headedness of desire generated but not contained by my loins; I pass from sober-lipped silence and eyes on stalks aching to pop from their sockets to the flush-cheeked giddiness of young motherhood, the tipsiness of milk-heavy breasts; and I dare to sing, at last, to sing, to break into song as loud as my lungs and throat will bear, the ancient lullabies once sung to my own babies, how many years ago:

> *Hush-a-bye, little baby!*
> *Hush-a-bye, little baby!*

and again, and yet again:

> *Hush-a-bye, little baby!*
> *Hush-a-bye, little baby!*

until at last the crying fades.

Father and the others—my daughters, my man-grown sons, yes, and other busybody kin too—murmur together these days, perhaps it has been these months, worriedly, fearfully, and it's of me—Mother—they murmur, such offensive words as *hearing things, change of life, not herself*, such futile questions as *why?* and I scorn to defend

myself against them for the baby's crying is not for their ears seemingly, it is not for them to bear witness to the secret sorrow of the
world, and, as I've said, out of prudery and caution, and selfishness
too, I have long denied the sound to them, professing innocence,
professing ignorance, at times frank annoyance, countering with
questions put to them: Do *they* hear it now? Has it passed from *me*
to *them*?

But they spy on me. Shameless persecutors, though flesh of my
flesh and blood of my blood, they steal silently into the house to
surprise me in the midst of my housecleaning and singing . . . my
lullabies . . . steal upon me in a long droopy-lidded kitchen reverie
or one of those reveries of the cellar steps, always twilight there,
and gravity seemingly in abeyance, equidistant between the foot and
the head of the old wooden stairs. "Mother, what are you doing?
Mother, is something wrong?"—those frightened half-accusatory
voices I scorn to answer yet of motherly obligation, though no longer
love, must.

" 'Wrong'? What is 'wrong'? Why do you use that word 'wrong'?"
"But, Mother, you seem so—"
" 'Seem'?"
"—seem so *strange*."
" 'Strange'? But why? And how? In terms of who? In terms of
you?"

And whichever one of them it is has dared approach me, one of
my daughters, one of my staring sons, grim-faced Father himself,
one or another female relative bearing my own features, I banish
them: beat them back.

Laughing contemptuously: "Must I be 'normal,' then, in terms of
you?"

For my old humor has returned, a scouring pad sort of humor,
good for harsh scrubbings, no sentiment and no tears. And I stand
foursquare on my ground, beneath my roof, protective of the secret
life beneath my roof, all that is newly entrusted to me. All that befits
my coarse graying curls, the single hairs that grow stiff and mischie-
vous from my chin, the big-boned skeleton that bears me erect each
day, the fleshy bulk of bosom, belly, hips, haunches, and my mica-
gleaming eyes.

"Mother," they insist, "we want only what is best for you," they insist, and: "Who is the judge of that?" I reply, standing my ground. For I swear I will have to be axed down, and hauled pulpy from the house, before I surrender secrets to enemies or to family alike.

Now it is true, as I have been too preoccupied to note, that thirty years ago in this house (tall, shingled, steep-roofed, this sparely renovated old farmhouse has been sufficient to bear the freight of my husband's and my issue, as midwestern as the cornfields and the dull little town adjoining) my first pregnancy ended in what's called "miscarriage"—fancy word for the surprise of bloody clotted tissue. That it was my first pregnancy I could not have confidently foreseen, the first of so many, thus I suppose came tears, and hurt, and a bit of rage, for the young woman who was then was more emotional than the one who is now. But the miscarriage came a mere six weeks into the term and was not truly life, and unnamed, though for a decent while mourned, more as a malady of flesh than a loss of life, still less *identified* life; but I am not a sentimental woman, nor do I come from sentimental stock, and for the long busy remainder of my motherhood I gave no thought to that loss, I swear—being, should you not know by now, hardly one of your whiny rheumy meek-Christian females, all faints and falls, weak ankles and weak head, a nagger, a snuffler, a weeper-into-Kleenex, quick to bleed and slow to heal. I am another kind of woman altogether, old American stock, standing five feet ten in my stocking feet, carrying my pride in my posture, and will I cringe and cower before my own children, or my potbellied husband, or old ranting God Himself on His high throne? I will *not*.

So it is a foolish business, and futile, seeing connections where there are none or may in fact be many, too many for the mind's eye, explaining the fact of Y in terms of X, so tidily, with so parsimonious a spirit, and never Y in terms of Z to follow; and if you had not X but did have Y (and all that precedes Y—yes, and shading off into infinity), would you have deduced X from it? Certainly not. With certainty, *not*. Thus with what ignorance compounded by insolence they tried to explain the ghostly music of our household (or is it perhaps in its essence "my" household?) in terms of a young woman's miscarriage of thirty years ago, that discharge of mere mute tissue-dappled blood as much embarrassment as grief, and as much simple physical discomfort as either, soaked up in sanitary rags and wrapped in newspaper, bundled off with the trash. For had I remained childless into this, my fifty-third year, would they not say, making their clucking pitying wet noises, that *that* was the explanation?

But the mean grubby things they say, they say, and so long as such things are outside my hearing I do not hear, for I have my secret knowledge, a voiceless cry intimate as the tiny bones of my inner ear or my sharp eye in its socket, regarding them with pity on *my* side, preparing their meals as I have always done, overseeing the household laid out so properly, in order, beneath the midwestern sky, washing walls, scouring, in season ridding the eaves of hornets' nests and what all else grow like mad embroidery above our heads, amused, bemused, singing the baby to sleep when there is no danger of being overheard, no spies on the premises, all's *mine*.

And when my eldest daughter-in-law, Elsie, she's called, my eldest son's wife, bland as a white-meated fish and as slyly fitted out with tiny bones, came in the summer with her infant, my grandson, to nurse him in the kitchen, all the while chatting happily with me, inveigling me to coo and grin and kiss and laugh flush-cheeked as silly grandmothers do, my son—but scarcely, now, *my* son—looking foolishly on, I perceived the stratagem behind it: that the living baby's noises, including, as his diaper was changed, a furious fit of wailing, would erase forever the noises of the other, the invisible baby—I saw, and took in stride, making no comment, knowing what I know.

And overheard, when at last they left, baby adrowse on Elsie's plump shoulder, such murmurings as "There isn't a thing wrong with your mother, Fritz!" and "She doesn't seem at all different to me—how is she different?"—and when they were gone I tore open the collar of my dress and laughed.

And then, in worry and in wonder, I walked quickly through the rooms of the house, panting up the stairs into the attic, huffing down the stairs into the cellar, brooding that, yes, my infant grandson with his squawling lusty lungs might have banished the other—and how pungent the odor of baby shit, which you do well not to forget. But early next morning the crying returned, faintly at first, as if teasingly, in the kitchen, then by degrees shifting to the parlor, then to the wallpapered wall behind the stairs. For I was alone in the house and the anguished thrumming in the old plasterboard like the beating of invisible wings was not unwelcome. "Who are you?" I cried. "What do you want of me, why have you done this to me?"—but content there would be no answer, now or any morning of my life, for the remainder of my life, and if I descended to the cellar and took up the sledgehammer in my trembling hands—better yet, Father's old pickax—and if I possessed a demon's power to smash through the very foundation of the house, every haunted fiber and nail, and bring its bulk clattering on my head, there would be no answer, never a whisper of reply. Happiness is this side of oblivion only.

WHY DON'T YOU COME LIVE WITH ME IT'S TIME

T he other day, it was a sunswept windy March morning, I saw my grandmother staring at me, those deep-socketed eyes, that translucent skin, a youngish woman with very dark hair as I hadn't quite remembered her, who had died while I was in college, years ago, in 1966. Then I saw—of course it was virtually in the same instant—I saw the face was my own, my own eyes in that face floating there not in a mirror but in a metallic mirrored surface, teeth bared in a startled smile, and seeing my face that was not my face I laughed; I think that was the sound.

You're an insomniac, you tell yourself: there are profound truths revealed only to the insomniac by night like those phosphorescent minerals veined and glimmering in the dark but coarse and ordinary otherwise; you have to examine such minerals in the absence of light to discover their beauty, you tell yourself.

Maybe because I was having so much trouble sleeping at the time, twelve or thirteen years old, no one would have called the problem insomnia, that sounds too clinical, too adult, and anyway they'd said, "You can sleep if you try," and I'd overheard, "She just wants attention—you know what she's like," and I was hurt and angry but hopeful too, wanting to ask, But what am I like, are you the ones to tell me?

In fact, Grandmother had insomnia too—"suffered from insomnia" was the somber expression—but no one made the connection between her and me. Our family was that way: worrying that one weakness might find justification in another and things would slip out of containment and control.

In fact, I'd had trouble sleeping since early childhood but I had not understood that anything was wrong. Not secrecy nor even a desire to please my parents made me pretend to sleep; I thought it was what you do: I thought when Mother put me to bed I had to shut my eyes so she could leave and that was the way of releasing her, though immediately afterward when I was alone my eyes opened wide and sleepless. Sometimes it was day, sometimes night. Often by night I could see, I could discern the murky shapes of objects, familiar objects that had lost their names by night, as by night lying motionless with no one to observe me it seemed I had no name and my body was shapeless and undefined. The crucial thing was to lie motionless, scarcely breathing, until at last—it might be minutes or it might be hours; if there were noises in the house or out on the street (we lived on a busy street for most of my childhood in Hammond) it would be hours—a dark pool of warm water would begin to lap gently over my feet, eventually it would cover my legs, my chest, my face. . . . What adults called "sleep," this most elusive and strange and mysterious of experiences, a cloudy transparency of ever-shifting hues and textures surrounded tense islands of wakefulness, so during the course of a night I would sleep and wake and sleep and wake a dozen times, as the water lapped over my face and retreated from it; this seemed altogether natural, it was altogether desirable, for when I slept another kind of sleep, heavily, deeply, plunged into a substance not water and not a transparency but an oozy lightless muck, when I plunged down into that sleep and managed to wake from it shivering and sweating with a pounding heart and a pounding head as if my brain trapped inside my skull (but "brain" and "skull" were not concepts I would have known, at that time) had been racing feverishly like a small machine gone berserk, it was to a sense of total helplessness and an exhaustion so profound it felt like death: sheer nonexistence, oblivion; and I did not know, nor do I know now, decades later, which sleep is preferable, which sleep is normal, how is one defined by sleep, from where in fact does "sleep" arise.

When I was older, a teenager, with a room at a little distance from my parents' bedroom, I would often, those sleepless nights, simply turn on my bedside lamp and read; I'd read until dawn and day and the resumption of daytime routine in a state of complete concentration, or sometimes I'd switch on the radio close beside my bed—I was cautious of course to keep the volume low, low and secret—and I'd listen fascinated to stations as far away as Pittsburgh, Toronto, Cleveland; there was a hillbilly station broadcasting out of Cleveland, country-and-western music I would never have listened to by day. One by one I got to know intimately the announcers' voices along the continuum of the glowing dial; hard to believe those strangers didn't know *me*. But sometimes my room left me short of breath; it was fresh air I craved: hurriedly I'd dress, pulling on clothes over my pajamas, and even in rainy or cold weather I went outside, leaving the house by the kitchen door so quietly in such stealth no one ever heard, not once did one of them hear—*I will do it: because I want to do it*—sleeping their heavy sleep that was like the sleep of mollusks, eyeless. And outside, in the night, the surprise of the street transformed by the lateness of the hour, the emptiness, the silence: I'd walk to the end of our driveway, staring, listening, my heart beating hard. *So this is—what it is!* The ordinary sights were made strange: the sidewalks, the streetlights, the neighboring houses. Yet the fact had no consciousness of itself except through *me*.

For that has been one of the principles of my life.

And if here and there along the block a window glowed from within (another insomniac?), or if a lone car passed in the street casting its headlights before it, or a train sounded in the distance, or, high overhead, an airplane passed, winking and glittering with lights, what happiness swelled my lungs, what gratitude, what conviction; I was utterly alone for the moment, and invisible, which is identical with being alone.

Come by any time, dear, no need to call first, my grandmother said often. *Come by after school, any time, please!* I tried not to hear the pleading in her voice, tried not to see the soft hurt in her eyes, and the hope.

Grandmother was a "widow": her husband, my step-grandfather, had died of cancer of the liver when I was five years old.

Grandmother had beautiful eyes: deep-set, dark, intelligent, alert. And her hair was a lovely silvery gray, not coarse like others' hair but finespun, silky.

Mother said, "In your grandmother's eyes you can do no wrong." She spoke as if amused but I understood the accusation.

Because Grandmother loved me best of the grandchildren, yes, and she loved me best of all the family; I basked in her love as in the warmth of a private sun. Grandmother loved me without qualification and without criticism, which angered my parents since they understood that so fierce a love made me impervious to their more modulated love, not only impervious but indifferent to the threat of its being withdrawn . . . which is the only true power parents have over their children, isn't it?

We visited Grandmother often, especially now she was alone. She visited us: Sundays, holidays, birthdays. And I would bicycle across the river to her house once or twice a week or drop in after school. Grandmother encouraged me to bring my friends but I was too shy, I never stayed long; her happiness in my presence made me uneasy. Always she would prepare one of my favorite dishes—hot oatmeal with cream and brown sugar, apple cobbler, brownies, fudge, lemon custard tarts—and I sat and ate as she watched, and, eating, I felt hunger; the hunger was in my mouth. To remember those foods brings the hunger back now, the sudden rush of it, the pain. In my mouth.

At home Mother would ask, "Did you spoil your appetite again?"

The river that separated us was the Cassadaga, flowing from east to west, to Lake Ontario, through the small city of Hammond, New York. After I left, aged eighteen, I only returned to Hammond as a visitor. Now everyone is dead, I never go back.

The bridge that connected us was the Ferry Street bridge, the bridge we crossed hundreds of times. Grandmother lived south of the river (six blocks south, two blocks west), we lived north of the river (three blocks north, one and a half blocks east); we were about three miles apart. The Ferry Street bridge, built in 1919, was one of those long narrow spiky nightmare bridges; my childhood was filled with such bridges, this one thirty feet above the Cassadaga, with high arches, steep ramps on both sides, six concrete supports, rusted iron grillwork, and neoclassical ornamentation of the kind associated with Chicago Commercial architecture, which was the architectural style of Hammond generally.

The Ferry Street bridge. Sometimes in high winds you could feel the bridge sway. I lowered my eyes when my father drove us over; he'd joke as the plank floor rattled and beneath the rattling sound there came something deeper and more sinister, the vibrating hum of the river itself, a murmur, a secret caress against the soles of our feet, our buttocks, and between our legs, so it was an enormous relief when the car had passed safely over the bridge and descended the ramp to land. The Ferry Street bridge was almost too narrow for two ordinary-sized automobiles to pass but only once was my father forced to stop about a quarter of the way out: a gravel truck was bearing down upon us and the driver gave no sign of slowing down so my father braked the car, threw it hurriedly into reverse, and backed up red-faced the way we'd come, and after that the Ferry Street bridge was no joke to him, any more than it was to his passengers.

The other day, that sunny gusty day when I saw Grandmother's face in the mirror, I mean the metallic mirrored surface downtown, I mean the face that had seemed to be Grandmother's face but was not, I began to think of the Ferry Street bridge and since then I haven't slept well; seeing the bridge in my mind's eye the way you do when you're insomniac, the images that should be in dreams are loosed and set careening through the day like lethal bubbles in the blood. I had not known how I'd memorized that bridge, and I'd forgotten why.

The time I am thinking of, I was twelve or thirteen years old; I know I was that age because the Ferry Street bridge was closed for repairs then and it was over the Ferry Street bridge I went, to see Grandmother. I don't remember if it was a conscious decision or if I'd just started walking, not knowing where I was going, or why. It was three o'clock in the morning. No one knew where I was. Beyond the barricade and the DETOUR—BRIDGE OUT signs, the moon so bright it lit my way like a manic face.

A number of times I'd watched with trepidation certain of the neighborhood boys inch their way out across the steel beams of the skeletal bridge, walking with arms extended for balance, so I knew it could be done without mishap, I knew I could do it if only I had the courage, and it seemed to me I had sufficient courage; now was the time to prove it. Below, the river rushed past slightly higher than usual; it was October, there had been a good deal of rain; but tonight the sky was clear, stars like icy pinpricks, and that bright glaring moon illuminating my way for me so I thought *I will do it*, already climbing up onto what would be the new floor of the bridge when at last it was completed: not planks but a more modern sort of iron mesh, not yet laid into place. But the steel beams were about ten inches wide and there was a grid of them, four beams spanning the river and (I would count them as I crossed; I would never forget that count) fourteen narrower beams at perpendicular angles with the others, and about three feet below these beams there was a complex crisscrossing of cables you might define as a net of sorts if you wanted to think in such terms, a safety net; there was no danger really, *I will do it because I want to do it, because there is no one to stop me.*

And on the other side, Grandmother's house. And even if its windows were darkened, even if I did no more than stand looking quietly at it and then come back home, never telling anyone what I'd done, even so I would have proven something *because there is no one to stop me*, which has been one of the principles of my life. To regret the principle is to regret my entire life.

I climbed up onto one of the beams, trembling with excitement. But how cold it was! I'd come out without my gloves.

And how loud the river below, the roaring like a kind of jeering applause, and it smelled too, of something brackish and metallic. I knew not to glance down at it, steadying myself as a quick wind picked up, teasing tears into my eyes; I was thinking, *There is no turning back: never*, but instructing myself too that the beam was perfectly safe if I was careful for had I not seen boys walking across

without slipping? Didn't the workmen walk across too, many times
a day? I decided not to stand, though—I was afraid to stand—I
remained squatting on my haunches, gripping the edge of the beam
with both hands, inching forward in this awkward way, hunched over,
right foot and then left foot and then right foot and then left foot,
passing the first of the perpendicular beams, and the second, and the
third, and the fourth, and so in this clumsy and painful fashion forcing
myself to continue until my thigh muscles ached so badly I had to
stop and I made the mistake—which even in that instant I knew was
a mistake—of glancing down, seeing the river thirty feet below: the
way it was flowing so swiftly and with such power and seeming rage,
ropy sinuous coils of churning water, foam-flecked, terrible, and its
flow exactly perpendicular to the direction in which I was moving.

"Oh, no. Oh, no. Oh, no."

A wave of sharp cold terror shot up into me as if into my very
bowels, piercing me between the legs rising from the river itself, and
I could not move; I squatted there on the beam unable to move, all
the strength drained out of my muscles, and I was paralyzed, knowing, *You're going to die: of course, die*, even as with another part of my
mind (there is always this other part of my mind) I was thinking with
an almost teacherly logic that the beam *was* safe, it was wide enough,
and flat enough, and not damp or icy or greasy, yes certainly it *was*
safe. If this were land, for instance in our back yard, if for instance
my father had set down a plank flat in the grass, a plank no more
than half the width of the beam, couldn't I, Claire, have walked that
plank without the lightest tremor of fear? boldly? even gracefully?
even blindfolded? without a moment's hesitation? not the flicker of
an eyelid, not the most minute leap of a pulse? *You know you aren't
going to die: don't be silly*, but it must have been five minutes before
I could force myself to move again, my numbed right leg easing
forward, my aching foot; I forced my eyes upward too and fixed them
resolutely on the opposite shore, or what I took on faith to be the
opposite shore, a confusion of sawhorses and barrels and equipment
now only fitfully illuminated by the moon.

But I got there; I got to where I meant to go without for a moment
exactly remembering why.

Now the worst of it's done: for now.

———

Grandmother's house, what's called a bungalow, plain stucco, one-story, built close to the curb, seemed closer to the river than I'd expected. Maybe I was running, desperate to get there, hearing the sound of the angry rushing water that was like many hundreds of murmurous voices, and the streets surprised me with their emptiness—so many vacant lots, murky transparencies of space where buildings had once stood—and a city bus passed silently, lit gaily from within, yet nearly empty too, only the driver and single (male) passenger sitting erect and motionless as mannequins, and I shrank panicked into the shadows so they would not see me; maybe I would be arrested: a girl of my age on the street at such an hour, alone, with deep-set frightened eyes, a pale face, guilty mouth, zip-up corduroy jacket, and jeans over her pajamas, disheveled as a runaway. But the bus passed, turned a corner, and vanished. And there was Grandmother's house, not darkened as I'd expected but lighted, and from the sidewalk staring I could see Grandmother inside, or a figure I took to be Grandmother, but why was she awake at such an hour? How remarkable that she should be awake as if awaiting me, and I remembered then—how instantaneously these thoughts came to me, eerie as tiny bubbles that, bursting, yielded riches of a sort that would require a considerable expenditure of time to relate though their duration was in fact hardly more than an instant!—I remembered having heard the family speak of Grandmother's sometimes strange behavior, worrisome behavior in a woman of her age or of any age; the problem was her insomnia unless insomnia was not cause but consequence of a malady of the soul. So it would be reported back to my father, her son, that she'd been seen walking at night in neighborhoods unsafe for solitary women, she'd been seen at a midnight showing of a film in downtown Hammond, and even when my stepgrandfather was alive (he worked on a lake freighter, he was often gone) she might spend time in local taverns, not drinking heavily but drinking, and this was behavior that might lead to trouble, or so the family worried, though there was never any specific trouble so far as anyone knew, and Grandmother smoked too, smoked on the street, which "looks cheap," my mother said, my mother too smoked but never on the street. The family liked to tell and retell the story of a cousin of my father's coming to Hammond on a Greyhound bus, arriving at the station at about six in the morning, and there in the waiting room was my grandmother in her old fox-fur coat sitting there with a book in her lap, a cigarette in one hand, just sitting there placidly and with no mind for the two or three others, distinctly odd, near-derelict men, in the room with her, just sitting there reading her book (Grandmother was always reading, poetry, biographies of great men like Lincoln, Mozart, Julius Caesar, Jesus of Nazareth), and my father's cousin came in, saw her, said, "Aunt Tina, what on earth are you doing here?" and Grandmother had looked up calmly and said, "Why not? It's for waiting, isn't it?"

Another strange thing Grandmother had done—it had nothing to do with her insomnia that I could see, unless all our strangenesses, as they are judged in others' eyes, are morbidly related—was arranging for her husband's body to be cremated, not buried in a cemetery plot but cremated, which means burnt to mere ash, which means annihilation, and though cremation had evidently been my step-grandfather's wish it had seemed to the family that Grandmother had complied with it too readily, and so immediately following her husband's death that no one had a chance to dissuade her. "What a thing," my mother said, shivering, "to do to your own husband!"

I was thinking of this now, seeing through one of the windows a man's figure, a man talking with Grandmother in her kitchen; it seemed to me that perhaps my step-grandfather had not yet died, thus was not cremated, and some of the disagreement might be resolved; but I must have already knocked at the door since Grandmother was there opening it. At first she stared at me as if scarcely recognizing me; then she laughed, she said, "What are *you* doing here?" and I tried to explain but could not, the words failed to come; my teeth were chattering with cold and fright and the words failed to come, but Grandmother led me inside, she was taller than I remembered and younger, her hair dark, wavy, falling to her shoulders, and her mouth red with lipstick; she laughed, leading me into the kitchen where a man, a stranger, was waiting. "Harry, this is my granddaughter Claire," Grandmother said, and the man stepped forward, regarding me with interest yet speaking of me as if I were somehow not present: "She's your granddaughter?" "She is." "I didn't know you had a granddaughter." "You don't know lots of things."

perceive

ACNE

) WORLD

ROWILD

MAIACNE

MARÚN

UN

PLIE

To plant

Lilies

Hostma

Helintrobentia

1 Yalari magatia

1 witch hazel

Sir John gilloy

Hosta Krosuna — divide plant

+ ??

Pot up containers for:

Clematis

plant Nf 6 perennial bed

And Grandmother laughed at us both, who gazed in perplexity and doubt at each other. Laughing, she threw her head back like a young girl, or a man, and bared her strong white teeth.

I was then led to sit at the kitchen table in my usual place, Grandmother went to the stove to prepare something for me, and I sat quietly, not frightened yet not quite at ease though I understood I was safe now, Grandmother would take care of me now, and nothing could happen. I saw that the familiar kitchen had been altered; it was very brightly lit, almost blindingly lit, yet deeply shadowed in the corners; the rear wall where the sink should have been dissolved into what would have been the back yard but I had a quick flash of the back yard, where there were flower and vegetable beds. Grandmother loved to work in the yard, she brought flowers and vegetables in the summer wherever she visited; the most beautiful of her flowers were peonies, big gorgeous crimson peonies, and the thought of the peonies was confused with the smell of the oatmeal Grandmother was stirring on the stove for me to eat. Oatmeal was the first food of my childhood, the first food I can remember, but Grandmother made it her own way, her special way, stirring in brown sugar, cream, a spoonful of dark honey so just thinking of it I felt my mouth water violently; almost it hurt, the saliva flooded so, and I was embarrassed that a trickle ran down my chin and I couldn't seem to wipe it off and Grandmother's friend Harry was watching me, but finally I managed to wipe it off on my fingers, and Harry smiled.

The thought came to me, not a new thought but one I'd had for years, but now it came with unusual force, like the saliva flooding my mouth, that when my parents died I would come live with Grandmother—of course, I would come live with Grandmother—and Grandmother at the stove stirring my oatmeal in a pan must have heard my thoughts, for she said, "Claire, why don't you come live with me, it's time, isn't it?" and I said, "Oh, yes," and Grandmother didn't seem to have heard for she repeated her question, turning now to look at me, to smile, her eyes shining and her mouth so amazingly red, two delicate spots of rouge on her cheeks so my heart caught, seeing how beautiful she was, as young as my mother or younger, and she laughed, saying, "Claire, why don't you come live with me, it's time, isn't it?" and again I said, "Oh, yes, Grandmother," nodding and blinking tears from my eyes; they were tears of infinite happiness, and relief: "Oh, Grandmother, *yes.*"

Grandmother's friend Harry was a navy radio operator, he said, or had been; he wore no uniform and he was no age I could have guessed, with silvery-glinting hair in a crew cut, muscular shoulders and arms, but maybe his voice was familiar? maybe I'd heard him over the radio? Grandmother was urging him to tell me about the universe, distinctly she said those odd words, "Why don't you tell Claire about the universe," and Harry stared at me frowning and said, "Tell Claire what about the universe?" and Grandmother laughed and said, "Oh—anything!" and Harry said, shrugging, "Hell, I don't know," then, raising his voice, regarding me with a look of compassion: "The universe goes back a long way, I guess. Ten billion years? Twenty billion? Is there a difference? They say it got started with an explosion, and in a second—well, really a fraction of a second—a tiny bit of tightness got flung out; it's flying out right now, expanding"—he drew his hands, broad stubby hands, dramatically apart—"and most of it is emptiness, I guess, whatever 'emptiness' is. It's still expanding, all the pieces flying out; there's a billion galaxies like ours, or maybe a billion billion galaxies like ours, but don't worry, it goes on forever even when we die—" but at this Grandmother turned sharply; sensing my reaction, she said, "Oh, dear, don't tell the child *that*, don't frighten poor little Claire with *that*."

"You told me to tell her about the—"

"Oh, just *stop*."

Quickly Grandmother came to hug me, settled me into my chair as if I were a much smaller child sitting there at the kitchen table, my feet not touching the floor; and there was my special bowl, the bowl Grandmother kept for me, sparkling yellow with lambs running around the rim; yes, and my special spoon too, a beautiful silver spoon with the initial C engraved on it which Grandmother kept polished, so I understood I was safe, nothing could harm me; Grandmother would not let anything happen to me so long as I was there. She poured my oatmeal into my dish; she was saying, "It's true we must all die one day, darling, but not just yet, you know, not tonight, you've just come to visit, haven't you, dear? and maybe you'll stay? maybe you won't ever leave? *now it's time?*"

The words *it's time* rang with a faint echo.

I can hear them now: *it's time: time.*

Grandmother's arms were shapely and attractive, her skin pale and smooth and delicately translucent as a candled egg, and I saw that she was wearing several rings, the wedding band that I knew but others, sparkling with light, and there so thin were my arms beside hers, my hands that seemed so small, sparrow-sized, and my wrists so bony, and it came over me, the horror of it, that meat and bone should define my presence in the universe; the point of entry in the universe that was *me* that was *me* that was *me*, and no other, yet of a fragile materiality that any fire could consume. "Oh, Grandmother—I'm so afraid!" I whimpered, seeing how I would be burnt to ash, and Grandmother comforted me, and settled me more securely into the chair, pressed my pretty little spoon between my fingers, and said, "Darling, don't think of such things, just *eat*. Grandmother made this for *you*."

I was eating the hot oatmeal, which was a little too hot, but creamy as I loved it; I was terribly hungry, eating like an infant at the breast so blindly my head bowed and eyes nearly shut, rimming with tears, and Grandmother asked, *Is it good? Is it good?*—she'd spooned in some dark honey too—*Is it good?* and I nodded mutely; I could taste grains of brown sugar that hadn't melted into the oatmeal, stark as bits of glass, and I realized they were in fact bits of glass, some of them large as grape pits, and I didn't want to hurt Grandmother's feelings but I was fearful of swallowing the glass so as I ate I managed to sift the bits through the chewed oatmeal until I could maneuver it into the side of my mouth into a little space between my lower right gum and the inside of my cheek, and Grandmother was watching, asking *Is it good?* and I said, "Oh, yes," half choking and swallowing, "oh, *yes*."

A while later when neither Grandmother nor Harry was watching I spat out the glass fragments into my hand but I never knew absolutely, I don't know even now, if they were glass and not for instance grains of sand or fragments of eggshell or even bits of brown sugar crystalized into such a form not even boiling oatmeal could dissolve it.

I was leaving Grandmother's house; it was later, time to leave. Grandmother said, "But aren't you going to stay?" and I said, "No, Grandmother, I can't," and Grandmother said, "I thought you were going to stay, dear," and I said, "No, Grandmother, I can't," and Grandmother said, "But why?" and I said, "I just can't," and Grandmother said, laughing so her laughter was edged with annoyance, "Yes, but *why?*" Grandmother's friend Harry had disappeared from the kitchen, there was no one in the kitchen but Grandmother and me, but we were in the street too, and the roaring of the river was close by, so Grandmother hugged me a final time and gave me a little push, saying, "Well, good night, Claire," and I said apologetically, "Good night, Grandmother," wondering if I should ask her not to say anything to my parents about this visit in the middle of the night, and she was backing away, her dark somber gaze fixed upon me half in reproach. "Next time you visit Grandmother you'll stay, won't you? Forever?" and I said, "Yes, Grandmother," though I was very frightened, and as soon as I was out of Grandmother's sight I began to run.

At first I had a hard time finding the Ferry Street bridge. Though I could hear the river close by; I can always hear the river close by.

Eventually, I found the bridge again. I know I found the bridge, otherwise how did I get home? That night?

LADIES AND GENTLEMEN:

Ladies and gentlemen: A belated but heartfelt welcome aboard our cruise ship S.S. *Ariel*. It's a true honor and a privilege for me, your captain, to greet you all on this lovely sun-warmed January day—as balmy, isn't it, as any June morning back north? I wish I could claim that we of the *Ariel* arranged personally for such splendid weather, as compensation of sorts for the—shall we say—somewhat rocky weather of the past several days. But at any rate it's a welcome omen indeed and bodes well for the remainder of the cruise and for this morning's excursion, ladies and gentlemen, to the island you see us rapidly approaching, a small but remarkably beautiful island the natives of these waters call the Island of Tranquility or, as some translators prefer, the Island of Repose. For those of you who've become virtual sailors with a keen eye for navigating, you'll want to log our longitude at 155 degrees East and our lattitude at 5 degrees North, approximately twelve hundred miles north and east of New Guinea. Yes, that's right! We've come so far! And as this is a rather crucial morning, and your island adventure an important event not only on this cruise but in your lives, ladies and gentlemen, I hope you will quiet just a bit—just a bit!—and give me, your captain, your fullest attention. Just for a few minutes, I promise! Then you disembark.

As to the problems some of you have experienced: let me take this opportunity, as your captain, ladies and gentlemen, to apologize, or at least to explain. It's true for instance that certain of your staterooms are not *precisely* as the advertising brochures depicted them, the portholes are not quite so large; in some cases the portholes are not in evidence. This is not the fault of any of the *Ariel* staff; indeed, this has been a sore point with us for some years, a matter of mis- understandings and embarrassments out of our control, yet I, as your captain, ladies and gentlemen, offer my apologies and my profoundest sympathies. Though I am a bit your junior in age, I can well under- stand the special disappointment, the particular hurt, outrage, and dismay that attend one's sense of having been cheated on what, for some of you, probably, is perceived as being the last time you'll be taking so prolonged and exotic a trip—thus, my profoundest sym- pathies! As to the toilets that have been reported as malfunctioning or out of order entirely, and the loud throbbing or "tremors" of the engines that have been keeping some of you awake, and the negligent or even rude service, the overcooked or undercooked food, the high tariffs on mineral water, alcoholic beverages, and cigarettes, the re- ported sightings of rodents, cockroaches, and other vermin on board ship—perhaps I should explain, ladies and gentlemen, that this is the final voyage of the S.S. *Ariel* and it was the owners' decision, and a justifiably pragmatic decision, to cut back on repairs, services, ex- penses, and the like. Ladies and gentlemen, I am sorry for your inconvenience, but the *Ariel is* an old ship, bound for dry dock in Manila and the fate of many a veteran seagoing vessel that has out- lived her time. God bless her! We'll not see her likes again!

Ladies and gentlemen, may I have some quiet—please, just five minutes more?—before the stewards help you prepare for your dis- embarkment? Thank you.

Yes, the *Ariel* is bound for Manila next. But have no fear, you won't be aboard.

Ladies and gentlemen, *please.* This murmuring and muttering be- gins to annoy.

(Yet, as your captain, I'd like to note that, amid the usual whiners and complainers and the just plain bad-tempered, it's gratifying to see a number of warm, friendly, *hopeful* faces and to know that there are men and women determined to enjoy life, not quibble and harbor suspicions. Thank *you*!)

Now to our business at hand: ladies and gentlemen, do you know what you have in common?

You can't guess?

You *can* guess?

No? Yes?

No?

Well, yes sir, it's true that you are all aboard the S.S. *Ariel*; and yes, sir—excuse me, *ma'am*—it's certainly true that you are all of "retirement" age. (Though "retirement" has come to be a rather vague term in the past decade or so, hasn't it? For the youngest among you are in their late fifties—the result, I would guess, of especially generous early-retirement programs—and the eldest among you are in their mid-nineties. Quite a range of ages!)

Yes, it's true you are all Americans. You have expensive cameras, even in some cases video equipment, for recording this South Seas adventure; you have all sorts of tropical-cruise paraphernalia, including some extremely attractive bleached-straw hats; some of you have quite a supply of sun-protective lotions; and most of you have a considerable quantity and variety of pharmacological supplies. And quite a store of paperbacks, magazines, cards, games, and crossword puzzles. Yet there is one primary thing you have in common, ladies and gentlemen, which has determined your presence here this morning, at longitude 155 degrees East and latitude 5 degrees North: your fate, as it were. Can't you guess?

Ladies and gentlemen: *your children.*

Yes, you have in common the fact that this cruise on the S.S. *Ariel* was originally your children's idea and that they arranged for it, if you'll recall. (Though you have probably paid for your own passages, which weren't cheap.) Your children—who are "children" only technically, for of course they are fully grown, fully adult, a good number of them parents themselves (having made you proud grandparents—yes, haven't you been proud!)—these sons and daughters, if I may speak frankly, are *very* tired of waiting for their inheritances.

Yes, and *very* impatient, some of them, *very* angry, waiting to come into control of what they believe is their due.

Ladies and gentlemen, please! I'm asking for quiet, and I'm asking for respect. As captain of the *Ariel*, I am not accustomed to being interrupted.

I believe you did hear me correctly, sir. And you too, sir.

Yes and you, ma'am. And *you*. (Most of you aren't nearly so deaf as you pretend!)

Let me speak candidly. While your children are in many cases, or at least in some cases, genuinely fond of you, they are simply impatient with the prospect of waiting for your "natural" deaths. Ten years, fifteen? Twenty? With today's medical technology, who knows; you might outlive *them*!

Of course it's a surprise to you, ladies and gentlemen. It's a *shock*. Thus you, sir, are shaking your head in disbelief, and you, sir, are muttering just a little too loudly, "Who does that fool think he is, making such bad jokes?"—and you, ladies, are giggling like teenaged girls, not knowing what to think. But remember: your children have been living lives of their own, in a very difficult, very competitive corporate America; they are, on the face of it, well-to-do, even affluent; yet they want, in some cases desperately need, *your* estates— not in a dozen years but *now*.

That is to say, as soon as your wills can be probated.

For, however your sons and daughters appear in the eyes of their neighbors, friends, and business colleagues, even in the eyes of their own offspring, you can be sure that *they have not enough money*. You can be sure that they suffer keenly certain financial jealousies and yearnings—and who dares calibrate another's suffering? Who dares peer into another's heart? Without betraying anyone's confidence, I can say that there are several youngish men, beloved sons of couples in your midst, ladies and gentlemen, who are nearly bankrupt; men of integrity and "success" whose worlds are about to come tumbling about their heads—unless they get money or find themselves in the position of being able to borrow money against their parents' estates, *fast*. Investment bankers, lawyers, a college professor or two—some of them already in debt. Thus they decided to take severe measures.

Ladies and gentlemen, it's pointless to protest. As captain of the *Ariel*, I merely expedite orders.

And you must know that it's pointless to express disbelief or incredulity, to roll your eyes as if I (of all people) were a bit cracked, to call out questions or demands, to shout, weep, sob, beg, rant and rave and mutter—"If this is a joke it isn't a very funny joke!" "As if my son/daughter would ever do such a thing to me/us!"—in short, it's pointless to express any and all of the reactions you're expressing, which have been expressed by other ladies and gentlemen on past *Ariel* voyages to the South Seas.

Yes, it's the best thing, to cooperate. Yes, in an orderly fashion. It's wisest not to provoke the stewards (whose nerves are a bit ragged these days—the crew is only human, after all) into using force.

Ladies and gentlemen, these *are* lovely azure waters—exactly as the brochures promised!—but shark-infested, so take care.

Ah, yes, those dorsal fins slicing the waves, just beyond the surf: observe them closely.

No, we're leaving no picnic baskets with you today. Nor any bottles of mineral water, Perrier water, champagne.

For why delay what's inevitable? Why cruelly protract anguish?

Ladies and gentlemen, maybe it's a simple thing, maybe it's a self-evident thing, but consider: you are the kind of civilized men and women who brought babies into the world not by crude, primitive, anachronistic chance but by systematic deliberation. You planned your futures; you planned, as the expression goes, your parenthood. You are all of that American economic class called "upper middle"; you are educated, you are cultured, you are stable; nearly without exception, you showered love upon your sons and daughters, who knew themselves, practically in the cradle, privileged. The very best—the most exclusive—nursery schools, private schools, colleges, universities. Expensive toys and gifts of all kinds; closets of clothing, ski equipment, stereo equipment, racing bicycles; tennis lessons, riding lessons, snorkling lessons, private tutoring, trips to the Caribbean, to Mexico, to Tangier, to Toyko, to Switzerland; junior years abroad in Paris, in Rome, in London; yes, and their teeth were perfect, or were made to be; yes, and they had cosmetic surgery if necessary, or nearly necessary; yes, and you gladly paid for their abortions or their tuition for law school, medical school, business school; yes, and you paid for their weddings; yes, and you loaned them money "to get started," certainly you helped them with their mortgages, or their second cars, or their children's orthodontic bills; nothing was too good or too expensive for them, for what, ladies and gentlemen, would it have been?

And always the more you gave your sons and daughters, the more you seemed to be holding in reserve; the more generous you displayed yourself, the more generous you were hinting you might be in the future. But so far in the future—when your wills might be probated, after your deaths.

Ladies and gentlemen, you rarely stopped to consider your children as other than *your* children, as men and women growing into maturity distinct from you. Rarely did you pause to see how patiently they were waiting to inherit their due—and then, by degrees, how impatiently. What anxieties besieged them, what nightmare speculations—for what if you squandered your money in medical bills? nursing home bills? the melancholic impedimenta of age in America? What if—worse yet!—addle-brained, suffering from Alzheimer's disease (about which they'd been reading suddenly, it seemed, everywhere) you turned against them, disinherited them, remarried someone younger, healthier, more cunning than they, rewrote your wills, as elderly fools are always doing?

Ladies and gentlemen, your children declare that they want only *what's theirs.*

They say laughingly, *they* aren't going to live forever.

(Well, yes: I'll confide in you, off the cuff, in several instances it was an *in-law* who looked into the possibility of a cruise on the S.S. *Ariel*; your own son/daughter merely cooperated, after the fact as it were. Of course, that isn't the same thing!)

Ladies and gentlemen, as your captain, about to bid you farewell, let me say I *am* sympathetic with your plight. Your stunned expressions, your staggering-swaying gait, your damp eyes, working mouths—"This is a bad joke!" "This is intolerable!" "This is a nightmare!" "No child of mine could be so cruel—inhuman—monstrous" et cetera—all this is touching, wrenching to the heart, altogether *natural.* One might almost say *traditional.* Countless others, whose bones you may discover should you have the energy and spirit to explore the Island of Tranquility (or Repose), reacted in more or less the same way.

Thus do not despair, ladies and gentlemen, for your emotions, however painful, are time-honored; but do not squander the few precious remaining hours of your life, for such emotions are futile.

Ladies and gentlemen: the Island of Tranquility upon which you now stand shivering in the steamy morning heat is approximately six kilometers in circumference, ovoid in shape, with a curious archipelago of giant metamorphic rocks trailing off to the north, a pounding hallucinatory surf, and horizon, vague, dreamy, and distant, on all sides. Its soil is an admixture of volcanic ash, sand, rock, and peat; its jungle interior is pocked with treacherous bogs of quicksand.

It *is* a truly exotic island, but fairly quickly most of you will become habituated to the ceaseless winds that ease across the island from several directions simultaneously, air intimate and warmly stale as exhaled breaths, caressing, narcotic. You'll become habituated to the ubiquitous sand flies, the glittering dragonflies with their eighteen-inch iridescent wings, the numerous species of snakes (the small quicksilver orange-speckled *baya* snake is the most venomous, you'll want to know); the red-beaked carnivorous macaw and its ear-piercing shriek; bullfrogs the size of North American jackrabbits; two-hundred-pound tortoises with pouched, intelligent eyes; spider monkeys playful as children; tapirs; tarantulas; and, most colorful of all, the comical cassowary birds with their bony heads, gaily-hued wattles, and stunted wings—these ungainly birds whom millions of years of evolution, on this island lacking mammal predators, have rendered flightless.

And orchids: some of you have already noticed the lovely, bountiful orchids growing everywhere, dozens of species, every imaginable color, some the size of grapes and others the size of a man's head, unfortunately inedible.

And the island's smells, are they fragrances or odors? Is it rampant, fresh-budding life or jungle-rancid decay? Is there a difference?

By night (and the hardiest among you should survive numerous nights, if past history prevails), you'll contemplate the tropical moon, so different from our North American moon, hanging heavy and luminous in the sky like an overripe fruit; you'll be moved to smile at the sport of fiery-phosphorescent fish frolicking in the waves; you'll be lulled to sleep by the din of insects, the cries of nocturnal birds, your own prayers perhaps.

Some of you will cling together, like terrified herd animals; some of you will wander off alone, dazed, refusing to be touched, even comforted, by a spouse of fifty years.

Ladies and gentlemen, I, your captain, speak for the crew of the S.S. *Ariel*, bidding you farewell.

Ladies and gentlemen, your children have asked me to assure you that they *do* love you—but circumstances have intervened.

Ladies and gentlemen, your children have asked me to recall to you those years when they were in fact *children*—wholly innocent as you imagined them, adoring you as gods.

Ladies and gentlemen, I now bid farewell to you as children do, waving goodbye not once but numerous times, solemn, reverential. Goodbye, goodbye, goodbye.

FAMILY

The days were brief and attenuated and the season appeared to be fixed—neither summer nor winter, spring nor fall. A thermal haze of inexpressible sweetness (though bearing tiny bits of grit or mica) had eased into the valley from the industrial regions to the north, and there were nights when the sun set slowly at the western horizon as if sinking through a porous red mass, and there were days when a hard-glaring moon like bone remained fixed in a single position, prominent in the sky. Above the patchwork of ex-cavated land bordering our property—*all* of which had formerly been our property in Grandfather's time: thousands of acres of fertile soil and open grazing land—a curious fibrillating rainbow sometimes ap-peared, its colors shifting even as you stared, shades of blue, tur-quoise, iridescent green, russet red, a lovely translucent gold that dissolved to moisture as the thermal breeze stirred, warm and stale as an exhaled breath. As if I'd run excited to tell others of the rainbow, it was likely to have vanished when they came.

"Liar!" my older brothers and sisters said, "—don't promise rain-bows when there aren't any!"

Father laid his hand on my head, saying, with a smiling frown, "Don't speak of anything if you aren't certain it will be true for others, not simply for yourself. Do you understand?"

"Yes, Father," I said quietly. Though I did not understand.

This story begins in the time of family celebration—after Father made a great profit selling all but fifteen acres of his inheritance

from Grandfather; and he and Mother were like a honeymoon couple, giddy with relief at having escaped the fate of most of our
neighbors in the Valley, rancher-rivals of Grandfather's, and their
descendants, who had sold off their property before the market began
to realize its full potential. ("Full potential" was a term Father often
uttered, as if its taste pleased him.) Now these old rivals were without
land, and their investments yielded low returns; they'd gone away
to live in cities of ever-increasing disorder, where no country people,
especially once-aristocratic country people, could endure to live for
long. They'd virtually prostituted themselves, Father said, "—and for
so little!"

It was a proverb of Grandfather's time that a curse would befall
anyone in the Valley who gloated over a neighbor's misfortune but,
as Father observed, "It's damned difficult *not* to feel superior, sometimes." And Mother said, kissing him, "Darling—you're absolutely
right!"

Our house was made of granite, limestone, and beautiful red-
orange brick; the new wing, designed by a famous Japanese architect,
was mainly tinted glass, overlooking the Valley, where on good days
we could see for many miles and on humid-hazy days we could barely
see beyond the fence at the edge of our property. Father, however,
preferred the roof of the house: in his white suit (linen in warm
weather, light wool in cold), cream-colored fedora cocked back on
his head, high-heeled leather-tooled boots, he spent most of his
waking hours on the highest peak of the highest roof, observing
through high-powered binoculars the astonishing progress of construction in the Valley—for overnight, it seemed, there had appeared
roads, expressways, sewers, drainage pipes, "planned communities"
with such melodic names as Whispering Glades, Murmuring Oaks,
Pheasant Run, Deer Willow, all of them walled to keep out trespassers, and, even more astonishing, immense towers of buildings
made of aluminum, and steel, and glass, and bronze, buildings whose
magnificent windows winked and glimmered like mirrors, splendid
in sunshine like pillars of flame . . . such beauty, where once there'd
been mere earth and sky, it caught at your throat like a great bird's
talons. "The ways of beauty are as a honeycomb," Father told us
mysteriously.

So hypnotized was Father by the transformation of the Valley, he often forgot where he was; failed to come downstairs for meals, or for bed. If Mother, meaning to indulge him, or hurt by his growing indifference to her, did not send a servant to summon him, he was likely to spend an entire night on the roof; in the morning, smiling sheepishly, he would explain that he'd fallen asleep, or, conversely, he'd been troubled by having seen things for which he could not account—shadows the size of longhorns moving ceaselessly beyond our twelve-foot barbed wire fence and inexplicable winking red lights fifty miles away in the foothills. "Optical illusions!" Mother said, "—or the ghosts of old slaughtered livestock, or airplanes. Have you forgotten, darling, you sold thirty acres of land, for an airport at Furnace Creek?" "These lights more resemble fires," Father said stubbornly. "And they're in the foothills, not in the plain."

There came then times of power blackouts, and financial losses, and Father was forced to surrender all but two or three of the servants, but he maintained his rooftop vigil, white-clad, a noble ghostly figure holding binoculars to his eyes, for he perceived himself as a *witness* and believed, if he lived to a ripe old age like Grandfather (who was in his hundredth year when at last he died—of a riding accident), he would be a chronicler of these troubled times, like Thucydides. For, as Father said, "Is there a new world struggling to be born—or only struggle?"

Around this time—because of numerous dislocations in the Valley: the abrupt abandoning of homes, for instance—it happened that packs of dogs began to roam about looking for food, particularly by night, poor starving creatures that became a nuisance and should be, as authorities urged, shot down on sight—these dogs not being feral by birth but former household pets, highly bred beagles, setters, cocker spaniels, terriers, even the larger and coarser type of poodle— and it was the cause of some friction between Mother and Father that, despite his rooftop presence by day and by night, Father nonetheless failed to spy a pack of these dogs dig beneath our fence and make their way to the dairy barn where they tore out the throats— surely this could not have been in silence!—of our remaining six Holsteins, and our last two she-goats, before devouring the poor creatures; nor did Father notice anything unusual the night two homeless derelicts, formerly farmhands of ours, impaled themselves on the electric fence and died agonizing deaths, their bodies found in the morning by Kit, our sixteen-year-old.

Kit, who'd liked the men, said, "—I hope I never see anything like that again in my life!"

It's true that our fence was charged with a powerful electric current, but in full compliance with County Farm and Home Bureau regulations.

Following this, Father journeyed to the state capital with the intention of taking out a sizable loan, and re-establishing, as he called it, old ties with his political friends, or with their younger colleagues; and Mother joined him a few days later for a greatly needed change of scene—"Not that I don't love you all, and the farm, but I need to see other sights for a while!—and I need to be *seen*." Leaving us when they did, under the care of Mrs. Hoyt (our housekeeper) and Cory (our eldest sister), was possibly not a good idea: Mrs. Hoyt was aging rapidly, and Cory, for all the innocence of her marigold eyes and melodic voice, was desperately in love with one of the National Guardsmen who patrolled the Valley in jeeps, authorized to shoot wild dogs, and, when necessary, vandals, arsonists, and squatters who were considered a menace to the public health and well-being. And when Mother returned from the capital, unaccompanied by Father, after what seemed to the family a long absence (two weeks? two months?), it was with shocking news: she and Father were going to separate.

Mother said, "Children, your father and I have decided, after much soul-searching deliberation, that we must dissolve our wedding bond of nearly twenty years." As she spoke Mother's voice wavered like a girl's but fierce little points of light shone in her eyes.

We children were so taken by surprise we could not speak, at first.

Separate! Dissolve! We stood staring and mute; not even Cory, Kit, and Dale, not even Lona who was the most impulsive of us, could find words with which to protest—the younger children began whimpering helplessly, soon joined by the rest. Mother clutched at her hair, saying, "Oh please don't! I can hardly bear the pain as it is!" With some ceremony she then played for us a video of Father's farewell to the family, which drew fresh tears . . . for there, framed astonishingly on our one hundred-inch home theater screen, where we'd never seen his image before, was Father, dressed not in white but in somber colors, his hair in steely bands combed wetly across the dome of his skull, and his eyes puffy, an unnatural sheen to his face as if it had been scoured, hard. He was sitting stiffly erect; his fingers gripped the arms of his chair so tightly the blood had drained from his knuckles; his words came slow, halting, and faint, like the faltering progress of a gut-shot deer across a field. *Dear children, your mother and I . . . after years of marriage . . . of very happy marriage . . . have decided to . . . have decided. . . .* One of the vexatious low-flying helicopters belonging to the National Guard soared past our house, making the screen shudder, but the sound was garbled in any case, as if the tape had been clumsily cut and spliced; Father's beloved face turned liquid and his eyes began to melt vertically, like oily tears; his mouth was distended like a drowning man's. As the tape ended we could discern only sounds, not words, resembling *Help me* or *I am innocent* or *Do not forget me beloved children I AM YOUR FATHER*—and then the screen went dead.

That afternoon Mother introduced us to the man who was to be Father's successor in the household! and to his three children, who were to be our new brothers and sister—we shook hands shyly, in a state of mutual shock, and regarded one another with wide staring wary eyes. Our new father! Our new brothers and sister! So suddenly, and with no warning! Mother explained patiently, yet forcibly, her new husband was no mere *step*father but a true *father*, which meant that we were to address him as "Father" at all times, with respect, and even in our most private innermost thoughts we were to think of him as "Father": for otherwise he would be hurt, and displeased. And moved to discipline us.

So too with Einar and Erastus, our new *brothers* (not *step*brothers), and Fifi, our new *sister* (not *step*sister).

New Father stood before us smiling happily, a man of our old Father's age but heavier and far more robust than that Father, with an unusually large head, the cranium particularly developed, and small shrewd quick-darting eyes beneath brows of bone. He wore a tailored suit with wide shoulders that exaggerated his bulk and sported a red carnation in his lapel; his black shoes, a city man's shoes, shone splendidly, as if phosphorescent. "Hello Father," we murmured shyly, hardly daring to raise our eyes to his, "—Hello Father." The man's jaws were strangely elongated, the lower jaw at least an inch longer than the upper, so that a wet malevolent ridge of teeth was revealed. As so often happened in those days, a single thought passed like lightning among us children, from one to the other to the other, each of us smiling guiltily as it struck us: *Crocodile! Why, here's Crocodile!* Only little Jori burst into frightened tears and New Father surprised us all by stooping to pick her up gently in his arms and comfort her . . . "Hush, hush little girl! Nobody's going to hurt *you!*" and we others could see how the memory of our beloved former Father began to pass from her, like dissolving smoke. Jori was three years old at this time, too young to be held accountable.

New Father's children were tall, big-boned, and solemn, with a faint greenish-peevish cast to their skin, like many city children; the boys had inherited their father's large head and protruding jaws but the girl, Fifi, seventeen years old, was striking in her beauty, with pale blond fluffy hair as lovely as Cory's, and thickly lashed honey-brown eyes in which something mutinous glimmered. That evening, certain of the boys—Dale, Kit, and Hewett—gathered around Fifi to tell her wild tales of the Valley, how we all had to protect ourselves with Winchester rifles and shotguns, from trespassers, and how there was a mysterious resurgence of rats on the farm, as a consequence of excavation in the countryside, and these tales, just a little exaggerated, made the girl shudder and shiver and giggle, leaning toward the boys as if to invite their protection. Ah, Fifi was so pretty! But when Dale hurried off to fetch her a goblet of ice water at her request, she took the goblet from him, lifted it prissily to the light to examine its contents, and asked rudely, "Is this water *pure?* Is it safe to *drink?*" It was true, our well water had become strangely effervescent, and tasted of rust; after a heavy rainfall there were likely to be tiny red-wriggly things in it, like animated tails; so we had learned not to examine it too closely, just to drink it, and, as our attacks of nausea, diarrhea, dizziness, and amnesia, were only sporadic, we rarely worried but tried instead to be grateful, as Mrs. Hoyt used to urge us, that unlike many of our neighbors we had any drinking water at all. So it was offensive to us to see our new sister Fifi making such a face, handing the goblet back to Dale, and asking haughtily how anyone in his right mind could drink such—*spilth*. Dale said, red-faced, "*How?* This is *how!*" and drank the entire glass in a single thirsty gulp. And he and Fifi stood staring at each other, trembling with passion.

As Cory observed afterward, smiling, yet with a trace of envy or resentment, "It looks as if 'New Sister' has made a conquest!"

"But what will she do," I couldn't help asking, "—if she can't drink our water?"

"She'll drink it," Cory said, with a grim little laugh. "And she'll find it delicious, just like the rest of us."

Which turned out, fairly quickly, to be so.

Poor Cory! Her confinement came in a time of ever-increasing confusion . . . prolonged power failures, a scarcity of all food except canned foods, a scarcity too of ammunition so that the price of shotgun shells doubled and quadrupled; and the massive sky by both day and night was crisscrossed by the contrails of unmarked jet planes (Army or Air Force bombers?) in designs both troubling and beautiful, like the web of a gigantic spider. By this time construction in most parts of the Valley, once so energetic, had been halted; part-completed high-rise buildings punctuated the landscape; some were no more than concrete foundations upon which iron girders had been erected, like exposed bone. How we children loved to explore! The "Mirror Tower" (as we called it: once, it must have had a real, adult name) was a three-hundred-story patchwork of interlocking slots of reflecting glass with a subtle turquoise tint and, where its elegant surface had once mirrored scenes of sparkling natural beauty, there was now a drab scene, or succession of scenes, as on a video screen no one was watching: clouds like soiled cotton batting, smoldering slag heaps, decomposing garbage, predatory thistles and burdocks grown to the height of trees. Traffic, once so congested on the expressways, had dwindled to four or five diesel trucks per day hauling their heavy cargo (rumored to be diseased livestock bound for northern slaughterhouses) and virtually no passenger cars; sometimes, unmarked but official-looking vehicles, like jeeps but much larger than jeeps, passed in lengthy convoys, bound for no one knew where. There were strips of pavement, cloverleafs, that coiled endlessly upon themselves, beginning to be cracked and overgrown by weeds and elevated highways that broke off abruptly in mid-air, thus, as state authorities warned travelers, they were in grave danger, venturing into the countryside, of being attacked by roaming gangs—but the rumor was, as Father insisted, the most dangerous gangs were rogue Guardsmen who wore their uniforms inside out and gas masks strapped over their faces, preying upon the very citizens they were sworn to protect! None of the adults left our family compound without being armed and of course we younger children were forbidden to leave at all—when we did, it was by stealth.

All schools, private and public, had been shut down indefinitely. "One long holiday!" as Hewett said.

The most beautiful and luxurious of the model communities, which we called "The Wheel" (its original name was Paradise Hollow), had suffered some kind of financial collapse, so that its well-to-do tenants were forced to emigrate back to the cities from which they'd emigrated to the Valley only about eighteen months before. (We called the complex "The Wheel" because its condominiums, office buildings, shops, schools, hospitals, and crematoria were arranged in spokes radiating outward from a single axis and were ingeniously protected at their twenty-mile circumference not by a visible wall, which the Japanese architect who'd designed it had declared a vulgar and outmoded concept, but by a force field of electricity of lethal voltage.) Though the airport at Furnace Creek was officially closed we sometimes saw, late at night, small aircraft including helicopters taking off and landing there; were wakened by the insectlike whining of their engines, and their winking red lights; and one night when the sun remained motionless at the horizon for several hours and visibility was poor, as if we were in a dust storm yet a dust storm without wind, a ten-seater airplane crashed in a slag heap that had once been a grazing pasture for our cows, and some of the older boys went by stealth to investigate . . . returning with sober, stricken faces, refusing to tell us, their sisters, what they had seen except to say, "Never mind! Don't ask!" Fifteen miles away in the western foothills were mysterious encampments, said to be unauthorized settlements of city dwellers who had fled their cities at the time of the "urban collapse" (as it was called), as well as former ranch families, and various wanderers and evicted persons, criminals, the mentally ill, and victims and suspected carriers of contagious diseases . . . all of these considered "outlaw parties" subject to severe treatment by the National Guardsmen, for the region was now under martial law, and only within family compounds maintained by state-registered property owners and heads of families were civil rights, to a degree, still operative. Eagerly, we scanned the Valley for signs of life, passing among us a pair of heavy binoculars, unknown to Father and Mother—like forbidden treasure these binoculars were, though their original owner was forgotten. (Cory believed that this person, a man, had lived with us before Father's time, and had been good to us, and kind. But no one, not even Cory, could remember his name, nor even what he'd looked like.)

Cory's baby was born the very week of the funerals of two of the younger children, who had died, poor things, of a violent dysentery, and of Uncle Darrah, who'd died of shotgun wounds while driving his pickup truck along a familiar road in the Valley; but this coincidence, Mother and Father assured us, was only that—a coincidence, and not an omen. Mother led us one by one into the drafty attic room set aside for Cory and her baby and we stared in amazement at the puppy-sized, florid-faced, screaming, yet so wonderfully alive creature . . . with its large soft-looking head, its wizened angry features, its smooth, poreless skin. How had Cory, one of us, accomplished *this*! Sisters and brothers alike, we were in awe of her, and a little fearful.

Mother's reaction was most surprising. She seemed furious with Cory, saying that the attic room was good enough for Cory's "outlaw child," sometimes she spoke of Cory's "bastard child"—though quick to acknowledge, in all fairness, the poor infant's parentage was no fault of its own. But it was "fit punishment," Mother said, that Cory's breasts ached when she nursed her baby, and that her milk was threaded with pus and blood . . . "fit punishment for shameful sluttish behavior." Yet the family's luck held, for only two days after the birth Kit and Erastus came back from a nocturnal hunting expedition with a dairy cow: a healthy, fat-bellied, placid creature with black-and-white-marbled markings similar to those of our favorite cow, who had died long ago. This sweet-natured cow, named Daisy, provided the family with fresh, delicious, seemingly pure milk, thus saving Cory's bastard-infant's life, as Mother said spitefully—"Well, the way of Providence *is* a honeycomb!"

Those weeks, Mother was obsessed with learning the identity of
Cory's baby's father—Cory's "secret lover," as Mother referred to
him. Cory, of course, refused to say—even to her sisters. She may
have been wounded that the baby's father had failed to come forward
to claim his child, or her; poor Cory, once the prettiest of the girls,
now disfigured with skin rashes like fish scales over most of her body,
and a puffy, bloated appearance, and eyes red from perpetual weeping. Mother herself was frequently ill with a similar flaming rash, a
protracted respiratory infection, intestinal upsets, bone-aches, and
amnesia; like everyone in the family except, oddly, Father, she was
plagued with ticks—the smallest species of deer tick that could burrow secretly into the skin, releasing an analgesic spittle to numb the
skin, thus able to do its damage, sucking blood contentedly for
weeks until, after weeks, it might drop off with a *ping*! to the floor,
black, shiny, now the size of a watermelon seed, swollen with blood.
What loathsome things!—Mother developed a true horror of them,
for they seemed drawn to her, especially to her white, wild-matted
hair.

By imperceptible degrees Mother had shrunk to a height of less
than five feet, very unlike the statuesque beauty of old photographs,
with that head of white hair and pebble-colored eyes as keen and
suspicious as ever, and a voice so brassy and penetrating it had the
power to paralyze any of us where we stood . . . even the eldest of
her sons, Kit, Hewett, Dale, tall bearded men who carried firearms
even inside the compound, were intimidated by Mother and, like
Cory, were inclined to submit to her authority. When Mother in-
terrogated Cory, "*Who* is your lover? Why are you so ashamed of
him? Did you find him in the drainage pipe, or in the slag heap?—
in the compost?" Cory bit her lip and said quietly, "Even if I see his
face sometimes, Mother, in my sleep, I can't recall his name. Or who
he was, or is. Or claimed to be."

Yet Mother continued, risking Father's displeasure, for she began
to question *all males* with whom she came into contact, not excluding
Cory's own blood-relations—cousins, uncles, even brothers!—even
those ravaged men and boys who made their homes, so to speak,
beyond the compound, as she'd said jeeringly, in the drainage pipe,
in the slag heap, in the compost. (These men and boys were not
official residents on our property but were enlisted by the family in

times of crisis and emergency.) But no one confessed—no one ac-knowledged Cory's baby as his. And one day when Cory lay upstairs in the attic with a fever, and I was caring for the baby, excitedly feeding it from a bottle in the kitchen, Mother entered with a look of such determination I felt a sudden fear for the baby, hugging it to my chest, and Mother said, "Give me the bastard, girl," and I said weakly, "No Mother, don't make me," and Mother said, "Are you disobeying me, girl? *Give me the bastard*," and I said, backing away, daringly, yet determined too, "No Mother, Cory's baby belongs to Cory, and to all of us, and it isn't a bastard." Mother advanced upon me, furious; her pebble-colored eyes now rimmed with white; her fingers—what talons they'd become, long, skinny, clawed!—out-stretched. Yet I saw that in the very midst of her passion she was forgetting what she intended to do, and that this might save Cory's baby from harm.

(For often in those days when the family had little to eat except worm-riddled apples from the old orchard, and stunted blackened potatoes, and such game, or wildlife, that the men and boys could shoot, and such canned goods as they could acquire, we often, all of us, young as well as old, forgot what we were doing in the very act of doing it; plucking bloody feathers from a quail, for instance, and stopping vague and dreamy wondering what on earth am I doing? here? at the sink? *is* this a sink? what is this limp little body? this instrument—a knife?—in my hands? and naturally in the midst of speaking we might forget the words we meant to speak, for instance *water, rainbow, grief, love, filth, Father, deer-tick, God, milk, sky* . . . and Father who'd become brooding with the onset of age worried constantly that we, his family, might one day soon lose all sense of ourselves as a family should we forget, in the same instant, all of us together, the sacred word *family*.)

And indeed, there in the kitchen, reaching for Cory's baby with her talonlike fingers, Mother was forgetting. And indeed, within the space of a half minute, she had forgotten. Staring at the defenseless living thing, the quivering, still-hungry creature in my arms, with its soft flat shallow face of utter innocence, its tiny recessed eyes, its mere holes for nostrils, its small pursed mouth set like a manta ray's in its shallow face, Mother could not, simply could not, summon back the word *baby*, or *infant*, nor even the cruel *Cory's bastard*, always on her lips. And at that moment there was a commotion outside by the compound gate, an outburst of gunfire, familiar enough yet always jarring when unexpected, and Mother hurried out to investigate. And Cory's baby returned to sucking hungrily and contentedly at the bottle's frayed rubber nipple, and all was safe for now.

But Cory, my dear sister, died a few days later.

Lona discovered her in her place of exile in the attic, in her bed, eyes opened wide and pale mouth contorted, the bedclothes soaked in blood . . . and when in horror Lona drew the sheet away she saw that Cory's breasts had been partly hacked away, or maybe devoured?—and her chest cavity exposed; she must have been attacked in the night by rats and was too weak or too terrified to scream for help. Yet her baby was sleeping placidly in its crib beside the bed, miraculously untouched . . . sunk in its characteristic sleep to that profound level at which organic matter seems about to revert to the inorganic, to perfect peace. For some reason the household rats with their glittering amaranthine eyes and stiff hairless tails and unpredictable appetites had spared it!—or had missed it altogether!

Lona snatched the baby up out of its crib and ran downstairs screaming for help; and so fierce was she in possession she would not give up the baby to anyone, saying, dazed, sobbing, yet in a way gloating, "This is my baby. This is Lona's baby now." Until Father, with his penchant for logic, rebuked her: "Girl, it is the family's baby now."

And Fifi too had a baby—beautiful blond Fifi; or, rather, the poor girl writhed and screamed in agony for a day and a night before giving birth to a perfectly formed but tiny baby weighing only two pounds that lived only a half hour. How we wept, how we pitied our sister!—in the weeks that followed nothing would give her solace, even the smallest measure of solace, except our musical evenings, at which she excelled. For if Dale tried to touch her, to comfort her, she shrank from him in repugnance; nor would she allow Father, or any male, to come near. One night she crawled into my bed and hugged me in her icy bone-thin arms. "What I love best," she whis-

pered, "—is the black waves that splash over us, endlessly, at night,—
do you know those waves, sister? and do you love them as I do?"
And my heart was so swollen with feeling I could not reply, as I
wished to, "Oh *yes.*"

Indeed, suddenly the family had taken up music. In the evenings
by kerosene lamp. In the predawn hours, roused from our beds by
aircraft overhead, or the barking of wild dogs, or the thermal winds.
We played such musical instruments as fell into our hands discovered
here and there in the house, or by way of strangers at our gate eager
to barter anything they owned for food. Kit took up the violin shyly
at first and then with growing confidence and joy for, it seemed, he
had musical talent—practicing for hours on the beautiful though
scarified antique violin that had once belonged to Grandfather, or
Great-grandfather (so we surmised: an old portrait depicted a child
of about ten posed with the identical violin tucked under his chin);
Jori and Vega took up the piccolo, which they shared; Hewett the
drums, Dale the cymbals, Einar the oboe, Fifi the piano . . . and the
rest of us sang, sang our hearts out.
We sang after Mother's funeral and we sang that week a hot
feculent wind blew across the Valley bearing the odor of decomposing flesh and we sang (though often coughing and choking, from
the smoke) when fires raged out of control in the dry woodland areas
to the east, an insidious wind then too blowing upon our barricaded
compound and handsome house atop a high hill, a wind intent upon
seeking us out, it seemed, carrying sparks to our sanctuary, our place
of privilege, destroying us in fire as others both human and beast
were being destroyed . . . and how else for us to endure such odors,
such sights, such sounds, than to take up our instruments and play
them as loudly as possible, and sing as loudly as possible, and sing
and sing and sing until our throats were raw, how else?
Yet, the following week became a time of joy and feasting, since
Daisy the cow was dying in any case and might as well be quickly
slaughtered, when Father, surprising us all, brought his new wife
home to meet us: New Mother we called her, or Young Mother, or
Pretty Mother, and Old Mother, that fierce stooped wild-eyed old
woman was soon forgotten, even the mystery of her death soon

forgotten (for had she like Cory died of household rats? or had she, like poor Erastus, died of a burst appendix? had she drowned somehow in the cistern, had she died of thirst and malnutrition locked away in the attic, had she died of a respiratory infection, of toothache, of heartbreak, of her own rage, or of age, or of Father's strong fingers closing around her neck . . . or had she not "died" at all but passed quietly into oblivion, as the black waves splashed over her, and Young Mother stepped forward smiling happily to take her place).

Young Mother was so pretty!—plump, and round-faced, her complexion rich and ruddy, her breasts like large balloons filled to bursting with warm liquid, and she gave off a hot intoxicating smell of nutmeg, and tiny flames leapt from her when, in a luxury of sighing, yawning, and stretching, she lifted the heavy mass of red-russet hair that hung between her shoulder blades and fixed upon us her smiling-dark gaze. "Mother!" we cried, even the eldest of us, "—oh Mother!" hoping would she hug us, would she kiss and hug us, fold us in those plump strong arms, cuddle our faces against those breasts, each of us, all of us, weeping, in her arms, those arms, oh Mother, *there*.

Lona's baby was not maturing as it was believed babies should normally mature, nor had it been named since we could not determine whether it was male or female, or somehow both, or neither; and this household problem, Young Mother addressed herself to at once. No matter Lona's desperate love of the baby, Young Mother was "practicalminded" as she said: for why else had Father brought her to this family but to take charge, to reform it, to give *hope*? She could not comprehend, she said, laughing incredulously, how and why an extra mouth, a useless mouth, perhaps even a dangerous mouth, could be tolerated at such a time of near-famine, in violation of certain government edicts as she understood them. "Drastic remedies in drastic times," Young Mother was fond of saying. Lona said, pleading, "I'll give it my food, Mother—I'll protect it with my life!" And Young Mother simply repeated, smiling so broadly her eyes were narrowed almost to slits, "Drastic remedies in drastic times!"

There were those of us who loved Lona's baby, for it *was* flesh of our flesh, it *was* part of our family; yet there were others, mainly the men and boys, who seemed nervous in its presence, keeping a wary distance when it crawled into a room to nudge its large bald head or pursed mouth against a foot, an ankle, a leg. Though it had not matured in the normal fashion, Lona's baby weighed now about thirty pounds; but it was soft as a slug is soft; or an oyster, with an oyster's general shape—apparently boneless; the hue of unbaked bread dough, and hairless. As its small eyes lacked an iris, being entirely white, it must have been blind; its nose was but a rudimentary pair of nostrils, holes in the center of its face; its fishlike mouth was deceptive in that it seemed to possess its own intelligence, being ideally formed, not for human speech, but for seizing, sucking, and chewing. Though it had at best only a cartilaginous skeleton it did boast two fully formed rows of tiny needle-sharp teeth, which it was not shy of using, particularly when ravenous for food; and it was often ravenous. At such times it groped its way around the house, silent, by instinct, sniffing and quivering, and if by chance it was drawn by the heat of your blood to your bed it would burrow beneath the covers, and nudge, and nuzzle, and begin like a nursing infant to suck virtually any part of the body though preferring of course a female's breasts . . . and if not stopped in time it would start to bite, chew, *eat* . . . in all the brute innocence of appetite. So some of us surmised, though Lona angrily denied it, that the baby's first mother (a sister of ours whose name we had forgotten) had not died of rat bites after all but of having been attacked in the night and partly devoured by her own baby.

(In this, Lona was duplicitous. She took care never to undress in Mother's presence for fear Mother's sharp eye would discover the numerous wounds on her breasts, belly, and thighs.)

As the family had a time-honored custom of debating issues in a democratic manner—for instance should we pay the exorbitant price a cow or a she-goat now commanded on the open market, or should the boys be given permission to acquire one of these beasts however they could, for instance should we try to feed the starving men, women, and children who gathered outside our fence, even if it was food too contaminated for the family's consumption—so naturally the issue of Lona's baby was taken up too and soon threatened to split the family into two warring sides. Mother argued persuasively, almost tearfully, that the baby was "worthless, repulsive, and might one day be dangerous,"—not guessing that it had already proved dangerous; and Lona argued persuasively, and tearfully, that "Lona's baby," as she called it, was a living human being, a member of the family, one of *us*. Mother said hotly, "It is not one of *us*, girl, if by *us* you mean a family that includes *me*," and Lona said, daringly, "It is one of *us* because it predates any family that includes *you*— 'Mother.' "

So they argued; and others joined in; and emotions ran high. It was strange how some of us changed our minds several times, now swayed by Mother's reasoning, and now by Lona's; now by Father who spoke on behalf of Mother, or by Hewett who spoke on behalf of Lona. Was it weeks, or was it months, that the debate raged?— and subsided, and raged again?—and Mother dared not put her power to the vote for fear that Lona's brothers and sisters would side with Lona out of loyalty if not love for the baby. And Father acknowledged reluctantly that however any of us felt about the baby it *was* our flesh and blood and embodied the Mystery of Life: " . . . its soul bounded by its skull, and its destiny no more problematic than the sinewy tubes that connect its mouth and its anus. Who are we to judge!"

Yet Mother had her way, as slyboots Mother was always to have her way . . . one March morning soliciting the help of several of us, who were sworn to secrecy and delighted to be her handmaidens, in a simple scheme: Lona being asleep in the attic, Mother led the baby out of the house by holding a piece of bread soaked in chicken blood in front of its nostrils, led it crawling across the hard-packed wintry earth, to the old hay barn, and, inside, led it to a dark corner where we helped her lift it and lower it carefully into an aged rain barrel empty except for a wriggling mass of half-grown rats, that squealed in great excitement at being disturbed, and at the smell of the blood-soaked bread which Mother dropped with the baby. We then nailed a cover in place; and, as Mother said, her skin warmly flushed and her breath coming fast, "There, girls—it is entirely out of our hands."

And then one day it was spring. And Kit, grinning, led a she-goat proudly into the kitchen, her bags primed with milk, swollen pink dugs leaking milk! How grateful we all were, those of us who were with child especially, after the privations of so long a winter, or winters, during which time certain words have all but faded from our memories, for instance *she-goat*, and *milk*, and as we realized *rainbow*, for the rainbow too re-appeared, one morning, shimmering and translucent across the Valley, a phenomenon as of the quivering of millions of butterflies' iridescent wings. In the fire-scorched plain there grew a virtual sea of fresh green shoots and in the sky enormous dimpled clouds and that night we gathered around Fifi at the piano to play our instruments and to sing. Father had passed away but Mother had remarried: a husky bronze-skinned horseman whose white teeth flashed in his beard, and whose rowdy pinches meant love and good cheer, not meanness. We were so happy we debated turning the calendar ahead to the New Year. We were so happy we debated abolishing the calendar entirely and declaring this the First Day of Year One, and beginning Time anew.

ACKNOWLEDGMENTS

The stories in this volume, with two exceptions, were originally published in the following magazines: "House Hunting" in *The Kenyon Review*; "The Knife" in *Redbook*; "The Hair" in *Partisan Review*; "Shopping" in *MS.*; "The Boyfriend" in *The Massachusetts Review*; "Passion" in *GQ*; "Morning" in *Arrete*; "Naked" in *Witness*; "Heat" in *The Paris Review*; "The Buck" in *Story*; "Yarrow" in *TriQuarterly*; "Sundays in Summer" in *Michigan Quarterly Review*; "Leila Lee" in *Northwest Review*; "The Swimmers" in *Playboy*; "Getting to Know All About You" and "Capital Punishment" in *The Southern Review*; "Craps" in *Boulevard*; "Death Valley" in *Esquire*; "Twins" in *The Ohio Review*; "The Crying Baby" in *New England Quarterly*; "Why Don't You Come Live With Me It's Time" in *Tikkun*; "Ladies and Gentlemen" in *Harper's Magazine*; and an earlier version of "Family" in *Omni*. "Hostage" was originally published in the collection *Share Our Strength*; and "White Trash" in a limited edition from Lord John Press.